The Lady
and Her Doctor

D1636302

The Lady
and Her Doctor

BY
EVELYN
PIPER

Academy
Chicago
Publishers

Published in 1986 by

Academy Chicago Publishers
425 N. Michigan Avenue
Chicago, Illinois 60611

Copyright © 1956 by Harper & Brothers

Printed and bound in the USA

Library of Congress Cataloging-in-Publication Data

Piper, Evelyn.
    The lady and her doctor.

    I.   Title.
PS3531.I76L33   1986   813'.54   85-28716
ISBN 0-89733-194-X (pbk.)

The Lady
and Her Doctor

Chapter I

MAUREEN said, "You gotta hear me, Mom!"

"Everyone will hear you!" Jenny hurriedly closed the kitchen door. "Pipe down, Maureen, you'll wake Uncle Miltie."

"But you gotta hear me my poem, Mom!"

Buddy said, "Hear ye, hear ye! Oyez, oyez!"

Jenny told Bud to shut up and stop teasing his sister. She told Maureen that she had plenty of time before school. "If you wake up poor Uncle Miltie, Maureen, I'll hear you in a way you won't like. I want Milt to get his sleep."

Milton didn't thoroughly awaken until Jenny said, "I want Milt to get his sleep," but that got him up, that woke him like a fire alarm woke a fire horse. What Jenny wanted, Milt didn't want.

Maureen said affectedly, " 'A Psalm of Life,' by Henry Wadsworth Longfellow."

Buddy said, "By Henry Wadsworth Shortfellow," imitating her recitative flourish.

"You shut up, Buddy Krop!

"Art is long, and Time is fleeting,
And our hearts, though stout and brave,

Still, like muffled drums, are beating
Funeral marches to the grave.

"Now that's a cheerful little number, isn't it, Mom? 'Still, like muffled drums, are beating funeral marches to the grave.'"

Milton sat up, threw off the covers and swung his feet off the Hide-a-Bed. His heart was pounding.

Jenny said, "I hear Milt. You woke him, Maureen, with your poem. I don't know what to do with you, Maureen, you'll be the death of me!"

"The death of me," Milton thought. "'Still, like muffled drums, are beating . . .' Muffled drums nothing," he thought. "Tachycardia. I sat up too suddenly, that's all. Doesn't mean a thing. Awareness of the heartbeat, that's all. I get these palpitations all the time now, but they don't mean a thing." He stretched and rubbed his hands down his back where the crease in the Hide-a-Bed always made a crick. He heard Jenny coming down the hall from the kitchen and called out that he was up, hoping to keep her out of the room that way, although he should have known better. The only room she wouldn't just barge into was the john. Just because she used to be a nurse, she thought that gave her the right to barge in everywhere. The minute she barged in, as usual, she started telling him.

"Sleep good, Milt? Milt, Mrs. Antony called already. When you examine her, Milt—"

"Look, Jenny, are you the doctor here or am I? If I'm the doctor then let me decide how to run my practice."

"Now, Milt—"

"Now, Milt! Now, Milt!"

"I'm just trying to be helpful, Milt."

"You're just trying to run me."

"But Mrs. Antony will call another doctor if you pooh-pooh her again, Milt. I could tell from the way she talked on the phone."

"You could tell," he said. "You know everything, don't you?"

He walked to the open window and reached under the pulled-down blinds to close it. This was an Apartment Suitable for Physician. On the ground floor, which, since he slept in the living room, meant he could never have the blinds up nights. It wasn't a case of people seeing in but of potential patients learning that "the doctor" didn't have a bedroom and slept on a bed which turned into a sofa. Where he was supposed to sleep was another matter but perhaps the patients figured that a doctor's five and a half rooms were different from other apartments in the building just as a doctor was different from other people.

Jenny took a step toward Milton. "Aw, Milt—Milt!"

"Aw, Milt—I'll be the death of you, won't I?"

The word "death" hung in the air between them until Jenny swooped over the Hide-a-Bed and yanked the cover off Milton's pillow and threw it onto a chair, then stripped the sheets and blankets, grunting, lifting, shoving, to fill the air with these noises, to fold the bed away, death away. She looked everywhere but at Milton. "I better wash the sills before office hours. Honestly, you'd think, way out in Jackson Heights like this—"

She would wash the sills with the blinds down because she must not be seen doing them. Jenny was supposed to be his "nurse." The window sill washing was supposed to be done by a maid, the patients were supposed to believe this maid also cleaned and cooked for him. An invisible maid.

"Breakfast is ready, Milt." Jenny straightened up, stretching. When she raised her arms, the coachman's robe pulled tight across her firm breasts. No patient would have recognized her in that fancy ruffled pink robe as the tailored "nurse." (Actually she was his receptionist-secretary. She let the patients in and answered the telephone and collected his fees. If death came today, Jenny would know to a penny what was owing him. Owing her was more like it.) Jenny had fixed Milton's breakfast but she had not thought it necessary to clear the table of

Buddy's breakfast. Buddy had, as usual, eaten only the whites of his fried eggs. The two glazed yolks were like two glazed yellow eyes. Milton covered Buddy's plate with another and drank his orange juice. Jenny noticed the maneuver and smiled as if nothing was supposed to turn Milton's stomach.

"Take your polyvitamins, Milt."

He smiled at that.

"Go on, Milt, take your polyvitamins." She pushed the bottle of them toward him.

"Didn't Phil take his vitamins, Jenny? Is that why he died?" He waved the bottle of pills away. "Don't waste them on me. Save them for the kids."

"Aw, Milt, don't!" Jenny set the bottle back on the table. Her lips were trembling. Her brown eyes filled with tears.

The toast tasted like sawdust, cardboard—anyhow nothing like the bread his mother used to bake and which he and the boys used to eat in the old kitchen in Brookfield, Connecticut. For a minute, grinding the cardboard, sawdust, whatever it was, between his teeth, Milton could smell the bread and the kitchen and his three big brothers and he wanted—not to cry, but to pound his fist on the old scrubbed wooden table in the old kitchen and say, "Mom, hear me, Mom! Oyez, oyez, you got to hear me, Mom, it's like muffled drums beating!" He got the mouthful of sawdust down and put the rest of the slice on his plate, shoving his chair back. Jenny started to tell him he had to eat but he said he wasn't hungry. Jenny said, all right, he could eat after he made his calls. Halloran, Demitric, Cohen, Antony, and he said maybe he would. Business before eating— well, it was her business, too. She lived on it.

"Milt, drink your coffee, anyhow. You can't go out on an empty stomach that way."

She pushed his cup closer, leaning across the table so that he saw the shadows between her breasts. He lifted the cup more to keep from seeing Jenny than because he wanted coffee. She was

4

so damned healthy, so bursting with health. Jenny started taking dishes off the table, picking up Buddy's covered plate. In a minute she would scrape the dried yellow eyes off the plate into the garbage can. The thought of them made his stomach heave and he set his cup down. "I better get dressed."

The bathroom was where he dressed, his private suite, his private castle. The suit he had worn yesterday hung from a hanger on the hook behind the door. His shoes with the socks he had worn stuffed into them were on the laundry hamper. His undershirt, drawers, and one of the white-on-white shirts Jenny believed were suitable for a doctor were on a lower hook, his underwear hidden from Maureen, who also used the bathroom and, from the look of the sink, had just used it. Milton turned on the cold water tap full force so that Jenny and Maureen wouldn't barge in and stripped off his pajamas before he recalled that he had forgotten to stop off at the linen closet on his way here. The linen closet was "his" closet and he should have stopped and picked out clean socks and B.V.D.'s and, if the white-on-white shirt wouldn't do a second day, a white shirt. He shaved and washed naked, bending over the sink, and then, because when he dried his face he could see in the mirror over the medicine chest door his broad chest covered with strong curling black hair, so deceptively powerful, he could not wait to change his underwear, but to hide his heart, to forget it, to get out and see Cissie Parker for a few minutes and forget the whole damned business, he put the soiled undershirt on and over that yesterday's white shirt. By this action he had hidden his chest, but he could not help seeing his thick wrists, his big hands, the bulging farm-boy muscles of his calves.

"But the Doc looked strong as an ox," people would say. And so had his father who had died at forty-two, and Phil, and so had Don and so had Hut, although Hut didn't count since he had gone down in the South Pacific a year after graduation from medical school. All the Krop boys had looked strong as oxen!

5

The feel of the soiled socks drawn on his feet was like the taste in his mouth at facing another day.

The mailboxes for all the tenants were set into the wall on the right-hand side of the foyer and as Dr. Krop passed on his way out of the apartment house he looked into his and made sure the mail hadn't come yet. Somebody upstairs pushed the button for the self-service elevator and it could have been Cissie Parker and Milt didn't want her to know that he timed his leaving so that he would meet her, so he hurried out of the building.

Milton's Studebaker was barely two years old but because it was always parked outside, the finish had suffered. (It reminded him of his mother's skin because she, too, had stayed outside in all kinds of weather, and Milton hastily visualized Cissie Parker's skin in order to forget his mother's, but Cissie reminded him of his mother's canary that all the boys had chipped in for and bought her. It wasn't the only present they had bought his mother, but it had been the only useless one. So it reminded him of Cissie Parker—useless, useless, too.) The Studebaker was pastel green, but it was pastel dust-colored this fine morning. Buddy had volunteered to polish it when the old Studie had been turned in, but his enthusiasm had died down when he found that he could never hope to be repaid by having the use of it for any date he might have when he reached his sixteenth birthday. Even Jenny, who would give her right arm for Buddy, had been horrified at the suggestion. Her Buddy should have known a doctor's car, like a doctor, must be available at any time.

Milton unlocked the door of the car and, as he got in, heard light steps behind him on the sidewalk. Cissie. It wasn't surprising that he had noticed Cissie. There were God knows how many females in this one apartment house and in the four others on the block, but most of them were either pregnant, *post partum* or too old. There were more females around than you could shake a stick at, but damned if the kid wasn't about the only pretty one he'd seen. But it wasn't that, it wasn't the prettiness—she wasn't that pretty—it was the way he had caught her looking at him that first time, because she had noticed him first. A pretty little kid like that had noticed him first! He had been climbing into the Studie one morning, and when he turned she was looking at him that way and when he slid behind the wheel, like now, and drove away, he couldn't forget how she had looked at him. He'd made his calls and he couldn't forget it; then he knew why not. In Brookfield, the farm next to theirs had been owned by the Brownings. Unlike the Krops, Mr. Browning was a "gentleman farmer"; that meant he put money into the land instead of taking money out. The Browning girl wasn't there all year; a lot of the time she was away at boarding school. Then, after graduating, she went off a lot to Europe, to the Riviera, but when she was there, boy, was she there! You could see the Brownings' tennis court from their north field. Once when he and Hut were getting in the hay, Hut had pointed to a haystack. "This is a haystack, kid," Hut said, "and that—" pointing to the Browning girl playing tennis—"that's stacked." The way Cissie Parker had looked at him was the way he used to look at the Browning girl when, high on her brown mare, she had passed him high in the old Ford pickup truck.

First Dr. Krop started the Studie, then, accidentally on purpose, turned and "saw" Cissie Parker standing there, looking at him again the way he used to look at the Browning girl. He waved, leaned over and opened the door. Since the Parkers had moved into the apartment house, he must have given her fifteen, sixteen rides to the subway, but today she hesitated, color flared in her blond skin and she touched the blond hair on the right side of her small head uncertainly, then turned back and glanced up at the apartment house, at her window, Milt saw, at her mother who was leaning out of the window. Her mother was shaking her head, then Cissie shook her head at him but he said, "Get in," and she did. She would do anything he told her to. If the Browning girl had condescended to notice him enough to tell him to lie down on the dirt road and let her mare ride over him, he would have done it, and that's how it was with Cissie. He knew this even though he had never said more than hello and good-by to the kid.

Cissie usually gave a performance getting in the Studie and he usually enjoyed every wriggle of it, the leg show with chorus of gasps and flutters— He was always being shown women's legs, having their swollen bulk, their varicose veins, their ulcers and burns and bruises thrust at him. Cissie's concern with any disarrangement during her scramble into the car, the way her thin hands with the red nails touched and patted and repaired before she turned to him and gave him the Browning-girl look, always moved him by its very silliness, but today Cissie just plain climbed in. He liked the smell of her, compounded of every cosmetic ad she fell for, the perfumes of her deodorant, her bath powder, the stuff she sprayed on her blond hair to keep it in place, her lipstick, her pancake make-up. Today all her perfumes seemed fainter, as if her mother's disapproval had blotted them. Today Cissie sat biting her lip and, as the car moved off, glanced back nervously toward the window of her apartment and forgot to do all her little settlings and flutterings. "So your momma didn't want you to take a lift," he said.

"No, Doctor."

She seemed to think she had said enough, sitting quietly, denying him the sparrow act, the smell of her perfumes, all the things he would never have. "Why not, if you don't mind my being nosey?"

"Well, it's you're a married man," she said. "We didn't know you were a married man. We don't know the neighbors yet, so nobody told us. I don't know—I figured she was your nurse, because of course I saw her around. Mrs. Krop. I don't know,

8

I thought she was your nurse. Mom said I shouldn't think so much, I should find out."

Jenny was Mrs. Krop and Buddy was Buddy Krop and there was also little Maureen Krop. If Jenny had told Cissie's mother that she was Mrs. Krop, it was the truth and there was no reason Mrs. Parker shouldn't think she was his wife, but Cissie shouldn't have thought so. That she should think so— How could she think so? Milton started the car. She had a nerve! Who gave her the right to think he would marry Jenny, a woman like Jenny! Leaving out the four years she had on him, not even counting that. He saw Jenny as he had left her in the pink frilly thing—in any of the frilly stuff she wore out of office hours because, as she said, she'd had her bellyful of uniforms. If this kid here really looked at him the Browning-girl way she couldn't think he would marry a woman like Jenny, so he turned nasty. He wanted to hurt her. "You mean a married man can't give a single girl a couple lifts to the subway, is that it? Have I ever done anything else? Have I in any way propositioned you?" he asked. He pulled over to the curb and stopped the car. "Get out," he said, "go on, get out." He remembered how his mother used to put a dark cloth over the canary's cage when she wanted the bird to shut up; that was the effect of his anger on the kid. So long, Cissie, he thought. Married to a woman like Jenny, he thought. Beloved Husband of Jenny, it said on Phil's tombstone. When the time came, Jenny might as well save herself the expense of another stone and just tell Phil to shove over and plant him there alongside. No one in the whole world would know the difference, he thought. (Not Cissie.) No one in the whole world would know the difference, and neither would he, he thought. The life and death of Milton Krop. Which was which?

He had been heading toward Eighty-fifth, the Cohens', but, reaching the corner and too close to it to do it right, he made a

9

U turn. Not a U turn, he thought, a worm turn. Even a worm turns, he thought.

When Milton came back into the foyer, there were a couple of tenants at the mailboxes. He looked in his, but it was empty. As he put his key into the lock of the front door, he heard Maureen's voice just inside, not her reciting voice, but the usual high thin whine. ("Murine," Buddy called his sister. "Murine for sore eyes, Maureen for sore ears," Bud said.) Murine was in the hall whining while Jenny held her firmly with one hand and with the other wielded a hair brush on her daughter's brown hair. Murine was anxious to get to school. "Where's the mail?" Milton asked.

"I got it. You got a letter, Uncle Miltie. Mom, pul-lease! Let go, I'll be late, Mom!"

Jenny stopped brushing and released her daughter. "O.K., run along, Maureen. Look out crossing."

"Yes. Good-by, Mom. Good-by, Uncle Miltie."

He said, automatically, as usual, "Don't call me Uncle Miltie." Then he remembered. "Don't call me Uncle Miltie, just call me Pop!" Maureen looked interested, but Jenny shoved her toward the door and she left. "Where's my mail, Jenny?"

"Mail? What Maureen said you got, you mean? An ad. Nothing. How come you're back, Milt?"

"I came back for my mail. Where's my mail, Jenny?" She was walking down the hall, away from him, her hips firm in the thin robe.

"Mail! From drug houses and an ad for a new car. I threw them away. You're not in the market for a new car, are you, Milt?" She turned into the kitchen and began brushing the crumbs off the table. "No kidding, Milt, what did you come back for? You couldn't have made your calls yet."

"No kidding, I came back for my mail. You know what happens to people who tamper with the U.S. mails, Jenny?"

She had a temper. "Yes, and I know what happens to people who ask for it, Milt!" He stood there with his hand outstretched.

"I'll call the Equitable and find out," he said. "Give it to me, Jenny." She had hidden the letter in the electric percolator which needed rewiring. It had been opened. That didn't surprise him, of course. While he read it, Jenny went to the sink and began washing dishes noisily, but she heard when he crumpled the letter up because she turned around and faced him. She was crying.

"Why did you have to get more insurance, Milt? Why did you have to ask for it?"

He opened the garbage pail and tossed the letter into it. "I had to know. For sure. I feel so good, Jenny—tachycardia, that's all. If they gave me the additional ten thousand, it would mean it wasn't that certain." He let the lid of the garbage can fall. "Well, they didn't." He kicked the can. "Now I know."

"What for know? What for know?" Jenny came and stood in front of him. First she pounded her fists against her strong thighs, then against his chest. Tears were rolling down her cheeks. "I saw your application. I called Equitable, Milt. I begged them to tell you you could have the insurance. I begged them on bended knees. I'll sign a paper saying I don't get a penny of it, I said. I'll write out the premium checks, I said; they wouldn't do it." She looked at her fists. "But what for know, Milt? What will you do now you know?"

He said, "What do you think? Rob a bank."

"Something crazy!" She rubbed her hands together because they ached from pounding at Milton. "I won't be able to watch it again, Milt, not again!"

"The death of you, Jenny? Me," he said heavily, "me! Not you! Listen to me, the one thing I'm not going to do now I know for sure is go on this way until I drop in my tracks. Wake up. Make my calls. See the patients in the office. Go to Queens General, come back here. Pay the rent, pay the bills, pay what insurance I did get before they got smart on me—that's what I won't do."

She said, "Milt, don't talk like that, Milt. That's all you can do. Not for me, believe me, and not for the kids—for yourself. You got to work, go on working. You should do more work—on Phil's stuff that you dropped, for example, you should take it up again, Milt."

"Sure."

"Yes, sure." She began to wring her hands. "Milt, please, I know what it does to a man. I went through it with Phil, didn't I? Oh, my God, they make such a song and dance about the condemned criminal in the death cells, how they know to the minute when it's going to happen to them— How about when Phil found out about himself? Phil wasn't a criminal, and you're a good man, too. I know what I'm talking about, Milt, so listen to me for your own good."

"Stop trying to run me, Jenny. Your idea is I should wear blinders and go on in harness until I drop. Well, that's not my idea. And listen," he said, remembering, "I have another bone to pick with you." He pointed toward the window, toward the sidewalk outside where Cissie had stood each time he had offered her a lift. "What the hell do you mean telling people you're my wife?"

"People? Mrs. Parker. And I didn't tell her I was your wife."

"Mrs. Krop."

"I am Mrs. Krop." She touched his arm, stroked his sleeve. "I'm your dead brother's wife, Milt."

"Don't I know that? Have I ever forgotten that?"

She shook her head, "No, Milt."

" 'No, Milt!' Maybe you wanted me to forget it."

Her face turned bright red. "You don't know what you're saying, but don't, Milt!"

"Well, I didn't marry you," he said, feeling his own face burn, turning his face so Jenny couldn't see it. "Fed you, dressed you, slept you, but I didn't marry you, and I wasn't going to marry the Parker kid, either, so what did you have to break it up for? You didn't have to break it up. What was it?" he asked. "Some rides to the subway in the mornings. Why did you have to break it up? There was nothing between us, I tell you. The weather. The New Look in styles. The morning headlines, a little kidding. Nothing."

She said, "The first time I saw Phil in the hospital, they sent me up to his lab with a specimen. He said, 'What is it, nurse?' And I told him what it was; that was all Phil and I said and it wasn't nothing, Milt. You shouldn't do it to the kid, Milt, because she's only a kid, that's all she is." Jenny rubbed her palms down her robe. "It isn't good to be a widow, Milt." She flung one hand out. "It isn't—nice—"

As Milton walked away from Jenny he heard the telephone ringing, but he wouldn't pick it up. "Still, like muffled drums, are beating funeral marches to the grave." Now he knew. Well, now he knew. (He had known before, but now he knew.) "Well, what will you do now you know," she said. "I know what it does to a man," she said. "Work," she said. "Go on working. Work harder," she said. "Drop dead working!" He began to pace up and down in time to the beating of his heart.

Jenny had to clear her throat several times before she could produce her "nurse" voice for the telephone. "Miss Folsom?" she said. "Immediately?" She rolled her eyes at Milton. "Is it an emergency, Miss Folsom? I'm asking because you said it was an emergency when you called the doctor out of his bed at 3 A.M. and there was no reason for it."

Milton, pacing, couldn't help listening to Jenny. (He had been trained to listen.) He had thought it was a good idea, since he couldn't come running with a hypodermic every time the old lady thought she had pain, to give her a bottle of placebo. The label on it was purposely impressive. CAUTION. POISON. DO NOT OVERDOSE. The last emergency call from the

Haunted House had been when the old lady had taken a placebo and become violently nauseated, scaring the girl to death. If this was going to happen every time the girl gave the old lady a sugar pill, he better take them out of their hands.

"Miss Folsom, the doctor is out on his calls, right now. I can try to reach him if you're certain—"

Jenny would be mad as hell if she knew he had given the old lady the bottle free, dispensed it himself because she was such a miser and raised such a stink about what druggists charged. Jenny thought patients respected a doctor more if they had to plunk down good money for the druggist; she thought if he didn't come running the old lady might scrape up at least what his other patients paid him.

"I really don't think I can reach the doctor, Miss Folsom. He'll see your mother around noon at the earliest. That's the best I can do."

The best she could do for Miss Folsom, anyhow. Jenny didn't like the way Miss Folsom talked. What did he care what Jenny liked? What did he care about Miss Folsom? Jenny put down the phone and walked over to him. He could tell from her expression that she was going to try to forget what had happened, try to con him into just going on.

"You didn't eat any breakfast, Milt. Come on and have a cup of coffee and a piece of toast at least before you make your calls."

Because she had asked him to have coffee, Milton walked out of the kitchen and down the hall.

"Halloran, Demitric, Cohen, Antony and the Haunted House, Milt. O.K.?"

Because she had told the girl in the Haunted House he wouldn't get there until noon at the earliest, Milton decided to go there first. The least he could do, he thought, now that he knew, the least he could do was stop doing exactly what Jenny told him to do.

When he parked in front of the big iron gates, he saw that, as usual, when it was at all possible to keep kids out, there were the baby carriages parked on the sidewalk. The *Kaffeeklatsch* was in full force, sitting on the canvas camp stools they had brought, their backs against the iron fencing. There was nothing but cement here for the kids to play on, but here at least the kids could see the grass and bushes and trees behind the gates. Dr. Krop took his medical bag from the car and locked the car door.

"Good morning, Doc."

"Good morning." Mrs. Levinson. False croup. She expected him to ask about her little Michael. "How's Mike been?"

"If he'd had any more trouble, Doc, you'd be the first to know." She had a tooth missing in the front and before laughing always covered her mouth with her hand. She did so now. "You're the doctor, Doc!"

He was supposed to laugh at the joke. "I guess I would at that." Was he really just going on doing what was expected of him?

"You're going into the Haunted House, huh, Doc? What's it like inside?"

"You want more inside dope, you go see the doctor. There's just the old lady and her daughter in all those rooms, is that right, Doc?"

He nodded.

"What's the daughter like? Somebody, I forget, told me she used to see the old lady around before she was bedridden, a regular Maggie Sugarbum— How about the girl? What kind of girl lives like that in a house like that?"

"What kind of girl?" He thought for a minute: hair skinned back, big nose. Skin color like a mushroom from being under glass all the time. Cat had her tongue when he was around. "Well," he said, "she's always reading poetry." The women started shaking their heads at each other when they heard that. Milton realized that each time he came to see the old lady and wanted to sit down on the chair pulled up to her bed and had to lift one of Miss Folsom's little brown books of poetry off it, he shook his head the same way. The house was crammed full of furniture. Once he asked the old lady why she didn't sell it. "My dear man," she said, "you couldn't. At present it is in disrepute." That meant it was old but it wasn't antique. It certainly wasn't "colonial," he knew that much.

"Mrs. Levinson, we're keeping Doc out here talking and meanwhile the old lady could be dying in there."

"Better get to my patient," Milton said and opened the gates. He walked briskly, putting on a doctor act for the *Kaffeeklatsch*.

What they had called the Haunted House was a brownstone turreted pile with bay windows bursting through the flat face like boils. (Jenny went to a place and bought magazines second-hand for the waiting room. *The New Yorker* magazine had the Charles Addams cartoons, like this house. It was like a Charles Addams cartoon.) The Haunted House had been left over from the old time before Jackson Heights had been built up. If it had once had companionable neighbors, it had none now; what were not big apartment houses were small five-room bungalows built in the twenties. It had about three acres of grounds, with a brick path and a brick drive and the remains of landscaping, a fountain, statues, even the ruins of a little wooden gingerbreaded bridge over the ghost of a stream. The old lady said her grandfather had built the house for his wife, so the grandfather must have had plenty; but now, Milton thought, the old lady and the girl were probably living on the remains of the last mortgage or on the charity of the bank or whoever held the mortgages, until they decided to foreclose and throw them out of this pile and build another apartment house on the site. Now the old lady lived on bread and water and family pride and, one of these days, today, tomorrow, next year, five years from now, the old lady would be carried out feet first. (But she didn't *know*, Milton thought, stumbling. She didn't know for sure that it would be within a couple of years, so it wasn't the same thing.) He walked more carefully up the overgrown path, hearing the murmur of the women's voices behind him. When he had seen the pictures of the villa in Antibes lying on the old lady's bed that time, he had even figured she'd dreamed she'd be well enough sometime (and rich enough) to take a trip to the Riviera. The pictures had been cut out of some magazine—"steps cut into the living rock descend from the cliff-top house down to the sea," he remembered. He had figured the old woman had dreamed—and asked her, but she said, "Oh, that's my daughter's." So the daughter, poor kid, was the one who wanted to go down to the sea in dreams. So the daughter and the doctor had that in common, he thought—dreams.

The grass which had forced itself up between the bricks was tall enough to bend and wave in the breeze. The lawn looked like a wheat field. What had been plump rhododendron bushes were so tall and stringy that they were like withered, arthritic arms with leaves clutched in the deformed fingers. Why couldn't the girl get herself a pair of blue jeans and get out here and clean up the grounds for exercise? It would do her a world of good to get out from under, to get away occasionally from the old lady's beck and call. He played with the idea of giving the old lady a good talking-to about the daughter being indoors so much. He remembered his mother reading from the Bible: "Honour a physician. . . . For of the most High cometh healing." The old lady didn't know her Bible very well because she certainly didn't honor him. He walked up the stone steps carefully for he always had the feeling the stone was ready to crumble, and the whole house, in fact, give way. With the old lady, he thought, he had no authority. He had a lot of foreign patients from the old country where they were supposed to bargain but they didn't, not about his fees, anyhow, while the old lady, the blue blood all-American family, did. "For of the most High cometh healing. . . ." Man in white. She probably called the Good Humor man a man in white. His mother must turn in her grave at the honoring the old lady did to him. Oh, God, he thought. Oh, God, if only his mother hadn't believed being a doctor was the greatest honor. Four years in college. Four years in medical school. Interning. All the Krop boys . . . And now that he knew for sure, what was he going to do about it?

He was just about to ring the bell when he saw that the door had been left slightly ajar; for him, no doubt, so the old lady must be really in a bad way, he thought, because they never left it open. The girl must not have wanted to leave her mother even long enough to answer his ring. He stepped inside, reminding himself not to be startled this time by the two suits of armor which stood one on either side of the wide hall, just inside the door, challenging him: Who goes there? It was dark inside. When the girl came down to open up for him, he generally heard her putting the light on along the way, for him, that is. She, he was sure, could find her way around without lights. Knew every inch by heart. Born here. Knew where the thin rugs scattered on the dark floor had tears in them. He moved cautiously down the hall, transferring his medical bag to his left hand so that with his right he could feel along the wall for the wall light he remembered was somewhere in the neighborhood, but he couldn't find it. Be damned, he thought, if he was going to die of a broken neck here. He called, "Miss Folsom! It's the doctor, Miss Folsom!"

He never did know what it was, what small sounds heard and translated subconsciously, or what sudden vacuum, what sounds indrawn, made him forget about breaking his neck and hurry along the dim hall and turn to the right into one of the dim rooms off it just in time to catch her tipping the bottle, spilling the pills into her palm. She was not looking at him but at the glass of water ready on the desk to wash the pills down with. Milton dropped his medical bag and ran across the room and

18

grabbed the bottle with one hand while he held her hand with the other. He then set the bottle down on the desk that had the water on it and took the pills she had spilled on her palm and transferred them to his left hand. Then he retrieved the bottle and, bending over to put the pills back, saw the suicide note. It read: *Amory, I am committing suicide because I poisoned Mother.* It was signed *Sloane*.

Milton discovered that while he had been reading the note he had put the six pills she had spilled out back into the bottle and screwed the top back on. Now he put the bottle into his jacket and the suicide note into the inside breast pocket where he kept papers, as if a suicide note was as dangerous to leave in her possession as pills. Then he turned back to the girl and said, "What's been going on here?" It seemed to him that his voice broke a long silence but actually it had been only a few minutes since he had called her name in the hall. "Well," he said, "come on, tell me, what's been going on here?"

She licked her lips. "You weren't coming until noon," she said.

It wasn't that he had walked in just as she was going to do it, not a coincidence, that is, and not a fake suicide, he was somehow sure of that. She had left the front door open because she didn't expect him until noon, when it would be all over and done with, and then she had heard him call and tried to get it over with. "Too bad I came earlier, isn't it?" Her lips began to tremble, then her whole body. He went to her and grabbed her arm, which stiffened at his touch and pulled her after him while he moved back into the hall again and toward the stairs.

He was hurting her arm. She said, "Please."

"No," he said, "come on up with me. I'm not going to leave you alone down here." He saw that her eyes were blurred with tears and set her hand on the banister rail so that she could guide herself up. "Come on." She started up obediently and he came after her, one step below. When they reached the half landing, he put his hand under her elbow and helped her up, then turned her toward the big room which was the old lady's and she came along nicely until they reached the open door; then she balked.

"Please," she said, "please."

"You don't want to go in?" She nodded, then she couldn't stop nodding and the violent trembling began again. "None of that," he said. "Listen to me. None of that!" He looked around the hall and saw the bathroom directly ahead and led her that way, then shoved her into it and came in after her. "Wash your face. Let the water run cold over your wrists." (What a bathroom—a museum piece!) He turned on the cold faucet and put her wrists under it and she stood that way, catatonic, bent over the sink. He opened the big brown door of the medicine cabinet and looked over what was in there. At first, in the trance she was in, she didn't understand; then she said, "Don't trouble, there's nothing poisonous there. Just what I gave Mother. I was going to take the rest of them."

He reached into his pocket and showed her the bottle. "This?" She nodded.

"Then what happened?"

She looked down at her wrists. "She hasn't—hadn't been feeling well. She said she was feeling very ill. Since yesterday, oh, groaning—breathing—" She lifted one hand to cover her ear, but when the cold water dripped, she shivered and put her hand back under the faucet. "Since yesterday—groaning—all night." She looked at him. "This morning, I gave her three of the pills. She wouldn't stop. I kept on giving them to her. Four more. Seven. I was going to take the rest."

"Can I leave you alone while I have a look at your mother?"

She nodded again. "It's not so easy—twice." She smiled at him. "One loses—momentum. . . . One wants to live."

One wants to live. Two want to live. Me, too, he thought.

He said, "Yes, one wants to live. Just let that cold water run. I'm going in to have a look at her." He left her staring down at the water running over her thin wrists.

From the doorway it was obvious that the old lady was dead. Milton went to the bed and examined the body briefly, then pulled the sheet up over the head. Considering how to handle the girl, just standing there figuring out how to handle her, he noticed the pile of papers lying on the chair pulled up to the bed where the girl generally sat, where the brown books of poetry usually lay, and he picked the papers up. Partly because the papers might give him a clue, partly to put off the moment when he must face the girl, he went to the window and took the papers with him. The top paper was a letter from the Brown Realty Company and offered Mrs. Folsom $110,000 for her property and requested, this time, the letter said, the courtesy of a reply since if Mrs. Folsom was determined not to sell at this date, the Brown Realty Company would negotiate for other equally desirable property in the vicinity. Then, of course, Milton got it. (He glanced around for the pictures of the house on the cliffside at Antibes, France.) The house didn't belong to the banks, for the love of Mike, it belonged to the old miser! She had had this offer from this firm. Not even "the courtesy of a reply" did it say? Miser, one of those misers! He looked back at the sheeted figure on the bed. "One wants to live." You bet. One kills to live, too. The old lady wouldn't let the girl live. She wanted the girl to go on in this rock pile, rat hole here. She wanted the girl to stay in this rut just like Jenny wanted him to stay in his rut, until the girl died, until he died!

What he felt first was sympathy for the girl, he told himself later, the first thing he had felt was sympathy for the girl.

Cautiously now, he tiptoed away from the window, the papers rustling richly, and set the papers back on the chair where they had been. He listened, but except for the running water there was no sound. Then he tiptoed back to the window, took the bottle out of his pocket again and studied it carefully. He screwed open the top and spilled the pills onto his palm. He smelled them, tasted them, made absolutely sure, in other words, that these were the ones he had dispensed to the old lady himself. The bottle of course was the same. The label was in his own handwriting. CAUTION. POISON. DO NOT OVERDOSE. "Now wait a sec," he told himself. "Hold on a sec. This is it! Look before you leap, Milt. Look the ground over and see what we're getting into, boy. It may seem foolproof but let's look before we leap.

"I'll start from the beginning, O.K.?" he told himself. "No druggist knows about these. I had them around the house. I dispensed them. I know the old lady didn't die of poisoning, so I'm O.K. in case anything happens. I'm in the clear. I'm no accessory to any crime, I'm an accessory to innocence, if there is such a thing. If there is any such animal! The old lady died a natural death, no matter with what provocation, or whatever the girl thought; about that there is no question. The only question is, what do I gain?

"A hold over the girl, that's what I gain, right? A hold over one hundred and ten thousand bucks.

"I didn't arrange this. I didn't plan this. It happened, and it happened today of all days! Boy, I tell you this much, a hold over anyone, yesterday, maybe tomorrow, would be out of my league, but not today. And it happened today. That counts!

"And just to me. Of all the people in the world it could only happen to me!" It was as if, for once in his life, all the stars in the heavens went and formed a design that spelled his name! A thing like this had never happened before and never would again, probably.

"The way I see this is it's my chance. I'd be a fool not to take it the way things are with me." He meant no harm to the girl. Morally the girl had killed her mother when she gave her the overdose of placebo, the same as if she had given her potent medicine. The mother had been dying of course ("the breathing") with less fuss this A.M. probably than many previous times. The girl wouldn't know that this was the genuine article, the stertorous breathing, râles, that this was it. So, she gave her three, and then four more. She had meant to kill, that was the point morally. By telling the girl the facts, he couldn't spare her guilty conscience; all he could do by telling the girl the truth was remove any fear of punishment—which was exactly what he was going to do anyhow.

The first thing he had felt, he reminded himself, was sympathy for the girl. "One kills to live"—he had said that before he knew. He had never felt closer to any girl than he had to her because she wanted to live, like he did. In a way, the two of them were a lot alike. Her mother had kept her in jail and his mother had kept him and the boys in as good as jail. He wanted some icing on his birthday cake, and so did she!

"There's no possible leak," he said. "Even Jenny doesn't know. Thank God Jenny doesn't know. 'What are you going to do, Milt? You'll do something crazy?' Well, this isn't crazy. This is my chance. I'm taking it."

It was funny how the big dim bedroom was different now that he knew how much money the old miser could have had by signing some papers. When you had very little money any room you lived in was a furnished room; your poverty furnished it for you. You were tied down to your pocketbook. Now he looked at the towering headboard of the bedstead with curiosity and respect—the brown wood, the carved yellow flowers inlaid in it. The old woman could have been so much more comfortable in a hospital, or even here in the hospital bed he suggested they rent, which the girl could have raised and lowered and could have made up without so much difficulty. Then she would not have had such a job giving bed baths. It was different now he knew the old lady could have had a private room in the best hospital (and the best doctor, he reminded himself, smiling).

He looked at the pleated newspaper shade on the lamp next to the bed, recalling how the old lady always held up her hand to her face because the light had bothered her but she made the girl pleat newspapers and stick them around the bulb until they singed, and then made her pleat a new one. . . . And there was no easy chair for the girl, just that straight one with the papers on it now. That old lady had handled the girl's life—her lifetime had been handled like the old lady's money! She had locked the girl's life away with the money in this old dark house. He crossed to the door and called out, "You all right there?"

"Yes," she said.

"Be with you in a minute, Miss Folsom." O.K., he told himself, one minute. Sixty seconds to make up your mind once and for all. *For all?* Milton snickered. For all of two years at the most! Who are you kidding? What have you got to lose?

She was standing exactly as he had left her. Milton turned the cold water faucet off and took a towel from the rack. When she made no move, he began to dry her hands for her. Aristocratic hands, you'd call them. Long, pale, thin fingers, flattened at the tips. Pale nails, rounded not pointed nails, not polished but moon shiny, a narrow palm, a wrist he could put his thumb and second finger around. He looked up from her hand to her face, also aristocratic. (It was not the money which had changed his opinion of her face; her face didn't look different to him since he knew about the money.) Her nose, he thought, wouldn't look so long and thin if she didn't pull her pale hair back so tight, and if she would show her mouth. A girl without lipstick positively had no mouth, he thought. Probably the old lady didn't go for lipsticks. Painted women. (Painted Cissie, he thought. Cissie had a baby nose and Cissie believed he was married to Jenny.) Miss Folsom was wearing a nothing skirt and blouse; all her clothes were nothing clothes—but if she put some of the $110,000 on her back?

She turned her head away from his stare. "Please—"

"O.K.," he said. "Let's go downstairs. Where's your telephone?"

"Telephone?" She moved out of the bathroom ahead of Milton. "I will show you—" She stopped in the doorway, wheeling. "Oh—the police. I will show you."

"Not the police, Miss Folsom, the mortician."

"Mort—"

He gave her a push to start her downstairs again. "Undertaker." She walked but turned her head back to stare at him. "I was going to recommend Dinton because they give you a decent funeral cheap but I just recalled a certain letter I saw on the chair in your mother's room. One hundred and ten thousand dollars for this house, it said. . . . If that's so, Miss Folsom, which mortician do you want me to call?" He wanted her to know he had read the letter.

"It doesn't matter, does it?" She held on to the railing, walking carefully.

"Sure?"

"Oh, please!" she said.

Angry at him. He touched her shoulder and she stopped in her tracks, he pressed her shoulder and she turned her face toward him. "Do you understand? I don't think you understand, Miss Folsom, not the police. No police. No cops. No suicide note. Do you understand? I'm going to write out a death certificate. Death by natural causes, as we say. Do you get it? Because even if you don't, I do. I get it. I understand. You have my sympathy. I would have done the same thing myself. A door opened in your face and she shut it in your face. I couldn't take it any more than you could, and I have nothing but sympathy for you, Miss Folsom." He paused expecting—what, he didn't know. Something feminine was as clear as he could get it—that she should bust out crying, something—but she just stood there on the stairs like a log, so he said, "Don't you get it? I'm going to bat for you." She still didn't give, but—you could see it hap-

25

pening—went limp, and he grabbed her and had to hold her up. "Don't be scared," he said, "I'm making myself a—what do you call it—accessory. Come on, let's get it over with before I change my mind." She still didn't do anything feminine, but there was no strength in her so he kept his arm around her in case she'd plunge down the rest of the stairs. But when he got to the bottom and saw the telephone back of the stairs in the hall, he let go of her and she leaned against the stair rail watching him. While he was dialing, he said, "Look, I've never lived either, see? I've been a farm hand since I was knee high to a weed. I worked my way through college and medical school and I've been a doctor. For five years I've supported my sister-in-law and her two kids and today I found out that Jenny's been telling people I'm married to her. Insurance in case I should try to grab a chance to live. Maybe you thought I was married to Jenny, too? She's the one you talk to on the telephone—Mrs. Krop." She shook her head, which meant she didn't think about him at all, she never gave him a thought. Well, she was giving him a thought now, all right. All the time he was talking to Joe Dinton he felt her thinking about him. You could feel it. He kept sticking his finger in between his collar and his neck because her eyes on him made him uncomfortable. What was she thinking of him? My hero? You saved my life? Damned if he knew.

In the way of business, Joe Dinton, Dinton's Funeral Home, treated Dr. Krop with extreme cordiality and respect. Joe's performance with the bereaved was one thing, but when, as between experts, he got confidential about his work— Maybe the little bastard could forget how soon it would be his personal corpse dumped into a wicker basket and worked over, but— Forget it, forget it, Milton told himself. Maybe now you're going to get a decent chance to forget it, he thought, giving Joe the information he needed, telling Joe the death certificate would be forthcoming.

"Now where can I sit down, Miss Folsom?" When she simply blinked, he walked down the hall, re-entering the room where he had found her with the bottle in her hand, picking up his medical bag from the floor where he had dropped it, moving to the desk where she had left the suicide note. When he opened his bag to take out a death certificate, he saw that there were many papers in the pigeon-holes of the desk. How little they resembled the papers in his own desk. Maybe these were money papers and that was the difference. Behind him, Milton could hear her steps. "Miss Folsom, come on over and give me some facts."

She came and standing with her hands clenched at her sides answered his questions. Then she said, "Why?"

Milton tapped his pen against the back of his hand, on the black hair that sprang there abundantly, vitally. "Why am I sticking my neck out for you, you mean?"

"Yes, why?"

"I told you. Because you have my complete sympathy, and, to be perfectly frank with you, I don't think I'm sticking it out very far. I was your mother's doctor a long time now. With her condition, she could have died today, tomorrow, five years from now. If I hadn't come in and seen what you wrote, that's what I would have assumed—that her condition killed her." He saw how she was digging her nails into her palms. "Have you any stimulants in the place?" Her eyes were pale blue.

"Stimulants?"

Wrong word? He had used it to sound high-toned. "Liquor. A shot." She shook her head. "Well, I'm going to give you a pill before I leave. To calm you down, sedate you." She shook her head again. "You will have to put yourself in my hands, Miss Folsom, because I've put myself in your hands, haven't I? Tit for tat. I can't have you breaking down when Joe Dinton comes, can I?" Now her eyes were a darker blue.

"No, of course not, of course not."

He put his pen down and took her hands in his. "Look, I'm on your team. I'm on your side." Her hands did not respond at all to the pressure of his. Cold hands. "We're pals," he said, but that sounded so crude, "we're birds of a feather, that's what we are, see?" She blinked and he dropped her hand and continued filling out the certificate in a businesslike way. When it was finished he said, "I could give you an injection—put you out. I could call the mortician, tell them. You could leave the door open and they'd remove her without disturbing you; then when you woke up from the injection it would all be over. How about that?"

She said, "I couldn't. No, thank you."

He pulled his medical bag toward him and rummaged in it, taking out a sample of sedative. "Then just take this. It won't do more than quiet you down." She barely nodded. "You have nothing to worry about any more. You understand that, don't you? You have nothing to fear."

"No, Dr. Krop."

No, Doctor, yes, Doctor! Why couldn't she be—feminine?

"But I don't like leaving you alone like this. Haven't you got somebody you could call and ask to stay with you?"

"No one."

"Maybe someone real close wouldn't be such a good idea— You might be tempted to get talkative— How about a distant relative?"

"There is no relative I could call on. Mother avoided relatives."

"Boy friend? Girl friend? A neighbor?"

She looked astonished. There were no neighbors as far as she was concerned, as far as Miss Folsom was concerned all the people in the apartment houses or in the bungalows didn't exist.

"I get around a lot, naturally," Milton said. "How about a lady patient of mine? There's a Mrs. Antenelli. . . ." (Right outside your gate this minute, even if you don't know it!) "She's a good-natured slob, be happy to oblige." (Jump at the chance to see the inside of the Haunted House.)

"Thank you, but I couldn't. If I'm not—not going to jail, I'll have to get used to being alone."

From habit, he thought, from the ways forced on her by the old miser. When he got up from the desk, Miss Folsom closed the flap, hiding from him the papers, the letters that looked and smelled like money. He said, "Now, now, you're not alone. You have me." He snapped his bag shut, giving her the certificate. "Wait a minute, when they're through here—it won't be long, they'll just ask a couple of questions about the funeral arrangements—suppose you lock up and go to a hotel for a while. Go on," he urged, "I prescribe it. Go to the Waldorf-Astoria, get yourself the royal suite." She was shaking her head. "Oh, go on, change of air—"

She said firmly, "It would look so odd. I must not do anything that would look odd."

All Milton could say was that he could see he could trust her. She had begun now to walk toward the front door, and all he could do was follow her. With his patients, he had discovered that the best way was to tell them when he would see them again, but she wasn't his patient, was she? What was she? Standing in front of one of the suits of armor, she held out her hand in a boy kind of way, and when he held his out, shook it.

"It would be absurd to thank you," she said.

He remembered Cissie thanking him for a lift to the subway, blushing, fluttering, patting. "You don't need to thank me." It seemed to him then that she gave his hand a little press before she dropped it, and he told himself that this was the same as Cissie kissing his hand, kissing his feet, just that darkening of Miss Folsom's light-blue eyes was the same as Cissie kissing his feet. "So long," he said.

Milton was aware, as he left her in the dim hall and went down over the path—keeping his eyes on it because the long grass might trip him and, in case she was watching from one of the windows, make him ridiculous—that he had not asked her to call or said he would get in touch with her. He hadn't deliberately done so, but now he thought he wanted it left up in the air. He, anyhow, was certainly up in the air. What would happen now? He didn't know. "Hold over her" was for a professional blackmailer, not for him; not, with his blood pressure, for him. For him, it couldn't be, "You give me XX dollars, or else—" For him, it had to be nice. So what? So he just didn't rightly know what the program was from here on. Search him. The prognosis, he thought, he didn't know the prognosis here. It wasn't one of the subjects he'd studied in medical school.

His face must have shown something because, the moment he pulled the gate to, behind him, Mrs. Antenelli said, "Anything wrong in the Haunted House, Doc?"

"The old lady is dead." He lowered his voice, frowning at the brilliant sunshine as though it should have dimmed in respect. "Mrs. Folsom was dead when I arrived," he said.

"Rest in peace. Oh, is that the name? Folsom?"

"Folsom."

"Rest in peace. What did she die of, Doc?"

He hadn't time to answer before Mrs. Levinson told Mrs. Antenelli that doctors weren't allowed to divulge about people's sickness.

"There's a law, isn't there, Doc?"

"Yeah, the unwritten law, isn't it, Doc?"

Mrs. Levinson was the first to stand and kick up the brake of her baby carriage, which she had been gently shaking, and then fold her canvas stool and hitch it behind the handle of the carriage. The others began lifting their charges from the sidewalk where they had been playing. Either they did not find it proper that their children's play should desecrate the house of mourning, or they instinctively wished to remove their kids from death.

No one wanted to be near death if he could help it. No one wanted to be contaminated by death; no one wanted to die.

Milton stood at the edge of the sidewalk, studying his watch, while the women, for once silenced, gathered the toys the kids had scattered around and moved away. When Milton got into his car and started the motor, he twisted around to see the old house in the sunlight. He wondered if the girl was thinking about him. Walking up and down the big dim rooms, perhaps the one with the money desk in it, stopping at the desk, touching the heavy carved flap with her thin flat-end fingers, wishing she could turn back the clock and have it that morning before she gave the old lady those pills? (He took one hand off the wheel to feel the bottle in his pocket, then, remembering, touched the breast pocket into which he had thrust her suicide note.) Well, she couldn't turn back the clock; only he could do that. This time—for once, that is—he was in control.

He turned into Roosevelt, now reasonably full of women on domestic business. He could not hear what the girls were saying, just their lips moving, but whatever it was each of them looked out for number one, so looking out for number one, for a change—what next? "Hold over" meant everything or nothing depending on what you did about it. The handshake she had just given him could be the kiss-off as far as Miss Folsom was concerned, if he let it be, so what it came down to was, was he going to let it be? Did he intend to let the girl sell the house for $110,000, go off to Antibes and lie on that beach in the picture there in one of the bikinis they wore in France and remember him in her prayers? Leave him something in her will, say?

Which was a hot one. Anybody leaving him something in their will had better kick off very soon.

He moved and heard the rich money-crackle of the paper on which she had written the suicide note. What had he taken that for? The bottle of placebo, yes, but why the suicide note?

To be on the safe side. If he had the note, he had the proof the girl had done it by herself.

But she hadn't done anything.

Just leave it that the letter was an ace in the hole. He didn't have to figure it out, just hold onto it and let it ride.

Let it ride? Yes, he thought, for once let it ride. Let it rip.

He found that he had driven back to the apartment without thinking. His car, like himself, kept in line. It wasn't in the Studie to go off on any joy ride, even on a day like this.

If all she was going to do, he thought, was leave him something in her will, then she had better try suicide a second time and with something more potent than a bottle of placebo.

He got out of his car and locked it, nodding professionally as he passed in answer to the greeting of the small gossiping group of housewives gathered in front of the big apartment house. All the women said "Hello, Doc." They all knew the Doc. Maybe no one knows the Doc, Milt thought, maybe they just think they know the Doc. He went into the house and paused before the rows of bells in the front vestibule, pressing the Doctor's Bell, which was different from all the others. Maybe the Doc was different from the rest of them at that, he thought. They're all sheep led to the slaughter, but maybe not the Doc, at that. The clicking started immediately and he let himself into the inner lobby.

Jenny was standing by their open door, waiting for him. She knew his ring. Because Jenny was in her "nurse's" uniform, she deferred to Milton, standing back and permitting him to go first, following him up the hall into the room in which he had slept and where now four patients waited. They all greeted him and Milton nodded and walked through to the door which, had this not been rented as a doctor's apartment, would have been the dining room. Jenny followed him in and held out her hands for his jacket. She picked up the white office coat to hold for him while he put it on. Jenny was putting on an act that nothing had happened because what else could she do? No matter how big she talked about everything being for his good, she was thinking of number one. There was no law that said he had to provide for Jenny and the kids. He could walk out on her—and did, leaving her holding the jacket. Jenny, the jacket still in her hands, followed him and he told her she'd better call the patients he was supposed to have seen that morning and tell them he had been delayed by an emergency call. She asked what emergency call but he said he'd tell her after she telephoned the patients. When Milton saw that she was at the telephone, looking up numbers, he went through the kitchen and into the hall near the bathroom, to "his" closet. His valise, where Jenny stored his woolen stuff in the summer, was up on the top shelf. He took it down, listening to Jenny's voice telling Mrs. Antony why he hadn't visited her that morning, opened it and felt the slit in the lining to make sure the note would go in without creasing. Then he wrapped the note in one of the clean handkerchiefs from a lower shelf and slipped it into the slit. The bottle he shoved into the pocket of an old pair of blue serge pants, then fastened the valise again and put it back where it belonged. (My God, even "his" valise had been Hut's valise first!)

As Milton walked back to the examining room, he heard the telephone ring. He got there in time to see Jenny put the phone back in its cradle and hunt for another number in the directory.

"That was Miss Folsom just now, Milt. Now she wants to talk to you. Free advice." Jenny sighed. "Honestly, Milt, no matter what they say about modern progress, doctors had it better before they invented the telephone. If you came to a doctor's office and took up his time, you felt some obligation at least. To a doctor the telephone will never replace the horse!"

"Well, she won't be wanting much more advice—free or otherwise—about the old lady. She was dead when I got there. D.O.A. That's where I spent most of the morning." Jenny "tsched." He knew she was subtracting the eight dollars a week from their regular income.

"That's how it goes," she said. "It was only to be expected with her. I told Miss Folsom you'd call back as soon as you could, but if the old lady's dead, what's the hurry?" In order to prevent Milton from calling the girl even if there was no hurry, she went to the waiting room and told the first patient to come in, the doctor would see him now.

The history charts of the four patients were laid out on the desk. While the first one was getting undressed, Milton could have made the telephone call, but he didn't want to, not knowing what to do next. Manna had fallen at his feet and he had bent and picked it up, yes, but what to do next he didn't know and he was scared he'd do the wrong thing. So he saw the four patients and that took an hour and a half. It was after twelve when he let the last one out the front door. Standing there, he could hear Maureen's whine, home for lunch and to beg Jenny to let her buy a new costume for tap dancing. He couldn't blame Jenny for giving in to the kid, he thought. You'd have to be made of iron to stand up against that whine, whine. Although since Jenny was Maureen's mother it might not sound so bad to her. Jenny, being their mother, thought that he or anybody else should be happy to slave his life away providing for Maureen and Bud. She had another think coming.

The telephone rang and he hurried back into the consultation room to answer it, calling to Jenny that he was getting it. If it was Miss Folsom calling again after he hadn't called her back, well, she would certainly think that as far as he was concerned he'd be satisfied to be remembered in her prayers. "Hello," he said, "Dr. Krop speaking."

Her voice trembled. "This is Sloane Folsom. They took—they just took her—but I didn't give them—the—certificate."

"But then they can't—"

"I said you wanted me to come to your office and get it—the

certificate—and then I would bring it to them. That you had to see another—" She paused. "I simply cannot allow—"

He said, "Now, now, now! I see you haven't taken the sedative I left, have you? You sound pretty hysterical to me, Miss Folsom."

"I cannot permit you to— It is too—too much."

"I better see you," he said. "I'll be right over. I better." He could not ask the girl to come over here, Milton thought, smelling the fish Jenny had cooked for their lunch, looking with distaste at his consultation room, hearing Maureen's high whine. Miss Folsom had never seen this place and he was glad of that. "Sit tight. I'll be right over." He went into the kitchen and told Jenny that the Folsom girl was in hysterics. "I'm going over there now."

Jenny shrugged. As he moved down the hall, she said, "Milt —no matter what, give her some medication, so she'll know it's not a social call. That's always the best thing. And then you better go to the clinic before you make your calls from this morning. They'll keep. Halloran, Demitric, Cohen, Antony. You should be back by five-thirty; there's a couple appointments in the office. You're going to be a little rushed since I gather you spent the whole morning at the Haunted House."

Jenny always *gathered*. She gathered this and gathered that. Maybe, for a change, he would gather, too. He said, "Is that what you gathered, goosie, goosie, gather!"

Maureen looked up from her lunch, giggling.

Miss Folsom was wearing a thin black dress instead of the skirt and shirt, and that was new to him as was the smaller room she led him into, on the other side of the house; he had never been in there. As they had never been before to his knowledge, the windows were open in here, and because they opened onto the grass and bushes and trees, he smelled weather again instead of cement and cars and people, which was new, also.

35

He stood at the window, breathing in while Miss Folsom repeated that she could not accept his sacrifice. She had thought it over and decided she had better go to the police. (It was a new voice.) He kept his face toward the window.

"What would they do to me?"

He turned. "That I couldn't say. I'm a doctor, not a lawyer. You could tell them the—mitigating circumstances," he said, "the provocation—that it certainly wasn't premeditated." He smiled. "You can tell I'm giving out with what I've read in the papers—the language—how should I know?"

"I've read the papers. Temporary insanity—"

"Temporary sanity," he said with feeling, "that's my opinion, for what it's worth—that's how I felt about it. All my sympathy, I told you—"

"You are—very kind sounds absurd. All my words sound absurd, Dr. Krop, for what you are willing to do, but I cannot let you do it."

"That's up to you," he said. "In the final analysis, that's up to you. I took too much on myself when I came down the stairs and told you your worries were over and I'd sign the death certificate. Kindred spirits," he said, the phrase coming to him, but sounding wrong, "kindred souls."

"But it is so much more dangerous than you think, Doctor! You think there is just the offer for the house. There is much more and that makes it more dangerous."

"Insurance?" Living on bread and water to pay the premiums, like he had to.

"No. The Folsom estate, Dr. Krop. Even now the Folsom estate does not merely mean this house—and the bulk of it goes to me. There are some bequests, of course, but the most part is mine. If there were no estate, I would allow you to—I don't want—I assure you, I don't want whatever will happen to happen."

"You want to live. I know. One day I saw some pictures cut

out of a magazine—a villa in Antibes, how it looked inside, outside, the beach— I asked your mother, as a joke, of course, whether she was planning a trip to the Riviera and she told me they were your pictures." She looked puzzled, which astonished him because every detail of the pictures was clear in his mind, even the description, "engaging villa . . . life divides between rooms coolly devoid of color and terraces set against the flamboyant hues of the Mediterranean—" The taste of the description was fresh in his mouth. "Côte D'Azur," he said, and she repeated "Côte D'Azur," pronouncing it differently, he noticed.

"That is my sister Amory," she said. "Amory lives in Antibes."

It was the first he had heard of any sister. No wonder. The sister lived on the Riviera, this one stayed home, "among the cinders," like Cinderella. "You stayed here and were the good kid. Like Cinderella."

"My sister had ways of prying money loose, Dr. Krop. Amory has had every penny out of Mother that was coming to her. She doesn't inherit."

"I see."

"So you see that it could mean trouble." She moved a step closer. "It is because of my sister that I cannot accept your help. She will come back, I assure you. She won't accept this."

"Why not? I don't get it. She knows your mother was sick. She knows people with hearts like your mother's die every day. Your mother could have died any day. Any doctor will tell your sister that. Let her ask any doctor—even a French one." Now he moved closer, staring into the girl's eyes. "Listen," he said, "if that's all, I'll handle her."

"Handle her?" She blinked, then stared.

"I'll take care of your sister if she comes around, I promise you that. Don't give your sister another thought." He moved closer. "Don't worry, don't worry," he whispered. She moved away and he frowned. "O.K.," he said, "let's face it. We don't know each other and we don't know what a jury would say about what happened here this morning. You have provocation, Miss Folsom. You could tell how your mother treated you. Take the jury for a tour of this rock pile. Show them. Maybe a jury with no personal interest would say not guilty, temporary insanity; you don't know that and you don't know whether you'd rather trust those twelve men or me, isn't that it? I might have a very personal interest."

"Dr. Krop!"

"No, let's face it, let's face it. Between this morning and now, you thought about that. You thought if you let me do this you'd put yourself in my hands. I'd have a hold over you. You thought that, admit it."

She said calmly, standing her ground, "Yes, of course I thought that."

This voice she used now was dry. She had squeezed all the panic and fear out of it. That's what money did, he thought. The minute I closed the front door after me and she calmed down a little, she realized that now she owned it all and that changed the picture. The Folsom estate. "That's what you thought, you admit it. After all, what do you know about me? That I'm an accredited, competent physician? I could be a— excuse me! I could be a big you-know-what for all you know."

"Yes," she said, "you could be."

"You're forgetting one thing, though. The minute that death certificate goes out, you have something on me. It works both ways. And let me remind you of one thing more. This should show you! Whatever I might do from now on, Miss Folsom, this morning—with no ax to grind—I saved your life! And you know how I happened to be able to save your life? Because I didn't come here *after* the other patients the way Jenny told you I would. Mrs. Krop. I was right there when she told you I couldn't get around to you until after noon, and the reason she told you that is Jenny doesn't have much use for you or your mother." He rubbed his thumb against his fingers in a money gesture. "As far as she knew and I knew, the Folsom estate paid us the sum of two dollars per call whereas my other patients paid three-fifty to five bucks. But I came here first for one reason and for one reason alone—because you've had my sympathy right along. Because before I knew a thing about you and your mother having more than two bucks between you—plus some books of poetry, Miss Folsom—I figured the banks were just letting you stay on in this house until they threw you out. Before it meant anything to my possible advantage, Miss Folsom, I came here first—for your sake!" He had gotten himself all worked up and when she didn't move, he did. Out of the room, into the hall, right to the telephone. Then he called her. "Get the cops," he said. "Call them up now. I'll tear up the death certificate." He heard her coming across the room, down the hall, and stared at the telephone he was holding toward her. So that was that, he thought, that was that. He hadn't been able to handle it. He had fumbled the ball. They had passed it to him but he couldn't hang on to it. When she reached him, he set the telephone down so he could dial "O," then handed the receiver to her.

"Police?" she said. "Is this the police? This is Sloane Folsom." She spoke slowly with her eyes boring into his face and he stood there giving her stare for stare. Hell with her. She told the police the address of the Haunted House. "There are some boys climbing our fence," she said. "Trespassing, yes. Please see that they leave. No, officer," she said, "I can't chase them myself. My mother died this morning in this house." She cleared her throat. "I said my mother died this morning so. . . . I will call out to them, officer. I'll say the police are coming, but if they don't leave I will call you again and then—" She set the receiver down without taking her eyes off him. "I did not distrust you, Dr. Krop. It was Amory—it was my sister, and if you will take care of her—"

Her voice faded away. She began to tremble, with increasing violence. He could hear her teeth chattering and she turned so pale he was sure she was going to pass out. When he came to her this time she clung to him and he picked her up and carried her to the room with the money desk in it where there was a couch and laid her on it. Her breathing was rapid and shallow, her skin moist. When he put his hand to the front of the black dress to loosen it, she grabbed his hand; then she used her other hand to pull him down to her.

At first he thought, "Gratitude." She had tested him and not found him wanting as the saying went. "That's O.K., gratitude," he thought, feeling her teeth as she pressed her lips against his in gratitude; then he thought, "Oh, well, hysteria."

Then he said to himself, "I'll be damned. Well, I'll be damned. Well, I'll be damned."

He said, "Look, don't blame yourself for this, Miss—say, I can't go on calling you Miss Folsom, can I?"

She looked up at him with her light blue eyes, now darker than he had ever seen them, and then closed her eyes. "Sloane."

"Sloan," he repeated. "Well, don't blame yourself for this, Sloane. Don't get thinking you're some kind of freak. I mean—believe me, I'm a physician and I know what I'm talking about. This sort of thing happens under strain more often than you think, even to shy kids like you. Reading poetry . . . Like they say, people are funny, Sloane." She kept her eyes closed. "You get my point, don't you? What happened to your mother—the shock, the scare and all—and making up your mind about me—this—what just happened—this is part of the—release from tension, that's all, chalk it up to that."

She opened her eyes wide and he saw that they were lighter blue again and that now she was smiling. Her lips twitched.

She said, "Oh, yes, release from tension."

"Well, all I wanted to say was these things happen. I wanted you to know these things happen." He wished, now that she seemed more herself again, she'd pull down her skirts and button up, but she didn't move.

"Ah," she said, smiling up at him, not moving though, "how funny you are! How sweet. Do you think with my mother's murder—do you think that Lady Macbeth was worried about the germs on her hands?" She held up her hand and then slid it into his shirt where it was unbuttoned, laying her palm flat against his bare chest. "Unseemly," she said, "*ungemütlich*. How sweet you are!"

"What?"

"Never mind. Hold me," she said, "you're sweet. Hold me."

So he held her. "O.K.," he said, "O.K., now, O.K." He told himself that it certainly was one way of breaking the ice, wasn't it?

He dropped Miss Folsom at the funeral home and then drove off and parked a block away while she brought the death certificate in so Joe Dinton could go ahead. She returned to the car in about fifteen minutes and when he asked her whether Joe had asked any questions she said, with assurance, no, of course not, as if nobody would ever question her. They started back toward the Haunted House and Milton didn't see what he could do except drop her there, but, a block away, she suddenly turned and asked him not to leave her, please. Because he hadn't expected this, because, he thought, he was still so damned well trained, he said he would like to stay with her but he really had to go to his cardiac clinic at Queens General.

She said, of course. The poor patients, she said. She touched his sleeve. "Take me with you."

"Take you—"

"Let me go with you."

"Today?"

She smiled. "Dr. Krop, visiting a hospital clinic couldn't possibly be called festive, if that's what's worrying you."

So Milton took Miss Folsom with him. He had worked in the clinic since he started practice, and most of the old-timer patients knew him. As he and Miss Folsom walked down the corridor past the rows of patients on benches toward the examining rooms, he was greeted many times. Their clinic visit was a big event in these people's lives, the doctors were VIP's to them; the way they greeted him showed that. Milton took this for granted until he noticed Miss Folsom looking at him with real respect and then he realized that by letting her come here he was showing himself up against the best possible background. (Maybe I'm better at this than I know, he thought, maybe I'm smarter than I know.) There couldn't be a better character reference than the way those patients looked up to him. It was only in the hospital clinic, where you worked for nothing, that there was any approximation of the glory that he and the boys had been promised by their mother in the kitchen in Brookfield when she started the four of them becoming doctors. Here Miss Folsom couldn't see Jenny, or the greasy bills she collected for him, or the Hide-a-Bed on which he slept, or the bathroom where he dressed or the linen closet where he kept his clothes. (And her suicide note. And the bottle of pills.) Just as his mother had promised, Miss Folsom, walking next to him, was looking at him as if he was Somebody! He felt, however, that if he went on and introduced her to the other doctors and she heard their shoptalk, it would be a letdown. God knows there were no knights in shining armor in Queens General! He stopped and waved at the benches and asked Miss Folsom to sit down and wait, he had to start examining. Miss Folsom saw the clinic nurse, Miss O'Connor, hurrying to him— "Oh, Doctor!"—and heard the social worker asking when he could discuss— Good, he thought, swell. He shrugged at Miss Folsom, who was choosing a seat on the patients' benches, and walked into the little cubicle and waited for the patients to be weighed and brought in to him.

Half an hour later, when Milton came out to bring a chart which hadn't been properly filled out, he looked for her and saw that of all the patients there, Miss Folsom had chosen to sit next to old Austen, the Limey, old sourpuss Austen. Old Austen was talking away and that struck him funny. (This was the day, all right!) In the four years that he had seen old Austen once every three weeks, he had never once seen her unbend to anybody. "Yes, Doctor; no, Doctor," that was all Austen ever said to a soul until now. The other patients didn't exist for her any more than the neighbors existed for Miss Folsom. ("Sloane," he reminded himself, smiling at her, and she smiled back even if old sourpuss didn't.) He left the chart on the desk with a note on it and returned to the cubicle examining stall.

All the time he was examining patients, taking cardiographs, making notes on charts and writing out medication slips, he was trying to decide what the next move should be. Would it be better to take it for granted that now—after what happened —it would happen again, or act as if it had never happened? Wouldn't that be the gentlemanly thing to do—act like what happened was "a closed book"? Talk about her mother? Never mention her mother? He examined, prescribed and listened mechanically to complaints. Shortness of breath. "If I didn't have them four flights to climb, Doc. How can I lose weight? Eat a lot of meat, she says. I'd like to see her eat meat on what they allow me for food, Doc. My legs are all swole up, Doc. Are you going to give me the needle today, Doc?" Milton was still up in the air when he and Miss Folsom walked out of the hospital together and got into the Studie, still didn't know. (He noticed, because it was so different from Cissie, how Miss Folsom climbed in, how she didn't give a damn what she showed getting in. Miss Folsom just got in and sat, he noticed.) She seemed to be waiting for him to make the next move and still he didn't know what it should be. As they approached the Haunted House and he still didn't know, he began to perspire.

43

He was afraid that with her thinking him so marvelous she would assume that this was all. Remember him in her prayers. He'd done his good deed for the day, and that was that. Of course he could have something to say about that—and if he had to— (He could do anything he had to. Today proved that.) But he'd rather have it smooth. No threats. No blackmail. No strain on his heart.

When he pulled up in front of the gates of the Haunted House Milton became self-conscious about sweating so much and rolled down the window. The air, rushing in, seemed to wake Miss Folsom and she began talking, but about, of all things, old sour-puss Austen. He was sure she had learned more about Austen in that one talk than he or anyone else at the clinic had learned in four years. To flatter her, he said as much and she smiled. She had approached Austen, she said, without in the least knowing why consciously, but apparently she had chosen to sit next to her because without being conscious of it, she had recognized the type. Austen was a servant, a genuine servant. The real vanishing redskins, she said. Austen, she said, should be preserved.

"In vinegar?"

She shook her head. If Austen was vinegary, it was because she so resented living on what she called the dole. Poor old creature, she said, she'd be as out of place in England now as she is here in New York. Mrs. Austen was living in a world she never made. It turned out, Miss Folsom said, that Austen had been cook at the Endicotts'—friends of Mother's—for over twelve years, wasn't that odd?

(What was odd to him was the way she could say "Mother's" so easily.)

Mother, Miss Folsom said, had probably eaten Austen's cooking many times. The Endicotts had been most particular, so Austen must be a splendid cook. She so enjoyed cooking. Austen had told her that she had gone on cooking after she knew she had heart disease but she had been forgetful about her restric-

44

lious and had become very much worse so that she had been forbidden to work, poor old creature.

"She's not the only poor old creature in Queens General," he said. "The place is lousy with them."

"I know!" She turned to him. "Could I help? It is going to be—hard," she said. "It will be twice as hard if I have too much time on my hands."

"Just while you're stuck in that house," Milton said. He could see she couldn't leave tomorrow; it would look funny. (She had a lifetime in front of her to live, he thought.) "Why don't you go out and work on the grounds there? That's good healthy work, and they sure could stand it!"

"But I like them that way," she said.

"Oh, they'll tear it all up anyway, when they build—"

She said, as if it didn't matter, "That's right. Do you know what I should do on the grounds though? I should see that the Victorian garden is preserved. I should see it is set up some-where—like the herb garden at the Cloisters. That should be preserved. I will work on that, yes." She clapped her hands. "I know now why I sat down next to Austen!"

"Why?" She looked ten years younger all of a sudden. She was holding out her hand so that he could see her black glove. "Why?"

"Because her gloves were darned like mine."

Why the poor kid, Milton thought. Now he remembered noticing—before—that her stockings often had a sewn-up run in them. He hadn't seen a sewn-up run since Caesar was a pup. Jenny wouldn't sew up runs; Jenny threw runnered stockings away the way she shoveled the two glazed yellow eyes of egg yolks into the garbage can. Milton was so sorry for Miss Folsom then that, without thinking was it the right thing to do, he took his hand off the wheel and pressed it against her thigh, and she took her hand and helped press his hand against her thigh, hard, meaning it. He saw that her eyes were that darker blue again, so it was going to be all right. She had asked to work in the hospital with him. Her hand was pressing his hand. It was going to be all right. "No more darns," he said, smiling at her. "You can count on me, you know that now, don't you?"

"I know I can." She put her hand up to her forehead. "I knew I could from the beginning. It was only Mother who was dubious about you, Dr. Krop. It was Mother who made me telephone you and—break up our partnership this noon."

"What?"

"Her ghost. Her ghost walked—up and down—not clanking chains, just pursing her lips the way she did when she didn't think much of an idea. Her nostrils always pinched, her mouth pursed— After you left Mother kept walking up and down with that dubious expression, telling me I was being a credulous fool to put myself in your power. Isn't that preposterous—Mother? Under the circumstances?"

Under the circumstances, he told her, the quicker she got rid of her mother's house and got out the better.

"It is not my mother's house, it is my house." Her nostrils pinched. Her mouth pursed. "It is my house, Dr. Krop."

Chapter II

MILTON should have guessed that Jenny would go and see Sloane. The evening before Jenny had been waiting up for him when he came home from an A.M.A. meeting. She had already opened up the Hide-a-Bed and made it up for him and was lying on it in her nightgown with what looked like Buddy's school sweater thrown over her shoulders. The thought of Jenny lying on his bed, warming the sheets for him, made him uncomfortable and he frowned at her. "Lie somewhere else, can't you?"

She didn't stir. "Where were you, Milt?"

"Did you need me?"

"No, as it happened, I didn't, but if I had needed you I wouldn't have known where to reach you."

"Well, as it happened, I took in a meeting at the A.M.A."

"That's right," she said, sitting up. "I forgot. A.M.A. meeting tonight, I forgot. Anyhow, you weren't at a meeting last night. You were at the Haunted House."

"For the love of Mike, Jenny, don't talk like the other biddies. It's not a haunted house."

"Well," she said, stretching her leg, pointing her toe, "you haunt it."

"How much do you charge to haunt a house? That was a joke, wasn't it, son? Lie somewhere else, will you?" She had red nail polish on her toes.

Jenny jumped off the bed and smoothed the blanket. Her hands had more flesh on them than Miss Folsom's had, and, of course, red polish.

"What do you charge to haunt a house, Milt? You must have made twenty visits since the old lady died, but I gather you don't charge anything or I'd have had a decent bill to send on the first. What gives, Milt?"

He should have guessed that when he wouldn't give Jenny any satisfaction she would go and find out for herself. Sloane told him right off that Jenny had come barging in that morning when he was safely making his calls.

Sloane said, "She called you 'Milt.' "

"Well, my name is Milton."

"Milton, yes, John Milton."

"Milt isn't as bad as what her kids call me. You can guess what they call me!" She couldn't, apparently. "From on television? Radio? 'Uncle Miltie,' you know." But Sloane had never heard of Milton Berle. "Well, I never heard of John Milton. Who's John Milton?" She told him. She put her hand over his eyes.

"Blind Milton! 'When I consider how my light is spent ere half my days in this dark world and wide.' "

The sense of the quotation hit Milton suddenly. "When I consider how my light is spent ere half my days—" He took the hand off his eyes and held it to his cheek. "Why did you say that?"

"Why, why? I don't know any more of it. Milton—John— isn't my boy!"

"Why did you say that to me? What did Jenny tell you about me?" They were in the small room downstairs which was where they generally stayed. It had four big windows, clear glass, not

48

stained like some of the others, so it wasn't as dark. The walls weren't panelled in here and it wasn't as crowded with big old dark furniture and breakable knickknacks. Here there were books on the tables and a mending basket (like the one his mother used to have) and a bowl with colored wools in it and some blue knitting Sloane was ripping out spilled over the side; it was more homelike here and he didn't mind this room as much as the others. "Tell me what Jenny said, Sloane."

"She told me the circumstances in which your brother had left her and the children and how you had nobly stepped in and supported them. Your sister-in-law had apparently heard some gossip. You have been seen coming in here—although by whom—"

The women at the gates weren't blind, deaf and dumb, he told Sloane. "That's by whom."

"It would seem that you are blind, deaf and dumb, blind Milton—about women, anyhow. You are a babe in arms where women are concerned. You are apt to mistake sympathy for love. A lot more of the same, she told me."

No, Jenny wouldn't have told her about him because you didn't tell patients about their doctor's life expectation. Unreasonable or not, patients didn't like a doctor who—well, physician, heal thyself, the saying went. How could you heal them, patients thought, if you couldn't heal yourself? No, Jenny cared too much about her bread and butter to spill about him.

"So Jenny thinks I've never been in love? I don't know from nothing?" Blind, blind Milton, she whispered, and because the quotation had really sent him, because she had quoted it as if she knew, because he did feel close to her, like her, he began talking about the Browning girl. If he had tried to make love he'd have done a lousy job, probably, but this way, with what the poem did to him, with talking about the Browning girl— Sloane must have been able to hear his sincerity because when

49

he stopped she laid the hand he had been holding against his lips, which was a soft, a real girl kind of thing to do.

"And I remind you of her—Browning?"

The brown mare, the Browning house, the parties, the convertible, the four-car garage, this one could have those things by lifting her little finger. Côte D'Azur, she could have that. "You reminded me of her from the first," he said.

"Your sister-in-law—"

"Jenny!" Jenny didn't consider how his light was spent. Jenny had to run him. Down to the ground. What did she want, Jenny? What was she putting her two cents in for? "My sister-in-law doesn't happen to know you have a nickel to your name. She's afraid you'll take the bread out of her mouth, my sister-in-law!"

"She told me about her boy—the plans she has. I could help with the boy."

"No," he said roughly, "none of that."

"I could help out with your sister-in-law."

That was a laugh, pay him off by giving Jenny money! "None of that."

Now she kissed the palm of his hand. "What can I do, then?" And when she saw how she had startled Milton by taking the initiative that way, going straight to the point, she began to laugh.

(He had been telling himself every time he saw her not to rush it. Three weeks was nothing, he had told himself, he'd ruin everything if he rushed it, he had to go slow—and now—) His face showed his thought. She pointed at his face.

"What a fix it has been in, hasn't it?" she asked. "Literally *The Doctor's Dilemma.* Shaw," she said, "Uncle Miltie Shaw, darling! The poor, poor doctor's been between Scylla and Charybdis. Certainly if you—couchezed avec a good girl you should make it right. But if the girl is in mourning—if the girl is rich. . . . But darling Milton," she whispered, "I am not really in mourning. Oh, there are bad dreams, darling, when I need you near me because you know, because you're the only one—and there are . . . other dreams when I also need you near me." His mouth was hanging open and she put her hand under his chin and gently closed it. "Don't bother puzzling it out, dear blind Milton—will you marry me?"

He sat with his arm around her and squeezed her to him. She leaned her head against him and he could smell the faint odor of her hair. She must shampoo it with Ivory soap, he thought. Ivory soap, for the love of Mike! Because that was one more thing he didn't understand about her. She was wearing the same old black dress and her hair skinned back the same old way and no make-up. Having asked him to come to see her right after lunch, having known what she was going to talk about, how could any female woman do so little to make herself attractive to a man? He could imagine what Cissie Parker would have done in similar circumstances.

"Yes?" Sloane asked.

He must have looked as if he was going to say something. "You know what I'm going to give you for an engagement present?"

"Not a ring, Milton, please. I don't ever wear jewelry."

"I couldn't afford to give you jewelry." He got off the sofa and knelt in front of her, taking her face between his two hands. "What is it you don't have? Anyhow, as far as I can see, you don't have it. What is it every other girl beginning at twelve years of age has? What did the Browning girl have that you don't have?" She couldn't seem to guess. He whispered, "A lipstick."

He was engaged. He hadn't fumbled the ball. He had to tell someone. He wondered what the women at the gate would say if he told them. He should tell them, he had one of them to thank for passing on the good word to Jenny. Mrs. Levinson, probably. He nodded to Mrs. Levinson and asked about her Michael, then got into the car and turned its nose toward home.

Home, hell!

Because he was excited, he didn't ring the bell but used his key and let himself in. The minute he opened the door there was a kind of scurry along the back hall, a door opened and was immediately closed. He got there quickly enough to see that it was his closet door she had opened and shut. Jenny was standing in the entrance to the bathroom.

"Oh, it's you," she said, "that's O.K. I thought it was Bud."

He flung his closet door open and reached up for the suitcase and felt to see if she had left the straps undone, but if she had opened them, she had fastened them again.

Jenny had come away from the bathroom and was standing right behind Milton. "What do you want out of the valise, Milt?"

"What did you want in my closet? My God, all the privacy I have in this place is in this closet, but you have to stick your nose in there, too!"

She said, "Now, listen here, Milt—" but then remembered that he had to be handled with kid gloves. "Now, Milt," she said, and reaching into the closet took out a bottle, showing him that it was peroxide. "All it was, I was touching up my hair, Milt. When you came in I figured it was Bud, so I wanted to quick hide the evidence." She held the open bottle of peroxide under his nose so he could smell it. "It's dumb, but I don't want Bud to know I touch up my hair a little."

He closed his closet door, shoving her back away from it.

"I won't go near your closet if it's so private. I thought you just kept clothes there. In the future, I won't go near it. You can put away your own clean socks and B.V.D.'s if that suits you better, Milt." She smiled at him. "I don't poke my nose where it doesn't belong."

"Don't you? Oh, boy!" But he was in a good humor. "Okay to come in?" He followed her to the bathroom.

"Sure, come in, Milt."

She had wrapped absorbent cotton around the rattail of his comb, he saw, but he should worry now about the way nothing was sacred to Jenny. "Oh, don't you poke your nose where it doesn't concern you!"

She laid his comb down on the sink and faced him. "I gather she told you I went there this morning."

"You gathered right, goosie, goosie, gather! Whither don't you wather! But you gathered wrong if you thought you were throwing a monkey wrench into the works this time. You gathered wrong if you thought if you went over there and made a poor mouth Sloane would have nothing to do with me!"

"Who?"

"Sloane. Sloane Folsom."

"Sloane!"

"It's a very high-class name, in case you don't know. Sloane Krop to be!"

Her face became red. Jenny had parted her hair to touch it up. Milt could see her scalp turning bright pink, like an infant about to cry, he thought.

"Milt— I saw her. Sure I went to see her because I had to make sure it was like I suspected. You suddenly paying attention to her this way, since the day I broke it up with the Parker kid. Aw, Milt, you told me yourself—a nothing, a mouse, a born old maid. You said that yourself. You said she never had a word to say for herself. And now I saw her, Milt—I saw for myself she's not for you, Milt. It's crazy. It's just rebound, Milt, that's all. She's not your type girl. It's all on account of what I did with the Parker kid, rebound and revenge on me!"

Milton smiled, picked up his comb, pulled the damp cotton off the rattail and flushed it down the toilet.

"Why do you want to cut off your nose to spite my face,

Milt? Hair pulled back, no make-up. I know what you like, Milt! Not like the little Parker kid— And don't think for a minute this one is weak and helpless just because she never has a word to say for herself. Maybe the reason she isn't married is men aren't fooled so easy."

"I can handle her."

"So you say."

"Without any help from you."

"Milt! Don't act as if I was your enemy."

"I only said stay out of my hair. I can get along without your help. I don't want your help."

"It's nuts to marry her."

"It's nuts she should marry me is more like it."

"Who are you telling that to? I saw her, Milt. Who do you think she is, the Venus de Milo?"

"I think she is Sloane Folsom, that's who I think."

"Please think it over, Milt. Please don't rush into this."

"This is so sudden, you mean, Jenny? That's for the bride to say. I'm not asking you to marry me."

"Don't be so fresh!" She began to cry and turned away. The peroxide was running down her forehead so she turned to the sink and began mopping it up with absorbent cotton, getting herself under control. "I'm glad we got the double Hide-a-Bed, Milt." (I told you so!) "That's one good thing, I'm glad I wouldn't listen to you with your single, single! I'll put Bud's things in with mine and she can have Bud's closet. Your wife. If you'd rather, you two can have Bud's room and he can sleep in the waiting room—only he's so sloppy with his things— Well, what I'm trying to say is we'll make out, Milt, if that's what you want."

"Already putting Dr. and Mrs. Krop where you think we should go, huh?" He walked out into the hall and gestured for her to follow him. "Nobody's asking you where we should go. Come on, sit down. You're going to get the shock of your life,

Jenny." He marched into the consultation room and sat behind his desk, motioning Jenny to take the patient's seat. He picked up the letter opener that said Merck and Company on it and tapped his palm with it, like a big businessman. "All set? Hold tight. We're not going to move in here."

"You're going *there?* To the Haunted House?"

"For the time being," he said, "for the time being!"

"But what about when they take it away? The bank? Whoever owns it?"

"Nobody's taking it away. I'm giving you all this, Jenny." He waved with the letter opener at the desk, the chair she was sitting on, the secondhand examining table he and Jenny had enameled, the old-fashioned glass instrument case, the third-hand diathermy, the fluoroscope he had just finished paying out for on time. "It's all yours. You can save this stuff for Bud, but if you'll take my advice, you'll get rid of it. Now this is what I'm going to do." He paused to savor that. He could count on the fingers of one hand the number of times he had been able to say, "This is what I'm going to do." "I'm going to turn over what I have in the bank to you. Every penny, because you'll need it. The insurance—well, being in your name, when the time comes, you get it. If you can get anything for my lousy practice, you're welcome to it, although I doubt that. In other words, Jenny, everything I have is yours—except me."

"You haven't got good sense, Milt." She leaned forward earnestly. "How will you live? What will you do? What is this, a marriage or a suicide pact?" She banged her hands down on her strong thighs. "If you ask me—which you're not—that's what I'd nominate your Sloane for—the girl I'd choose to commit suicide with! No, seriously, Milt, how will you live?"

He savored that. "How will I live? How will I live? I'll tell you, Jenny: I'll live. At least I'll begin to live before I stop." He pointed at Jenny with the letter opener. "You call this living? I don't call this living. But now—Jenny, Sloane is a rich girl,

55

an heiress. They are offering $110,000 for the house, Jenny, and that's just the beginning. She's loaded, get that through your head!"

Jenny put her hand to her head as if his command were an impossibility. "But I saw her," she said flatly. "What are you giving me, Milt? Rich? I saw the Haunted House. Rich! Loaded!"

"Her mother was one of those misers, Jenny. You read about them in the papers all the time—like those brothers, you know. Poor kid!"

"Poor kid—she's kidding you, Milt, she saw you coming! She's taking you for a ride and you're falling for it!" She leaned forward, staring into his face. "No?" He shook his head and something about him made her believe it. "She's an *heiress*? She's rolling in it?" They sat there like that, staring at each other, Jenny blinking, Milton smiling. When Bud shouted for Jenny, they both jumped. Neither of them had heard the door opening.

Bud, having come home from school, wanted something to eat. (He wanted something to eat every day right after school. He said they starved them in that lunchroom.) Jenny hauled herself out of the chair, completely exhausted. "O.K., Bud, I'm coming." She didn't even ask Bud why he couldn't fix something himself, which she usually did, but, needing time to think, hurried into the kitchen.

Bud said, "Hey, Mom, what's with your hair?"

Jenny was bent over the kitchen table stripping what was left of the chicken they had had last night. She was frowning.

"What's with your hair, Mom?"

"A touch-up. Peroxide," she said. "Shut up, will you, Bud?" She didn't even notice that Bud wasn't surprised. He had known about the touching-up for years; so had Maureen.

"Mom, put mayonnaise."

Sighing, Jenny got the mayonnaise. Three weeks ago Milt would have laughed in her face if she had said he would want

56

to marry the girl in the Haunted House. Milt hadn't known she was any heiress then. Two dollar calls, for heaven's sake. Three weeks ago—he was that way about the Parker kid three weeks ago and that was for sure. The day the old lady died in the Haunted House. Yes.

"Will you please give over that sandwich, Mom? I'm waiting."

"Shut up, Bud." That had been the day the old lady died, yes. That had been the day the letter came from the Equitable saying they wouldn't insure Milt. The same day. First the letter and then Milt being sore at her because she tried to keep him from knowing and getting desperate—

"But I'm starving, Mom."

"Here," she said, shoving it at him. When Bud stared because this wasn't like Mom, the way she was acting, Jenny picked up the chicken sandwich and slapped it into his hand. "Pour a glass of milk yourself. Go on to your rocm, son." He stared at her. "I said go eat it in your room, Bud. Turn on your radio. Do some homework for a change. Go on. Maureen will be back from school in a minute and then I won't be able to hear myself think. She has choir but she'll be back any minute."

"You got something there, Mom." Because he was still staring at his mother while he poured the milk, Bud spilled some of it on the floor, but even this didn't bring Jenny to. Bud spread the milk over the floor with the sole of his shoe and then went into his room.

Jenny lifted the chicken carcass, set it down on the table again, stared at a thickish piece of white meat left on the breast and, pulling it off, began nibbling at it. The day the old lady in the Haunted House died—because of the letter from the Equitable that morning, Milt hadn't been what you would call himself. (Her heart gave a thump and she wiped the grease off her hand on the kitchen tablecloth and pressed her breast.) She had known what it would do to him, to know. She herself had told him, "You'll do something crazy, that's what!" So anything could have happened that day that might not have happened other times. A crazy man. Who knows what a crazy man will do?

So Milt arrived at the Haunted House that way and it's touch and go with the old lady. The girl is hysterical, the girl is crazy, too, that day, don't forget that. When she had telephoned for Milt to hurry over, she had been hysterical, the girl. The girl, Sloane (what a name!) lets it out, or the old lady talks about the money she has. Some way Milt finds out there is money there. He is at the end of his rope and the girl is hysterical.

Why was the girl hysterical? Because of her mother's condition? Since when? Jenny thought. The girl had called up before that day thinking her mother was on her deathbed—two weeks before that day at three in the morning when the old lady had a drug reaction and the girl telephoned Milt emergency, was she hysterical then?

Like fun she was hysterical then! Jenny stared at the clean white skeleton of the chicken and shivered. Ten minutes before hadn't she said to Milt that this sounded more like a suicide pact than a marriage? If it was a kind of suicide pact—like psychic, she thought, like second sight! Of course, she thought, of course! Convulsively she tried to swallow the chicken meat because the skeleton of the chicken had become the skeleton of the old woman from the Haunted House. She felt a wave of nausea and ran to the sink to spit the chicken out, rinsing her mouth. Then she ran back to Milton in the consultation room. "Milt," she said, swallowing because the chicken corpse would not go down, "Milt!" She had to put her hand over her mouth because her lips trembled so. "Milt—I feel funny. Milt, I know you think I'm always patting myself on the back—but have I ever said I'm like psychic, Milt? Like second sight? Well, that's how I feel now, like second sight!"

He had been doodling with the letter opener on the blotter. "That's a new one. What's it got to do with me?"

"Everything, Milt. Suddenly—suddenly you're marrying this girl. Girl—she must be thirty!"

"Twenty-eight."

"Maybe. Three weeks ago you didn't know she existed, suddenly you're off to Buffalo. Suddenly she's rich. No, you don't have to be psychic, people won't need to be psychic to smell there's something funny going on! I've got to talk to you privately, Milt. You've got to listen to me. A minute, Milt!" She went to the door of the consultation room and called her son. When he answered she said that she and Uncle—Milt, she and his uncle wanted to have a private talk about the condition of a certain sick patient—private, and they didn't want to be disturbed. "When Maureen comes," she said, "you tell her go make herself one of her peanut butter and jelly sandwiches and leave us alone. Strictly alone, Bud, I mean it." Jenny closed the door, then opened it. "Bud, say I said she can have a Coca-Cola today instead of a glass of milk. It's all right with me, say; she doesn't have to come banging in here." She closed the door. "That will hold Maureen. She'll be in seventh heaven if I let her have a Coke between meals." She sat in the patient's chair. Milt still drawing circles with the letter opener worried her—it was like Bud when he should be paying attention for his own good —and she reached for it but Milt pulled it away and shook his head.

Milton didn't even bother looking up. He drawled, "Well, we're private. When is the séance going to start, Mahatma Gandhi?"

"It starts now, Milt. She did it. Sloane." (How can you call a girl "Sloane"?) "The old lady was D.O.A. but you find out the girl did it. You find out she's an heiress. You tell her you'll cover for her because what have you got to lose? You were fit to be tied that day, Milt, so you figure if the police find out— and maybe they won't, maybe no one ever will—but if they find out, you can end it then, both of you, a suicide pact as I said before. You think: a short life and a merry one. You're a doctor, after all, Milt, there's always morphine." Now he was at his prescription pad with the letter opener, but listening. He was listening, all right. "What do I care about the old lady, Milt? From all I know about her, whatever she got she probably deserved. Anyhow, she's dead and buried. Rest in peace," Jenny said, shivering, feeling with her tongue for any remaining bits of chicken.

"Amen."

"It's you I'm thinking about, Milt, you should know that. Look, I should worry what the girl did or didn't do; I'm no eager beaver running to the cops. I'm not my sister's keeper in other words."

"Just your brother-in-law's keeper in other words. Jenny, if I did what you think I did I should be behind bars. You should go to the cops with your second sight, Jenny, not to me."

"Milt!"

"Go to the cops. Put up or shut up."

"You know you have nothing to fear from me, Milt."

"My good angel, my good angel!"

"Yes, your good angel. If I'm your good angel, maybe she's your bad angel. Sloane." She stroked the desk because he would not let her touch him. "Listen, Milt, I saw her. You're putty in her hands, Milt. 'Ha-ha-ha,' he says! Milt, you're too used to me. My bark is worse than my bite and that's what you're used to. I talk. So when you meet up with a girl like that, you naturally think because she doesn't say much—Milt, with me you know what I'm thinking, do you think you know what she's thinking? Like fun, Milt! With me you know where you stand. Like fun you know where you stand with a girl like that, Milt!"

He put down the letter opener and shoved his chair back. "Go to the cops or shut up, I don't give a damn what you do. No, wait a minute, there's just one thing. Sloane isn't a doctor or a nurse. If you go to her and tell her about me—you know—

if you tell her about my blood pressure, she won't believe it doesn't make a damned bit of difference what I do, within reason, with the time I have left to live. She—cares for me, Jenny. It's no suicide pact, it's love. If you tell her about my condition, she'll make an invalid out of me. Some honeymoon with the bride scared every night she'll wake up and find hubby dead in the bed! I have enough liabilities as it is, maybe she won't even marry me if she knows that. So if you tell her that, if you go there and open your big mouth and tell her that, until I give you permission, anyhow, if you blab, whether it breaks it up between us or not, you won't get one penny from me. There's no way you can get a cent out of me unless I want to give it. Bud can get a job and support you, he'll be sixteen. Maureen can have a latchkey and make her own peanut butter and jelly sandwiches after school every day. She can have a Coke by herself and you can go back to nursing, Jenny. You're healthy if I'm not." He stood up and walked toward the door.

"Milt," Jenny said, "I wouldn't. Milt, I wouldn't." He opened the door of the consultation room. "Milt, I wouldn't, anyhow," she said.

"Hello, I would like to talk to Dr. Mayberry, please."

"Dr. Mayberry? Dick? This is Jenny Krop, Dick. Phil's widow. Phil Krop, Dr. Philip Krop. Yes," Jenny said, "still Phil's widow. No," she said, "I never got married again. Oh," she said, "you mean Milt, Phil's younger brother? No, he just lives here with me and the kids, or rather we live with him. What? Go on! Is that a proposal, Dick, or a proposition?"

"Well," she said, "I didn't call you for an offer, Dick. You've got a good wife and you're no marriage bureau that I know of. It's a medical question, Dick. What? Oh, 'shoot,' you said. It's funny you should say 'shoot.' You'll see what I mean. It's this way. You know how it is if you were a nurse and married to a physician, people always think you should know medicine. Well,

I have a friend, she's a writer, Dick, and she wants to know—She writes those detective stories, she wants to know is it possible to poison someone with something so it can't be found out?"

"Yes," Jenny said, "undetectable. Somebody is poisoned in the book and she wants to know is there such a thing as a poison they can't find out."

"Thank you, Dick," she said, "I'll tell my friend. Thanks a million. If poison is suspected, if it isn't a case of a dumb coroner passing anything up—yes, I remember the Faulkner case, that's right. So if the body is actually autopsied by some medical examiner who knows his business, as far as you know they can't get away with it. Have I got it straight?"

"Who?" she asked. "Milt? Oh, Milt doesn't want to be bothered with my questions these days. Milt's going to be married October fifteenth."

Chapter III

THE wedding was the only ceremony. Milton had figured there would be a "reading of the will" but Sloane said it hadn't been necessary. She knew what was in the will. If Milton was interested— "Not interested," he said. The letter with the nice round $110,000 figure was enough for him, enough for a merry life if a short one, and that was all he was interested in. Jenny, of course, was interested in everything. She wanted to give a dinner for Sloane. She said a dinner would not only show Sloane she, Jenny, had nothing against her, but for the kids' sake, so they wouldn't think it peculiar, their uncle marrying a stranger, all of a sudden.

"Maureen cried," Jenny said. "You know how she adores you, Milt!"

Maureen cried again when she found she wasn't going to be a flower girl at Uncle Miltie's wedding. It wasn't going to be that kind of wedding, Jenny explained, just a civil ceremony at City Hall because Sloane's mom had just died.

Jenny asked Milton if Sloane would like to have her go with her shopping for the wedding gown.

"She's not getting a wedding gown." He, too, had wanted to go shopping with Sloane for her trousseau. It would be like in

63

the movies, he thought, models parading in front of you, no looking at price tags. Jenny and Maureen staring at him in astonishment at this information looked comically alike. (He had also been astonished. "But Milton, darling," Sloane had said, "I make my things. There's no dressmaker who knows me as well as I know me." He couldn't see what knowing had to do with it, but she said she knew herself, she knew clothes. Like hell she knew. "Come on, Sloane," he had said, making a joke of it, "you don't thnik you look like the pictures in Vogue, do you?" "The last thing in the world I want," Sloane said, "is to look like the pictures in Vogue." Whatever she wanted to look like, she looked like nothing in the world he had ever seen. For twenty-nine fifty you could buy a decent dress, but he had never seen anything like Sloane's dresses for any money, and nobody else had, either.) Jenny was talking to him again, asking whether he knew if Sloane had bought herself one of those new peignoirs they showed for trousseaus. He shook his head, not daring to tell Jenny that Sloane had goggled at him when he asked about her "trousseau," as if she had never heard the word mentioned in the presence of a lady. "You know," he had said, "white bride stuff, lacy—very-thin—" "Don't be vulgar, darling," she said. Vulgar!

"That's good," Jenny said, "then we'll get her a pretty one. You can come shopping with me for it, Maureen. We'll go to Saks Fifth Avenue and do it right. And should we get her a nightie to match?"

Buddy grinned, "Now that's what I call a good idea, Mom! A nightie is what a bride needs most!"

"Why, Bud?" Maureen saw him grinning. "Bud, why?"

"Murine, if you'd use some Murine for your eyes maybe you wouldn't have to ask so many questions. Right, Uncle Miltie?"

"Mom, why?"

Jenny said, "Now I already told you about things like that. I told you, Maureen!" She saw her daughter's whine forming, mounting. "Maureen, if you say 'why' once more I won't take you to Saks Fifth Avenue!"

Since Sloane told nobody about her marriage, the peignoir was the only gift they received.

"How kind of Jenny," Sloane said, but although Milton privately thought that Jenny had really "done it right," all white and lace and white ribbons, and you could see through it when Sloane held it up, she held it up for one minute only, then folded it back into the Saks Fifth Avenue box, laid back the tissue paper which had covered it and that was the last Milton saw of the peignoir.

Milton was one hundred per cent for the marriage at City Hall with Jenny for one witness, an official hanging around and a couple who were there for their own license for the rest. Walking down the aisle dressed in a monkey suit wasn't his idea of a good time, but he certainly figured they'd have a honeymoon. Bermuda, he figured, or Florida, even, having given up the Riviera for the honeymoon since they had to wait for the house to be sold to get hold of money that wasn't tied up in the estate. He had looked up the names of the best hotels in Bermuda and Palm Beach. Once, at a medical convention in Atlantic City, Milt had stayed at the Traymore Hotel. A bride and groom had gone up in the same elevator with him. The groom said to the bride that he had had champagne and caviar sent up to their suite so they could have some before going down to dinner, O.K.? Milton was thinking about that bride and groom when he asked Sloane how about Bermuda for their honeymoon.

Sloane said, "I beg your pardon?" They were sitting together in the smallest room downstairs. She had ripped the blue wool which had been in the basket on the table the day her mother died, knitted it into a short thick cape, and now she was threading it with black velvet ribbon, making small black velvet bows.

"How about Bermuda, I said, for our honeymoon." He saw her expression. "We are getting married, right? Bride and groom, honeymoon, it rhymes. It's in all the songs."

"Do leave it in the songs, please." She held up the cape, frowning at it.

"What do you call a honeymoon?"

"I say wedding trip, darling."

So he said "wedding trip." What hotel, where, for their wedding trip, and she said, "Oh, please, no hotel, darling!" She said hotels made everything that shouldn't be—public. People who went to hotels at these times invited the other residents in, she said, ugh—from the bellhops to the manager—and she threw the blue cape away from her in disgust and came to him, running her finger over his cheek. "It makes my blood run cold," she said. "You don't want my blood to run cold, do you, blind Milton?"

He had not quite acknowledged to himself that it was his own blood running cold that he was afraid of, that he had counted on the hotel people looking at him the way they had looked at the couple in the elevator at the Traymore to give him a lift, a kick. That first time, that first day, he had been so sorry for her that day, he had believed she was like him, beaten down like him, hungry like him for life, and that first time he had wanted her. Without any trimmings, he thought.

If he wanted to go away, Sloane was saying, Cousin Etta's place would be perfect. Cousin Etta would be delighted to have them stay as long as they chose. All they needed to do was ask. Cousin Etta kept the house staffed all year round and it was good for the staff to have people descend on them occasionally since Cousin Etta hardly got out there at all any more. "It's a lovely old place," Sloane said, "and oh, Milton—Cousin Etta's beach!"

"A private beach?" When Sloane said it was a private beach, Milton saw a strip of white sand fenced off with big signs reading PRIVATE, NO TRESPASSING and innumerable public bathers crowded together with hardly room to stretch out in (like Coney Island) looking over the fence and envying him and Sloane, wondering who they were to rate a private beach, which would give the honeymoon the kind of lift he needed. But then he remembered the time of year. "Hey," he said. "No one goes to beaches the middle of October, Sloane!"

"No one but us. October is when it is wonderful—the solitude, the wind, the whipped surf—undomesticated. When I was there last there was a windstorm; it had blown, blown. . . . It had a Brontë-ish, moorish quality otherwise sadly lacking on Long Island. Ah, Milton," she said, touching his mouth, "Cousin Etta's place will be perfect for our honeymoon."

She was riding him, saying "honeymoon," of course, but you certainly couldn't call from Queens to Long Island a trip!

The house was big, all right, but it gave you the creeps. It was clean as a pin, nothing neglected or falling down, but the covering on the furniture, the drapes, even the pictures on the walls had had all the colors sucked out of them by years of sun, or maybe, he thought, blown off by the rough wind Sloane thought so marvelous. You could see patterns of flowers and leaves on the furniture coverings, but the flowers were now the same as the leaves. It all gave him the creeps and Sloane liked it. (No lipstick, no nail polish, no wedding gown, no color!) She said, well, perhaps a room should have—she said it in French; in English it meant "one spot of red"—so she marched into the kitchen, came back with a big orange cooking pot and stuck flowers in it. And he wasn't at all sure she did it to kid him. The bedroom Sloane chose for them had six windows and you could see the private beach from them and there was a private balcony you could step out on, but who wanted to step out when you had to clutch the railing to keep from being blown off the balcony just to see an empty beach? (Sloane wanted to. She made him come out and stand there in the wind and say, "Wild west wind." An "incredible sensation," she said.) The bathroom that went with the room, now that was incredible for you, Milton thought, and the staff was two old people (the man with a well-developed Parkinson's) who obviously resented Cousin Etta's little scheme for keeping them on their toes. They knew Sloane from the times she had stayed here, but although she told them he was her husband and a doctor, he was "Mr." Krop and she was "Miss" Sloane. The staff fed them three meals a day and kept the place clean and made the bed up, but with no frills attached—which symbolized everything so far. He was plain married to Sloane with no frills attached. Sloane herself provided no frills—no lipstick, no frills. She certainly felt no need to be feminine. It astonished Milton —a girl who read poetry all the time. You would think a girl like that would be poetic, way off in the clouds somewhere, but she was anything but.

She left the lacy peignoir Jenny gave her at home and took what she called her "Jaeger." Her Jaeger was the ugliest damned bathrobe Milton had ever seen. Sloane adored it. She even rubbed the sleeve of it against his cheek to show him how soft the wool was, and he gave it that; it was soft, but surely that wasn't all a bride's negligee was supposed to be, soft? And she was so proud that it was twelve years old. (Wasn't it the man who supposed to be attached to old clothes?) Everything Sloane had brought with her was old: old flannel slacks, old mannish shirts to wear with them, the older the better. It was so sad to Sloane that just when a shirt got really good, it fell to pieces. The first night they were there, Milton had gone into the crummy bathroom and pulled off the new silk striped pajamas he had bought for the occasion because it turned out Sloane didn't have a nightie to her name. Never wore them, she said, and if she didn't wear nightgowns how could he wear pajamas?

As he had told her, Milton had put down what had happened the afternoon her mother died to hysteria, to shock; he had felt broad-mindedly that anything could happen on a day like that, but this didn't hold for Cousin Etta's place. He was no Romeo but he was no monk either; yet Sloane certainly surprised him. The second day they were on Long Island, an unexpectedly warm day, like June, so that they could go down to the private beach and lie in the sun, he was so—surprised at her—that she noticed. She rolled away from him and lay on the sand with her forearms under her head and said very .calmly, "Now I've shocked you, Milton, darling."

And he had been so shocked that he said what he was thinking. "Well," he said, "a girl who's always reading poetry!"

She began to laugh, "Oh, darling Milton, perhaps you should read some poetry, too. Say, Baudelaire—but no, because he is supposed to be wanton. Read the Sonnets—but everyone knows what Shakespeare is full of, besides quotes. No, you should read John Donne—"

She knew, of course, that he didn't know John Donne from a hole in the wall.

"He was a seventeenth-century divine. A clergyman, Milton. A minister! Yes, he's the one for you to read." She began to recite: "Come, Madam, come . . . oﬀ with those shoes—" She pushed herself up from the sand, scrambled around and started yanking off his shoe. "Off with those shoes, Milton!" Her eyes were dark blue, her voice curled, cuddled. When she saw Milton's face, she flung his shoe over her shoulder and threw herself down on top of him, tickling him to make him laugh. "Does it want wose-colored silk shades on the lamps? Does it want to turn the wamps down, one by one? Does it like the curtains dwawn?"

No man could stand that sort of kidding, naturally, but that was anger, for Christ's sake! And what a hell of a thing, he couldn't help thinking, what a hell of a thing!

He did not know that when, as right after the beach episode, he made some reference to her mother, saying in this case that, for the love of Mike, neither of them should take any chance of being hauled into court right then, that he was punishing her, bringing her to with a bang, frightening her so that she would become helpless and feminine and look up to him and remember what he had done for her and cut out the horseplay, but he had to do it quite often. Even when she sobered up, though, she would not discuss the future. This time was time out, she said, and he guessed it was supposed to be; he had to give in, but when the honeymoon was over, when they were an old married couple, he would start the ball rolling. He knew some poetry himself, John Milton, if not John Donne. He knew, "When I consider how my light is spent ere half my days. . . ."

After that one warm day on the beach, it rained three days steadily. Sloane liked to walk in the rain and when he said they shouldn't, they would catch cold, she said surely, as a doctor, he knew better than that. "What does one catch cold from, Doctor?" They walked in the rain three days; in the damp gray that followed it, three more days. They ate the meals the staff prepared for them. Sloane read herself poetry out of the brown books she had brought. (A decent library—the one deficiency in Cousin Etta's lovely place, according to Sloane!) They played some honeymoon bridge and Sloane played the piano while he read the newspapers. He did not want to read newspapers but there was nothing else to do and, except for the ads and the obits, he read them through.

Today Sloane played the piano even longer than usual ("Chopin, Milton, cum Sloane, cum Cousin Etta's piano!") so he finished the news sections. It occurred to Milton, sitting on the bleached cretonne chair, that besides the news and the obits, there were the entertainment section and the society news. (He would never again have to leave his name at the box office in Loew's!) His wife, it occurred to him, was society, if she chose to be, wasn't she? She had the name and the dough. And there was also, he remembered, turning the pages quickly, Apartments for Rent. Surely he could now discuss where they were going to live? He waited until Sloane finished the number she was playing, although he didn't know whether it was the finish or whether she just stopped, and he suspected that Sloane wouldn't call what she was playing a "number." He folded the paper, tucked it under his arm and went and sat next to Sloane on the piano bench, giving her a playful shove with his hip. He took up one of the thin hands which was no longer quite the mushroom color it used to be and began to spread the long fingers apart, first because then she couldn't start playing the number again, and second because she liked him to touch her. (You "touched" people for a loan, he thought; well, he was going to "touch" her, all right. It was about time.) He pushed her four fingers together so roughly that she swung her head round and stared. "Sloane, we've been here a week," he said. "Let's give Cousin Etta's place back to the Indians. It looks like more rain and I'm sick of rain, I'm sick of wet sand—"

"We'll go home tomorrow," Sloane said. She freed her hand. "All we have to do is pack and—oh, better tell Edwards so Mrs. Edwards doesn't plan to feed us—and their tips. Let's see." She sat playing one note with one finger while she went into deep thought. Then she stopped playing and said, "Five dollars."

Milton asked whether she thought she was John D. Rockefeller. "Five dollars now is a dime then," he said.

Sloane smiled. Cousin Etta would be annoyed if they gave too much. It would set a bad precedent. He must leave that sort of thing to her, she said. Overtipping was a sign of social insecurity. Since it apparently bothered him to give five dollars, she would attend to it herself. She put both hands on the keyboard again, but he wouldn't let her start playing.

She said, "You're sick of Chopin, too, poor Milton!"

"No, I want to read you something." He found the ad in the paper and read it. "How does it sound to you?"

"Duplexes always sound like Monsieur Jourdain to me, Milton."

"Huh?"

"A 'duplex' apartment. Monsieur Jourdain, Milton. *Le Bourgeois Gentilhomme*, Milton, being so amazed to discover that he had been talking prose all his life. Duplex means stairs. Why pay for stairs in an apartment?"

He could see that she might have had her bellyful of stairs and began to read another. When he finished he asked where she thought they should live until "everything was settled."

"At home," she said. "Of course."

He laughed. "Kid, you're like a little bird!"

"A what?"

"A little bird, I said." Bird? No wonder she thought she hadn't heard straight! Cissie Parker was the little bird, the ducking, dipping, flirting sparrow. This one (I got it!) an eagle—with that beak! After swimming, when she came out of the water—because she wouldn't wear a swimming cap any more than a nightgown or lipstick—and her hair was plastered. A bald eagle, he thought while he repeated what he had told her, anyhow. "Like a bird, a little bird who was kept caged up so long—and then when the door opens and it's free, the bird can't believe it. The little bird just sits there in the cage until someone boots it out. Well, I'm the one to give you the boot! You're free, kid! You don't have to stay cooped up in the old dump any more. The Haunted House!"

"Is that what they call it?"

What did she care what they called it.

"Milton, not yet. We can't leave yet."

"Not yet? 'When I consider how my light is spent'—John Milton, you told me that! Listen, I don't want to settle down in the Haunted House!"

She took the paper from him and studied the ad he had read her. "Sutton Place—but, don't all your patients live in the vicinity?"

"When we came here I told Jenny to tell my patients I was retiring." She looked shocked, now *she* looked shocked! "You wouldn't worry about them if you knew them. The clinic patients you saw are a horse of a different color, Sloane. They're really sick and they're really grateful; them I won't give up, but what I thought I'd do was take a rest from practice. We can live wherever we want because I can start practicing wherever we are. Sutton Place, why not?" (He had no intention of practicing, but figured it was smarter not to say so. One step at a time.)

He shook his head at her playfully. "Now, listen, kid, you know it's true you can love a rich girl as much as a poor girl, don't you? I do," he said, smiling at her. "Well, it's also true you can cure rich people as well as the poor slobs. They get just as sick as the poor slobs, Sloane." She hadn't unbent an inch. "You remind me of my mother—was she romantic about doctors! As a matter of fact, Sloane, I haven't saved one life since I've been in practice. It's just a case of making a dollar like any other job, so let them take their psychosomatic bellyaches and their varicose veins and their ingrown toenails to someone who needs their three-buck office visits!"

She left the piano and walked to the window, turning her back on him, tracing the path of a raindrop down the pane, and began to talk about working for nothing. Certainly he no longer needed to support himself, that was true. She began on the charity work the Folsoms had done, apparently they had gone around handing out doughnuts and coffee to the underprivileged on the *Mayflower*. That was O.K. with him. He let her talk until she ran down, then he said, fine, fine, but since she agreed he was no longer tied to the neighborhood, they didn't have to stay where they were. It didn't have to be a duplex and it didn't have to be Sutton Place—wherever she liked. He held up the paper: Central Park South, Park Avenue, Fifth Avenue, if you didn't have to worry about the rent, there were apartments all over.

She was still tracing raindrops. "That's precisely the point, Milton, dear, there are apartments all over. Common." Her voice quivered. "But houses like mine are not common. Oh, surely you don't think it's chic to be a mob? Our house is us, Milton. Emerson said it: 'Insist on yourself; never imitate.' I assure you, Milton, the really fashionable thing in New York is a big house like ours!"

A big house, he thought, like the Brownings' house. With the grounds fixed up. Landscaped. He saw a long line of cars stretching from the big iron gate to the front door as he had once seen them at the Browning place in Brookfield. The Browning girl and her father had been standing in the lighted doorway that evening with the door open behind them, welcoming the guests. That night he had been driving past in the Ford, but this time he would be the one standing in the lighted doorway of the big house with his Browning girl standing there with him. Class. All the lights in the house would be on. He had never seen the Haunted House really lighted up, nor had anyone else. All the biddies would come crowding to the gate to find out what was going on in the Haunted House. One of them would tell Jenny, of course, and she'd come running quick enough. She'd see him standing in the doorway, home-town boy makes good. There would be flowered curtains in the window and rugs so deep the old floors wouldn't creak every step you took. He would have a tux made to order, or tails, as the case might be. "May I have the pleasure of the next dance?" Did anyone say that except in books? Jenny would say, "Poor Milt," the way she did, and one of the biddies would look at her like she was nuts. "Poor Milt?" It might not be a bad idea to stay where they were until they went to Europe. "Well, O.K.," he said, "but there'll be some changes made! We'll get a gardener and a couple." He pointed to the piano. "Live it up in the Haunted House, presto changeo! Can you play, 'There'll Be Some Changes Made'? It's not Chopin!"

"Changes?"

"You're so used to the dump you don't even see it, Sloane. My God, the taste!" He described what he thought the Browning house must have been like on the inside. He had seen what he thought it was like in the *House and Garden* magazines Jenny bought secondhand for the office. Chintz, bright color, comfort.

"Preposterous," Sloane said.

"What's preposterous is staying there like it is; that's what's preposterous!"

"Milton, I do assure you—"

"Assure me, nothing!"

"In its manner, the house is a gem. I assure you."

"Ha ha ha."

"Are we quarreling? Our first quarrel? I don't want to quarrel with you on our *honeymoon*, but you mustn't be so conventional, Milton, darling!"

"Some honeymoon!"

"Milton, call a decorator to see the place; ask him. That's fair."

"I'll pick the decorator. I'll ask him. I'll pick the best."

"Yes, darling, do. Now I want to be conventional," she whispered. "How does it go? 'I like quarreling because it's such fun to make up.' Make up, Milton!" She ran to him.

Her hands were icy from the cold windowpane, her voice throbbed, her eyes gleamed; he held her off. "You'll do whatever the decorator I pick says? Promise me?"

Later he thought that it was the wife who was supposed to want something, a mink coat, a diamond, a new car, and it was the man who wanted her to "make up" and it was the woman who "made up" after the man promised her whatever she wanted, but they left Aunt Etta's place immediately after lunch, and he could forget about making up in the excitement and relief at leaving Long Island.

Milton did not see Jenny for two weeks. Then he thought he should and drove over after lunch on Friday, before going to the clinic. Jenny, who was alone, came to the door in her pink fluffy robe, which she never would have done while there were patients to consider. She put her hand to her breast.

"Milt! What's wrong?"

"Nothing is wrong. Why should anything be wrong?" He laughed at her expression. "Don't tell me you still have that crazy idea of yours? Did you think the cops were after me so I came running to you? Well, there are no cops and if there were I wouldn't come here running, so get that out of your head. This is just a social call. How are the kids?"

"They miss you, Milt. We all miss you."

"That's nice. You have to leave to be appreciated, I guess. What else is new?" She told him that she was going to stay on in the apartment until the school term was over and then, if she could get Maureen to agree—she hated to give up her tap class and all her little friends—go live with an uncle she had in Trenton who would keep them free if she kept the house and cooked for him. "The uncle who's a widower?" Milton whistled.

"You stop that, Milt!"

"She's blushing," Milt said. "O.K., I'll stop that. Near Trenton, New Jersey, isn't it? Then Bud can go to Princeton, that's in New Jersey. Bud can be a Princeton man!"

"You don't have to make fun of Bud, Milt. Bud never did you any harm." Nor me either, she thought. "What are you going to do now the honeymoon's over?"

"Well, when the house is sold, we intend to travel." He reached into his pocket and drew out an official-looking envelope, handing it to Jenny, who took it but kept it in her hand, staring at it. "Look in, look in," Milt said. "I'll bet you never saw a passport before!" He pulled the envelope away from her and showed the passport to her. "We're going to France—the Riviera, Italy, Spain, Paris, London, Rome, Naples. Did you ever hear the saying, 'See Naples and die? That's me; see Naples and die happy!"

"Milt!"

"Where's your sense of humor, Jenny? And remember that is strictly between you and me."

"You haven't told her yet?" When he shook his head, she wondered if that was funny, too, Milt's not telling his own wife. She didn't know. She had thought and thought—what else did she have to do these days, for heaven's sake—but she hadn't come up with any answers. She still knew there was something funny about it and she still didn't know what. She was still sure the girl had killed the old lady and that Milt had it on her, but if he wasn't afraid of the cops—if there was no poison they couldn't find out, if there was no such animal— "You leaving soon, Milt?"

"When the house is sold."

"But you told me she had a firm offer?"

So he told her what Sloane had told him, except putting Sloane's words into his own mouth. The offer was not the last offer. You did not take the first offer. People like the Folsoms got their money by hanging on to real estate until the right moment. Jenny certainly was no businessman, had no head for business. You didn't jump when a firm raised its little finger, you didn't look too anxious. For the time being, they were going to stay just where they were. Make themselves comfortable. Psychology.

"In the Haunted House? I wouldn't live in the Haunted House for all the psychology there is. I'd rather stay here."

He said, "And that's how much you know, Jenny! What you

call a Haunted House is a genuine museum piece. It is historical, Jenny! For example, there's one room—well, an ancestor of my wife's was in the shipping business to China, Hong Kong. There's one room with the furniture he ordered made for him in China at the time. I'm not saying it's beautiful, Jenny—and it's certainly not comfort you get." (The seats were made of marble inlaid with mother-of-pearl, for God's sake!) "But stuff like that has to be preserved."

(The decorator said: combination of Victorian taste and Chinese craftsmanship produced marvels of transcendental monstrosity which should be seen to be believed. The decorator, picked by him so he couldn't accuse Sloane of putting him up to it, had said a lot of things which had to be heard to be believed, but he had heard them so he had to believe that it would be sacrilege to touch this house, useless to tone it down, impossible, in fact. Mrs. Krop, the decorator said, bowing toward the other room where Sloane had gone, is one of the heroines of fashion—*fantaisiste*. Mrs. Krop (my dear Doctor) makes her own style. "I would as soon touch this house," the decorator said, "as cover up that face with—pancake—*pancake!* I would as soon hang flowered chintz here as obscure that miraculous hairline with curls!" The decorator said that Sloane was a real beauty although she could certainly walk down the street and not get a single whistle—"except mine, when I was young enough, and yours, of course!" Then he put his glasses on and looked at him with his eyes hanging out. "Oh," he said, "not your whistle, either, Doctor? What a pity," he said, "what a dreadful pity!")

"We wouldn't touch the house, Jenny. In fact, when we sell, we're going to give a couple of the rooms, walls and all, to a museum!" Jenny's eyes were hanging out now the way his had when he first heard this. "Of course it's more comfortable since we got servants." He hoped she wouldn't ask questions about these, and she didn't. She thought all you had to do to get servants was pay their wages. He hoped, what with the decorator and the museum and the servants and the passport, that Jenny would talk on the other side of her face about the Haunted House.

"Milton, Milton," Sloane said. "Wake up, Milton, you've been asleep. Napping. After lunch. It's two o'clock. What can you have been dreaming of? You're at home. I'm Sloane. Your wife. Your bride of six weeks. It's November twenty-sixth and two o'clock and time to go to the clinic. I'm going with you."

He shook his heavy head.

"Just today, Milton. I have to talk to you."

He lumbered upstairs and she followed him into the bedroom, waiting there while he washed up, standing behind him while he brushed his hair and changed his jacket which had become rumpled because he must have slept so restlessly. (What had he been dreaming of?) On the stairs, going down, he was about to ask Sloane what she wanted to talk to him about, but she put her long finger over her pale mouth.

She began talking as soon as they got into the Studie. "She's leaving. Helga."

He belched.

Sloane said that was a most appropriate response considering Helga's cooking. "No two weeks' notice, Milton; an annunciation, while you were napping."

"So long, Helga, then. Call the agency." She shook her head, meaning this was useless. "Call another agency."

"No use, Milton. I knew it was no use the moment I saw the look on the little faces of the first man and wife when I showed them through the house. Oh, Milton, when I showed them the servants' quarters—like two Queen Victorias!"

"Come again?"

"They were not amused. They didn't even unpack their luggage, remember? And you telephoned the agency and since the

79

man and wife hadn't returned and reported, the agency was most apologetic and bewildered. They simply couldn't understand, could they, and I said to you, 'They will, Oscar, they will.' "

"Come again?" It wasn't so cold but everybody was walking like winter.

"Something Whistler said to Oscar Wilde. The point is, darling, I told you then."

"You told me, you told me!" The stove had settled it for the next couple, a combination coal stove and range. Sloane said Cook used to love it—Cook was Swedish and adored her coffee, and could keep a pot of it on the back of the stove and have a cup whenever she felt like it—and the woman of the couple looked at her man and said, "She was Swedish, madam? Passed on, madam? Perhaps she had too many cups of coffee." Maybe it hadn't gone quite like that but it was the story they now told each other. Anyhow, the man of that couple had worn a white coat and looked more like a lab assistant than a butler. And then Helga had arrived with the other woman to do the cleaning and serving; then the other woman left and now Helga was leaving. "Maybe you told me, but I don't see that solves anything."

"It settles the question of calling another agency, Milton. None of them have servants to offer, not real servants."

"I think you're glad Helga is leaving." He swung the Studie around the corner grimly, the rubber making more or less the sounds he would like to be making. "Well, I give up. What do you suggest?"

"You really give up? Splendid. Now, as I have told you, only genuine servants will do for our house—and I have one. I can get us a real cook. She'll know how to manage any char we can pick up and then we'll be all right."

"Swell. Why didn't you say so in the first place?"

"We had to finish with agencies first, Milton, darling. The cook I have in mind was trained at old Mrs. Vinton's. You don't know Mrs. Vinton, but she was the last chatelaine in the United States. She would come down to the kitchen every morning and go over the menu with the cook, weigh out what was needed and lock up all the rest."

"My God," Milton said.

"How I wished I could do that with Helga, Milton! Anyhow, this particular cook is accustomed to working in a kitchen like ours on a stove like ours in a house like ours. She is used to our ways. She would look down her nose on the kind of employer that the Helgas respect, and vice versa."

"Then our troubles are over. Grab her."

"Well, there is a drawback."

"Aha!"

"Milton, you actually said 'aha'! All right, I'll be serious, but I am so glad to get Helga out of the house that I could dance for joy. Now, I do think it can be worked out but you must tell me if it can."

The "real servant" she meant turned out to be Austen! Old Austen from the clinic! Old sourpuss!

Sloane, talking very fast the way she did when she wanted to convince him, winding him in her words the way she could, said, but Austen would be so grateful; if Austen could get a job again it would rejuvenate her.

He had never seen Austen grateful for anything. The other patients pretended to be. They said thank you and that you were the best doc and they were so glad they got you; maybe they said that to all the docs, but it went down good. Not Austen. She never praised and she never begged. She sat on the bench as if she were in church and never gave an inch. As far as she was concerned, she was supposed to do what the doctors told her to and the doctors were supposed to tell her. Tit for tat. He realized, trying to see Austen as their cook, that he really disliked the old woman. "Now wait a minute, Sloane—hold your horses! Austen can't be a cook for anyone any more, Sloane. She hung on to her last cooking job and got into real trouble with edema. She's on a strict salt-free diet and being a cook for people who can eat anything, you're bound to slip. And then she's got to keep off rich food, keep her weight down."

"But that's all to the good," Sloane said. "You've put on weight yourself with Helga's cooking; it will be all to the good not to have rich food. So if we cast our bread upon these particular waters, Milton darling, it will return a hundredfold in non-calories. And now I'll tell you our salt-free scheme. You must say if it will work or not."

There was to be no salt at all in the kitchen so that there would be no possible chance of an oversight. The old silver salt shaker on the table would be the only salt there was and they would salt their food themselves at the table. That made no difference to the taste. It was nonsense to say it did! Simple? Foolproof? The solution of old Austen's problem, and Austen the solution of their problem! "You say, Milton. It is your decision."

What else could he say? Sloane was right; they would never get anybody decent to work in the Haunted House and if he didn't agree it was back to Sloane's cooking. Eggs and more eggs and bread pudding for dessert.

"Oh, splendid! Let me go in and tell her." They had reached Queens General.

"I'll tell her." Quietly, so none of the others would know. God, what they'd say if they knew! "I'll tell her you want to see her out here and then you can explain the whole thing."

Sloane smiled, "That won't be necessary."

"You had this all fixed up between you?"

"Dear Milton, nothing can be 'fixed' without your approval. I told you that the first time I saw her I instinctively recognized her type. We gravitated toward one another, but that is all."

"I give up," Milton said, and that was how he felt. He gave up. His hands were tied.

"All you have to do is tell Mrs. Austen Barkis is willing."

"Who is Barkis?"

"You, Milton. Oh, Dickens! Just tell Mrs. Austen to come, bag and baggage, as soon as she can manage."

"You go on home, Sloane. You could catch the bus on the corner. I'm going to be two hours."

"I'll wait." She opened her purse. "See?"

Other women carried a million things in their pocketbooks—perfume, lipstick, eyebrow pencils, mascara, pretty handkerchiefs—but his wife had a book of poetry stuffed into hers. "I see. O.K."

Chapter IV

A T FIVE o'clock when the clinic was over and they came into the house, they saw Helga's two valises, just beyond the two suits of armor. They heard Helga's steps from the taipan room, where she must have been waiting for them. Sloane said, "You deal with her, Milton," and dashed past him, running along the hall and up the stairs.

"Doctor," Helga said.

"Just a sec. Sloane," he called, "Sloane, hold on, there!" She stopped at the half landing where the bronze woman with the torch in her outstretched arm lighted the stairway for Sloane and challenged him. "Hold on. If anything is due Helga—" I haven't got ten bucks, he meant, and hoped Sloane would understand and not make him say it in front of Helga. Sloane shook her head that nothing was owing and continued upstairs. Helga waited until Sloane reached the top, then came closer to him, smelling of perfume, whispering confidentially.

"She wouldn't give me a reference. What do you think of that, Doc? The madam wouldn't give me a reference—as if a reference from her—" She saw Milton's expression. "I mean in a case like this—"

"What do you mean, 'in a case like this'?"

"Well, Doctor—I mean coming into the kitchen throwing fits! You're not supposed to use paper towels, for example, to wipe out pots with. Rags, she said, and you had to scrub and boil them and use them again. And saving electricity. And if you should run out of butter! Wait until madam sees the reference I'm going to give her at the agency! If she thinks Mrs. Roberts will send anyone else to work in this lunatic asylum she's got another think coming! Reference!"

Milton jerked his head toward the door. "Get out, go on! I've heard enough out of you." When she didn't move, he started toward the stairs, but she moved after him.

"I'm sorry, Doctor. Sir, I just got my Irish up thinking of what I went through here, but I shouldn't get mad, should I?"

"Not with all that blubber you're carrying around; as a physician I can tell you that!"

"I shouldn't have talked like that. Excuse me." She began to whisper again. "Doctor, excuse me if this is fresh, but the way I figure it, you're a mental doctor, aren't you?" She made the old gesture indicating lunacy. "I mean—the madam— You're kind of her private doctor, I mean, aren't you? That's what I figure," she said.

She honestly believed Sloane was crazy. She wasn't just saying it in anger, she meant it. "You can figure what you like, it's a free country. And you can get out. Now."

She ducked her head and then handed him a piece of paper she was holding. "Yes, sir. Here's a telephone message I took while you were out this afternoon, Doctor." She shook her head over the slip of paper. "I almost forget it. You know, Doctor, in the sixteen days I been here, this was the only time the phone rang! That's another reference I could give if I wanted to. It's like a cemetery here."

He read what Helga had written. "What lady? What does this say?"

"Lady Constant. Lady Constant, she said. 'This is Lady Constant,' she said. She wanted to talk with Miss Folsom. F-o-l-s-o-m. This was Dr. Krop's residence, no Miss Folsom here, I said. I was sure it was a wrong number because it being the only time the telephone rang but it wasn't the wrong number. Dr. Krop's residence." Helga shook her head.

"What does this say?" Milton showed Helga.

"Her telephone number to call her back, the lady, and that is when she called, two forty-five. I marked it down."

"Lady Constant, Plaza 3-4968?" When she nodded, he waved at Helga to leave and, picking up her two suitcases, staring around the hall as if she didn't believe it was real, Helga left the house. As Milton stood there, the door banged behind Helga and immediately Sloane appeared at the head of the stairs.

"I was hiding under the bed. Has she gone?" She peered over the railing, then clasped her hands ecstatically. "Ah, darling, it's like having the exterminators in! That creature was a rodent! Gnawing at my vitals, Milton. Oh, the way she fixed eggs for herself for breakfast, darling, swimming in butter. She was a pig!"

Milton wouldn't have believed she could spit out a word like that.

"Stuffing herself, wasting, throwing away good food! It was her way of getting back at us, Milton—the waste. But she's gone, she's gone. I could dance with joy." She began to come down the stairs. "Aren't you joyful, Milton?"

He held up the paper. "I'm puzzled. Here's a telephone message to call a Lady Constant. Who is Lady Constant?" He had looked at the paper, not so much to refresh his memory but because he felt self-conscious about the title; when he looked up at Sloane she was bent over the banister rail as if she had suffered a severe cramp. He ran up to her. Her skin was clammy and her teeth were chattering. He put his arm around her. "Who is Lady Constant, Sloane?"

Her teeth chopped the words into syllables. "A-mor-y. My

sis-ter." She leaned against him. "What will I do? What will I do?"

He started to lead her downstairs. "Do what she asks. Call her." But she pulled away from his arm, holding to the stair rail as if expecting to be dragged off—to jail, he supposed. He was afraid that they would both tumble if he pulled at her and told her to go upstairs, then. Lie down. "Nothing has happened yet, Sloane. Let's not cry until we're hurt." She was weeping. He put his hand under her chin. "Look at me. Am I scared? If I'm not scared why should you be? Haven't I got as much to lose as you have?"

She looked at him and then, because her tears fogged her, because she wanted to make sure, wiped her tears away, blinked, stared at his face. Her voice whispered now. "You're not afraid. You're really not, Milton!"

"I'm not." He pried her hand off the rail. "Leave it to me. I'll handle her."

Under her breath she repeated that, "Handle her." She swallowed. "Milton—don't let her—"

"I won't let her."

She clutched his hand, drew it to her cheek. "She's wicked, worthless, vicious. I—I did what I did, but—"

"You know how I feel about what you did."

"But she's wicked. From the time she could reach out, she grabbed, Milton. She's always taken everything. What was mine. Anybody's. Mother preferred Amory, she always preferred Amory."

"Come on upstairs. Cinderella. You told me, and what you didn't tell me, I guessed."

Sloane, leaning on Milton, walked up the stairs. "Flourished like a green bay tree. Mother pretended to dislike what Amory did—she did dislike it, but admired it, too. Cinderella isn't such a trite story when you're the one it happens to, when you're the one who stayed here with mother—slaved. It isn't *fair*," she said,

87

weeping again, letting his hand go to cover her face. They walked upstairs together, slowly. "Never cared for anyone but herself," Sloane said, "her soft comfort. It is my money." Her breath caught. "Our money, Milton. If they find out they'll take it away and that's what she wants."

"All she wants now is for you to call, that's all." They reached the top of the stairs. Holding on to the wall, Sloane moved to their bedroom and once inside allowed him to push her down on the bed and then to give her a sedative which she obediently swallowed. As he was bringing the glass of water back to the bathroom, the phone rang.

Sloane made a grab at Milton. "Don't answer it! Don't!"

"But it must be your sister again."

"Don't answer."

"Someone has to. Helga is gone. Sloane, for the love of Mike, you'll put ideas into her head, that's what you'll do. Sloane, don't you see if you don't act natural, she'll certainly start thinking something is funny. A sister doesn't have to think a sister murdered their mother to come home from Europe and call her up. For Christ's sake, she just called you up! There could be a thousand reasons for that, a thousand reasons for her coming back—at least don't put the words into her mouth!"

She moaned, "Don't, don't!" but he got his jacket out from between her fingers and ran downstairs.

The telephone call was from Jenny. "Hold it, Jenny." He put his hand over the receiver so Jenny couldn't hear and called up to Sloane that it was Jenny, not her sister, but she didn't answer him. "What is it, Jenny? I'm in kind of a—"

"Now, Milt, have I been on your neck? I haven't seen hide nor hair of you since you came to see me, have I? I am reminding you that I haven't been on your neck so you won't tell me you're 'in kind of a—' before you hear why I called."

"O.K., Jenny."

"I'm only on this phone now because I'm worried about you."

The way he hissed, said she should mind her own business, how many times did he have to tell her to keep her nose out. "This is something to worry about, Milt! Listen, around three o'clock this afternoon I had a telephone call. I waited until now because I hear you're still attending the cardiac clinic, anyhow." ("You hear, you hear!" he said, but she paid no attention.) "You'll never guess who I had this call from, Milt."

But he did guess. Helga had said there was no Miss Folsom here, only Mrs. Krop, Dr. Krop's wife, Dr. Milton Krop. At first Sloane's sister might have figured Sloane had sold the house to a Dr. and Mrs. Krop, but Helga would surely have told her if they were new here. Helga certainly knew Sloane had lived here all her life. The old days, Sloane was always giving Helga, the good old days in this house when servants were servants. The sister waiting on pins and needles for Sloane—or whoever it was—to call back would certainly be curious about this, and why not look into the telephone books where his name was still where it always had been, Dr. Milton Krop. Perfectly natural. The sister would telephone his office and get Jenny.

"A call from a certain 'Lady,'" Jenny said. "I hope not a 'Lady' who means trouble, Milt, but I have my doubts. She turned out to be your wife's sister, from France. When she called, she asked for you, Milt, but why should I bother explaining you weren't in practice any more? I've had a bellyful of their complaining to me when I tell them that. She asked if I was your nurse. No, I wasn't your nurse, them days are gone forever. Secretary then? I said I was Mrs. Krop, since she had to know. Mrs. Krop? Dr. Krop's mother? I knew right then she wasn't just a patient. You know how you can tell when it's personal."

"Psychic. I know."

"Who said psychic? I told her I was Dr. Krop's sister-in-law and she said so was she your sister-in-law, she rather imagined! Rather imagined! She asked who your wife was, to make sure, and then on the basis we were both sisters-in-law tried to get

89

very chummy. All of a sudden, very chummy, you see? Are you beginning to smell a rat, Milton?"

"What rat?"

"The sister, of course, Milt! She tried to pump me! Until that minute she didn't know a thing about her sister getting married. Until that minute! All she knew was her mother was as usual, no sicker than usual, and then all she knew was her mother was dead and when the funeral was to be. What she hadn't known was her sister had married the doctor who had taken care of her mother. I didn't tell her—she remembered the name, Milt. As far as she knew, you were just her mother's doctor to her sister and now here you are married to her. She wanted to know a lot of things—how her mother died, for instance. Were you in attendance, any other physician? What kind of doctor were you, anyhow, a big specialist with a Cadillac? How long were you and her sister going steady before you were married? How long were you married?"

"Women are supposed to be curious. So what?"

"Aren't you curious, Milt?"

"About what curious?"

"About what I told her. Maybe I told her wrong, Milt, and if I did you can't blame me. If you'd only tell me what's what, Milt!"

"I don't care what you told her," he said.

Jenny tested that, silently repeating Milton's sentence for her inner guide. He meant it, she decided, he didn't care. She said quickly, "I didn't tell her anything." When the telephone rang, when this Lady called, Jenny had been reading about another teenage murder in the newspaper. There was an article explained these murders and how the atom bomb was partly responsible. The kids nowadays had no future they could count on like in the old days, the article said, and when you had no future you could easy become a killer. And neither did Milt have any future. The article explained Milt, too, didn't it? How he could have done something—funny; how he could not worry now over what might happen? She didn't need to worry over the teenager, Bud, but only over poor Milt.

"I didn't tell her anything, Milt, I sang your praises and maybe I shouldn't have done that because that way she found out you're not a big specialist with a Cadillac. I guess talking to me was enough to show her you weren't in the money, Milt; anyhow before you married her sister. And I'll tell you what else she said—that her mother never mentioned her sister and you in the same breath in her letters. She wrote about her doctor and she wrote about her daughter, but not in the same breath, so she knows you never went steady with Sloane, and then you got married so soon after the funeral, she knows that. Oh, Milt," Jenny said, "watch out, watch out, she's poison! I can feel it in my bones. She's suspicious."

"You know what she can do with her suspicions," Milton said, "the same thing you can do with yours. How many times do I have to tell you?" He could tell her and he could hang up on her, but that was all. Jenny was like a bulldog, he couldn't pry her loose. Although Sloane was still upstairs in the bedroom —she was hanging on to him also—he began to climb the stairs again. She did not move when he came into the bedroom, but she knew he was there, all right. He went to the bed and sat down and when he put his hand on her shoulder she shivered and turned so she could see him. "You see what happens when you let your imagination run away with you, Sloane? That was Jenny. Her reason for calling was your sister had called her— now don't start imagining about that! Your sister can look in a phone book, there's only one Dr. Milton Krop in Jackson Heights and it's a free country, she could call Jenny! And why did Jenny call? Not what you're thinking, kid. To make sure you really have royalty in your family so she can shoot her mouth off to the neighbors. Wait till Bud the Princeton man gets hold of this! You see? Now call your sister—a fishing expedition."

Sloane sat up in the bed, shoving her hair back, looking wild. "Milton—Amory wouldn't have come back unless she suspected, I assure you. Don't delude yourself."

"I'm not deluding," he said. "I'm just not crossing my bridges in advance." He could not smooth her hair just then—God, what fear did to a face, he thought—but he took her wrist. He could take her pulse. "I'm not going to let you call her. You should feel your pulse, kid! I'm going to call her. I'll say you're out somewhere, not home yet, but I just came in and found the telephone message. Naturally, I call up the minute I hear she's in town. Her brother-in-law." He patted her hand and laid it down neatly at her side, getting off the bed. "Sloane, what do I call her, Lady Amory?"

"Lady Constant."

"But I should sound like one of the family. A brother-in-law."

"Lady Constant. Why must you sound like one of the family? What do you mean, Milton?" She was watching him closely, her eyes narrowed watching him.

"I mean I should sound like one of the family. Not the butcher boy, I mean. Lie down again, Sloane. Give that sedative a fighting chance to work on you. I'll report back after I talk to her." He paused on the half landing and practiced saying "Lady Constant" to the damned bronze figure there; she was suspicious of him also, she was poison.

Sloane whispered, "Well? Well?"

"She didn't want to talk to me at all at first." He heard Sloane draw in a sobbing breath. "She said because she isn't feeling well right now, but if that was a lie it was dumb; I didn't let Lady Constant get away with that. 'Then I'm just the one you should talk to,' I told her, not fazed in the least. 'You're forgetting I'm a doctor, aren't you, Lady Constant?' " Sloane was watching his mouth as if she needed to lip read, as if she were deaf. " 'I'm coming over, Lady Constant,' I said. 'I'll look you over.' I wouldn't take no for an answer. After all, it's up to the doctor, isn't it? It's in the doctor's hands, I mean. I put it over, I'm going there now." He moved to the big wardrobe and when he opened it the door creaked as in a ghost story. He reached in and took his medical case from the floor of it and turned, holding it toward Sloane, blowing on it as if it were dusty. "So I'm going right now to take care of your sister." He set the bag down on the bed and opened it, his fingers touching the bottles lined up against the sides, each in its leather slot, then his sphygmomanometer, his stethoscope and his hypodermic case. He took out the stethoscope and, folding the rubber tubing, thrust it into his pocket. "Do I look like a doctor again?"

Sloane nodded.

"That's what I've got to look like."

"Milton—"

"She's waiting, Sloane. I don't think I'd better drive in— parking in midtown—the subway will be quicker. You lie down, go on."

She moaned, "How will I wait?" and threw her hands over her face.

On the dresser near the door there were a couple of her books. Milton tossed one onto the bed. "Read some poetry. Relax. Leave it all to me, Sloane, that's what I'm here for."

She lay where she was, hearing his steps down the hall, along the lower hall, hearing the door slam after him. She sat up on the bed and her hand went over her mouth. She felt for the book and found it, and touching the limp leather binding knew it was her Shakespeare.

> O! my offence is rank, it smells to heaven;
> It hath the primal eldest curse upon 't,
> A brother's murder.

She held the book for a moment more, then let it drop and

moved her body to the far side of the bed so that she would not touch it. She thought: mother's, brother's, primal eldest curse. The syllables racked her throbbing head.

"*Entrez!* Oh, come in, do!"

She looked so startled, sitting there in bed, that he actually took out his stethoscope to introduce himself. "Dr. Krop," he explained, waving the stethoscope. "I said I was coming right over, didn't you expect me?" He took a step into the room and she jumped out of the bed.

"I expected you to be announced."

"Them to first call up from downstairs, you mean? Well, I just said Dr. Krop and they rushed me right up here by elevator. I guess they thought it was an emergency. You know—doctors, priests, privileged characters." He closed the door with one hand and pointed to the bed with the other. "You'll freeze your tootsies. Go on, get back in bed, you look shaky." What she had on must be a peignoir set like Jenny had bought Sloane for a wedding present; except in the movies he had never seen stuff like that on anyone, not on his type patient!

"I do feel rather shaky."

Her hair must be tinted. Dyed was too harsh a word for the little that had been needed to change it from Sloane's mouse color to this; not blond, not red, not platinum. And, for the love of Mike, with some curls and waves in it, no matter what interior decorators said! Cut short, of course. He remembered Jenny telling Maureen about the razor cut. Razor cut. She probably had Sloane's eyes—too light blue for his taste—not really darker, just darkened, he thought. Wasn't there a black line drawn all around her lids? Did that do it?

She shivered under his stare and pulled the covers higher. "If you look at me that way, I'll think I'm very sick."

"It's that you look so much like my wife." He looked around for a chair to sit on. "So you're Sloane's sister!" The chairs were all covered with stuff, filmy, flyaway stuff like what she was wearing, dresses, a fur thing, another fur thing. Everything was covered with her stuff.

"Oh, there isn't any place cleared, is there? Well, I'm a lazy slut even when I haven't just gotten off a boat and even when I'm in health. But you know that, I'm sure; how Amory never lifts a finger and the maid here won't lift a finger for me. How do they know when you're stony? The stewardess from the boat must have checked a mark on my luggage after she had my tip —as tramps do on houses. Please just shove what's on that chair on the floor, Dr. Krop. How I miss Paulette—my faithful maid. Damn it, faithful unto debt, not death! You're not smiling! Don't you think that's a mot, Doctor Krop—faithful unto debt? It's the best I can do for the present, I'm afraid."

He could barely hear what she was saying, the mélange of the textures he was lifting off the chair, the softness, crispness, clinging, the very colors themselves made his fingertips tingle. "You just got off the boat, you said?"

"Fresh from Antibes. Oh," she said, "do you know Antibes?"

"The houses are up on cliffs and they have stone steps cut in the living rock down to the beaches there—"

"You've been to Antibes?"

"In my dreams," he said, "but we're going there, me and Sloane."

"Not Sloane! Surely not Sloane?"

"Why not? Now your mother is gone Sloane can go wherever she wants to, can't she? This Antibes, it's what it's cracked up to be, isn't it?"

"Cracked up?" She stared at him. "Well," she said, "if you're a romantic. The whole Riviera is polluted, of course—like the whole world, Dr. Krop—but still . . ." What it was to wake up in the big bedroom there, early-morning chocolate brought by the faithful unto debt Paulette. When she drew the curtains— they were curtains in the theater sense—when Paulette drew the curtains and revealed the set . . . Oh, modest except for the set. One made plans, she said, half of which one never troubled to carry out. "The swimming. Air like a fin—in the alcoholic sense—a state of constant semi-intoxication—pixilated so that the merest pubcrawling became enchantment—"

Milton sighed, then shook himself like a dog to free himself of the enchantment, the pixilation. "Why did you come back then? Why leave?"

She laughed. "Why indeed! My dear man, for the only reason I ever do anything, because I'm stony. Surely Sloane told you that elemental fact about me. How is Sloane?"

"She's out. Doesn't know you're in the United States yet. I came home and found your message. Sloane's all right. I was forgetting this isn't a social call. How you are is more the point, isn't it? Now, exactly what's bothering you?" He couldn't get "Lady Constant" out.

"I'm dizzy and nauseated."

"I see." He opened his medical bag and took out his thermometer, shook it down and, rising, gave it to her. When he began to examine her, she took the thermometer out of her mouth and tried to tell him, don't bother, just dizzy, just nauseated, but he stuck the thermometer back in her mouth and did a superficial examination. Her eyes dilated, staring at him, and he thought that she was going to work up quite a temperature if she didn't look out. He went to his bag and touched the little bottles, one after another, then the tubes, then removed the thermometer and read it and shook it down. "You take two of these," he chose the tube, opened it, "and you'll feel much better in half an hour."

She held out her hand for the pills and he gave them to her. There was a bottle of water by the bed table and he poured some of it into a glass and held the glass toward her. She took the water but set it down on the table again.

"You've been very kind, Dr. Krop. It was very good of you."

"You won't know how good until you take those pills." He lifted the glass again.

"Later. It really was very good of you to—" He moved the glass toward her. "Don't bully me, Dr. Krop!"

"Bully? I call it curing you. Come on, get them down."

She shook her head, smiling grimly. "Not now."

"I know how to shove pills down balky patients if I have to."

He smiled the same way she did; both of them smiled at each other, then she gave up.

"I'm not very good at being tactful, am I, Dr. Krop? I hated to tell you after dragging you up here like this, but I don't need the pills. You see, I had a brainstorm after you kindly— I'm an idiot to have forgotten, but one does, doesn't one? I'm perfectly sure that the dizziness and nausea are only what always happens to me the first day off a boat or a plane." She put the two pills on the bed table, holding her hand over them. "If I'm wrong, I'll take these later."

"I'll take them now."

"But, Dr. Krop—in case my diagnosis is wrong?"

"Uhuh. Back to Papa." He pulled her hand, which was so much like Sloane's, off the pills and took them away, dropping them into the tube again, screwing on the cover, shoving the tube back into its leather holder in the medical bag. "A first-year medical student knows better than to leave unidentified drugs around. It can lead to trouble."

"You're very—careful." He was coming toward her with another bottle from his bag.

"Dramamine," he said, "if what you have is landsickness, someone should have told you about Dramamine."

"But I know about it! My dear man, I lived on it! I wouldn't have survived." She pushed away the glass he was holding toward her.

"Whoever told you should have told you to take it a day

97

before you got on the boat and continue at least a day after. What's the matter? Do you like being dizzy and nauseated?"

She said, "Of course not, no, of course not!"

"Water stale?" He looked at the glass of it she would not accept. "I'll get you—"

"We'll ring," she said, jumping up. "I'll ring for ice water."

"I thought in Europe they didn't go for ice water." But he didn't open the bathroom door to get her the water. The door opened, startling him so that the water he was carrying slopped over his sleeve. "What the hell is this?"

The young man walked to the bed, pulling out a handkerchief so that Milton first figured he'd gotten some of the water; but, no, the handkerchief was to put the two Dramamine capsules in, to carefully wrap them in, to tuck them away in his pocket.

"So it's not the B.F.," Milton said slowly. "I thought B.F., but why you'd have to hide the B.F. from me—I'm your brother-in-law, not your hubby. So it's protection! A bodyguard, not a B.F.!" He wiped his face with his handkerchief and then wiped his wet sleeve. The two of them were staring at him. "I'm just going to sit down," he said to the man who had moved in front of Lady Constant because he had pulled something out of his pocket. "Now I feel—dizzy and nauseated, too. I'll let you know how I feel after you tell me why anyone needs protection from Milt Krop."

"Come now, Dr. Krop!" Lady Constant said, adding to the young man, "I keep thinking 'Dr. Fell.'"

"Amory!"

"Who's Dr. Fell?"

"Didn't you learn Dr. Fell as a child? 'I do not love thee, Doctor Fell, the reason why I cannot tell.'"

"I didn't ask you if you loved me; you don't have to love me, it's a free country. I'm asking why you have him hiding in the john? Why did you wrap up the Dramamine tablets like they were two-carat diamonds, as if I didn't know!"

"You do know then?"

"You don't have to be Einstein. That guy was here when I telephoned you. You tell me you're under the weather and being a good-natured slob as well as a physician, I dust off my little black bag and come running here—and that guy's in there so it's perfectly safe. Now tell me why he has to be there."

"You have a good nature and I have a suspicious nature, Dr. Krop. I'm afraid I was suspicious of your good nature. I suspected that your forcing your attentions on me—your purely medical attentions on me, I mean—might conceivably have significance."

"It had significance. Helpful Milt. Trying to help a lady out."

"Out," Lady Constant said. "Way out? All the way out?" She reached forward and tapped the pocket in which the young man had put the Dramamine.

"With Dramamine? The A.M.A. will be very surprised to hear that it's fatal."

"And Day and I will be very surprised to find it is Dramamine, won't we, Day?"

The young man had a habit of settling his jacket over his shoulders before he spoke; he did it now. "Dr. Krop, I would say that you know what this is all about. It seems to me you do know why Amory should feel she must protect herself against you. You certainly haven't suggested that her suspicion is a surprise to you."

Princeton boy. Talking through his nose. Brooks Brothers. "I haven't suggested it because it isn't true." He spoke to Lady Constant without using her title. He was damned if he was going to use that title. "How did my wife know you were in the United States before I did? When did you talk to my wife?"

"I haven't talked to Sloane."

"Is that the honest truth? I get it—she wrote to you! No? She telephoned you? I forget all you have to do to telephone the Riviera is pay the telephone bill."

"Except for a cable telling me of my mother's death and funeral I haven't heard from Sloane in any shape or form."

"You haven't?" Milton deliberately scratched his head. "Wait a sec—wait. I get it—at three o'clock today you spoke to Jenny, my sister-in-law, Mrs. Krop." Milton guffawed. "My *other* sister-in-law! Oh, my God, don't tell me it was Jenny who put these funny ideas into your head!"

"Has she funny ideas?"

"She's full of them usually; in this case I don't know. I'm not my sister-in-law's keeper."

"My dear Dr. Krop, I don't need to talk to Sloane and I certainly heard nothing but your praises from your other sister-in-law."

"Let's get one thing straight. We are talking about the same thing—the idea is you think that your mother—"

"I believe that mother was murdered, yes. Quite right; that is precisely what I think and I came to the conclusion all by my little self. If Sloane told you I was a moron she was mistaken."

Milton took a step toward Lady Constant. "How I would like to knock the chip off your shoulder," he said. "You get the chip off your shoulder, do you hear me? Who the hell do you think you are?" He retreated, felt for the chair with his hand, jerking his head from the young man to Lady Constant. "How long you known her?"

Lady Constant answered for the young man. "Day and I are old friends."

"How long have you known her?" He saw how the young man had stepped between him and Lady Constant. "Relax!" Milton said, and sat on the chair he had cleared. "Relax, I'm talking as a physician, mister. Have you known my wife's sister long enough and well enough—if you know what I mean—to tell me if she has these delusions about any other subject under the sun?"

"Delusions! Oh, my dear man! Delusions, Day! Do you call

it a delusion that my mother died so suddenly, unexpectedly? Do you call it a delusion that it was you who filled out her death certificate and then, a pitifully short time afterward— Oh, Sloane's the one for quoting about the funeral baked meats! It is certainly no delusion that you and Sloane were married. If Sloane had ever felt the slightest amorous interest in you, my dear Dr. Fell, I would have known of it from Mother. If Sloane thought you were—" she indicated how little, putting her red-polished thumbnail against the nail of her little finger—"*that* possible, Mother would have written and told me so. And you needn't tell me that my mother was a sick woman who missed a flaming love affair under her nose that everyone else knew about, because the one thing I did learn from your estimable praise-singing sister-in-law was that she had been as surprised by your marriage as I was!"

Milton tugged at his nose. "Mister—this whole cock-and-bull story she's worked out—take my word for it!"

"Take his word for it, Day, do!"

"Look. Look me up—call up the hospital where I work. Oh, hell, this has gone too far for that! Go on and have the Drama-mine analyzed; that's what you took them for. And when you find out that they are Dramamine and not arsenic, you'll begin to see things a little—" He wagged his jaw from side to side and stood up. The young man jumped to attention. "I'm just going for my bag." The young man got to it first. Milton said, "What the—" Then he laughed. "O.K. Carry it for me, will you? Be my caddy, see if I care! Take it all the way home for me; that bag is heavy—even if it isn't loaded." He reached the door, hearing the young man right in back of him. "That's a good one, isn't it? It's heavy even if it isn't loaded. That's as good as your joke about servants, in my opinion." He opened the door. "Go to a reputable lab for the analysis, O.K.?"

"The best," Lady Constant said spitefully, "the police lab!"

"So you're going to the police? You're going to tell them I

killed your mother with Dramamine which you were too smart to swallow!"

"Not necessarily the same pills."

"No, could be the others, like the first ones where I was too smart to leave you the evidence and wouldn't leave them hanging around. Tell them about those, too. When they laugh in your face and you find out you're quite safe with me, give me a ring! I came here today—forced my attentions on you as you put it—for different reasons than you figured, but I did want to talk to you, that much is true. So give me a ring after the Dramamine is analyzed." He walked into the corridor and held out his hand for the bag, but the young man came out with him. "I'm going, I'm going," Milton said. "Don't worry, I'm not going to use a hypodermic through the keyhole so when the duchess locks her door, she drops dead!"

"Doctor, I came out to apologize."

"Go on!"

"I don't know what makes Amory fancy herself as a detective."

"Lady Constant, Private Eye! Maybe she could get herself on television. Look, your girl friend—oh, nuts," he said and walked rapidly toward the elevator.

The young man placed himself between Milton and the elevator.

"Get out of my way," Milton said. "I'm up to here!"

"Dr. Krop, please—I wanted to tell you that Amory has already seen her lawyer. She gave him her reasons for suspecting you and he called the District Attorney. I think you should know that the District Attorney has already been in touch with some judge or other and that Amory's been told that the orders for exhumation of her mother's body will be filled out tonight. By now, probably."

The elevator came up and the young man stepped out of the way and Milton stepped into the car, then out.

"I thought I'd tell you," the young man said.

"Thanks. You meant well. I have something to tell you." The young man bowed in an English kind of way and ducked his head toward the duchess' room, but Milton shook his head. "No sense telling her, the way she feels. First, one thing, I don't give a damn about exhumation orders. What do you think I am? You think I like people accusing me of murdering a patient? I'd *ask* for exhumation myself—insist—except for one thing." He pointed at the young man's face. "Boy, you sure trust me, nix!" His heart gave a lurch because his mother used to say that, "nix." She used to toss her head. It made her look young when she tossed her head. Milton took a deep breath. "There's only one reason I don't want any exhumation and that's not for the reason you think. I give you my word. You can laugh yourself sick about my giving you my word; I should worry. But there's one thing I want to ask you. Will you go back to your lady friend— No, I better. Do you trust me enough to let me get close enough to her to ask her something? One thing. Leave my loaded bag outside. Who needs it? She didn't want a doctor, she wanted a murderer. Leave the bag and you can—what's that word?" He patted his pockets. "You know, you can see if I'm clean—frisk me, that's it. Frisk me first, if you want to."

"She can't call off the exhumation, you know."

"I don't give a damn about the exhumation!" Milton shouted this. The young man appeared to be listening to the echoes of his voice, as a piano tuner listens, then he nodded and started back to Lady Constant's room, but paused at the door, with his hand on the knob.

"Perhaps I'd better—" He went inside.

Milton leaned against the wall. He told himself that his mother saying "nix" had been saying "no." He told himself he had had enough "no's" in his lifetime. In his lifetime, he told himself. The door opened.

"Of course he's bluffing, Day, but it won't hurt. All right, it won't hurt, it won't hurt, Day!"

The young man stuck his head out of the door and Milton went in.

Lady Constant was standing by the window, looking down at the street. "One thing about Day, Dr. Krop, he cannot bear having his curiosity denied. What is it you want, Dr. Krop?"

"Not for me. I'm thinking of my wife—"

"Poor Sloane, poor conniving, murdering little Sloane!"

Milton said, "That's enough out of you about her. What you don't know about your sister would fill a book."

"I will find out soon, though."

"Listen to me—don't say any more about her. You have enough words anyhow you're going to have to eat, take my word for that. You said enough already so it's hard for me to stand here and not belt you one!"

"Amory, give the man a chance!"

"I'm controlling myself because of my wife."

"Oh, he's madly in love with her, Day! Day, you should have been in the room—the wall should have been made of glass then you could have observed the way he stared at me when he came in. How would it go in the appropriate literature—he *ate me up with his eyes!*"

Milton stammered, "I told you—you look so much alike!"

"And so different," Lady Constant said. "And Day, *vive la différence*—that's what was written all over his face, Day—*vive la différence!*"

Milton said, "I don't understand, is that Spanish, *vive?*"

"Pity. I assure you, Day—"

"You flatter yourself," Milton said, "boy, you flatter yourself, kid!"

"No, but I don't flatter you, either. And it would be extreme flattery to believe you were capable of appreciating anything about Sloane but Mother's property. I'm *courci*, Dr. Krop, and

I know it. That is a Spanish word for you, untranslatable, unfortunately, but it means—oh, dowdy-smart, a not-quite-quite! You couldn't possibly appreciate the *beauté du diable* which my sister has!"

"Just one look at me and you know what I like!"

"Just one look at me, Dr. Krop—just one look like the one you gave me when you came in and I certainly know what you like!"

Day said, "Amory, please—"

"Leave her alone. I don't care what she thinks. All I want is one thing. Will you do one thing for me?" He shrugged. "The condemned man's last request, only this isn't funny. I'm dead serious about this. Go ahead with the exhumation, exhume till you're blue in the face, but until you have the proof that what you think isn't a cock-and-bull story like I say it is, don't let my wife hear about it. Just don't tell her and don't let anyone else tell her what you suspect, O.K.?"

Amory drummed on the window sill, "Is that all?"

"Is that so much to ask?" Milton turned to the young man. "Have you any pull? Can you make her keep her trap shut to my wife until the medical examiner gets through—a couple of weeks, at least, if he's thorough."

"He's going to be thorough. He's aware that you're a doctor, Dr. Krop. He told me three weeks."

"Three weeks then."

"Why is it so important, Dr. Krop?"

"I think it's important, that's why! Look, give me your word on it you won't mention anything about this for three weeks and I'll give you my word I won't tell Sloane about it afterward. Never."

"Why should I? Why should I do anything you want? No, my dear Dr. Krop, I will not not tell Sloane. In fact I will tell Sloane now." She reached for the telephone.

Milton lunged for it but was too late. "Can't you stop her?"

he asked the young man, who had stepped in between himself and Lady Constant. "Don't let her do this now, when she's hysterical. Make her wait until she calms down, anyhow. Think it over. Wait—"

"Amory," the young man said, "wait!" He put his hand over the dial.

"One minute is all I ask. Just don't let her cut off her nose to spite her face. You get me," Milton said, nodding. "I can see you at least get me. Look, I'm going now. I'll go to my sister-in-law's. Will you call me and put me out of my misery? It's in the book under Dr. Milton Krop."

The young man nodded and Milton went out of the room again, but the door was still open and he could hear, first the young man, then the duchess.

"Amory, can't you wait until—?"

"No. Take your hand off that dial, Day!"

As Milton bent to pick up his bag he heard the click of the dial. "So nix," he thought, "so no, so nothing!"

"Hello?" she said, "Sloane?"

"Who else?" he thought, walking wearily to the elevator. Hello, Sloane. Good-by, Sloane. Hello and good-by, Sloane. Top of my hit parade, Lady Constant: Your hello Sloane is my good-by.

Schizoid personalities were very common, he thought, but not splits like his. Not usually split the way he was, he thought, noticing that he had walked from the hotel to the Fifty-ninth Street station of the Independent Subway, not usually through the middle. Not usually hello-good-by from the waist up, with the bottom part, the feet, walking to the subway station as if he could go back to the Haunted House now, as if there was any sense going back now. Milton held out for a moment against the stream of people flowing down the subway stairs, the hand without the black doctor-bag clutching the door, resisting the current, but it was too much effort to cling there for long so he let himself be shoved down the stairs with the rest of them, the way he had always been shoved, the way it had always been too much effort, the way it was going to be from now on out, he thought. A real man wouldn't take it lying down, a real man could have stopped that bitch some way, but he wasn't a real man, just Milt Krop, the nix-boy. He had known he was the nix-boy of the family from the time he could read, no, before that, from the time he could read the nix in his mother's eyes. He knew it, his mother knew it and Jenny knew it. Jenny knew it but good.

He was pressed against the doors of the subway car with the rest of them but he let them press even though the edges of his medical case were cutting into his thigh; no sense wasting energy using the old elbows. Save your strength. Conserve oxygen when you're trapped underground. Milton turned his face away from the glass door—it was all he could turn without shoving—and stared into the faces around him. There was death in each of them, not only in his, only not so soon and not so positively so soon.

And then he saw that he had not been schizoid, that the bottom part of him taking him to the subway had been connected with the top part of him that realized it was all over. Both parts had acted together getting him here because the only manly thing he could do was make it sooner and this was the best possible place for it, wasn't it? The Independent Subway in rush hour? Rushhour, rushhour, the wheels chorused obligingly. Accidents happened all the time in the subway. Nobody yelled: Stop the train, man overboard! He felt the wheels then rather than heard them, rushhour rushhour, the greasy, filthy, crushing wheels, and wished forlornly it could be man overboard from the Queen Elizabeth en route to Cherbourg, a luxury liner they called her, the luxury of clean green sea water, but no luxury liner for him. "What it was to wake up in the morning in the big bedroom," the bitch had said. Hello Riviera, good-by Riviera, where the Browning girl had gone!

It was funny the way he stayed on that packed train, going through, at each station, the scuffle necessary in order not to be pushed out with the crowd until he came to his own station. Go home to die. Well, they all did that if they could.

He was home. His station. He stood at the edge of the platform while the ones to whom this station was also home walked toward the stairs and up and out, waiting until the next train so that just before it reached him, he would let her rip. It would be no harder than learning to dive when the boys had taught him. Like everything else, diving was harder for him to learn than for the others. His body had rebelled against letting itself go in, head first. "You can do it, Milt," Phil had said. "If we can do it, you can do it," Phil had said. ("If we could die, you can die," Phil meant.) Milton set the black bag down, then picked it up again. Phil had also said, "I'm going to count ten, Milt, and then if you don't fall in, I'm going to shove you." He could feel the canvas of the diving board under his toe and he curled his toes around the edge, faintly hearing the next train. "Come on and shove, Phil," he said. "I need a shove. I need help, Phil."

Cissie, clutching the imitation patent leather hatbox, prayed he would look up at her. She could pray because she hadn't made this happen. She had kept away from the Haunted House. She had been a good girl, so she could pray. The last person she had expected to see across from her on the uptown side was him so she could pray with a clear conscience. "Let him look up," she could ask. Once. Look at me once more, Doctor. Just lift your head once, I want to see your face once again. (Her mother said what was he, no Clark Gable, not even a handsome face, her mother said.) "Oh, Doctor, just once look up before the train comes!"

If it had really been Cissie and not a hallucination, he thought, really Cissie standing there across the tracks on the downtown platform, the little bird, the little Cissie, then she had been sent. She had been sent like a vision, a message, a command. Phil had been telling him to keep his head down, but Phil was dead and if he had kept his head down and let go, he would be dead too, but he had looked up and across the tracks was life. Cissie was life. The train had come and divided them, Cissie or the vision of Cissie on the downtown side—he hadn't waited to find out which. With the train between them, hiding her, he had run, gasping, sweating, trembling, his legs almost unmanageable, along the platform to the steps and then up and out into the air.

He had not waited out on the street to see whether, if it had been Cissie, she would come out also, walk out of the downtown exit across the street there, no sense to that yet. Yet, he thought, putting the bag on the floor between his feet, feeling in his pocket for a dime. He closed the door of the telephone booth, slipped the dime into the slot and took off the receiver. BEFORE DIALING WAIT FOR THE— Before dialing—*wait!* All he had heard was "Hello? Sloane?" then he had run away. What she had probably said was that she suspected foul play and that the D.A. was going to exhume and find out if it was so. What else could she have said? She could have said that he didn't want her to tell Sloane what she was doing. Nothing wrong with that. Nobody would want his wife told such a thing. Was it good news?

She didn't have to wait, no point waiting—which was exactly what he was going to say to Sloane: that there was no point waiting around three weeks for the police to come and get them. What he was going to say was they shouldn't wait, not another day. They had their passports. They had the dough. Let them have their fling before the cops caught up with them. Give the cops a run for their money and see the world their slogan. Git up and git. He dialed the number and heard the phone ringing in the Haunted House. He counted: One, two, three. (It would have been dumb as hell to let Phil shove him before he got something out of this business, because so far—nothing. *And how*, nothing, he thought, picturing Sloane looking the way she did lying on the bed, hearing the telephone, going down to answer it.) "Hello?" he said. "Sloane?"

But it wasn't Sloane. He banged down the receiver. When he told the operator that he had dialed correctly but got the wrong number, his voice trembled with indignation.

"I'm sorry," the operator said. "If you will hang up—"

He wiped his hands down his trousers before he dialed again. The telephone was picked up on the second ring. "Hello? Sloane?"

"Dr. Krop's residence."

Milton said, "Who's this? This is Dr. Krop, who's this?"

"Dr. Krop's residence. Excuse me. Is it Dr. Krop speaking?"

"I'm speaking. Who's this?"

"Why, Dr. Krop, it is Mrs. Austen, Dr. Krop."

He had forgotten Austen. When he left Sloane in the car in front of Queens General she had told him to tell Austen to come as soon as possible, "bag and baggage." Austen, of course, had known Sloane was going to finagle it sooner or later, Austen had been all packed and raring to go, bag and baggage! His feet did a jig step on the floor of the telephone booth, a hope step. "How long have you been there, Mrs. Austen?"

"How long, Doctor?"

"How long, how long, were you there about an hour ago? Did you pick up the phone an hour ago?"

Yes, Austen had been there, had answered the telephone, had ascertained it was Lady Constant, had gone to madam who wasn't well and told her and madam hadn't been well enough to speak to Lady Constant.

"She *isn't* well enough, Mrs. Austen. She's sick. Am I glad you're there, Mrs. Austen! You've taken a load off my mind, I can tell you. Lifesaver," he said, "a real lifesaver!"

"Dr. Krop, why, Dr. Krop—sir— You must know what it meant to me, sir, when madam—"

"Madam and me both, Mrs. Austen. All of us, we're all just one happy family now you're there!" As for Austen, she went into quite a song and dance about how much it meant to her to be earning an honest living with gentlefolk again.

"Shall I call madam to the telephone now, Doctor?"

"Don't bother. If she heard the phone ringing and asks you tell her it was me; otherwise don't bother. And Mrs. Austen, if Lady Constant calls again— I'll bet you've been trained how to say 'madam is not at home' so they believe it! Well, madam is not at home if Lady Constant calls again, get me?"

"Yes, Dr. Krop."

"She's not home to anybody tonight. When I get back, I'll explain." There was a pause and when Austen said, "Yes, Dr. Krop" again, it was in the usual way, the usual snippy way. After Milton hung up he figured that one out: the Marster doesn't explain to servants. "Theirs not to reason why, theirs but to do and die." But nobody's going to die, Milton thought. Not tonight, anyhow. Not yet. While there's life, there's life, Milton thought.

It was Jenny's face which came to life when, answering the doorbell about fifteen minutes later, she saw Milton standing there with his medical bag. She reached for the bag with one hand and with the other, like the nurse she had been, moved to his side, grasped his elbow firmly and led him into the apartment.

Maureen called from the kitchen, "Mom, who is it?"

"Why didn't you get the door you're so anxious?" Bud said.

Jenny studied Milton's expression. "Never mind who it is, curiosity! You stay right there and eat your supper, Maureen!"

111

She should have known better. Before she could get Milt into the waiting room, she heard Maureen squealing that it was Uncle Miltie, Bud. "You'll see him later. You'll see Uncle—Milt, Uncle Milt later, Maureen. He's going to come in there and eat in a few minutes so now you eat." Jenny released Milton's arm to close the door of the waiting room so the kids wouldn't come there and stand gawking. If, at last, Milt had come to ask her help, they'd put him off. She could tell that right now he was in one of his moods where he was this way, that way; she didn't want the kids putting him off. Milt, when she let go of his arm, made straight for the Hide-a-Bed. Didn't that mean Milt was home again, that he'd come home because she had guessed right, that sister-in-law was poison? "Thanks God," she thought, and then quickly took the thought back. "I didn't mean that, not like that, not thanks God, he's in trouble, just thanks he came to me he can trust!"

"Aw, Milt," she said, and walking across the room, sat next to him on the Hide-a-Bed and laid her hand on his thigh. "Aw, gee, Milt, it's so good to see you home again!" Milt didn't answer, just stared at the waiting room. "It's kind of tatty," Jenny said. "I know. You get lazy keeping it right without the patients coming in. Without you, Milt. Will you listen to me," she said, laughing at herself. "I'm like talking about the weather. What do you care if the waiting room is tatty? Right, Milt? That's the last thing on your mind, right, Milt?" She had the feeling if he didn't spill soon, he'd never spill, so she shut up and patted his thigh encouragingly, but still he just sat there, waiting. For what? She studied him anxiously. He didn't look well, Milt! She jumped up then and hurried to his bag, fishing in it for his sphygmomanometer because maybe she was wrong, maybe it was his health, after all, and not the sister-in-law. When she came back to Milton and tried to pull his topcoat off, Milt came to and shook his head, so she folded the gray cuff neatly and put the instrument back into the medical bag.

This time, instead of sitting next to him again, she pulled a straight chair across the floor and set it in front of the Hide-a-Bed and sat where she could see him full, catch his eye and hold it. "Listen, Milt, don't you hear me?" Her tone seemed harsh to her, so she reached out and patted his thigh again. "Of course you hear me, you're not deaf, you're just in trouble up to here!" She touched his neck gently. "Well, maybe you are, maybe you're not, but two heads are always better than one, Milt." ("So give," she thought. "Give! Maybe there's not a minute to lose and you just sit there like a bump on a log!") "I can't help, Milt, if you don't tell me what happened. It's not a guessing game, Milt! I give up. I give up, Milt. I admit I can't guess the riddle, so you have to tell me, then I can help you, Milt. O.K.?" Now at least he looked at her instead of the room. "How many times have I helped you, Milt? We put our two heads together and we get the answer, right?"

"What right?"

"Let me help you. You're Phil's kid brother, Milt!"

Milton wet his lips. Everything wasn't so rosy. All that happened was Sloane didn't know yet, and what was that? Maybe if he did tell Jenny, laid it out for her, maybe she could tell him what to do next. Cissie had saved his life, but for what? Maybe so Jenny could tell him what to do. "Jenny," he began. It was the triumphant expression on her face, the victorious relaxation evident in the way her whole body slumped as he said her name, that stopped him. He swallowed hard and said it again, "Jenny—"

And then the telephone rang.

Jenny jumped but stayed her ground, "Yes, Milt? Yes, Milt?" But she couldn't help listening to see if Maureen or Bud was getting the phone, and so was Milt listening. They both sat listening until Maureen tapped down the hall, tapped a knock on the door and tapped until her mother told her to come in.

"It's a lady—a lady. A lady wants to talk to Uncle Miltie, Mom."

"I'll get it," Jenny said. "Some lady. I'll get it, Milt, don't worry."

He walked past Jenny and up to Maureen. "Some lady? What lady?"

Bud, picking his teeth, was behind Maureen in the hall. He took his finger out of his mouth. "That's no lady, that's his wife!"

"It is not his wife. It's a lady, Uncle Milt, that's what she said."

Jenny stared after Milt's back. He was staring at the telephone.

"You know what you said, you little dope, you said Uncle Miltie's wife wasn't a lady! Mom, Murine said Uncle Miltie's wife wasn't a lady!" But his mother wasn't paying attention to what the little dope said.

Milton talked quietly, as if he could be overheard by the party on the telephone. "Jenny, take Maureen and go in the kitchen again. Bud, close that door!"

"Milt, if it's the sister-in-law— Let me handle her, Milt! Don't you talk to her—"

"Out," Milton said. He waited until Jenny left and Buddy closed the door, then he went to the telephone. "Hello?"

"Dr. Krop? Lady Constant here."

"Yes?"

"I called to tell you that I've thought over what you wanted me to do. I won't tell Sloane about the exhumation until I know."

"You won't regret it. Thanks a million."

"You do understand that everything is going ahead just as I told you? This doesn't affect anything else."

"All I'm interested is that you shouldn't tell Sloane. I told you that before and I'll tell you that again; that's all I ask."

"Yes, but could you tell me why you don't want Sloane to know yet? It is only three weeks. Why is it so vital that she doesn't know, could you tell me that?"

"I could but I won't. Not after what happened up there. Let's not go into that or I'll see red again. The reason I came to see you—not what you thought by a long shot—the reason I came to see you was to tell you why I don't want you to let Sloane hear about this. Naturally, I couldn't jump in with both feet. I had to wait and make sure you had this wild idea of yours first—"

"Don't be under the misapprehension that I believe it a wild idea, Dr. Krop!"

"You still think I murdered your mother? I came to your room for murder number two— O.K. It's a free country, think what you want, just don't let Sloane know a thing about what you think."

"Now, Dr. Krop, you don't think I'm going to see Sloane, do you? Call on her? Leave cards? Come into my parlor, said the spider to the fly?"

"Wherever you see her. You could invite her to your hotel."

"I will see her precisely nowhere. She is at liberty to interpret my antisocial behavior any way she chooses, but I am not going to see Sloane until— I'll see Sloane in court, in other words."

"You're off your rocker, Lady Constant. Listen, the day you have the proof in your hands how off-your-rocker you are—in three weeks when they finish the examinations, give me a ring, then I'll tell you why."

"That will be the day," she said. "Good-by, Dr. Krop."

Milton walked to the window and pulled the blind all the way up, the way he had never been able to pull it when he slept here on the Hide-a-Bed. The raw new buildings opposite, the rather narrow street didn't look so bad with the blinds all the way up.

From the hall Jenny called, "You finished talking on the phone, Milt?"

"I'm finished talking." He wondered why Lady Constant had changed her mind, but, whatever it was, now he had three weeks.

"Can I come in?"

"Are you asking?"

"I'm asking."

Milton swung around. Jenny was standing there holding the chair she had pulled next to the Hide-a-Bed as if she didn't know where to put it. She apparently decided to leave it where it was and to sit on it.

Jenny repeated, "Well, I'm asking, Milt."

"Since when do you ask to come in a room?"

"Don't keep me on pins and needles, Milt. That's not what I'm asking and you know it. Milt, you were just going to tell me about her sister-in-law, the lady."

He scratched the back of his neck. "Yeah? Well, saved by the bell, boy!"

"Milt—"

He sat on the Hide-a-Bed opposite her. His knee hit her knee hard as he sat but although Jenny winced she did not move, as though it was necessary to show him how much she could take. "Am I finished talking on the phone—as if you didn't know! My dear sister-in-law Jenny, don't you think I know you listened in? All that bushwah about how I can trust you—listening in on a private telephone conversation! That should show me I can't trust you any further than I can throw a piano!"

"Now, that's not so, Milt!"

"No? Well, I won't argue with you. Suddenly I'm starving. Can I have a bite, Jenny?"

"Suddenly you're starving!"

"My appetite has returned—with a bang, that's right!"

"You come here like it's your last day on earth, Milt—like

the bloodhounds are after you—and then you find out they are after you and you're starving, suddenly! All right, so I listened in! For your sake and your sake only I listened in. That woman is having the mother's body exhumed and your appetite comes back!"

"You don't get it, do you?" He stood up and stretched lazily, hulking over Jenny. "It's Greek to you, isn't it?" He shook his head at her, smiling. "Come on, Jenny, Jenny, I thought you knew everything. You don't know everything? Well, I'll tell you, then. As I've been telling you since the first time I mentioned my wife to you, there's nothing to it. Listen—you had the same wild idea the sister had—"

"*Has*, don't you forget," Jenny said, looking up at him. "*Has!*" She gave him a light push and he stood up. Looming over her like that she couldn't talk to him the way she talked to Bud, and she had to. "Milt, I heard."

"Put it on ice."

"Milt, you can tell me to put it on ice, but you can't tell that one, her sister! She's out for your blood, Milt, you need me now."

"My good angel!"

"You need me, Milt."

"Angels at my head and feet."

"Not her."

"My good angel, my bad angel!" He saw how she planted her feet wide apart on the floor, strong. "My good angel with the long nose she's always sticking in my affairs. . . . All I want, angel, is for you to keep the nose out!"

"Milt, at least tell me what you won't tell her until after the autopsy!"

"You want to be *told?*" He put his little finger into his ear and shook it to clear his hearing. "You can't figure it out yourself?"

"No more riddles, Milt. I can't get the first one—how come you're not worried. Don't give me another one!"

"No riddle, no riddle, it's very simple. All I care about is Sloane's not finding out about the wild ideas some people have. Now I got the sister to promise she won't shoot her mouth off, and you won't, either, will you, Jenny?" She shook her head. She wouldn't go to Sloane, he knew that, the last one in the world Jenny would go to was Sloane. "So it's all right, now, see? Now, will you feed me or not?"

Milton stepped aside with exaggerated politeness, like a little gentleman, and waved her through the door first. She obeyed him and started up the hall to the kitchen, Milton following. When she turned and looked back at him he grinned with the exact same face he always had when he thought he'd put something over on her. She felt old and tired and the smell of the lamb stew coming from the kitchen turned her stomach, but that was all to the good since it would mean there'd be more for Milt. Milt had his appetite back. All Milt was worried about was his wife, his Sloane. (What a name for a girl!) Not the sister, not the cops, just his wife knowing. "Milt, I'm asking the same as her sister did—why is it so important your wife doesn't know?"

"Come on, Jenny, it's what makes the world go round—love! You see, Jenny, that's what you don't understand. For instance, you think Sloane's a mutt for looks. Well, there's looks and looks— It's too bad you don't know French."

"You do?"

"I'm picking up a little for when we go abroad. There's such a thing as beauté du diable. There's such a thing as despising how they look in Vogue!"

There's such a thing as Cissie Parker, Jenny thought. She would have stopped outside the kitchen door and tried once more to get Milt to talk, but he reached around her and shoved the door open. The kids were sitting at the table, poor kids.

Milton said, "Hello, Maureen—Bud. Say, Bud, how did that song go you used to sing until it came out of our ears? 'I'm in love, I'm in love, I'm in love'?"

Bud blushed. "I don't know what you mean, Uncle Milt."

"How he's going to get through med school with a memory like that! 'I'm in love, I'm in love, I'm in love—with a wonderful girl—' That's the idea, Jenny. At ease, Bud!"

Buddy's ears turned a bright red. "Listen here, Uncle Milt!"

"Stop riding Bud, Milt!"

"Bud's good angel! Well, stick to Bud, Jenny, and it will be O.K." Milton sat in the chair which used to be his, picked up Maureen's knife and fork and drummed on the table with them to the tune of "I'm in Love." "Jenny," he said, "I'm starving, no kidding. My mouth is watering for that lamb stew."

"Honest, is it, Uncle Milt?"

"Honest." He rubbed his belly. "Why shouldn't it?"

"But, Uncle Miltie, it's just lamb stew. You could eat steak every day now you're rich, Uncle Miltie!"

Bud said, "Steak!"

"Don't rich people eat steak every day, don't they, Mom?"

She was at the range, turning the light up under the pot of stew, and didn't answer.

Bud said, "No, dopey, not steak. They eat everything under glass."

"What's that, 'under glass,' what does Bud mean 'under glass,' Mom?"

Jenny said sullenly, "I never did know. Ask your uncle."

"Yeah, ask Uncle Milt, Maureen; maybe he knows, maybe not!"

Maureen forgot about "under glass" and shoved her chair back and ran over to her uncle and leaned against him coquettishly. "Gee, Uncle Miltie, I been missing you a lot. You're my real uncle, not like Uncle John in Trenton. I don't wanna go live in Trenton and never see you again, Uncle Miltie!"

Bud said, "Well, I do! Anything is better than hanging around here. Anything to get away from here, if you ask me."

Jenny, putting Milton's full plate in front of him, said, "You ate enough, Bud, why don't you go on outside with the gang?"

"No, thanks. I wouldn't go out for a million bucks tonight. If they see his car parked outside, they'll just start in on me the minute I get out. No, thanks!" He shoved his chair back, glared at Milton and left the kitchen, banging the door.

Milton said with his mouth full, "I didn't drive here so my car isn't outside but what's all that about, Jenny?"

"I know, Uncle Miltie! They say, 'How's your Uncle Milton D. Rockefeller, M.D.? Was that your millionaire uncle in his gold Studebaker I saw, Bud? Was that your uncle's millionaire wife I saw in the supermarket pinching the vegetables until they screamed?' Bud doesn't like it when they say those things, but I say 'sticks and stones will break my bones but words will never harm me!' "

"That's enough, Maureen. You ate enough, too. Go on in and get your dresser drawer tidied up like I asked you ten times!" Reluctantly Maureen left. "Don't blame Bud, Milt. I guess he shot off his mouth before his friends when you got married. It's only human nature, and they just get back at him. Of course the kids get it from their folks—your ex-patients, Milt. They didn't like it when you gave up practice that way. If you'd moved to a duplex on Park Avenue, they'd understand that, but when you live in the Haunted House and they see you working in that yard there like a ditch digger in overalls, they don't like it that you seem to rather dig ditches than be their doctor."

"I'm not digging ditches. I used to be a farmer, remember?"

"I remember you became a doctor the minute you could! I get it, Milt, you're in love with your wonderful wife and you're in love with the Haunted House, too. If I can swallow one, I can swallow the other!"

"Hold your horses, hold your horses, Jenny!" He began to mop up the stew gravy with a piece of bread.

"Sure—it's all for the time *being!* The time being! You know what they're doing around here, Milt? They're laughing at you. You're only getting what you deserve, they're saying. Her turning out to be a miser after you only married her for her money— Other people besides myself see her pinching vegetables and they think she's no beauty whatever you call it, either! In the supermarket, they imitate her!"

"That's European," Milt said, hoping his face wasn't as red as it felt. "These people are too ignorant to know that's how the rich biddies do in Europe. They take a manservant to carry the basket, but they personally go to the market themselves and each apple and onion they buy has to be perfect!"

"Like those two brothers died in that filthy dirty house, that's what they say around here—"

"Jenny, look—" He put the sopped bread down, unable to eat another mouthful. "Don't be crazy, Jenny. The mother was, sure—but not Sloane; don't be crazy!" What he had eaten was coming up on him. "A thing like this takes time, Jenny. You got to have time to get over the mother's influence. Believe me, from what I heard the two of them could have eaten off what you scrape into that garbage pail, Jenny; well, it takes time to get over that. Sloane has to learn she can live it up with the money now. You know what she's like, Jenny? I told her. A little bird, like a little bird who's been in the cage so long when you open the door it takes time for her to catch on she's free, that's all."

Jenny saw how he couldn't eat any more. Watching his face, she could almost taste the sour taste of regurgitation; she saw him blush, and thought: Maybe she's got time, but how much time you got, Milt? Like the kids with the atom bomb—what future? She must have made Milt some big promises to get him to help her with her mother. (Milt was a good boy.) But promises are cheap, she thought. What's going to happen if she won't live up to what she promised him?

"Mom! The phone is ringing!"

"Answer it, answer it!" She wiped her hands down her skirts as if, when they were clean, she could go to Milt and pull his head against her and watch over him.

"It's for you again, Uncle Milt!"

Jenny said, "That Lady, Maureen? Is it that same Lady again?"

"It's a man. He wants to speak to Uncle Miltie."

"It's a man, Milt."

"I'm not deaf, Jenny." Milton went to the extension telephone. It took him a moment to realize that Dayton Mills was the man who had been in Lady Constant's room. "Hold the wire a sec, Mr. Mills." Milton walked to where Jenny was standing and took her by the arm. Maureen watched with great interest as Milton walked her mother to the front door of the apartment. "You too, Maureen! Open that door. Step outside, Maureen. Now you, Jenny!"

"Now, listen, Milt!"

"This is the only way I know to keep you from listening in. Just stay out until I call you. It won't hurt you." He shut the door in Jenny's indignant face and locked and bolted it, then returned to the telephone. "Yes, Mr. Mills?"

"I wanted to tell you that it was I who convinced Amory to do as you asked."

"Thanks. Damn glad you did."

"I was convinced that you weren't bluffing about not giving a hoot in hell that Amory had instigated this exhumation thing."

"I wasn't."

"Amory thought you might be stalling for time."

"Three weeks? Did you have the Dramamine analyzed? Let me know."

"One of these days Amory and I expect to be married."

"Where's Lord Constant?"

"Sir Alfred? Amory and he have been divorced for years. Dr. Krop, providing of course that the exhumation shows nothing, if Mrs. Krop never finds out how—how far off the course Amory's suspicions went—she won't be prejudiced against Amory, will she? I told Amory that very strongly, and I put it to her that if she did what you wanted now, you would put in a good word with your wife and then Amory would have what is rightfully hers."

"I certainly will put in a good word, but, according to what my wife told me, your girl friend already got what was coming to her and a lot more."

"That's true, Doctor, except, of course, for the house itself."

"According to my wife, her sister got her half of that, too."

"Yes, she did, but the point is that Mrs. Folsom had come to believe that it was unfair for Amory to get only what it had been valued at ten years before. When she found she could get $110,000, she weakened, Amory says. At first she had been adamant when Amory asked for a more realistic fifty per cent but Amory believes that, had she not died when she did, she would have given in. Amory is quite sure that when she sold the house her mother would have given her the money, but, of course, she died."

Of course she died. "The old lady was about to sell the house when she died? I didn't hear you."

"That's right; that's what Amory thinks, anyhow. She can't prove it in the courts—not a hope. But although all the rest of her mother's estate was tied up for her sister, Mrs. Folsom could have given Amory the difference between what Amory got for her share of the house and what it could have been sold for. The reason Amory left Europe in such a tearing hurry was because it seemed peculiar to her that her mother should die just when she was having this change of heart, when she was ready to sell. It seemed too much of a coincidence to Amory—and this, of course, was all she had to go on before she found out her sister had married you. Well, you know what Amory believes. I don't, as I told you. I believe that Amory will find out that she's invented a murder out of the whole cloth. In my opinion there's a lot of projection involved."

"Projection?"

"In the psychiatric sense." He cleared his throat. "I dabble in psychiatry, as you may have guessed, and I really think that the—the vigor of Amory's imagination here is in part due to her projecting onto her sister some of her own death-wishes against the old lady, her mother. As a doctor, of course, you'd know more about that than I would! Are you there, Dr. Krop?" Dr. Krop made a sound between a gasp and a grunt. "Well, that's all I had to say, really, but, if you should need me. . . . I always have the use of a little pied-à-terre in New York. I'm in the telephone book: Dayton Mills. In case you should wish to send a Message to Garcia."

"Thanks. She still won't touch me with a ten-foot pole, huh?" Milton tried to laugh. "Well, she'll change her mind in three weeks." He hung up. Milton got his coat and hat and walked to the front door, which he was surprised to find locked and bolted. He unlocked and unbolted the door and walked out. He was so deep in thought he did not even notice Jenny and Maureen standing there.

"Milt? You going? Wait! You have to wait!"

He shook his head.

"Milt—you have to. Milt, wait, you forgot your bag!" She took his arm and led him back, whispering. "Don't go out there now, Milt. Mrs. Parker is there. Cissie's mother. She's going to make a big hullaballoo if she sees you!" It seemed to Jenny that Milt came to when she mentioned Cissie. "I'm in love with a wonderful girl," she thought. Ha! Ha! Once inside the apartment, she sent Maureen to find Uncle Milt's doctor bag. "I think it's in the kitchen. You look." It took Maureen a long time to find anything, even if it was at the end of her nose. "Milt, when I was standing out in the lobby, I ran into Mrs. Parker. She turned pale as a ghost and charged at me and said she thought so, she thought my brother-in-law was around! I would have denied it—on general principles the way she was so pale—but before I could shut her up, Maureen let the cat out of the bag. Mrs. Parker started to holler that she knew it, she knew it! I shut her up and made Maureen stand outside—I hope she doesn't catch her death—and Mrs. Parker started on me hot and heavy. She's a nervous woman, Milt. Her Cissie had a big date tonight, she was going to the Stork Club with this boy Mrs. Parker thinks is the cat's whiskers—such a future— Naturally, she boasts to me every chance she gets! Anyhow, Cissie was going out with him formal. She had her formal in a hatbox and she was going to a friend who lives in Manhattan to dress. I guess this boy Mrs. P. thinks is so wonderful doesn't own a car—and a taxi from here to the Stork Club! Anyhow, Cissie went to go to this friend's to dress up and all of a sudden she's home again with the hatbox and she isn't going to any Stork Club and all she would say was she changed her mind. Are you listening, Milt? Mrs. Parker is sitting in her window trying to figure out what made Cissie change her mind and she sees you —she thinks. She goes into the lobby, sniffing around, and then you throw me out of my house and I get Mrs. Parker's complaints right in the face."

"I have to go home. I'm not responsible for Mrs. Parker, Jenny."

"And you're not responsible for Cissie, either."

"Are you on that again? No, I'm not responsible for Cissie, either."

"That's what I told her mother. It's a free country, I said. You can come to see your sister-in-law, what's that got to do with her daughter, but according to Mrs. Parker, Cissie is still head over heels about you and if she saw you that was all she needs. (Probably in the subway, right, Milt?) To hell with the Stork Club and this nice steady boy with a future and Cissie is sitting upstairs in the apartment now. Here's Maureen with your bag, Milt. Wait now—Maureen, you go to the front window and tell us when Mrs. Parker goes inside the house."

"Like the F.B.I.?"

"Like the F.B.I. Hurry up, Maureen. You better wait a little, Milt. It won't look good if she starts accusing you right in the street at the top of her lungs. It could get to your wife; you know how people are."

"I'll wait a couple of minutes."

Jenny brushed a thread off his lapel. "Milt, that's one reason I feel so responsible. I wish I'd let you and Cissie, Milt—" He didn't register much. He was filing the thought of Cissie away, she thought, like Maureen stowing away candy bars in her dresser drawer for when she needed something sweet.

"I'm going now."

"Wait for Maureen, Milt. Take my advice."

"Take my advice, take my advice, you're like a broken record."

"Mom—she went away. Mrs. Parker. Not into the house, Mom."

"Thanks for the lamb stew, Jenny. You make a good stew."

"Any stew I make, you can eat it without worrying. I wish I could say the same for the stews you make for yourself, Milt. One of these days, you're going to get yourself in so deep—"

Chapter V

*T*HE telephone rang only four times before it was picked up. Milton, who expected to wait long enough for Mrs. Austen to come downstairs, who had prepared for her and not for Sloane first off, was thrown off balance, so that all he could think of was to ask where Mrs. Austen was.

"It's quite all right. She's not about. Oh, Milton, Milton, I've been waiting!"

"Yes. First of all, Sloane, you were right. She was suspicious."

"Tell me," she said, as if he hadn't spoken at all. "Tell me!"

"What do you think I'm doing?"

"Tell me."

He began to talk rapidly and with increasing forcefulness, what he said coming to him as he said it, repeating, enlarging what the Mills guy had told him, sounding, he thought, good. "I'm no psychiatrist, Sloane, and I don't pretend to be but— Well, first I listened to her spiel—you know how a doctor does when the patient reels off his symptoms. They're all new to the patient but to the doctors it's an old, old story. That's how I listened, as if it was nothing but what I expected, as if I was diagnosing. You know what projecting is, don't you, Sloane? You put onto someone else, or to something else, what you feel yourself. Your sister certainly had plenty death wishes against your mother. What I did was read her the riot act with the projection idea as a base."

"Milton, *will you tell me!*"

"I just told you, Sloane. She was suspicious. I just told you how I handled it."

"How you handled it! How you handled it!"

She sounded as if she were choking and then, bang, she hung up! She hung up on him. Milton closed his eyes and rested his forehead against the telephone, tamping down the heat which was rising in him, the beat. When he had himself in hand again, he found another dime in his pocket and put it into the slot. He was about to dial when he saw Cissie standing there, right outside the glass of the door. In the subway she had saved his life, she had stopped him—now what? What was she going to change now? He dialed his number, smiling at Cissie while he waited. "Sloane? What's the big idea hanging up? You didn't let me finish. I know what to do but you didn't let me finish."

"Finish then," she said, as if she weren't at all interested any longer.

"This explanation I gave her shook her, but even if she thinks it could be projection, that wouldn't be enough and I never thought it would. What do you take me for?"

"Please get on with it. I think I'm more—shaken up—than Amory is."

"God, you've got faith in me, haven't you?"

She said, "I had."

"Leave it to me. Now, your sister is crazy for this place, An-tibes. She raved about it and maybe it wasn't raving—not talk, see what I mean? Maybe she was hinting. Now, we give her some money and send her back where she came from. My psychiatric explanation will hold out a good deal longer if she's busy doing what she likes and isn't sitting in a hotel room here staring at the four walls, going over and over what I said, what I didn't say."

While Milton waited for Sloane to respond he nodded to Cissie. Sloane would get it. He would tell her he wasn't going to let her come face to face with her sister at all. He was going to handle the whole thing the way he had promised her. He'd be the go-between, and then, when she gave him some money—her hands would be tied. She couldn't possibly go to the cops and tell them he'd walked out with her money. (And he was her husband, don't forget that!) What she would think was that he had gotten cold feet because her sister had come on the scene and had walked out on her and what could she do? All she could do was wait, then when the ax fell in three weeks—In three weeks you could cover a lot of territory if you had enough money! You could find a house on a cliff in the sun on a beach nobody ever heard of! Cissie was looking at him with her heart in her eyes—three weeks with Cissie, Cassie in a bikini on a beach? She was leaning against the soda fountain, folding a straw nervously into accordion pleats. Still Sloane said nothing. "Well, the next thing is you get hold of some dough and give it to me. I give it to your sister. I see her and her projections off on the next plane out. How does that sound, Sloane?"

"Preposterous."

"Now, wait a sec!"

"Idiotic. If she is suspicious now, she'll be sure then!"

"Now that's just where you're wrong; why don't you give me credit for some brains? If she could take it for bribery, of course not. Out of a clear blue sky, dough—of course not! But that doesn't happen to be the case, does it? I'm suggesting that you give her just what she thinks is coming to her legitimately, what she thinks is owing her, what your mother was going to give her from the sale of the house. You give her the difference between what she got as her share of the house and what you can get for it, anyhow what your mother expected to get for it—"

Now came the picture of Sloane the prisoner in the Haunted House, her mother's prisoner in the Haunted House, the little bird unable to get out of the cage. He smiled at Cissie and waited. Maybe the whole story about the mother and the sale of the house was a put-up job; if Sloane now told him so, he'd go into another spiel about projection, the sister indulging in wishful thinking, projecting what she wanted onto truth— In the closed-up telephone booth, he was inside the muffled drum beating funeral marches to the grave.

"I won't give her a penny."

"But if your mother was going to sell the house—was she, Sloane?"

"Of course. As if a person can sell his share of the—the pottage and then years later— To sell is to sell, once and for all, isn't it?"

"I was under the impression your mother wouldn't sell."

"Were you?"

"I figured you were the one—" He remembered how he had told her that he knew all about it, knew what life had been for her in the Haunted House. He understood her, he had said, both of them two of a kind, he had said. Like the biddies in the neighborhood were saying, she'd been laughing up her sleeve at him the whole time. Using him. They were all laughing at him except Cissie. He looked straight at Cissie and she raised her eyes to him. Cissie the little bird, Cissie. He wanted the money to fly away with Cissie. "Sloane, what difference does it make whether your sister sold her birthright for a mess of pottage or not, whether it's right she should want more or not; we're entitled to a little peace of mind, aren't we? Listen, this could be a life and death matter, couldn't it? Give me the money. The hell with the money, you have enough left. Let me take it to her!"

"Preposterous."

He said, "Well, that's my best suggestion." She gave such a

peculiar laugh—like hell, *laugh*—that he found himself staring at the earpiece from which the sound had come.

She said, "Is it?"

"You have a better suggestion?" This time she was really laughing. Crying? "Well, come on, you're so smart!"

"I'm so smart? I'm stupid, incredibly, abysmally stupid, Milton!"

Then she clapped down the receiver again, leaving Milton still staring at the earpiece, hearing, "*Stupid*, Milton! *Stupid*, Milton!" StupidMilton, stupidMilton, hearing the speech she hadn't made, everything she hadn't said but had thought he understood from the first time he had told her he did understand, from the time he had promised her he would "handle" her sister, don't worry! What she had understood the whole time was that he meant he would kill her sister. She had figured, had understood he would become a murderer, just like her! "Birds of a feather," he had called them, himself, he had said it, stupidMilton! Birds of a feather flock together, he had told her.

Milton stumbled out of the telephone booth walking right by Cissie at the counter.

She had calmly expected him to kill her sister.

The sister had calmly expected him to try to kill her.

They were the pair, the birds. Folsom birds. What a pair, he thought.

Jenny, too, he thought. Jenny figured he was a killer, too. Nothing would convince Jenny he wasn't a killer.

All of them, all the girls knew more about Milt Krop than Milt Krop. All the girls knew Milt Krop was a killer. Well, he thought, could be they were right, at that.

His hands were on the door of the drugstore but they were on Sloane's throat. He had her down, his knees on her chest. As he choked her, he banged her damned head against the floor.

He told all of them, striding along the street, his coat flapping like wings, what happened when you gave a dog a bad name. Maybe they didn't know that, the girls!

Cissie stood at the soda fountain, the folded-up straw hanging from her fingers. Then she saw that the doctor had left his doctor bag in the telephone booth.

When the doorbell rang again, Jenny got off the Hide-a-Bed and hurried to the hall, muttering that it was a busy night for a change but not meaning that she minded because she thought it was Milt again. "Mrs. Parker!"

"Yes, it's Mrs. Parker, Mrs. Krop!'"

That was a sly dig at her for the time she had let Mrs. Parker think she was Milt's wife. "Please, Mrs. Parker, I had enough out of you. It's been a busy night."

"I just want to know one thing."

"Ask Information, I'm not Information."

"You're a mother. You have a mother's feelings. All I want to know is he still here. The doctor, is he still here?"

"I don't see what business—"

"Yes, business! My Cissie likes chocolate ice cream. Whenever she got sick and took her medicine like a good girl, I'd send her papa out for a pint of chocolate ice cream. If her papa was alive today I wouldn't be here in your place begging you to tell me one little thing. If I had my man to look after this! After I talked to you before, I went to get my Cissie ice cream from the Greek's. They have home-made. Two blocks. It didn't take me fifteen minutes by the clock and she's gone. I came up and I called her, 'Cissie, Cissie,' and she's gone."

"Call the Stork Club, then."

"Cissie's not at any Stork Club. She said she wasn't going and I know Cissie, wild horses wouldn't drag her there. All I'm asking is if he's gone, too!"

"If I tell you my brother-in-law left, you'll figure he was with Cissie. You're hysterical, Mrs. Parker, that's what you are!"

"He left, he left! I knew it!"

"He left. He went home to his wife where he belongs, that's where he went. He came to see his sister-in-law and he had supper here—lamb stew—and then he left like a respectable married man."

"Cissie must have seen him leave, I tell you. She must have followed him!" Mrs. Parker started to open the door, but Jenny pulled her back.

"It's a free country, think what you like, that's your privilege, but that's all is free. You can't run over to my brother-in-law's house and tell his wife—"

Mrs. Parker began to cry that she didn't know what to do, she was out of her mind. The last thing she wanted was to make trouble. "All I want is Cissie should be happy. She has this fine steady boy. He has a good job in a shoe factory, Assistant Manager. He's crazy for Cissie. I don't want to make trouble!"

"You're going to have trouble without making it if you're not careful!" Jenny pushed up Mrs. Parker's coat sleeve and took her pulse, not timing the beats, just shaking her head as if it was rapid and irregular. "I am a mother, right. I have a mother's feelings, right; so come in here." Now Mrs. Parker was sitting on Milt's Hide-a-Bed. Jenny stooped and scooped up both Mrs. Parker's thin legs. She then sat on the Hide-a-Bed and took Mrs. Parker's wrist again. "You're going to lie right there until your heart is down to normal. You're not sixteen any more; you want your Cissie to be an orphan on both sides?" She was going to keep Mrs. Parker there as long as she could. The way the poor thing was now, she would run straight to Milt's wife. Jenny was positive that Cissie had done just what her mother figured. Mrs. Parker attempted to sit up. "I'm a nurse, don't forget. I know whereof I speak." You could still see where Cissie got her looks. Mrs. Parker was forty-five, anyhow; she'd had a hard time from the look of it; her coat hadn't cost more than fifty bucks new; but even so, if you came right down to it, Mrs. Parker was better looking lying there with her hair gray a lot and crying than the wonderful girl Milt said he was in love with!

"—only trying to do the right thing. Nip it in the bud. When she found out he wasn't married— Never once, not since she was born, did my Cissie talk to me like that!"

But Cissie couldn't have taken it, Jenny thought. Cissie wasn't strong like she, Jenny, was. A little thing. What did Cissie know what it was like to be a widow with kids?

"It costs a fortune to go to the Stork Club, but Cissie wanted to go. All she has to do with Sidney is say. The sky's the limit where Cissie is concerned with Sidney!"

Jenny glared at the weeping Mrs. Parker; Stork Club, her and her Stork Club! Oh, God, if the girl was with Milt. If they were standing in the shadows, somewhere, close together and him with that wife he was so much in love with, ha ha— And him with a couple of years at most to live. Like the article said about teenagers and the atom bomb. Oh, God! You couldn't keep your nose out like Milt wanted—a little silly kid like Cissie Parker. A—a teenager like Milt! You couldn't!

"Doctor," Cissie called, almost breathless from having chased him, "Doctor, oh, please!"

Then Milton heard her. He turned and watched her, so caught by the way she moved that he didn't notice what she was carrying.

Cissie held it toward him. "In the telephone booth—you forgot your doctor bag."

"What's that?" He noticed the bag. "Yeah, that's right, I did!" Forgot his medical bag, forgot he was a medical man. Looking up from the bag to Cissie's face, to her worshipful eyes, to her Browning-girl eyes which said he was wonderful, marvelous; he could do anything, she thought, so he could do anything. He was a doctor, he had forgotten that. Maybe Sloane wasn't so smart thinking she could laugh at a doctor. Maybe that wasn't the same as laughing at an ordinary man, maybe a doctor could have the last laugh. Certainly he still didn't know yet how he could kill Sloane because even though it would give him the greatest satisfaction to put his hands around her throat and choke the life out of her, to bang her damned head against the floor, that wouldn't be enough to burn for. He still didn't know, even though he had that suicide note all prepared, even though he had the best possible motive for Sloane's committing suicide—remorse over having "killed" her mother, suicide while of unsound mind—he still didn't know, but for the second time that day, Cissie, standing like that, looking at him like that, made everything O.K. "Aw, Cissie!" he whispered.

After a little while, she pushed herself away from him, shoving both her hands against his chest. "Why did you marry her? Why did you have to marry her? Momma says for the money. She says if you're so perfect why would you marry a wife for the money?"

He transferred his bag to his left hand and stretched out his right one, smoothing back her soft hair. "Did you think that was why, Cissie? You know better than your mother, don't you?"

"I told Momma, no! Then, why?" she asked, waiting confidently to be told.

And he would tell her and she would tell her momma and her momma would tell the world. "I'll tell you, Cissie. Not what your mother thinks—or my sister-in-law Jenny, who thinks she knows everything—you have the right to know, Cissie. Why? Because I pitied her so. 'Poor little rich girl,' did you ever hear that expression? Because I'm so sorry for her, poor kid. I was pretty sore at you. Why didn't you have faith, Cissie—thinking

Jenny was my wife! Why shouldn't I help her then? Be of some use to humanity, that's why. They think they know it all!"

"Momma," Cissie whispered, nodding.

"They don't know. You know who knows, Cissie? Whoever's lived with my wife—in the same house, I mean. We had this cook, Helga, she quit the job today. Helga knows the real reason even if she's only an ignorant woman. She came to me today and she asked was I a mental doctor—a kind of private psychiatrist for my wife. My wife's a little—unbalanced, Cissie. That's why I married her and spend all my time and knowledge on her. You just saw me on the phone. I was talking to my wife. Did you notice she hung up on me, twice? She's hysterical. I told her to take another sedative—to quiet her. My God, I was only visiting my own sister-in-law for once, having lamb stew, for the love of Mike! But she won't take sedatives unless I'm in the house with her. She needs me, see, Cissie? I have to stand by there. For example, she's scared she'll overdose herself—you know why? Because she half wants to. That's psychiatry, Cissie; you wouldn't understand. She's scared to death of what she might do in a wild moment—because the desire is there, do you see?" She nodded uncertainly, taking in every word. "I have to go now."

"Not yet! You thought I'd forget you. I can't forget you. I'll never forget you."

"You have to, Cissie, and I have to go now."

"Not yet. Oh, I want to be with you once, just once!"

"We wouldn't want to have it on our conscience if anything happened to my wife, Cissie!" He shook his head at her gently. "I can't tell you what it means to me to get this chance to explain to you how things were, Cissie."

"I can't see you ever?"

"Go on home now, Cissie. No, you can't see me." Cissie did what he asked her to, started home. Cissie would always do what he asked her to; a word from him was all she needed.

136

Milton watched her slowly moving off and could tell from her back that she was crying. "Cissie," he called. She turned to him and she was crying.

"Yes?"

"I just wanted to know. It's funny, I don't know—what's your real name, Cissie?"

"Cecilia."

"'Does your mother know you're out, Cecil-ia?'" He would not move toward her, touch her again, but he didn't need to touch her. "Does your mother know you're out—" he sang.

"You're so good," Cissie sobbed. "You're so good—"

"A saint? You're the saint, Cissie. St. Cecilia, little Saint Cecilia with the golden hair!" Even in this light, without touching her, just because his hand moved out he could see her color change, just seeing his hand; then she sobbed and moved away. Milton stood and watched the way she walked until he couldn't stand it and then started toward the Haunted House again. He held his wrist watch out under the next street light. Back by nine.

By nine o'clock Mrs. Parker had fallen asleep on the Hide-a-Bed and Jenny went and stood by the window. If she went outside this room, Bud or Maureen would want to talk to her and she needed some peace right now, so she just stood there quietly until she saw Cissie on the sidewalk outside the apartment house. Because she had been thinking the word "peace" when she saw Cissie, Jenny thought, "Peace, it's wonderful!" That was from Father Divine. Who remembered Father Divine any more? Peace, it's wonderful, she thought, not because of Father Divine, but because of Cissie's ecstatic face seen under the two lights in front of the house, because of the way she was walking. Jenny turned to Mrs. Parker. If Mrs. Parker saw her daughter Cissie with that face on her, no amount of talk from Jenny was going to convince her that Cissie hadn't been with Milton or that Cissie would ever go to that Stork Club with that Sidney boy. Moving as quietly as possible, Jenny crossed the room, opened the door and went out of the apartment, intercepting Cissie in front of the self-service elevator. "Hello, Cissie, no use your going up to an empty house. Your mother is in my place." She laughed. "Don't look at me that way, I didn't kidnap your mother, she came in my place under her own power. In fact I couldn't stop her!"

"Is Momma sick?"

"At heart, sick at heart—maybe in the head. Maybe she's sick in the head, Cissie. She came to my place because of my brother-in-law, Dr. Krop. I believe you heard that name before?"

"Why should she go see you?"

"Come on in and ask her. You ask her and then she'll ask you. Sauce for the goose. You ask her why she's in my place and she's going to ask you where you've been. She went to get you some ice cream and when she came back you were gone, so she came in my place to see if my brother-in-law left so she could put two and two together."

"Oh."

"She put two and two together. Did she get the wrong number?"

"Of course."

I hope you can kid your mother better than you can kid me, Jenny thought; you're not much of a liar with your thoughts showing through that blond skin of yours! She kept talking, however, to give Cissie time to get a story together, because someone had to watch over such a little fool. (A pair of fools!) "Your mother's been lying down in my place, she was in such a state. She'd have run straight to my brother-in-law's wife the state she was in!"

"How awful! How awful! You must excuse Momma. I don't know what's got into her. All she is is upset because I wouldn't keep a date, that's all. She got herself all worked up over nothing. Can I see Momma now?"

Jenny opened her door, waved Cissie in and pointed out the door to the waiting room. "Help yourself. I'll be in the other room."

"Thank you," Cissie said fervently. "I can't tell you how I thank you!"

She had forgotten how sore she was at me, Jenny thought. All is forgiven. All is forgiven, why? With a girl, for one reason only, because all must be O.K. All made up. All forgotten. But Milt's wife couldn't be forgotten, could she? But divorced. Jenny told herself she mustn't let her imagination run away with her. She told herself to stop biting her nails, shaking her big hand in the air; she had bitten the pinky one off, to the quick. Quick, a divorce, she thought, why not? On what? she wondered. In what? The two-year old suit from Howard's? The old Studie? Her hand stopped waving in the air, went to her hip; she looked like a virago, warning an imaginary Sloane, "You stupid or something? The devil makes mischief for idle hands, you never heard that? You can't keep a doctor's hands busy digging ditches in your old yard, don't you know that? If you don't get Milt some real work to do—soon—"

Chapter VI

For a minute Milton thought that one of the two suits of armor had moved toward him as he came into the house, that it knew what he was going to do to Sloane, that the movement would end in its bringing the sword it held down on his skull. "Who's that?" he called sharply, veering away from the suits of armor nevertheless, staring down the hall where he heard someone. "I see you standing there!" It wasn't Sloane. "Oh, Mrs. Austen!" Now he could see her sour face. "What are you doing—up?"

"It is just past nine o'clock, Dr. Krop!"

He had started to say, "What are you doing *here*?" because he had forgotten that she would be here, he had counted on being alone in the house with Sloane. "I know it's nine o'clock, but you're not a well woman, Mrs. Austen!" He stepped nearer her. "You look done in." He shook his head at her.

Mrs. Austen began to tremble. "Doctor. Doctor, please— You haven't changed your mind? That isn't what you're going to say, is it, Doctor? About having me here? On the telephone, sir, you said it would be satisfactory. You said—"

"I just about said you saved my life, but I'm not going to save my life at the expense of yours, Mrs. Austen!"

"Dr. Krop—sir—if you turn me out—if I have to go on the dole again—that is no life, sir. Sir, if I have to go I would rather—"

Rather die with her boots on, poor old biddie! He shook his head at her again, to show he wasn't satisfied. "Where is Mrs. Krop?"

"Madam is in her room, Dr. Krop. I've kept your dinner hot, sir. If you'll just go into the dining room, I will serve it. You'll see, sir, I'm a good cook!"

If he ate, he wouldn't have to face Sloane yet. "O.K." Mrs. Austen hurried away and he walked into the godawful dining room. The dining room was, maybe, the worst room. It had red flock paper and the walls were loaded with oil paintings in gold frames, all of them pictures of storms at sea, shipwrecks, waves bouncing off jagged rocks. Cheerful. The only light came through the one big window, which was all different-color glass. With that light on those pictures—did old lady Folsom want to make people seasick? Was the old lady's idea to make people so seasick they couldn't eat much? Or Sloane's idea! To save on food that way? It could be Sloane, he knew that now!

Austen came in with a tray, trying so hard to show how easily she could manage that the tray jiggled in her old hands. She waited for him to sit, then put the tray on the sideboard and brought him the serving dish with—oh, God, stew on it!

"It is a particular ragout I used to cook when madam's mother dined at the Vintons' house, sir. Please try it."

Milton helped himself to as little as possible, then pointed with his knife to the next chair. "Sit down, go on, sit down. I want to talk to you." She obeyed him reluctantly and he lifted a forkful of the ragout (stew, he decided) and pretended it hit the spot but he didn't fool Austen, who immediately jumped out of her seat and moved the big silver condiment set within his reach.

"You forgot, sir!"

141

"What's that?"

"You forgot the salt, sir." She lifted the silver saltcellar out of the condiment set and handed it to him. "It's just the first time, Dr. Krop! You will get accustomed to it, sir, I'm sure you will. Madam assured me you would get accustomed to it, sir."

Milton stared at Mrs. Austen, at the big silver saltcellar trembling in her hand.

"Didn't madam tell you, sir?"

"Madam—?" Milton took the saltcellar from the old woman, turning it in his hands thoughtfully; then he smiled. "I sure did forget," he said, "but now I'll remember!"

"You do think it will work out, sir?"

He nodded vigorously. "Yes, I do think it will work out. Yes." Mrs. Austen was blinking at him, poor old biddy, with her heart in her eyes, because if it didn't work out, she'd rather be dead, she had as good as said so. Milton knew that he must seem to pass it over, not show her he was giving it another thought. Plenty of time to work it out when those beady old eyes weren't trying to take him apart. He salted the ragout vigorously, then put the silver shaker out of the way on the condiment tray. (For the time being out of the way!) "Now," he said, putting a forkful into his mouth, chewing, "now then—" The old hag was looking disgusted at him. (Talking with his mouth full!) He pointed with his knife at his mouth, meaning when he got it swallowed. Since he had to chew, he also chewed the idea over: only salt in the house. Sloane would have to use it. Sloane to eat a meal without him there. He out of the house and alibied for the time. He puts the what looks like salt? What pours like salt? It mustn't have too much taste and has to be fatal in small amounts. He would find it—what the hell was he a doctor for if he couldn't find one drug in the whole materia medica to suit his purpose? Come home. With witness. Find Sloane dead. He had the suicide note all ready, upstairs in the lining of his valise, all handy. All he had to do when he came back with his alibi witness was get hold of that saltcellar there, empty the poison down the john, replace it with salt. He nodded at Austen, swallowed and told her that you couldn't tell the salt had been added after cooking. "Fine," he said, pointing at the ragout on his plate but, oh boy, oh boy, meaning something quite different. "Fine!" He ate as much as he could take, then crossed his knife and fork on the plate and remembered that wasn't how to do because of the way the old woman kind of twitched her nose at him. (Sloane could also make him feel everything he did was wrong; two of a kind. See both of them in hell and gone, he thought.) Even though he remembered Sloane never did it, he gave his plate a shove, to indicate he was through. "That was good eating, Mrs. Austen!" She took his plate to the tray on the sideboard. "If eating was all I had to worry about here, we'd be all set with you in the house!"

"Sir?"

"I'm worried about—the madam. You saw her; how did she seem to you? Depressed?"

Mrs. Austen said primly, "Madam did not seem herself, sir."

"She was herself. She's got two selves, Mrs. Austen: Mrs. Jekyll and Mrs. Hyde." She brought him another plate, but he waved it away. "I'm too worried to eat much right now, Mrs. Austen. Don't bother. I don't want to eat, I want to talk to you while we have the chance. I know you're so happy to have a job again you'll overlook a lot, but you will have to overlook more than you bargained for!"

"Sir—"

"Don't get the idea I don't want you here, Mrs. Austen. I was a little worried could you take it—but since you explained what it means to you, I'm going to be selfish. I want you, but do you know how many in help we had here already?"

"Madam had told me, Dr. Krop, but they weren't real servants, none of them! They don't understand the work, sir!"

143

"Maybe yes, maybe no. Listen, Mrs. Austen. Helga, the one who left earlier today—"

"Wasteful. Madam had complained."

"O.K. Wasteful, but not so dumb as you might think. Do you know what she said to me today? She said I must be a mental doctor! She meant a psychiatrist, Mrs. Austen."

"These—girls—don't understand ladies, sir!"

"Now, Mrs. Austen, my wife told me—the minute you and she laid eyes on each other in the clinic, you felt you knew each other all your lives. Fine. Swell. For my own selfish reasons, that couldn't be better. When a feller needs a friend—" Milton saw Mrs. Austen stiffen up all over, but he did not know he had violated her code in which employers and servants could not be friends. Milton never learned when he offended Mrs. Austen. "Don't kid yourself that you know my wife because you're familiar with her background!"

"I wouldn't presume—"

"This Helga knew my wife a little better than you did and she told me she thinks madam is nuts. Now, that's putting it a little strongly, Mrs. Austen, but this much is true: my wife is a very disturbed girl. I'm worried stiff, Mrs. Austen!"

"I don't quite understand, sir."

"Disturbed. How shall I give it to you? Moody—up and down —subject to depressions, Mrs. Austen, serious depressions. I don't want to get too technical with you, you're not a nurse, but can I ask you—like I'd ask a nurse—to keep an eye on her in case I'm not around? You'll see I'm around most of the time. I've given up my practice to take care of her. That's why Helga figured I was a mental doctor, see; my wife's private psychiatrist! I'll be with her most of the time, but in case I'm not you let me know if she goes into depression again, will you?"

"Yes, Dr. Krop."

"Thanks a million."

"I'll bring your coffee and there's *pain perdu*, sir."

"There's what?"

"Madam mentioned that there was so much bread thrown out, sir. *Pain perdu* is a kind of a bread pudding, sir."

I might have known it, Milton thought, bread pudding again! "Just the coffee. Just pour a cup and bring it in and go on up and rest. I'll wash up the cup and saucer myself. We don't want you to overdo." She picked up the tray after carefully arranging what was on it, taking so damn long about it Milton could have shoved the plates down her throat. He wanted her to get the lead out of her pants, to git. He wanted to be alone and work over the scheme, step by step, see if it would hold water, where the cracks were, if any. Any minute Sloane might take it into her head to come downstairs.

Austen came back with the tray and a big silver pot and a cup and saucer. He could ask her to pour a cup in the kitchen from now to doomsday but she knew the right way to do things, even if he didn't, was the idea. She could "yes, sir, yes, Doctor" from now until doomsday, he could treat her like a human being instead of a robot until he dropped, but he was still the scum of the earth and bringing coffee in the pot was one way of showing him. He pretended he didn't remember he had asked for a cup, lifted the silver pot and smiled at the old woman because what did he care, whatever she thought of him, she was going to come in damn handy.

Milton stared at the doorknob that had turned but not opened the bedroom door. That, he thought, was a hot one, that really was a hot one! He had stalled downstairs as long as he dared, putting off the evil moment, he had tiptoed upstairs, turned the knob as if it would explode in his hand, had hardly breathed. In other words he had done everything possible in the dim hope that for once Sloane would be asleep when he came into their bedroom, and that he would not have to face her until morning, only to find she had locked the door on him. He stood there almost sick with relief and then, looking up at the third floor, seeing from the crack of light up there that Mrs. Austen was still awake as, from the crack of light under their bedroom door that Sloane was awake also, he saw how he could use this. "Sloane!" he called. "Sloane! Sloane!" He didn't need to shout, the old woman was a cardiac, not deaf. "Answer me. All I want to know is if you're all right, Sloane!" Silence, the silent treatment and locking the bedroom door as a punishment! "If you don't answer me, I'll break the door down!" ("Listen, old biddy up there!") He rattled the knob. "Just talk to me and then I'll go sleep in the next room; just speak, that's all I want, Sloane!"

"I'm quite all right."

He turned from the door, hunting for his handkerchief, pretending to be surprised to see Austen at the top of the third flight. He pantomimed his relief, mopped at his brow, turned to the door again. "Sloane, if you're still—nervous, will you take another of those pink capsules, those sedatives? The ones I gave you? If you're still jittery, Sloane, it's O.K. to take another now. I'm here and I have some stuff can pull anyone out of an overdose in two shakes of a lamb's tail!" He pantomimed to Mrs. Austen up there that overdosing was one of Sloane's neurotic fears.

"No."

"O.K., then. It's up to you. I'm going to bed in the next room, but if you can't sleep, take the pill or wake me and I'll take care of it. O.K., Sloane?" If the old woman remembered this, fine, if she didn't, nothing lost but a little breath and that much breath he could afford to lose in a good cause. "Good night, Sloane."

When Milton awoke the next morning, he didn't know where he was, but anywhere, he thought, getting out of the bed in a hurry, feeling that the griffins carved on the headboard were getting ready to pounce, anywhere was better than where he had spent the night in his dreams. He had never had such dreams in his life—but then he had never before put himself to sleep by going over a plan to murder his wife either. He stood by the side of the bed rubbing the cricks in his back, repeating his litany: she tried to kill an old woman—her mother—because the old lady was going to give her own sister part of what she thought should be hers; she knew all along I figured different. ("You're like a little bird, kid," he had told her.) But she let me kid myself, she laughed at me; she wanted me to kill her sister; she was going to let me be the patsy!

He went to the window and pushed the dust-smelling curtains aside and looked out while he reviewed the plan again. No, even by daylight, even when he looked out beyond the crazy grounds of the Haunted House, over the gate to where he could see the biddies sitting there in real life, the plan was O.K. He could do it. (Milt? Milt kill somebody?) He could do it and he could get away with it, too.

He had slept in his underwear and now he wanted to get out of it, to take a cold shower and scrub himself clean of his dreams. (Of his plan? Of the murder?) He gathered up the suit he had worn and opened the door carefully. Downstairs there were sounds. Sloane and Mrs. Austen. Upstairs, nothing. He hurried into the bathroom to shave, needing to use the old Rolls razor he hadn't used since Jenny and Bud and Murine had given him the Remington which now lay in its case in his dressing room. Here he had a dressing room but no plug in the john for an electric shaver. He ran the water. Brown again. Every day the water ran brown here, which, for all he knew, might make it worth being put in a museum like the furniture. A brown antique Victorian bathroom wasn't enough, yet; they had to have brown Victorian water to match!

Milton's foot had just touched the fourth from last step so he could see Sloane's black nothing-dress in the sitting room. Out of the corner of his eye, he saw the black moving toward him but pretended he was unaware of her and turned to his right into the seasick dining room. The door to the pantry was open and, as he approached the table, Mrs. Austen came out of the pantry. She was wearing a gray-and-white striped dress, probably some kind of cook's uniform, he decided, but, no kidding, more like a costume. He wondered as he said good morning when it dated from. (Austen fitted into this house like wallpaper on a wall!) Mrs. Austen asked what he wanted for breakfast and he asked for orange juice, two scrambled eggs—wet—and crisp bacon and two cups of coffee. Austen never wasted words on him anyhow, although she had been gassing away with Sloane earlier, so she nodded and started back toward the pantry, but halfway there, turned and reminded him not to forget the salt on his eggs. "Don't you worry about that," he said. (Let me do the worrying!) As he pulled out his chair, he heard Sloane behind him.

"Good morning, Milton. Did you sleep well?"

"Sure thing." He studied her. "From the look of you, I wouldn't say you did."

"No, I didn't sleep. I want to give you something, Milton."

She started backing out of the room so he followed her. She went to the desk and took an envelope from it and handed it to him. "What's this?"

"Please read the note."

It was the same stationery she had used before. It made the same rustle, the money sound. "—to say that my husband, Milton Krop, had absolutely nothing to do with the death of my mother . . . when Dr. Krop arrived it was a *fait accompli*—" Milton hit the foreign words with his forefinger, showing them to Sloane. "What's that?"

"Accomplished fact," she explained. "I should imagine I wrote *fait accompli* because I expect Amory to be the one to read it. I will change that. I'll rewrite the whole thing, Milton;

what I want is a document to prove— I want you in the clear," she said.

Milton said, "You're out of your mind," in a normal tone of voice and then heard the words he had said and remembered the open pantry door. "You're out of your mind, Sloane!" he repeated, but much louder, as if he were being driven out of his. Snapping the letter against the air, Milton started back to the dining room.

"It seemed sensible to me, Milton. Since I can't do what you suggest, I must be fair to you. Where are you going?"

"To eat breakfast. Get some food inside me." He marched to the table, ignoring Sloane, who had followed him and had one finger to her lips to remind him of the open pantry door. "Fair to me," Milton said. "You call that fair to me?" He took the letter and tore it down the center, then across, then across, making as much noise as possible doing it so that the old woman wouldn't miss it.

"It seemed to me the best solution—"

"Best solution! Best solution! You listen to me, will you? Your life isn't your own, you hear me? You hear me, Sloane? You can shut me out of your room but I'm still here! You're married to me now, don't forget that, so what happens to you happens to me! 'Fair to me!' "

"Milton—"

He now acknowledged her signals that Mrs. Austen was in the vicinity. "I don't care who hears me, I'm your husband and we two are one, as they say. What happens to you happens to me and I'll shout that from the housetops!" He fell into his chair and put the torn bits of paper on his bread-and-butter plate. "Mrs. Austen? You ready with that orange juice? Why don't you have some breakfast, Sloane? I'll bet you had some black coffee." When Mrs. Austen came in he asked her whether madam had had more for breakfast than a cup of black coffee and when she indicated that was all, asked for some eggs and toast. "Pay no attention to the madam, Mrs. Austen. A person doesn't sleep all night and then has nothing but coffee—an empty stomach gives some wild ideas, Mrs. Austen." He glanced at the torn bits of paper and then deliberately pulled some matches out of his pocket and set fire to them. If Austen didn't think it was a suicide note he'd burned, he'd eat his hat.

This time when Mrs. Austen went into the pantry, she closed the door after her. Mrs. Austen was too high-minded to eavesdrop, Milton thought. It wasn't her fault she had heard all she had; damn right, it was Milton's fault! He said to Sloane, "Now what?" She smoothed back her hair as if her head hurt her. "What do we do now I've turned down your first idea? Nothing? Your sister is in New York and she's suspicious but we do nothing about it?"

"Your suggestion was—"

"Preposterous. O.K. Say no more, my lady! No, don't tell me why it's preposterous, I don't want to hear. Let's talk about something else. Talk about the weather? Like winter, the weather. How is it with Mrs. Austen, will it work out? Everything settled, wages, hours? Same as Helga? Same days off, Thursdays and every other Sunday?" This was what he had to know, Austen's time off, because that figured in it. Mrs. Austen, Sloane told him in a dead kind of voice, her eyes looking past him, was to have the same wages as Helga and the same days off with one exception. Because, with her salt-free diet, she couldn't eat out in restaurants and because she had nowhere much to go, she preferred every Sunday, but would stay both Thursday and Sunday until she had her dinner. All that was left of Mrs. Austen's family and friends had emigrated to Canada, which was where she wanted to go to end her days, but which was too far, obviously, for days off. That was all Milton heard: *immediately after her dinner Thursdays and Sundays.* That was all he needed to hear because Thursday would be the day.

Mrs. Austen came in again and Milton caught the look she and Sloane exchanged and it gave him a scare. Two kindred spirits. He waited until she had gone and then warned Sloane that even though Mrs. Austen was grateful as hell about this job, she was only human after all. "I think it would be a bad mistake to get chummy, if you know what I mean."

Her nose went into the air. "I do not know what you mean."

He entwined his second and third finger. "I wouldn't get too chummy." Sloane's eyebrow went up and she repeated the word "chummy" as if it was a dirty word, while, for example, he wouldn't say what she was now saying to save his life: "mistress." The relationship between a servant and a mistress was a complicated one and did not include becoming chummy, she was saying. Milton shrugged. "I wouldn't know, would I? East is east and west is west and never the twain shall meet." As far as he was concerned, that was all right. He didn't want to meet the servant or the mistress at all—except on Thursday. Today was Saturday; Sunday, Monday, Tuesday, Wednesday, Thursday.

It was still too early for the lights to be on, so the bulbs in the Loew's marquee were a dull dirty yellow, but they did spell Thursday (Thursday to Saturday: Gregory Peck in *Moby Dick*) and that was enough to light the bulbs for him, Milton thought. He walked on toward the Schulte's next door, feeling in his vest pocket for the dime he had put there. He had not intended to go out and telephone Jenny yet, but he just hadn't been able to wait it out. He and Sloane had supposedly been working on the grounds, digging out the good specimen plants to be shipped to some old relative of hers somewhere, but Sloane wasn't working. She was clipping the bush he had dug to lessen the shock of transplanting and he could hear the shears, click then pause, click then pause. He could feel that she wanted to talk to him again. Since Saturday he had managed to hold her off, sleeping each night in the next bedroom, saying "May I" and "Not at all." He had dammed her up, pretty well, and he knew why: he wanted to keep what had happened on Friday fresh in his mind; he wanted to remember how she had hung up on him, what she hadn't said but what she meant. He had staved Sloane off in order to keep strong enough to do it and perhaps he was now calling Jenny early for the same reasons. He wanted Jenny to start telling him what to do and what not to, to get that fresh in mind, because if he didn't have the strength, in three short weeks he'd be back with Jenny telling him again, back on the old Hide-a-Bed until death do us part. Milton put the dime in and dialed the old number; what he would say was, "Jenny? This is Milt!" What he actually said when Jenny picked up the phone was, "Jenny?"

Jenny herself said, "Milt, what is it?"

"When can I see you?"

"Any time. Now."

"I mean alone. No offense, but without Bud or Maureen."

"Sure, without the kids. I can send Maureen to her friend Tessie."

"There's Gregory Peck at Loew's; does Maureen go for Gregory Peck?"

"At this stage she goes for anything in pants. Milt, this isn't just a social call, is it?"

"Not a social call, no. I want you to help me, Jenny."

"Oh, Milt!"

Leaped at the chance, Milton thought. Like a shot. She thought he was coming to throw himself at her feet and confess. (She thought he could kill—Milt Krop! She thought he could kill but she thought he didn't know from nothing; he could kill but he couldn't wipe his own nose. Women!) "This is what I want you to do, Jenny. Listen carefully: Call me right after dinner. Right after, get it, that's important. Get the kids off to the early show. I'll see Sloane answers the phone then and you tell her you want me to come over right away. Right away, do you get it?"

"Why? I mean if she asks—"

"She won't. She's not nosy like some people. I didn't mean that, Jenny. She won't ask because she's kind of wrapped up in her own troubles right now; if she asks say it's about Bud."

"Him being an adolescent, all the stuff you read in the papers nowadays." Jenny was thinking about Milt, really.

"Don't spin any yarns, just say it's about Bud and shut up. The idea is to see me, not to tell her about adolescents."

"I was just trying to get it to sound legitimate, Milt. Your wife is no fool, you know. How come all of a sudden I need to see you? How many times have I seen you since you married?"

"Let's not start that now." The old Jenny. She knew best. "Now, do you have it straight?"

"Now, Milt—lis-ten!"

"That's what you say to me, 'Now do you have it straight, Milt?' I wish I had a dollar for every time you talked to me as if I was a Mongolian idiot! What's sauce for the goose isn't sauce for the goosie goosie gander, is it?" She could get him so mad! (Even now. Today!)

"I have it straight," Jenny said meekly. "I call the Haunted House—excuse me!"

"It's haunted," Milton said. "Call right after supper." Right after supper for Jenny would be seven-thirty on the nose because he had had evening office hours for so many years. It wouldn't occur to poor old Jenny that in the Haunted House he didn't even sit down to the table until seven-thirty, quarter of eight. He had made sure that by seven Austen would be ready to leave. She would have eaten her supper at the kitchen table and their dinner would be all ready, the leg of lamb he had asked for on the platter, the cold vegetables, the mashed potatoes in that keep-hot thing. Austen would come in and ask if everything was all set for her first night off. He would say good-by, then kind

153

of look at the old biddy and stand up and say he would drive her to Roosevelt where they had the escalator so she wouldn't have to climb the long flight here. The old biddy would probably refuse, but he would insist—doctor's advice, she'd better take it. Sloane would almost certainly put her two cents in and make Mrs. Austen take the hitch; if she didn't, he could force it through.

On the way, he would ask Mrs. Austen whether Sloane had confided to her what had been troubling her this past week. Besides wanting to save Mrs. Austen the stairs, he had offered her this hitch to get the chance to find out; otherwise, as she well knew, he didn't like leaving the madam. Mrs. Austen might not want to admit she knew about him tearing up the "suicide" note and telling his dear wife that "that way was no way out, that she wasn't alone any more, what concerned her concerned him," but she had overheard, all right, and his question would bring it to mind.

Drop Mrs. Austen at the subway.

Come back. Seven-fifteen. By seven-thirty telephone rings. "Hell," he says. "No, you get it, Sloane. Every time it rings I think it could be your sister. You're handling that department now since you wouldn't take my advice. I'm not answering the phone when Mrs. Austen isn't here." While Sloane was out talking on the phone, put the picrotoxin in the saltcellar.

Sloane reports Jenny needs him right away. Reluctant to go, but sees his duty and does it. He tells Sloane she better go ahead and eat; Jenny, he says, is nothing if not long-winded. "Wait a minute," he says. Remembers that this is certainly after supper for Jenny. He takes up two pieces of bread and carves himself some meat off the leg of lamb. (Milt to Austen: "Now, I like leg of lamb, Mrs. Austen, but, funny, I like lots of garlic to hide the lamb taste. Lots of garlic on the lamb, Mrs. Austen," he had ordered, and garlic covered a multitude of tastes!) While he carves himself a piece of lamb, like a little gentleman he carves a couple of slices for the madam. He puts the madam's slices on the madam's plate and puts his slices between the pieces of bread. He salts his—but not all of his. He holds his sandwich by the unsalted part. When he gets out of sight he tears off the poisoned portion and disposes of it. (A sewer?) The part he throws away he is supposed to have wolfed on the way to Jenny's, the rest he eats in Jenny's presence so that she can witness that he ate the same meat and bread Sloane did. (Let them analyze the rest of the joint, the vegetables—the whole damned supper!)

Without knowing it he had walked out of Schulte's and was standing in front of a jewelry store looking at diamond rings. He hadn't even known he was looking into the window, but when he turned away he could, by closing his eyes, see every ring on the tray. He could even pick out the square diamond with the little oblong ones on the side he would buy Cissie. Now that he was aware that he was walking, he couldn't go so fast but held back, looking in the florist's window—Funeral Wreaths a Specialty, now that was a handy little bit of information! He knew he should go back to the Haunted House, that he must keep up his act of not leaving the madam alone for more than a half hour at a time for Mrs. Austen's benefit, but now that it was almost finished it was even harder to do. He had to force himself to turn the corner and go home.

The baby carriage brigade had not left for the day. When he was more than a block away, one of them—he wasn't close enough to see which biddy it was—saw him and told the others, evidently. The others, except for the one who was scrubbing at her child's leg where he had fallen, all looked up at him. The mixture of talk and giggles which he had come to expect from the baby carriage brigade rose to meet him. He didn't know what they were saying, of course, but he got the general idea: "That's the doctor coming. Did you hear the latest? The other day she had him on his hands and knees digging in the dirt behind the fence in the cold. For this a man studies ten years to be a doctor?" That was the general idea and the sounds now diminishing as he approached meant they were snickering at him for marrying money and being turned into a ditchdigger for his trouble. From now on, he thought, it would be different. Today let them laugh at him, let their faces stiffen with embarrassment as he reached them because to them a doctor who became a ditchdigger was in a class with a minister who became a drunk. You snickered, maybe, but at the same time you were ashamed and maybe a little scared. Today he smiled as he passed them. He didn't stop and talk but he didn't stiffen up and hurry past as he had been doing.

Milton expected Sloane to be out in the yard, but she wasn't there. He took his time walking up the path, expecting until he reached the steps that he might have missed her, that she could be behind that bush or working on the one behind the maple tree. Until he opened the front door, Milton expected her to sneak up at him, kind of begging him with her whole body to give in about her sister because that was what had been happening all week. He had not let her talk, but every movement she made, every look she gave him, begged him to get rid of the sister. ("Do me a favor," her eyes said, "do me a slight favor, kill my sister!")

The two suits of armor had developed a new trick in the past week because the light came in at a different angle: now, as the door opened, they seemed to turn their shining heads. So let them. He heard Mrs. Austen's steps coming toward him from the kitchen side of the house and, although he didn't want to, he called, "Sloane?" He hurried in Mrs. Austen's direction as if he couldn't tell the difference between the slow cautious steps of a cardiac old woman and the elastic tigery walk of his wife. "Sloane? Oh, Mrs. Austen," he said, "I thought you were the madam. Where is she? Upstairs?"

"Madam is out."

"Still out? I didn't see her there."

156

"Madam went somewhere, Dr. Krop. She didn't say. I was to tell you she would be back at six."

"You don't know *where?*" He was so frightened that he shouted at the old woman. Suppose she had gone to her sister? Suppose the sister had told her even though she had promised she wouldn't for three weeks? Austen was staring at him. He turned on his heel and walked back to the telephone. The telephone book slipped out of his hands and the thump it made on the floor set his heart pounding. As he bent to pick it up, he saw Austen's feet planted. He called out, "How did she seem?" He wet his thumb so that he could turn the pages of the directory. "Particularly—?" He found Lady Constant's hotel number and dialed it, waving at Mrs. Austen to wait until later to answer his question. She disappeared discreetly.

Milton was happy to find that he could say "Lady Constant" without clearing his throat.

The moment he finished talking to Lady Constant, he called Mrs. Austen and repeated his question about the madam. Had she seemed particularly depressed? All she could tell him was that the madam said she would be back at six; she hadn't seemed any—different. "I'm going upstairs and lie down," Milton said. "And conserve my strength," he added, but to himself. Sloane had not gone to her sister, her sister hadn't told Sloane; it was O.K. From the half landing the bronze woman with the light in her hand bent toward him as suspiciously as usual. He withdrew his hand from the rail until he passed her, remembering the nasty gash he had once received from the sharp tip of the bronze shoe. Bitch, he thought, the bronze bitch and the iron bitch!

The door to Sloane's room was open and he looked inside, deliberately evoking the hatred which invariably welled up when he visualized himself lying there in that bed, sucked slowly into the valley in the middle where Sloane always lay waiting. The anger against what Sloane had done to him came into his mouth, from his guts, he thought, as sour, as bitter, as acid as ever. But if he stood there too long, if he overcharged his battery with the hatred, he would not be able to wait. As it was, he couldn't be still but went to the next room and, walking up and down it, went over the plan from the moment when, sandwich in hand, he walked into Jenny's apartment, at about seven forty-five, sat down on the good old Hide-a-Bed, ate the edible part of the sandwich and began telling Jenny how worried he was about Sloane, about projection, about her condition (attested to by good old Helga) about the suicide note (witnessed by good old Austen). He would break down and admit to Jenny that he had bitten off more than he could chew. ("I told you so," Jenny would say.) He would make a good long story of it because the picrotoxin was fatal in from one-half to three hours. He would spin it out and Jenny would love every minute of it: Milt coming to her at last; Milt admitting Jenny knew best. He would tell Jenny that he had come to her because, after all, she had worked on the psychiatric wards, she knew something about this terrible business, more than he did, probably—if you came right down to it, what training had he had? He was no psychiatrist and although neither was Jenny, one advantage was, he could have her look Sloane over without Sloane thinking it was anything more than a social call. (Sloane won't ask why you're here, he would tell Jenny; she was too wrapped up in her own troubles these days. But if she did, Jenny was to say that Bud had barged in on them so they couldn't talk in her place and had come to the Haunted House to finish.) He would tell Jenny that he couldn't go it alone another day. He wanted her to come back with him and see whether she agreed that he must not defer to Sloane any longer and call a psychiatrist in no matter how much she objected.

Jenny would eat that up. Boy, how Jenny would eat that up— and he would eat up his nice sandwich!

If he timed it right, the kids would come back and he would

let Jenny get them to bed and hear Maureen's prayers and by the time he got back to the Haunted House—

When Milton had gotten that far with the review, his ears did a kind of double take on the noise he had been making, walking up and down the big room, and he pulled off his jacket and shoes, yanked his tie loose, undid his collar button and forced himself to lie down on the bed. He did not want Austen testifying afterward that he had been pacing up and down or it might look funny, his running out on Sloane to go to Jenny's, no matter what she wanted about Bud. He must seem worried, of course, but no more than usual. Lying stretched out, his whole body twitched, and he remembered a patient, a Mrs. Knudsen, a blonde whose husband was a traveling man in more ways than one, according to her. She had described how her whole body twitched as she lay in bed nights and he found himself apologizing to her now because he hadn't given her enough sympathy. "Excuse me, Mrs. Knudsen!" ("Excuse me, Mom. Excuse me, Phil—")

He couldn't make his mind a blank so he went over the whole thing again, step by step, examining each move, trying to anticipate even more minutely than he had, but that wasn't such a good idea because he started going too far, anticipating trouble without knowing where it would come from or how to prevent it. It was better, since he had it all letter perfect, to give himself a thrill, to see in his mind's eye the villa on the cliffs of Antibes. He let himself walk down the steps "cut into the living rock" and felt it warm under his feet. He was wearing bathing trunks and a shirt to match. Didn't they call those outfits Riviera outfits? On the beach—in bikinis—and if that wasn't what was being worn on the Riviera any more, by gum, one girl— his girl—was going to be wearing one if he had the say-so. And he would have the say-so! The guy who had the green stuff had the say-so and, for once, he would be the one with the green folding stuff.

He felt the bills in his wallet, then he felt the warm sand under his back. He closed his eyes and saw "the blue of the Mediterranean" and soon the twitching stopped so that he must have looked asleep because when Sloane came and opened the door she closed it again after her, softly, softly, so as not to disturb him. He lay as quietly as possible, hearing Sloane move around her room. (It sounded as if she was taking her clothes off. What for? She was always taking her clothes off, he thought, any time—in broad daylight—before lunch! She'd take off her clothes at the drop of a hat, he thought, and the hatred welled up inside, but although that made it harder to lie still, although it made the twitching come back, he welcomed the hate. He had to feel it. The hate was necessary.)

He lay as quietly as possible until he heard Mrs. Austen toil up the stairs, pausing at each step. When she was almost at the second floor, he got off the bed, walked across the room and threw the door open, standing there in his stockinged feet, stretching. "I guess I dozed off," he said. "What time is it?"

"About six-forty, sir."

"Is Mrs. Krop home?"

"Yes, sir. Madam returned at six. She is in her room." Mrs. Austen took a deep breath and started up the third flight to her room.

"Mrs. Austen, you shouldn't go upstairs when you have to come right down again. You should arrange things better than that." Mrs. Austen turned to him, about to explain that she was going up for her hat and coat: Milton snapped his fingers. "I forgot! Thursday, isn't it? Your night off. Had your dinner?" She nodded. "All ready to go?" She nodded again. "Have a good time."

"Thank you, Dr. Krop." She sighed.

The sigh was supposed to mean that there wasn't a chance in the world she'd have a good time, but he chose to interpret it as a sigh of weariness. "You look tired." He snapped his fingers again. "Get your hat and coat and I'll run you over to Roosevelt. They have the escalator there: save you the stairs. Go on, no trouble at all!" He nodded toward Sloane's door, meaning because he was grateful to Mrs. Austen for helping out with Sloane, and ducked into his room. He got his shoes on, pulled his tie tight, ran his hand through his hair and grabbed up his jacket before the old woman reached her bedroom, then he knocked on Sloane's door. "Sloane? I'm going to drive Mrs. Austen to Roosevelt so she has enough moxie left to paint the town red. I'll be back in ten minutes." Before she could say anything, he started downstairs. He was so afraid Sloane would somehow manage to stop him that he did not wait for the old woman but went downstairs and out.

He was standing on the top step waiting when he realized that the table in the dining room had not been set. He had glanced into the room as he passed, but it hadn't registered until now. He had the shakes so bad he couldn't get his door key out, and had to wait until he heard the old woman inside. He rang the bell. "Forget my car keys," he said to her, shooting past. It was true; the table wasn't set. Dark, the finish gleaming, the huge table was bare except for the condiment set and the silver candlesticks.

He was afraid to trust himself to ask, so he waited, saying nothing as he shepherded Mrs. Austen around to where the car was. Whatever had happened, he had to drive her to the station, which would give him time to ask in a way that wouldn't look suspicious. "Nothing like a cat nap to get you hungry! From the appetite I've worked up, I must have been digging ditches in my dreams. What's for supper, Mrs. Austen?"

"I don't know, sir."

Never heard of supper. Hadn't heard Sloane plan it with her in the morning: cold roast lamb (with plenty garlic, he had said, remember?) leftover string beans from yesterday mixed with leftover peas from the day before with some kind of fancy dressing, potatoes in the hot thing, anemic custard topped with stewed fruit from Monday's supper. "You mean you haven't fixed dinner? I thought it was understood that in the condition Mrs. Krop is, she isn't fit to—"

Nobody ever accused me of skimping my work, her voice said. "It was madam herself, Dr. Krop. Madam said I was not to fix dinner tonight."

"That's news to me!"

"Yes, sir, just before madam went out she gave me her orders. It was not my doing, sir."

"Of course not," he said. And they had reached the subway station, thank God. He pulled up to the curb and managed a smile, but that was about all he could manage. *Sloane knew!* The old woman didn't smile back at him. She hated him. He saw it on her face there before he bent to release the brake, before she pulled her servant's face back on. *Sloane knew!*

He had to pull up a block away because he was shaking like a leaf. "Take it easy," he said. "Don't jump to conclusions. All you know for a fact is she canceled the meal, that's all you know for a fact!"

"Oh yeah?" he said, "that's all? Just tonight, just tonight of all nights since we got married, for the first time she cancels the supper: just like that! The leg of lamb would dry out, the fancy dressing on the vegetables would turn rancid—just tonight, though, she doesn't give a damn about waste!" He put his head down on the wheel, dizzy with a panicky desire to start the car and head for the Canadian border.

"Wait a minute," he said. "One step at a time." He raised his head cautiously: it felt full of fluid. "She can't know!" He touched the envelope of picrotoxin in his jacket pocket. "There's no possible way for her to know." It was difficult to think because he felt so dizzy and nauseated. He said aloud, "Lady Constant!" Sloane had been there after all! Lady Constant had lied to him. The autopsy report had come through carly and she had told Sloane. So Sloane knew that much, but not that he meant to poison her tonight! So it was all over, finished, but that was all. She could only throw him out; she couldn't throw him into jail. Sloane was finished with him and the Riviera was finished. To quiet his churning stomach and swimming head, he took a deep breath of air—the usual Queens air, full of the exhaust of cars, of food, of small, dull lives.

He was back where he had been, that was all. Back with Jenny. Jenny had been right, he thought, the sour taste of failure filling his mouth; he couldn't manage without her. The two birds of a feather, the Folsom girls, had gotten together against him. He had always been out of their class; class showed. The Folsom birds against the sitting ducks, he thought, the Folsoms against the Krops.

At seven-fifteen, Jenny would be telephoning the Haunted House. He better stop her. He better say don't bother, that he'd explain some other time, just don't bother. That way it might be possible to keep Jenny from hearing the whole damned business which otherwise Sloane might tell her. If he had to go back and sleep on the Hide-a-Bed again, flatter himself back into his lousy practice again—and what else could he do besides starve or cut his throat—it would be best if Jenny didn't know. Since Jenny now owned every penny he had scraped together, what else could he do but go back? He had better stop Jenny before he had to crawl back on his knees and listen to her laughing at him until he dropped dead!

Milton climbed wearily out of the car—as cautiously as old lady Austen, he thought—and locked the car door, noticing that this was a No Parking place but too weary to give a damn. If his license didn't save him from a ticket, let them give him a ticket. He plodded to the drugstore on the corner and gave Jenny the spiel he had planned. For once, she didn't try to make him tell her, merely begged him to get in touch. Milton rested his head against the telephone and, standing like that, looking through the glass door that way, he naturally remembered Cissie. No bikini any more. No beach any more—but no reason now he couldn't see Cissie. If he wasn't going to poison Sloane, if he and Sloane were washed up, why not Cissie?

Milton wondered how he knew her number by heart that way. If Cissie wasn't home—if the mother answered? He didn't give himself time to plan what then. He was sick of planning. What the hell had all his planning gotten him, anyway? He dialed the number he hadn't realized he knew and waited. If it was the mother, who cared? Pretty soon now, Cissie's mother, the whole baby carriage brigade, the whole neighborhood, would know Sloane had thrown him out and he was back home to Momma.

Cissie answered the telephone. "Cissie, it's me," Milton said, "it's the doctor. I changed my mind. I got to see you just once, Cissie."

She said, "Oh, yes!"

He could see her lips forming the words. He could almost feel her sweet breath on his hot cheek and touched his cheek there, a vast recklessness coming over him. "Cissie," he said. "I kept you from the Stork Club, didn't I?"

"I don't care about that. Who cares about that?"

But she did care about her mother finding out and arranged their date for Friday a week when it would be safest. "Cissie, I'll meet you at the Stork Club Friday a week, nine thirty."

"Yes," she said. "Yes, yes!"

He heard himself laughing at her. "All you can say is yes, huh?" All she could say was yes. All she could do was look at him as if he was the be-all and end-all and say yes! "See you, Cissie!" He hung up before she could say that last "yes," but heard it anyhow, and that was enough to make him forget Jenny's "no," Sloane's "my dear Milton," which meant the same thing, his mother's "no," his brothers' "no," his whole god-damned life which, when you came right down to it, had been one long "no!"

Cissie's "yes" was enough to give him the strength to go back and face the music because what could Sloane do to him, after all? And he knew what he could do to Sloane: tell her, tell her off, once and for all, tell her what he thought of her, what touching her did to him. "Tightwad," he would say. "Miser! If you're the upper classes, give me vanilla! If you and your sister are the Four Hundred give me vanilla! Nympho," he would say. "Pervert, that's what you are! A man's supposed to be the dirty-minded one! You're an excuse for a woman! Narrow-minded, am I?" She had called him narrow-minded. He should read Kinsey, she told him. "Lowbrow, high loin," she said, "highbrow, low loin, my dear Milton!"

There was no parking ticket on the car. Too bad. He felt like tearing it up. Tearing into a cop. Busting someone in the nose. He got into the car, made a wide defiant U turn (worm turn!) and drove back to the Haunted House at forty-five miles an hour which could have gotten him another ticket, but nobody stopped him.

He drove up to the house and parked under the porte-cochere and nobody told him to get his lousy lowbrow Studie away from there. He walked up the steps and they didn't crumble under his middle-class feet and he unlocked the door and nobody had changed the lock on him. He socked the left-hand-side suit of armor with his open palm and it rattled helplessly. He looked into the big empty dining room which was tipsy with the last light coming through the crazy-colored glass panes, into the sitting room, the morning room, the drawing room, the library, the empty kitchen. As he started upstairs, he heard movement. Was the sister with her? Both of them up there laying for the Krops? Well, what went for one went for both of them!

"Milton? Is that you?"

"That's right, Milton. Milton and not the blind poet; the blind, dumb oaf, Milt Krop!"

She was standing in the doorway to her bedroom. It was dark

inside. She was holding onto the door with her long narrow fingers.

"It's Milton, it's Milton! You were calling me?"

She nodded. Her hair was let down and when she bent her head some of it fell over her face and she pushed it back with her hand and backed inside the bedroom. "Amory," she said, and backed away still more.

So the sister was there in the darkened bedroom? That guy, too, laying for me, too? He finished the flight of stairs and followed Sloane into the room. He could handle the three of them. "Milt Krop! *In* person!" No one was in the room except Sloane. "Where is your sister?"

"Milton—why did you think she was here? What has happened?"

"Why did I think—?"

"Milton!" She moved toward him.

"You said 'Amory'!"

"Yes. I telephoned her. Amory."

"So I thought she'd be here."

"No, no! I don't want her here! I never want to see her! I will never see her again, Milton. You are to deal with her! You said you would." She came closer to him, her voice came closer. "Don't you understand?"

"I understand. I understand."

"No," she said, "apparently not. I telephoned Amory." His stance was so hostile that she retreated to her bed. "Darling Milton, I am going to do what you asked. I am going to give Amory the money from the house. I went this afternoon to the realty firm and told them I would accept the offer." She lay on her bed and held out both her arms to him. "My darling, I am doing what you asked. Come to me, Milton. Darling Milton! Come here. We are all alone. Austen is gone."

"I know Austen is gone." Now one hand patted the mattress next to where she lay. "Wait a minute—wait a minute. Austen

166

said you told her not to fix dinner. Why didn't you let her fix dinner?"

"Oh, my dear," she whispered, ignoring his question. "You're shy of me. Are you shy of me, Milton?"

"Why no dinner? Are you sick?"

" 'Stay me with flagons, comfort me with apples: for I am sick of love.' Comfort me, darling, for I am sick of love!"

"You must be sick of something, to waste a good dinner—I figured God knows what it was for you to waste a good dinner!" Then Milton began to laugh because it looked like even Sloane would rather waste a dinner if it meant being murdered. Waste of a good murder was one waste even Sloane wouldn't mind! He couldn't stop laughing.

Sloane crept out of the bed toward him. "No dinner," she whispered, pressing her body against him. "No dinner yet, love!" She was kissing his cheek, rubbing his cheek with hers, her mouth whispering soft. "Dinner later, darling. A celebration dinner, a gala. We celebrate my being—how do you say, Milton? A good little wife. Love, honor and obey."

He could not stop laughing. "Dinner out? Eat out?"

"To celebrate my being obedient."

"Giving me the money?"

"Amory."

"Giving me the money to give your sister, Amory."

"Doing whatever you want. Whatever, whatever, whatever you want, you want—"

He said, "Sloane!" and put his arms around her hard. "Oh, my God, Sloane!" he said, hugging her, using her name without self-consciousness because she was giving him what he wanted, for once the little bird with the yes note, like Cissie, for once like Cissie, loving her for once because he didn't have to kill her. "Sloane!" he whispered, not laughing now, because he was happier than in his whole life that he didn't have to kill her. "Come, Sloane!"

For the first time Milton did not feel like the shambling bull led by the ring in his nose to the female. It did not occur to him that Thursday evening that it was the woman and not the male who was supposed to "be kind." ("Be kind," Sloane whispered. "Now I've done what you want, you will be kind, won't you, Milton, darling?") It was the man who was supposed to do what the woman wanted in order that she would no longer sleep alone in the next room, but Milton didn't remember that, then.

"Where will we go?"

She would not move.

"Sloane, where will we go to eat? I'm starving."

She stretched like a million dollars.

He had gone into the next bedroom and returned carrying his pencil-stripe suit. It wasn't much but it was the best he had. He held the suit up for Sloane to see. "They won't throw me out of a decent restaurant in this, will they? How about the Stork, Sloane?" She was sitting up in bed, hugging her knees. "How about the Stork since we're celebrating?"

She put her feet over the side of the bed and studied them. "I beg your pardon?"

"The Stork. The Stork Club!"

She came over to him naked as the day she was born and began to pull his hair playfully. "Darling Milton! The Stork Club!"

"What's wrong with it?"

Naked as the day she was born, she danced over to the mirror over the dresser and struck a pose. "Do I look like the sort of person who goes to the Stork Club?"

"Well, you'd have to put a little more on but not much more from what I hear. Why not the Stork Club, huh?"

"Because."

"Because" meant the usual reasons, probably; vulgar and middle class were the usual reasons with Sloane, but how could the Stork Club be vulgar and middle class? He was, however, too happy right then to give a damn. "How about the Automat; that's more your speed, is it?"

"Infinitely more preferable, yes." She gave his hair a last mocking tug. "You think I'm not serious, don't you, darling? Ask a gourmet about the meat pies at the Automat, or that coffee. Did you know they won a gourmet's prize for their pastry?"

"Okay. The Automat it is."

"Of course not. You'd hate it!"

What did he care? Let her remember afterward. He would send her a picture postcard from one of those famous places on the Riviera. "Not as good as the Automat but better than the Stork," he would write. "Come on, come on, get dressed!"

They ended up going to a French restaurant on Fifty-second Street. He asked was it the one she had told him about where you ate in the kitchen, but she squeezed his arm and said, "Oh, no, darling. It may take a mere three generations to go from shirt sleeves to shirt sleeves, but it takes at least six to go from eating in the kitchen routinely to eating in the kitchen avec plaisir."

"Avec what?" He asked her what he should do if the waiter started talking in French but she said they wouldn't unless he indicated that French was what he preferred. (Would that be ill-bred and vulgar?) When they reached the restaurant, it turned out to be swell. ("Posh," Sloane said.) He didn't even have to pretend he could read the menu because Sloane announced to the waiter that she would order for both of them and she did, but although she made a big deal of it, it wasn't caviar or champagne and what they had wasn't under glass, or "pressed." They had some kind of fish fillets, with grapes, Sloane explained. (Grapes?) They had a Salade Gaulois and some "perfect" Camembert and fresh fruit to finish. (No coffee.) There was some clear soup first Sloane raved about. "It looks like barely

169

tinted water but when you taste it—like a prism! It breaks on the palate into a rainbow of flavor." It did, he got what she meant, and the fish also was out of this world. Milton asked Sloane to tell him what he was eating so he could order it again, but she said, why bother, she would always be there to order for him, wouldn't she? (Like hell she would!) Then Milton realized that he had exactly four dollars in his pocket and he told Sloane she certainly would have to be around, he couldn't get the tab, otherwise, and you would have thought she would take the hint and pass him some dough under the table but Sloane only smiled and paid the waiter herself. (Vulgar to slip him the money so at least the waiter would think he could pay for it if he couldn't order it?)

French restaurants like that didn't have the food ready-cooked so, what with the conferences with the wine waiter about the wine and the rest of it, it was eleven when they finished eating. Milton felt too high to go straight home and suggested a midnight movie. How about they should look for an old Cary Grant on Forty-second Street? (When he pictured himself walking down those steps carved out of living stone, he always pictured himself kind of a Cary Grant type; that was why he wanted to see him tonight.)

"A Grant?" Sloane asked.

She didn't know who Cary Grant was any more than Milton Berle. "Not Ulysses S. Cary Grant is a tall guy; tall, dark—a smoothie." But Sloane didn't want to see a smoothie. She didn't want to see any movie except documentaries or good foreign ones and to hell with them. Milton suggested that since they were downtown like this, they drive around looking at the Great White Way, but Sloane said they should leave the Great White Way to the people who went to the Stork Club. This time he asked Sloane if the Great White Way was supposed to be vulgar, and she said, "Yes, darling, the acme of vulgarity," so they drove to Riverside Drive and then up the Drive and when they came to Lookout Point she asked him to stop and park and she would have been perfectly willing to sit there necking and if that wasn't the acme of vulgarity, what was? When she leaned against him, he made out his arm had gone to sleep. He began to yawn and said they better be starting back to Queens.

"I suppose so," she said, "tomorrow's Friday. There's your clinic."

Nothing could have been further from his mind than the clinic. "We may be too busy, tomorrow. I can skip the clinic for once." She looked into his face inquiringly. "I figured we'd go to the real estate office tomorrow."

"They will come to us, Milton."

He had figured, get the deal over with in the morning. Get to the banks before they closed. He saw himself with a check, stepping up to the cashier, not actually being asked whether he wanted it in thousand-dollar bills, but almost. He had figured Sloane would peel off what was coming to her sister and give it to him to take. He had figured he would get into his car and stop off at Saks Fifth Avenue and buy himself enough clothes for the boat—all he needed to leave the house with was his passport—go down to the steamship line and take any boat they offered. Get on the boat. Get going. "Can't they close the deal immediately?"

"Milton, dear! We aren't dealing with a four-room bungalow, you know!"

You didn't get $110,000 for a four-room bungalow. "That's right."

"If you go to the clinic, you can take Austen."

"Why bother? She doesn't need to go all the way to the clinic now she's working for us. I can examine her at home."

"No, Milton."

She was starting on the "no's" again, but he should worry. "Why not? You mean she's shy all of a sudden?"

"No." She put her hand on his knee. "Never mind, you never will understand Austen; don't try."

"What the hell," he said, "it's no skin off my nose." If it was the acme of vulgarity to try to save the old woman a trip to the hospital and a wait on the benches, she could go with him. It won't be long now, he thought, yawning. "If you say so, Sloane, I'll take her in the car tomorrow."

"Every third Friday," Sloane said. Then she yawned, too. "Sweet Milton!"

Chapter VII

*F*OR ONCE Milton had wanted Sloane to stay beside him in the big bed after they woke, because it was Thursday again and it made him feel good to lie there next to her warm body, pulsing and alive on this Thursday after last Thursday, but for once, because it was Thursday, Sloane wouldn't stay in bed. If Mrs. Austen was to leave when she fixed their dinner tonight, there would be a lot to do, Sloane said, and if he, Milton, wanted to be a dear, he wouldn't lie in bed much longer, either, but would come down to breakfast so that Mrs. Austen could get started on the bedroom. "We're not working her too hard, are we?" he asked, because he even felt grateful to the old woman on this Thursday after the last.

"She just dusts this room and makes the bed. No, we're not working her too hard."

Sloane tied the belt of her robe in that way she had he hated, as if she were a package and not a woman at all. (Cissie's little fluttery hands, touching, patting, prettifying.)

Sloane paused at the door. "Don't forget to air the room before coming down, Milton."

Cissie's fluttery little fingers touching him— He couldn't lie in bed then, and pulled up and out of it and dressed. In the

Stork—if they were seated on those kind of benches along the wall, if he could sit next to Cissie he could hold her little hand while he told her this was their "one night of love." He could let her fingers curl and tremble against his palm while he told her. She would start to cry but he would ask her to save the tears. "I'll Cry Tomorrow," like that book. Milton, bending over the big dim mirror to knot his tie, remembered that he hadn't engineered the, say, thirty, forty bucks he would need to hold Cissie's fluttery hand in the Stork Club, and, flipping the tie too hard, hit himself in the eye with the end. He was rubbing the flicked eye when, with the other, he caught sight of the pin, brooch, what-you-may-call-it, which had slipped down between the mirror and the top of the dresser. He picked it up and examined it. The brooch didn't look like much, like nothing next to some of the junk jewelry Jenny had, but anything Sloane had was the real thing, the coiled-up snake was real gold, those two eyes weren't rhinestone and the red fangs were real rubies.

He went to the window, turning the pin over in his hands. In the first place, Sloane wore the thing so rarely that she probably wouldn't miss it for weeks; in the second place, if she did miss it, she certainly wouldn't suspect him. In the third place, how else would he get to the Stork Club? He flung the window open to winter then, and not because Sloane had asked him to, but because it had become airless in the big room. His face was burning and he stuck it out of the window because he had been trained right; it wasn't easy to steal a piece of jewelry and pawn it. You could say it wasn't stealing—"What's mine is thine," you could say—but it was stealing and Mom wouldn't like it. (Would Mom like murder? Blackmail? Hell with that!)

Downstairs Sloane was frowning over her mail. Some papers had come from the real estate firm and she said they had omitted something. They had promised to make the wreckers wait for the museum in Boston to send their man down to see whether they would accept the gift of the drawing room, the

174

library and the dining room. (The museum sure looked this gift horse in the mouth, and Milton certainly didn't blame them!) Sloane wanted to go and see that the phrase was inserted before she signed. Milton said he wouldn't go with her and Sloane laughed and said perhaps better not since it was quite obvious what he thought of preserving anything about the place. Milton said what he wanted to preserve was their necks —if she didn't hurry up and get the money to her sister, that might not be so easy. Sloane said no time would be wasted, the provision had merely been overlooked, she would sign the contract this morning.

That gave Milton time to go to the pawn shop. He could have gotten more than the forty bucks he asked, but that was all he needed and he preferred leaving it forty bucks so in case he had to redeem it, he could.

Milton's first thought when he saw Sloane's face was that the real estate firm had backed out because of the clause she had been so stubborn about, but, no, it was nothing like that; it was the pin, the snake brooch. Her great-grandmother's snake brooch. It was missing.

It would turn up, Milton said. "Tell me about the deal."

She could only talk about the brooch. In the middle of a sentence she stopped and ran to the window to see if, in shaking out the sheets, the pin had been dropped. She went outside to search the grounds under the bedroom window, not stopping to put on a coat. She ran upstairs again and ran her hand across the window sill, getting her palm and fingers filthy and then staring at them as if she couldn't imagine why. No, it was not that valuable, Sloane said. Her eyes were big with misery. It was that she couldn't *bear* to have anything missing. Yes, she did feel precisely as if the world were coming down around her; that was it precisely. To have anything—as he blandly put it—just disappear pulled the props from under her! It might be a big house to him, but not to her. She knew every inch of it. The pin was not "somewhere"; she had been over every inch of the house where the pin might conceivably have gotten, been dropped, pushed, shoved, mislaid, and it wasn't in any of them. Yes, she had been over the whole house "with a fine-tooth comb" as his mother always said!

"On the third floor?" Milton asked.

Sloane gasped.

"Well, now listen. If you're so certain the pin wasn't misplaced—Mrs. Austen does clean the bedroom. Did you ask her about the pin being missing?"

Of course she had asked Mrs. Austen; both she and Mrs. Austen had been over the house looking!

"Ask her to look up on the third floor. Go in and tell her that I'm going through my bureau drawers—in among the shirts and socks, handkerchiefs. And I'll go through the laundry hamper, too. So if I can look, she can look, can't she? Or is she better than I am?"

"How is it different?" he asked. "If I can look why can't she? Why just because she is a servant? All right, then," Milton said, "you and she are so chummy but you can't ask her a simple thing like that! If you can't ask her, I can!" He left Sloane in the little room.

Mrs. Austen was sitting in the kitchen on the old rocking chair which she had pulled into the sunlight near the window. She was sitting with her knees apart and a yellow bowl between her knees, shelling peas into the bowl. When she saw him, she pushed herself out of the chair and stood up with the bowl held to her and her striped apron with the pea pods in it wrapped around it. He was very friendly about the whole thing, telling her first about him going up to look-see if the pin was among his stuff—the madam had asked him and the madam was also asking her. While he talked to Mrs. Austen, the color changed in

176

her face, the skin turning to a yellow as mustard-color as the thick bowl in her arms.

Austen talked through stiff bluish lips. "Does madam wish me to go through my things?"

"That's the idea." He made nothing out of it.

"Madam wishes—" She put down the bowl of peas, still clutching the apron full of pods, then pulled it off clumsily and laid it carefully on the table next to the bowl. Then she walked right past Milton toward the hall.

Milton went back to the little room. "My God," he said, "you should have seen her, Sloane! You would think you were accusing her of putting poison in the *pain perdu!*"

Sloane's face was white. "Milton, you said it was my idea that she should go through her things?"

"Sure. Why not? Come on, now, tell me about the deal." She said nothing. "It's going through?" She nodded. Her eyes were fixed on the door. All her attention was on the old woman toiling upstairs, as if she were going to the electric chair. To get her mind off Mrs. Austen, Milton asked Sloane to help him go through his things, unless, that is, she had already done so, and she gaped at him and said, "I beg your pardon? Of course not!" Milton said, "Why of course not?" They were married, weren't they? Sloane's lip curled. She wouldn't deign to answer that!

When he got her upstairs she simply stood by while he emptied the shirts and stuff out of his drawers, listening, he could see, to the old woman walking back and forth in her room on the third floor. "Nope," Milton said, shoving the last drawer back in. "Not in my stuff."

The old woman was no longer moving around, either. She, too, had finished looking.

Sloane sighed and sat on the edge of the bed. "Milton, we must call the police."

"And I thought what worried you was the old lady's feelings!"

"Precisely. We must call the police immediately, before Austen goes out, so that it will be impossible for her to have moved the pin out of the place."

"And I thought getting Austen here was the answer to your prayers! A real servant, a real antique Last of the Mohicans!" The police, he thought, my God, the cops in on it! It wouldn't take the cops long to go through the pawn shops and locate the pin and when Sloane found he had stolen it, all hell would break loose. Oh, God, he thought, I'm just too damn dumb to live! Jenny was right, he thought, too damn dumb! I didn't even have to take the pin. Why did I have to tell Cissie we'd meet at the Stork Club? The corner drugstore would have been Stork Club enough for Cissie, what did she care about Stork Clubs where he was concerned, but no, he had to show off, he had to steal the pin! A poem Maureen had learned and made all of them learn came back to him—Dum de dumm dumm—"for the sake of a horseshoe the battle was lost." Dumb. Dumb. Dumb. For the sake of showing off, he had lost everything! Sloane was staring at him from the bed there. "For the sake of a lousy pin you'll lose Austen, the Last of the Mohicans!"

She shoved her hair back. "But it isn't for the pin!"

"Oh, no! Oh, no! The principle of the thing! The sentimental value, I suppose! I heard that one before!"

"I'm afraid we'll lose Austen if we don't do it. How can I make you understand—" She shook her head at him. "You and Austen are worlds apart, how can I make you understand? I am calling the police because that is what Austen will want under the circumstances! Since you told her I suspected her, Milton, it is the only thing to do!"

"She wants you to call in the cops? Now I heard everything!"

"It is the only way to end this honorably."

He said, "It will end it! It will end it!" And then it came to him, dope that he was! It took all that blood, sweat and tears for him to see the way out. "For Austen's sake? Maybe. As you said, we're worlds apart. I'll never understand Austen. O.K. Now, how about for our sake? How about that? You must be nuts, get the cops in! Sure, let the cops get started going over this house with a fine-tooth comb! One lousy pin misplaced—sent to the cleaners maybe. We've got to tell her this minute we sent it out to the cleaners, but for the love of Mike don't let the cops set foot inside this house!" He saw Sloane's eyes fill with tears. "No, I don't know exactly what they might find, but I do know we'd be nuts to give them an engraved invitation to come in here without a warrant. For example, how do we know that your sister didn't go to the cops? How do we know the only reason they haven't been here already is because they couldn't get a warrant on what they have, but, go on, give them an engraved invitation! Invite them here for tea!"

"Milton!"

"Tea and crumpets for the duchess and the cops!"

"Poor old Austen," Sloane whispered. "Poor old girl. Poor old thing!"

"Just tell her the pin probably went out to the cleaners."

"You tell her," Sloane whispered. "Poor old thing!" She lay down on the bed, face down, and pressed her hands over her ears.

Obediently Milton went upstairs. The door to the room was open and he went inside. He hadn't been up here since Austen came and as he entered he decided it smelled of clean old woman. She was sitting on a straight chair with her hands in her lap and even though he signaled her not to, when he came in, she stood up beside the chair, as if lined up for inspection. A moth-eaten old suitcase lay open on her bed. It was such a pathetic old wreck of a suitcase that Milton couldn't look at it and turned to the stand-up pictures in old-fashioned frames she had set out on her dresser. Probably all dead and gone. His voice was very gentle when he told the old woman that the madam

179

was pretty sure now she must have sent the pin out with stuff for the cleaners.

Austen folded her lips. "Madam goes through everything."

"Madam can forget once in a lifetime, so you can forget it, too! Come on, forget it, Mrs. Austen!" Her lips were still bluish; she licked them with a pale tongue.

"Dr. Krop, I am sure you mean well, but, please—my good name, sir! Dr. Krop, at Mrs. Vinton's a valuable piece of silver, a silver and crystal epergne, disappeared— I beg you to call the police in before I leave this house today!"

The suitcase was lying open for the cops. The old woman was lined up for inspection by the cops. "Now, Mrs. Austen, this isn't Mrs. Vinton's house, is it? You got a different madam now and this madam doesn't want to call any cops in and insult you!" The bluish lips were saying, "Madam? Madam?" silently, the head wagged. "Yes, madam!"

"I will talk to madam, sir."

He stepped in front of Mrs. Austen. "That you will not!"

"Sir—"

Even though Milton knew how Sloane and Mrs. Austen felt about yelling from one floor of the house to the next, he went to the head of the stairs and yelled for Sloane to tell Mrs. Austen, "with her own lips," that she wanted Mrs. Austen to forget it and had no intention of calling in the cops. "Just tell her, Sloane! Sloane!" he called, reminding her by his tone what the cops could mean.

"That's right, Mrs. Austen," Sloane said.

Mrs. Austen seemed to be shocked into immobility; then her head, which had been wagging, nodded. She whispered to Milton, "I forgot how she was, Doctor, I forgot!"

Nuts, she meant. Psychotic, suicidal. Milton had forgotten also how hard he had worked to make Mrs. Austen think so; it was coming in handy, now. He had the crazy feeling that it meant so much to the old lady that without her thinking that about Sloane, she might have called in the cops herself. "Go on, shove the suitcase back under the bed and rest up for your night out and forget the whole thing!" The way the old lady looked at him, the way her mouth curled, she could have been Sloane standing there looking at him as if he was dirt, saying, "You don't understand. You don't understand!"

"How is she?" Sloane asked, without moving.

"She'll live. Now come on downstairs." He took her wrist but she pulled it away, which meant "You don't understand." "Kid," Milton said, "I'm going to give you a sedative. Get some sleep; when you wake up this will be a thing of the past." She took the sedative and Milton closed the door on her and went downstairs by himself.

When she heard Dr. Krop walking downstairs, Mrs. Austen, sighing, went over to her suitcase, smoothed down the sheet of tissue paper which covered her "things" and closed the lid, leaning on it. She fastened the left-hand clasp and it immediately sprang open, nicking her palm. Because she was so shaken, so miserable, not quite certain, that is, whether she was standing on her feet or her head, the springing lock scratching at her palm felt like Tawny. Tawny used to do that, spring at her playfully, not scratching hard—he wouldn't scratch hard—but nicking that way, and Mrs. Austen sat on the bed next to the suitcase and began to cry, wishing Tawny, her orange Tom, was with her again, knowing he never would be, knowing that this place could not be a home any more than her furnished room had been a home, knowing that this wasn't a real job because madam had only hired her because madam wasn't—quite—feeling that with madam not quite it wouldn't last anyhow, and that soon it would start all over again: the dole, the investigators, the questions, the furnished rooms. She heard her own helpless sobbing as an outrage, the last terrible wicked letting-down of her standards, and she reached out and undid the right-hand clasp of her valise and, shaking with the sobs, felt in among her "things." Mrs. Austen had packed and unpacked the valise so often that she knew where everything was without needing to see, knowing just where she had laid each of her "good" things carefully wrapped in venerable tissue paper, the hand-made lace collar from her mother, her mother's bits of Meissen china, the six pairs of kid gloves Mrs. Vinton had given her, one pair each Christmas, the Italian silk camiknickers from Mrs. Vinton's silly niece to get on her good side which were too young, the cat's-eye pin which was supposed to have brought her good luck, and way down underneath, right under the bottle she wanted, the length of fine Irish linen Mrs. Vinton had brought her from Ireland that she was saving to be buried in. Mrs. Austen took the linen out and then the bottle. She wiped her eyes to read the label and make sure it said CAUTION. POISON. DO NOT OVER-DOSE. NO MORE THAN THREE PILLS DAILY. The bottle was almost full of the red wicked-looking pills because she had only taken six, one each day; then when she had told Dr. Krop at the clinic how they upset her stomach and didn't help her chest pains any, he told her to stop. Since it didn't help the chest pains, there was no point in putting drugs into her system and upsetting it, he told her. The pills hadn't helped. Nothing had helped, not madam, not the last hope she had. Nothing. Nothing would ever help and she was tired. Mrs. Austen tipped the pills into her palm and counted out twelve. Twelve little red devil pills. The thought of swallowing more was too nauseating to contemplate, and if three was the most you should take in one day, twelve at once should—

Twelve should *help*, she thought, almost smiling.

Mrs. Austen tipped the pills from her palm to the pin tray on the dresser so they wouldn't roll and went to the bathroom down the hall with her glass, waiting patiently for the water to stop running brown, returning to her room with the glass of water.

She swallowed the pills methodically, two at a time. "One, two—buckle my shoe," memory said. "Three, four, shut the door. Five, six, pick up sticks." She took eleven only. "Ten, eleven, go to heaven."

"My God, forgive me," Mrs. Austen whispered, and shoving the suitcase aside, lay down on the soft bed with the length of fine linen over her, her arms clamped over it so that madam, poor soul, would understand she wanted to be buried in it.

Milton had his dinner by himself. Alone, he could forget Emily Post and which forks for what. You would think that some of the things Sloane did—planting her elbows on the table for instance—would have made Emily Post throw a fit, but he knew damn well Sloane thought she had perfect manners and he didn't have any. He tried not to see any of the seasick pictures on the dining-room walls. On the Riviera, he thought, you probably ate out on terraces a lot. Moonlight would turn the food pale, pallid, but on your tongue, the way Sloane had said about the soup in the French restaurant, it would break into a riot of flavor.

Milton did not even think of Mrs. Austen again until, at ten, he went upstairs and woke Sloane. Sloane thought of Mrs. Austen the first thing, and it wasn't until she said something about Mrs. Austen being out that he remembered that she hadn't gone out. (Surely he hadn't been that far "out" himself so he wouldn't have heard her going by the dining room?)

Sloane shot up in the bed and began to wring her hands. "She didn't go out! She didn't go out!"

"So what?"

"Please go up there! Please!"

He was kind of annoyed and told Sloane the way she was acting you'd think the old lady might have committed suicide

—and Sloane was nodding "yes" at him, nodding! "Because we wouldn't call in the cops, you mean? I never heard of such a thing! Because we wouldn't call in the cops!"

Sloane shoved her hair back and glared at Milton. "Even you have heard of hara-kiri, Milton? That particularly atrocious way of committing suicide, and why? Because one has lost face, Milton, you've heard of that?"

"Mrs. Austen is no Japanese."

"She is a servant, a servant, a servant! To be trusted is her *raison d'être*, her stock in trade! We have made her lose face!"

Mrs. Austen's "good name"! Milton started out of the room. Fast.

The old lady must have been asleep, because when he knocked and came in, she was sitting up in bed staring at him as if he were a ghost. "It's me, Mrs. Austen. You all right?" She stared around the room. "You're in your own room, Mrs. Austen. You must have dropped off. It's after ten. You missed your evening out, I guess, but probably a nice long nap is the best medicine you could have taken, right?"

"Medicine?"

"I didn't mean real medicine, Mrs. Austen, that was just a manner of speaking. You're not awake yet, are you?"

She said, "Not real medicine! I'm awake, sir."

If looks could kill! Milton considered asking the old woman what she had against him, what had he done, for the love of Mike? The "good name" business had upset her so much, she appeared to be in such a state, that for once she might forget herself and tell him, but then he thought: Ishkabibble. Hell with her, and went downstairs. He considered asking Sloane to ask Mrs. Austen what she had against him, but that would be asking for trouble; there was no telling what the old lady might tell Sloane once she broke down and got started. He said to Sloane, "You tell her yourself you wouldn't call in the cops, but that makes no difference. It's my fault even if it's your doing. That old woman hates my guts and I've never done her any harm! She never did have any use for me—but what have I done now? When I went up there, Sloane, she gave me such a look! Well, ishkabibble! I should worry. What can she do? Sue me?"

"She can leave," Sloane said. "I suppose she will, now."

"Go on!"

"She'll leave, Milton, I assure you."

"Ishkabibble, so she'll leave." He didn't need her now, let her leave. Good riddance. "Get off that bed, Sloane, forget the old biddy; come on down and have a bite to eat."

Sloane put her feet off the bed. "I hate letting her down. *Noblesse oblige*. I've failed her!" She held up her hand. "Please," she said, "don't say 'ishkabibble' again!"

If he got her downstairs, got her mind on something else, he might find out about the house deal at least. She was so miserable about her "*noblesse oblige*" that he had to hand her her robe, her slippers, a handkerchief from her drawer. It was his own idea to hand her a mirror and a lipstick; then they went downstairs.

Milton had left the table as it was, so, because Sloane kept sighing and shaking her head and acting beat, he had to clear the table a little, heat up the coffee, pour it into the silver pot and put some cold meat and salad on a plate for Sloane before he could sit down and start on the house deal. It was settled? Signed, sealed and delivered? Sloane nodded because she was eating. "Good!" He rubbed his hands. "So all we have to do now is go to the bank, get the money, hand what belongs to your sister over to her, and we can forget the whole thing."

"Bank?" Her dark eyebrows shot up as if she hardly knew what a bank was.

"They're not going to give you the $110,000 in cash, are they? So we'll have to go to the bank, right?"

Now she laid down her fork and stared. Milton counted ten first and then, in a careful voice, went over it.

"My dear Milton—"

"You were just kidding me? You're not going to give her her share? You were just kidding me?" The drumbeats began in his ears, the funeral beats. He clutched the table.

"Milton, Milton, I am going to do precisely what I said, precisely what you wanted! Of course I'm not kidding!"

"Well, then?"

"I most certainly never said I would give Amory cash—preposterous!" Such an idea had never entered her head. How could he have thought cash? If he thought cash it only proved how little he knew how things were done. Certainly Amory never for one moment imagined that the money was going to be done up in a neat little parcel and tied in a pink ribbon and—

He had to talk loud to hear himself over the drumbeats, but he kept hold of himself. He said that Sloane seemed to be treating this as if there were nothing more to it than a little family argument between herself and her sister about some money which her sister felt was still coming to her!

"Precisely," Sloane said. "Isn't that precisely what it purports to be? Be reasonable, Milton! Won't it defeat the whole purpose of your plan if we don't carry it out as if it was just that? A sum of money which Amory feels mother promised her and which I have now agreed she should have? What she had decided to give Amory was the difference between what Amory had received from her share of the house and what Sloane was getting for it now, correct? Yes, it had to be done to the last cent, accurate, yes! With Amory's lawyer acting for Amory and the family lawyer acting for them! Yes, there had to be all the red tape and papers signed, sealed and delivered—signed and sealed before delivery. Amory would most certainly suspect the worst if it were not done that way. "But how could you be so naïve? How could you be so infantile as to imagine that all that

186

was necessary now was to trot to the bank and get the cash and tuck it into your little trouser pocket and trot over to Amory with it? Where are you going, Milton? Milton?" He stumbled out of the dining room and talking, talking, she came after him. "Wait for me, please!" She began cajoling. "Come, now, Milton, we mustn't leave the table this way tonight of all nights. We don't want to give Austen an excuse to leave in the morning, do we?"

He was walking as fast as he could. His legs felt like lead, he kept bumping into the edges of furniture, knocking against things as if he were blind. Blind Milton. "When I consider how my light is spent—" Sloane never had any intention of giving him cash. She had just let him talk about cash. She had never "dreamed" he meant cash. She meant lawyers and red tape and gold seals and he wouldn't get a smell of the money. Only an infant would have thought go to a bank. Nice crisp century notes. Fold the folding money. "Tuck it into your little trouser pocket and trot over to Amory with it." And he had thought just that. (He blushed.) And he had thought that Austen would be relieved if they didn't call in the cops. And he had thought ishkabibble. And by next Thursday Austen wouldn't be there. He wasn't going to get a smell of the money this way and next Thursday Austen would be gone and the other way the whole thing depended on Austen. The autopsy report would come in. The two sisters would get together; no money, no Riviera, nothing, precisely nothing!

"Milton!"

"Go to hell," he called, standing at the big window, putting his palms against the glass, lifting them off.

She was right behind him. She stamped her foot. "Why do you want me to go to hell? Why does the manner in which Amory gets the money concern you?" She put her hand on his shoulder as if she could pull him around to face her and he flung off her hand. "Why do you want to bring Amory cash?"

She stood next to him at the window, her hand on the pane beside his hand, her face turned, trying to read his averted face; then she gasped. "And I called you naïve! Infantile! I called you naïve when I have always known—always, always known—that your preference is for the girlies, the pin-ups, the girly-girlies! Froufrou! Why, Amory is your meat! My dear sister Amory is just your meat! How could I not have seen? The Lady Constant—when you drooled over her title, Milton, the *gentil, parfait* Lady-lover!"

She began to bang her palms against the glass, making him blink. She'd go through the glass, he thought, cut herself to pieces, he thought, blinking, and turning to warn her he saw how her face had changed, the nose sharpened like her cutting voice.

"You couldn't walk off with the cash for Amory, how could you under the circumstances? I couldn't stop you if it was my money, how could I? My hands are tied, but dear sister Amory would be at the police station if you ran off with her money quicker than you could say Jack Robinson. And that would be too bad for you as well as for me since you're my accessory in crime, aren't you? But if you went off with Amory and the money? If you had arranged between the two of you that day to do that very thing? Cahoots," she said, banging the pane, "cahoots, cahoots! You planned that day to—how would you say it, ishkabibble—double cross me! It was to be a double cross, wasn't it, Milton? You and Lady Constant!"

He took both her hands off the window so that they wouldn't go through it and dropped them. "Me and Lady Constant? You're nuts! You think she'd have me? Would you have had me if not for what happened? Did you ever look at me before it happened? Listen," he said, "as far as I'm concerned, you and Lady Constant can both go to hell!"

The only reason he didn't leave the house then, that minute, walk out and leave the house then, was Jenny. He started upstairs, not pausing for breath at the half landing because there the bronze lady peered and grinned with the grin that would be on Jenny's face. Behind him he could hear Sloane following, but he made the bedroom next to theirs and shut the door in her face and locked it.

At least he would never have to undress and get into that bed in the next room again and wait for her to climb in and lie next to him and put her hand on his shoulder, slip closer to him, start that kind of talk.

He lay down on the bed and at first he thought it was that kind of talk, and through the door at that, touching the door instead of him, inching up on the door, pressing against it, because she was using that kind of voice, but actually all she was saying was she was sorry, he was right, she must have been mad, literally, completely unrealistic, always had been where Amory was concerned, he had guessed that, hadn't he? Mad jealousy where Amory was concerned, always. "Ah, darling Milton," she was saying now, pawing the door that way she had, "I knew before the words left my lips how insane—"

Milton thought: No, kid, the last thing in the world—him and Lady Constant. *Last*, he thought, blocking out the pleading voice, *last chance*. By next Thursday, next maid's day off, Austen would probably be gone, but tomorrow, the way Sloane had talked, she'd still be here. Tomorrow, Friday, when he and Austen went to the clinic? How about it?

He sat up.

It wasn't really different from last Thursday's plan except lunch would be the "last" meal instead of supper. He and Austen would leave the house together to go to the clinic. He would call Jenny as soon as he got to the clinic, same as last time. All he had to do was figure out some way both he and Austen could eat before Sloane tomorrow. At the last minute, some way to keep Sloane from sitting down at the table with him so that when he and Austen left for the clinic, Sloane would be alone eating the lunch left by Austen for her.

"Milton, Milton," Sloane said through the door, "you must give me a chance!"

Only if he had a chance, he thought; otherwise, the hell with her. She could stay outside that door until hell froze over because she refused to give him a chance. She took away his chance and laughed in his face. "Preposterous," she said, laughing in his face. "Naïve, infantile, impossible!" He had to shut his ears against the real voice pleading outside the door and repeat his litany against Sloane: murdered her mother (as good as), wanted him to murder her sister for her, be the patsy, promised him a life with her and just lay in that bed there using him, using him in bed, in the garden, in the Haunted House, giving him nothing.

"Please forgive me, Milton!"

Tomorrow morning put the picrotoxin in the saltcellar after breakfast, work with her getting the specimen bushes ready for shipping. Keep at it and keep her at it. Make out he forgot about the clinic in the afternoon. Dig out a lot more bushes than he could ball the roots of, say it was last chance before a real freeze. Get her to work wrapping them up so they wouldn't freeze. Why not lunch later for her? She didn't have to go to clinic. Tell Austen why madam was working while he ate. Eat salt-free lunch. Tell Austen madam had worked outside in the cold enough. Dish out for her. Call Sloane in and leave with Austen. It should work, why not?

"Oh, Milton!"

She was going to cry now. He went to the door, turned the key, turned the knob.

"Oh, Milton, Milton!"

Milton was awakened at four by a bad dream. He was in Paris watching the genuine can-can dancers. One of them came off the stage to where he was sitting on the aisle and danced especially for him, but laughing at him, and when he saw her face close it was Jenny laughing. When the dancer saw he recognized her, she turned her back and flipped the billowing skirts insultingly, hitting his face with the ruffly edge of them. He woke with his heart pounding and found that the can-can skirt was Sloane's hair which had drifted over his face. He moved away from Sloane and lay quietly, going over the part of the plan which concerned Jenny. (To make her laugh on the other side of her face!) Having called her the minute he arrived at the clinic, told her he must see her right away, having given her the spiel about Sloane being psychotic, maybe requiring psychiatric help immediately, having timed it so their arrival coincided with the fatal action of the picrotoxin, they come to the Haunted House. Leaving Jenny in the hall near the two suits of armor, he goes into the rooms downstairs to find Sloane. In the dining room, he picks up the silver saltcellar with his handkerchief, to preserve fingerprints, and puts it in handkerchief into his pocket. She is not downstairs, so he goes up to look for her. Call Jenny upstairs, show her, then say, "Excuse me—" Lurch out of bedroom, head toward the john. Jenny would ask where he was going. Tell Jenny. In the safety of the john, get rid of stuff, flush toilet. He would have the real salt in an envelope in his pocket. Refill saltcellar three quarters full, put it back in his pocket, fingerprints intact. All he had to do which mustn't be seen was put the saltcellar back where it belonged and that shouldn't be hard.

The morning came gray and damp, but soft, Sloane said. "Soft as forgiveness. You really have forgiven me, Milton?"

He was dressed for working on the grounds. Would he be willing to dig up those damn bushes if he hadn't forgiven her? he asked. "Finish your coffee and let's get going. There aren't going to be many days as warm as this."

"Yes," Sloane said, "but—"

But first she had to go over the linens and see what was to be kept and what given away. It wouldn't take long, Sloane said, and it couldn't wait. She would join him outside the moment she finished.

The reason that Milton went up to the linen room an hour later to get Sloane was, he knew as well as the next one, to recharge his battery of hatred. Working with plants, spading up bushes, neatly balling the roots had its inevitable philosophical effect. It softened him up too much. (If his mother hadn't made a doctor out of him? If he'd stayed on the farm the way he should have?)

Even the voices of the baby carriage brigade outside the gates began to sound like birds did.

Sloane was sitting on a stepladder stool near the high window. The gray day flattered Sloane, endowing her momentarily with color. Sloane raised her head as Milton entered and smiled.

"Have you come to collect me? I've been longer than I expected." She smoothed the sheet she was examining and began to fold it back along its creases, then let it drop onto the floor. "I find it so difficult to condemn them, Milton—the older the more delicious—but the reason I'm still at this is I took the opportunity of trying to make my peace with Austen." She waved at him to close the door because the linen room was on the third floor, near Austen's bedroom.

"She's in the kitchen," Milton said. "She's not mad at you any more for not calling in the cops?"

"You're the one she's furious with."

"What did I do? Did she tell you what I did?"

"We would hardly discuss her feelings toward my husband, Milton, no, but it was quite obvious. Why, she won't even go to the clinic with you today! I don't mean merely not ride with you; won't go, won't attend!"

Milton turned to stone.

"What Austen said was that now she is being paid a wage, she will go to a private doctor, not be a charity patient any more."

Milton made the enormous effort required to speak. "That's nuts! Listen. We understand her condition at the clinic. She'll go to some ignoramus—I can imagine— He'll kill her, Sloane, you've got to explain that to her!"

"My dear! I did!" Sloane stood up. "She wouldn't listen to me. All I could get out of her was that you had made a fool of her at the clinic."

His gesture meant "how?" Sloane shrugged. Sloane smiled. Milton forced his legs to move toward the door. "I'm going to ask her."

"You'll get nowhere, Milton. She's set her mind against you and the clinic and nothing will shift her." Sloane moved toward Milton, easily. "Oh, come, Milton, you've done everything you can for Austen. If you argue with her, she'll walk out on us. Let her be, your conscience is clear!"

"Yes," he said, "my conscience is clear, all right, my conscience is clear."

Sloane picked up the sheet she had dropped and handed the two corners of one end to Milton. "Here, be useful, darling!" She backed away with her two ends of the sheet, folded the sheet lengthwise, signaling Milton to do the same, then walked up to him and handed him her folded ends, then backed away, again.

The room was perfectly quiet and tinted with the inimitable, never-to-be-forgotten smell of clean linen. It wasn't until Sloane had put the folded sheet on the shelf, touching it lovingly the way she touched all old things, and picked up the next one to be folded that she broke the silence. "What is it, Milton?" She gave him the two ends of the sheet. "Tell me!"

"Nothing." If Austen won't come to the clinic, I can't do it.

"Something. Tell me."

193

He was so afraid that he might tell her that he said the first thing that came into his head. "I used to do this with my mother. In the kitchen at home." Tenderly touching, Sloane gave him her folded corners, blacked away from him, softly. She had never before looked so feminine to him as she did now, motherly. If she had conceived—

"You've never told me very much about your family, Milton."

"It wasn't because they weren't Folsoms. Nobodies."

She came toward him with the soft sheet. "Of course not. Tell me now."

He told her about the farm. What it had looked like, how neat, everything old but in good repair. When you bought stuff thirdhand to start with you had to keep it in good repair. The hours the boys had spent on the pickup truck. They could do anything, the boys. One fall—it was snowing, too, on the way to market with winter produce—the Ford had broken a rear axle and the boys had built a fire by the road and forged an axle.

"Yankee ingenuity," Sloane whispered. "You should be so proud."

"Proud?" He broke the softness with harsh laughter. "You know what I think when I think 'farm'? Cold. That's my word association: cold, frozen feet, my ears burning with cold. I can see my breath on the way to the school bus, stamping and flapping my arms to keep the circulation going. Cold. Being the youngest, I always warmed the bed up for the others, and for later—for medical school—hot! Sweating in the apartment, in the tenement. . . . We were only four blocks from Sutton Place, what do you think of that? You say medical school and I say 'hot.' I froze my way through childhood and sweated through medical school!

"Working your way through, they say! Through school, after school, all summer vacations working for other people who didn't need to work so they could go back to school when it opened! Four in the morning to get the farm chores done so we could get off to school!" He told Sloane how his father had died of high blood pressure when he, Milt, was four. If you were sentimental you would say his father had died in his mother's arms, but it hadn't been his mother's arms, it had been on the floor of the old barn, lying there in the cow droppings he had been cleaning up when he had his stroke. He, Milt, had been the only one home, the youngest, so he had been the only one to see his father lying there in the cow droppings, something to be proud of! His mother had sent him to the Clarkes' down the road where they had a telephone, but his father was cold by the time the doctor got there. When he came back, his mother took him on her lap and he smelled the cows on her, too. Maybe other people associated death with fancy flowers, but he, Milt, associated with cowflop, dung, with the tangy smell of urine. Proud!

His mother believed to her dying day that his father had died because the doctor couldn't get to him in time. It was because of this, Milton explained, because of the memory of his father in the cow dung in the barn, that his mother had wanted them to become doctors, and the funny part of it was—as he now reconstructed, ten specialists in attendance couldn't have helped his father!

"Ah, Milton!" Sloane whispered.

"Mom had the farm clear and two hands and four strong kids. Making us all doctors was her—"

"Religion."

"Mania, compulsion, the textbooks would call it! What any one person could do, my mother could do. She could have driven a dynamo with her will power alone, I tell you; four kids were nothing, a snap! She was quite a woman. I suppose your mother, or your nurse, your what-you-may-call-it, governess, told you fairy tales before you went to bed, didn't she?" (What did he care what her governess told her?) He saw his mother in the kitchen with the draft in the range making it go red, then pink, as if it were breathing, sitting there after a day's work near the oil lamp with her legs spread, wearing his father's shoes which she used for outdoor work and his father's dungarees, using, he now decided, what must have been his father's gesture of hitching up her pants. (And when one of them got out of line, she used his father's belt on them, too!) "My mother told us fairy stories too, nights in the kitchen: When all us boys would have our M.D.'s. When all us boys were doctors—the way she said that word it was a holy word, to my mother a doctor was holy! The fairy stories my mother told us was how it would be when we all were doctors! For instance, in sixth grade I wanted a chromatic harmonica—a kid in school had a beauty. God, how you want things when you're a kid at school! Well, she wouldn't get me a chromatic, but she'd tell me when I was a doctor I could have a gold harmonica. She used to say she'd live a thousand years with four sons doctors!

"She was fifty-five when she died. She was a woman, after all, and not a work horse, and although two of her kids were doctors then, they weren't magicians. Or holy.

"I don't need to go into what it took to get the four of us through medical schools. You can imagine. We were just ordinary guys, except for my brother Phil, no Phi Beta Kappas except for Phil, anything we learned we had to plug. Phil was the one should have been a doctor—like in the movies—dedicated. Dedicated until the day he died at thirty-nine which is why Jenny and the kids were left with exactly beans. Phil was too wrapped up in his research!"

"But, Milton, to be dedicated!"

"His kids couldn't eat on it. They ate on me. I took over Phil's obligations when he died. That's how we had been trained up to do: one for all and all for one, a regular Three Musketeers! We lived in that apartment near Sutton Place, don't forget. While Mom was alive she stayed on the farm. We could have made a good thing of it if Mom would have given up on one of us, even. But no! One of us had to go out every Saturday and put in a good eight, ten hours after classes and on Sunday. Come back to New York Sunday dog-tired and bone up for Monday's classes. Circles under the eyes, yawning— Some of the medics thought we had a high old time in our place weekends the way we'd stagger into the nine o'clock lecture Mondays, a regular love nest they thought we had—near Sutton Place! And vacations—I remember one Thanksgiving. In November you wouldn't think there'd be too much to do on a farm. I remember the ignition had gone bad on the truck. There was a patch had to go on the siding. The pigs had to have a new farrowing pen. I had promised Mom new laying-boxes for the hens. I remember listening to the fellows gassing about what they did Thanksgiving.

"Mom would cook up a lot of stuff and whoever went would hike back a load of food and we'd eat good the first half of the week. One for all and all for one! I tell you if the Reds were like the Krop boys— So we all got our M.D.'s! All four—and then there were three and then there were two. The Japs got Hut so he doesn't count. Phil and then me. The cheese stands alone! 'There's something rotten in Denmark!' " He struck his chest. "Me, Sloane! The cheese! I'm rotten, Sloane! I'm damaged goods! You know about high blood pressure? How it can run in a family? Pa, the boys—now me! The iron man! A regular peasant, right, Sloane?" He dropped the sheet which he had been clutching all along and flexed his right arm, then pointed to Sloane's face which had gone white. "I'm the last of them and soon there'll be none, that's what the man said, Sloane; then there'll be none!"

Her lips moved but no sound came. "Mil-ton, Mil-ton," she was saying. She held out her arms and he came to them. She dropped to the floor, kneeling on the soft sheets, and dragged him down with her, rocking him, crying now, "Milton, Milton!"

197

She whispered. "That's why when you came here and found Mother— What I had done— That explains how you dared take such a chance with your life with a stranger!"

He pulled out of her embrace. "Life? What life? Who're you kidding?" He grinned at her. "Now you won't be grateful!"

"Now I won't be suspicious!"

"When you said that poem to me: 'When I consider how my light is spent'— Like a ton of bricks!" he said.

"My darling, my darling!"

He touched her tears with his fingertips. He wanted to eat her tears. Her closed eyes were beautiful to him, her wet mouth, her shaking body. "Now you see how it is," he said. "Sloane. I want to live it up a little before I go. Sloane! Maybe I want to live it up for the four of us. Did you ever see a title of a book: A Lust for Life? I have a lust for life, Sloane! I didn't want to drop in my harness, making my calls, office hours, sleeping on a Hide-a-Bed. I'll sleep long enough on a Hide-a-Bed, do you see, Sloane? I never talked like this to anybody in my life!"

She took his face between her two hands. "You should have. What do you want?"

"Precisely," Milton said, making fun of her word, kissing her, "precisely, precisely? I want to get on a big boat, Sloane. Walk up the gangplank. I want to lie in a deck chair and be fed tea by a steward. Sloane, I want to live like a travel folder! I want to get some real service—real servants! I want to be waited on hand and foot. I want someone to turn on the bath water for me. I want my chairs pulled out. I want my grapes served peeled! I want to eat the kind of meals you read about. Soft beds and soft winds. I want the sun to shine every day. I want to see flowers like in catalogs! You remember the pictures your sister sent? The villa in Antibes—the steps cut out of living rock, that's what I want!" He looked at her. "Sloane?"

"Not Sloane," she whispered, "Ruth. From now on, Ruth. Whither thou goest—whatever you want!"

The envelope with the salt in it was in his pocket. When he got up to lock the door, he pulled off the jacket and hung it over the doorknob. It swayed a couple of times, it kicked a couple of times, like when a man is hanged, then it was still; then it was dead. Finished.

Chapter VIII

MILTON hated to do it just a couple of hours after he and Sloane had gone down to the Cunard Line and reserved a suite on the *Queen Elizabeth* for the nineteenth. Two cabins and a sitting room! It was the slack season and Sloane could have gotten them just an ordinary cabin for two, but she wanted to do it right. She had done it right.

Milton hated to pick a fight with the suite fresh in mind but he had to, and he had picked on old lady Austen because wanting her out of the house was kind of buying life insurance for Sloane in a way, and it would be easier to work up a mad against Sloane about Austen than about anything else. Milton waited until old lady Austen brought in the dessert; then, when she went back into the kitchen, asked Sloane to give the old lady her walking papers today. Right off.

Sloane frowned.

"I have my reasons. Come on now, Ruth, Ruthie!" Milton put his hand over Sloane's as it lay in her lap, but she pulled her hand away.

"That's cruel and unnecessary. Surely, unless she leaves of her own free will, she can stay until we go on the nineteenth?"

"Give her a bonus, a big send-off, but o-u-t, now! Out tomorrow morning."

"What possible reason can you have—"

"The best, believe me! I say the best, isn't that enough for you? Can't you take my word for something?"

"You must be reasonable, Milton."

"Don't use that tone to me! Don't talk down to me as if I was halfwitted; I don't want any more of that!"

Sloane delicately pushed his compote dish nearer to him.

"And don't tell me when to eat!"

"Tell me why?"

"Why? All right, why should I have to live another one of my limited days in the same house with an old cow you said yourself hates my guts? Why should I? Who needs it? Every time she looks at me, she—if looks could kill— You know it's true! Who needs it?" Sloane was wagging her head "no" at him as he had known she would. "So the old lady comes first around here, is that it?"

"Now, Milton—"

He was out of the house flinging down the path before she could stop him. If he just didn't come back now, he could meet Cissie at the Stork Club at nine o'clock and Sloane would think it was because he was sore at her putting poor old Austen before him. He walked rapidly, not looking back at the house in case Sloane had decided to come after him, not daring to stop to take the car in case she should catch him. He began to smile because the old lady would be furious if she knew she had done him a good turn with the delay. He took off an imaginary hat and tipped it toward the old lady. "A thousand thanks, old thing," he said.

Sloane wouldn't like him staying out but it would show her that she better live up to the letter of the law, better be R-u-t-h, that is, and no ifs, ands or buts about it! He would see Cissie again, one last time they would never forget, and he would teach Sloane a lesson. Two birds with one stone, the little yellow bird and the bald-headed eagle!

"Mrs. Krop? Jenny? This is Sloane. I hope I haven't waked you."

"Waked me? My God, it's only ten-fifteen!" Jenny wanted to ask had the world come to an end that Sloane should telephone little old her, but for Milt's sake she didn't want to get Sloane sore at her. "No, of course you didn't wake me."

"Good. How are you, Jenny? And the children?"

I'll bet she isn't sure how many children there are, Jenny thought resentfully. "We're O.K., thanks. How is Milt?"

At first, for a few minutes after Sloane hung up, Jenny felt good. It felt good to have Milt's high-hat wife call her up and give her condolences about Phil and all and ask her advice about Milt. It felt good to know that after Milt had told his wife how things were with him, she should turn to Jenny for help and advice; that she should tell her the plans she and Milt had and ask for Jenny's O.K. Then the satisfaction died down. There had been a funny little gap in the conversation that, now she came to think about it, rang a bell in Jenny. She had always had a feel for when she was being pumped. You couldn't count the number of patients she had nursed who had made those same funny little gaps when they wanted to pump her about something, prognosis, generally, whether the doctor had told them the honest truth or was he holding something back. Those patients, though, hadn't gotten anything out of her, not a thing, but she wasn't so sure, now she came to think about it, that Sloane hadn't. Jenny bit her knuckle; if only Milt would warn her! If only Milt would tell her what was what instead of holding out on her this way, she wouldn't open her big fat mouth and put her foot into it. Had that woman called for a different reason entirely? Had Milt told his wife he was going to be here this evening?

If Milt told Sloane he'd be here, then he's with Cissie, sure as shooting, Jenny thought. Did Sloane suspect about Cissie? It must be he was out with Cissie and Sloane had pumped her! Damn it, if Milt had only told her she would have sworn up and down he was there, made up some story about him taking the kids out for a sundae, but not even knowing he was out with Cissie or that he had wanted her to cover for him—

Jenny stood up, rubbing her wet knuckle down her skirt. She still didn't know if he was with Cissie!

"I'm doing this for Milt," Jenny said to her mirror, clamping her lips tight on a piece of Kleenex to get the excess lipstick off. She looked at the lipstick thoughtfully, snapped her fingers and took out the unopened bottle of Chanel Five Bud had bought her for her birthday. Wiping the powder from the drawer off its Cellophane wrapper, she thrust it into her pocket, and walked quietly out of the apartment so that Bud, studying in his room, wouldn't hear and want to know what was going on.

First Jenny went outside the house to the edge of the sidewalk where, by craning, she could see that there were lights in Mrs. Parker's apartment, in what was the living room. Then, hurrying through the cold, she went back into the vestibule and pressed the bell that said Parker and it buzzed back. She took the elevator up.

By the time Jenny reached 4A, Mrs. Parker had the door open on the chain. Jenny waved at Mrs. Parker and the door promptly closed, but then Jenny, thanking the Lord for Mrs. Parker's healthy curiosity, heard the chain being taken off.

"Yes?"

Jenny tried to see into the apartment, craning over Mrs. Parker, who blocked the way. "I'm right, aren't I? Cissie is out, right?"

"Cissie is out but I don't see that's any concern of yours."

"I wanted to make sure it was Cissie I saw leaving earlier." She reached into her pocket and pulled out the bottle of Chanel Five. "I came up because I want to give Cissie a little present, but I'm kind of embarrassed. I'd rather you gave it to her, if you don't mind, so that's why I waited until—"

"Cissie doesn't need your presents, thanks."

"You don't give because it's needed. Because you feel sorry for what you did."

"You don't need to feel sorry for Cissie, Mrs. Krop, not any more. In case you're interested, let me inform you Cissie came to her senses over your brother-in-law."

"Now that's good news!" She held the bottle toward Mrs. Parker. "Give it to her. Chanel Five. I guess even a pretty kid like Cissie can always use a little Chanel Five in a pinch." She waved the bottle under Mrs. Parker's nose. "She could have used it tonight, maybe!"

"I guess she could have." Mrs. Parker took the bottle, sniffing at it. "She's at the Stork Club tonight!"

"You don't say!"

"I told you she came to her senses." Mrs. Parker's triumph won over her anger at Jenny. "Boys like Sidney don't grow on bushes, but the more I said, the less she'd talk to Sidney when he called her. Anyway it must have soaked in because tonight she went with him to the Stork Club!"

"I wish I'd gotten a good look at her, then I would have seen this Sidney." Sidney! Some Sidney, Jenny thought.

"He didn't come here. She's meeting him in Manhattan like last time. Sidney is a Manhattan boy, and you can't expect a Manhattan boy to come all the way out to Queens to get a girl and also bring her back home, Cissie says. Maybe in my day they did, she says, but not nowadays. Cissie's dolling up at this girl friend's apartment in Manhattan like last time. Some girls might not mind going in the subway in a strapless, but not Cissie. Cissie's a very particular girl."

"She certainly is," Jenny said. She saw from Mrs. Parker's expression that what she meant had crept into what she said and changed her tone. "A prettier girl than Cissie is hard to find. You give her the perfume and say—" Jenny stopped short. Did she want Cissie telling Milt she had stuck her two cents in again? She shook her head. "Mrs. Parker, it just occurred to me, since Cissie has come to her senses like you said, maybe I should stay out of the picture?" Mrs. Parker gasped and held the bottle out toward Jenny, who waved it away. "No, you keep it! Maybe you and me don't get to go to the Stork Club but we can use Chanel Five, too, right? Listen, there's life in the old dogs yet!"

Jenny let herself into the apartment softly and tiptoed into what had been Milt's office and closed the door. She sat behind the desk where Milt used to sit during office hours and thoughtfully pulled the telephone closer. The life that was in the old dog surged through her body; she wanted to do something, to make a move, any move, but she forced herself to think it out since she didn't want to pull another boner.

Should she call Sloane? Milt wouldn't be back yet from the Stork Club, don't worry! Should she call Sloane and say she had been thinking over the advice she gave?

Maybe Milt, she could say, was entitled to find out for himself the devil made mischief for idle hands? After all, Milt was no babe in arms. (Cissie was! Damn fool Milt!) She could tell Sloane that people had to learn from their own mistakes, that was the way it had to be. If Milt was out now getting himself mixed up with Cissie Parker again, wouldn't it be better to let him go to Europe the way he wanted? Wouldn't that be best for Milt? To go off to Europe and "forget"?

Jenny put her finger tip in number nine on the dial and let it click back. If she was Sloane's friend, of course, there would be no question. She put her finger tip into number nine again and let it click back. If it was Milt's wife she was loyal to, she should call Sloane this minute and say, go to Europe the way Milt wants, stay in Europe, keep away from Queens, but what did she care about Sloane, calling her up about Phil dying so young and leaving her alone this way and asking advice about how to help Milt's poor remaining years when all she wanted was to pump, pump, pump?

Jenny Krop was Milt's friend first and foremost. No matter what Milt did, she was Milt's friend, one hundred per cent for Milt even if he didn't know it, and the best thing in the world for Milt was what she had told Sloane. Forget Europe. Stay here and keep going. He'd go off his rocker otherwise! What did Milt know what was good for him! (Cissie Parker!) Phil would have gone off his rocker hanging around in Europe with nothing to think about but himself; nobody knew that better than she did!

Let Milt take Cissie Parker to the Stork Club on Sloane's money, Jenny thought. Phil had had his work and he had her to come home to, let Milt have Cissie to go to the Stork Club with if that's what he wanted. Let Sloane look out for herself. Let Cissie look out for herself, Jenny thought, the little fool, the little fool! First and foremost Jenny was for Milt and what she had told Sloane was for him, so he wouldn't go nuts.

So let it stand, Jenny thought, and gave the telephone a shove out of reach.

Then she put her head down on the cleared space on the desk and let the tears come.

At first Milt thought that Sloane must have found out about the Stork Club although he couldn't imagine how. It was almost 2 A.M. when he got in, he hardly made a sound opening the front door, but the moment he stepped inside the hall she called him from upstairs. At first Milton thought it was anger and jealousy that electrified her voice like that, and while walking upstairs tried to figure out whether, as he was tempted to, it wouldn't be the best thing to tell her about little Cissie. One Night Of Love. A man is only human.

She was standing in the hall outside the bedroom. "Milton, Milton, Milton!" She ran to him, taking his two hands in hers, gripping his hands hard, dragging him toward the bedroom. Her long straight hair hung down her back and her eyes shone like a cat's eyes, and there were white circles around her thin nostrils.

He would have blurted it out about Cissie but she didn't give him a chance. All he got out was, "I'm sorry—" and then, pulling his hands with her cold ones, she led him to the bed, practically shoved him down on it, dropped his hands, started pacing up and down like a tiger, shoving her hair back the way she did because the bouncing way she moved got it into her eyes.

"Sorry, Milton?"

All desire to cry on her shoulder about little Cissie was gone. "Sorry I got sore about Mrs. Austen and ran out on you. I shouldn't have gotten sore when you've been so sweet." She made an expansive gesture which was plain enough to put an end to his apology because it signified so clearly that his running out didn't matter; whatever it was, she wasn't sore about that. As a matter of fact, now he took a good look, it was obvious that whatever she was, it wasn't sore.

"Milton! Amory called right after you left."

He couldn't get it out, couldn't ask her. The exhumation was finished? Of course. Why not? With his luck?

"I had Austen tell her that we were both out."

Sweat broke out all over his body. "Don't be frightened," he said. "Boy, you look scared! I'll handle her. I'll call her."

"No, not until Monday. On Monday you can call back, but until then I have left instructions with Austen that you'll be out. Promise?"

Milton, wiping his forehead, nodded.

"Now, listen to me! This is what we must do."

"We?"

"Not her, not Amory, please listen to me, please don't interrupt! I had an inspiration while you were gone— Oh, Milton, I feel as if you had been away a hundred years! A brainstorm!"

It was as if a cold wind had touched his sweated body. "Who needs brainstorms? Everything is settled!"

"A miracle," she said, "a miracle! Oh, listen to me! I am not sure, poor lamb, whether you have any idea how much money there is, Milton— So much money! This is what came to me, darling. I'm going to take the Folsom money and we'll create a medical foundation with it! To be called the—oh, not the Folsom Foundation, darling, the Krop Foundation, the Krop Clinic, I don't know, only that its name must perpetuate your name and your brothers' name! Thousands, perhaps hundreds of thousands, will bless your funny name, Milton! A place where, among other things—this will be entirely in your hands —the best scientific minds work together to find a cure for high blood pressure, yes! Too late for your brothers, darling, or for you, I know, poor, poor Milton, but for the others to come?

"Milton—listen—establish fellowships, scholarships, what is the proper term? Establish fellowships for just such young men as you and your poor brothers were—if you wish, for boys from farms, or from your state, Connecticut—so that those coming after you won't have as gruelling a time as you had!" Breathless, Sloane waited, her two hands now actually clasped.

The last thing, positively the last thing he could have figured! He said, "All this while I had a couple beers and cooled off!"

Sloane giggled. "Oh, I cheerfully admit I have only the vaguest notion of precisely what I mean by the Krop Foundation, but I have you to fill out, don't I? You will know. Well?"

"Sounds O.K. to me. Good idea." No skin off my teeth, he thought. There's more there than I'd want even if I could have it. "Let's sleep on it." He got off the bed and began to peel off his clothes, which now felt sticky.

"Sleep!" She began pacing the room, thinking about it again.

The walls hemmed her in, the big window was too narrow for her vision. "I couldn't!"

"I can. I'm tired out." He thought of how much he would enjoy taking a shower now—in the kind of bathroom he was going to have.

Sloane stopped pacing. "I'm afraid—visitations leave one in a fine frenzy! Milton, you must believe this: this idea came to me because I was thinking of you and your mother and your brothers!"

"I appreciate that. Honestly, kid!"

"As far as it is possible for me to be, I was selfless to start with. The—the personal plum in the institutional pudding—the dividend—did not come to me until later. I honestly did not realize what this would mean to me—selfishly—until afterward. Two things. Two plums. Have you seen them yet, Milton?"

He was standing with his back to her, undoing his pants. He shook his head.

"Think!" She stamped her foot.

"You're way ahead of me. I'm too tired to think, it's almost 3 A.M.!"

"Two things, surely you must see. First, something which has been haunting me all along, Milton, and I mean that literally—haunting! The fact is that under the law a criminal may not benefit from his crime. All along it has haunted me that if Amory is not bribed—if she doesn't stay bribed long enough—Should she go to the police for an autopsy and get it and should they, to coin a phrase, darling, find me guilty, the Folsom estate would go to Amory! Not to me, obviously, but not to you, either. As my accomplice, you would not be entitled to it and Amory would make sure you were so cited! I assure you, the nightmares I have had of Amory getting the money—" She laughed. "Far more terrifying than me in the electric chair—because more unjust? But, darling, if it is in trust for a humanitarian project like ours, she won't be able to touch it! That's the law!"

"Where did you find that out? Whom did you ask?"

"Heavens, Milton—I read a book once! Also, there was a series of articles in the *Tribune* last year about foundations and trusts! It's so, it's so! With the money tied up that way, whatever happens, Amory will not be able to get her predatory paws on it. Now isn't that a fat, juicy plum for us out of the pudding? Isn't it? 'He stuck in his thumb and pulled out a plum' and said what a good girl am I! Oh, Milton, Milton, I get my plum because I was a good girl, I wasn't self-thinking!"

Her words weren't grandoise, but her flinging gestures were, and the way she flung back her head. Her quotations were from Mother Goose but she proclaimed rather than spoke.

"Listen to me! Joan of Arc! Sloane of Arc!"

"Sloane of Arc's a good one!" While he had been at the Stork Club with Cissie, she had been here talking to her voices, seeing visions. Saint Joan. Saint Sloane. While he had been dancing at the Stork with little blond Saint Cecilia, his vision, not stone, not stone at all, Sloane at all. Cissie.

"—carry out your wishes, precisely, to the letter. What do I know about medicine, but you do. And you can consult men of standing in the field. Enough there to occupy you every moment and, as far as I am concerned, if—if I'm spared, Milton, which is an odd way of referring to escaping execution for my crime, I'll devote my every moment to it also!" Her smile darted like a dragonfly. "Much, much better than hying me to a nunnery hence!" Milton would teach Saint Sloane. Milton would show her. Milton would staff the foundation, would make the rules, lay out the plans for the staff, for the building, consult with architects, et cetera, et cetera. "Oh, Milton," she said, "to be kept so busy with such work that your days and nights and thoughts are filled with it rather than—"

Days and nights— "Wait a sec," he said, "hold on—I'm just

a plain garden variety medic—" The sudden jolting acceleration of his heart was making it difficult to talk. "You'll have to get the best men in the field. I'll look them up for you and we'll lay it on the line for them and exit. We've got a date with a lady named *Queen Elizabeth!* A previous appointment, like they say, velly solly!" He had to wait for breath. "A-deck, cabin number—"

"Cabin number! Cell number, darling, because that's what it would be for you. You would be as much in a cell as any condemned man in Death Row! This is the perfect thing to do, Milton!" She began to move again, touching objects, picking things up, her brush, her nail buffer, her mirror flashing in the light as she twisted it in her hands, laid it down.

His eyes were filled with burning sweat. He was afraid to move, afraid he would fall, he was trembling so violently, so he stayed where he was, comically holding his pajama bottoms which his hands could not button. "You promised me. You solemnly promised me. Remember? Remember? Ruth! Whither thou goest— What I say goes, in other words, remember? What I want, isn't that what you promised me? Well, you can have this foundation or what have you, sure, why not? I don't want to be any millionaire on your mother's money. I can't be even if I want to be—remember?"

"Of course, Milton. Certainly I remember."

"This Krop doesn't want a foundation. I told you what I want!" He pulled the two ends of pajama tight across his quivering abdomen and knotted them together. "Sloane," he came toward her, "you can't do this. You can't renege. I told you what this means to me. Listen, this means everything to me. Put the foundation second. Later. We must go away first." He stopped a few feet from her because she stamped her foot.

"You must not be so childish! You can't run away from yourself, surely you know that? Running away to the Côte D'Azur, the Blue Coast, to a mythical Blue Coast, Blue Bird! The bluebird isn't in Antibes, Milton!" She pointed out the window. "The bluebird is right there in your back yard! The blue coast, the azure coast is here in Queens!"

Beg her, grovel, kiss her feet? She wouldn't hear him begging, only her voices. Saint Sloane! What did she care what he wanted, what he was going to have was what her voices said, a golden crown, a halo, and how could the things he wanted stack up against that? Milton sat on the bed and began to beat his open palms against his thighs. "You were kidding me, weren't you? You were just sticking a pacifier in my mouth to shut me up? All this about inspiration while I was out—you never intended for one second to do what you said!"

"You're quite mistaken." She came toward the bed but his beating hands frightened her a little, her voice became more supplicating. "Darling, I was swept off my feet by your story— I lost all my sense of reality to your Côte D'Azur dream of never-never land. It took Jenny to bring me to my senses!"

"Jenny?" he said, springing up, "Jenny?"

She said, "Jenny assured me idleness would be the worst thing possible in your position."

"I might have known. Jenny!"

"I called her, Milton, after Amory phoned because I couldn't think where else you might be. Oh, that doesn't matter, does it? The point is, Jenny knows—tragically knows—your situation —tragic firsthand knowledge of predicament—knows what helped your poor brother—"

"I might have known. I might have known. Jenny!"

"—idling on the Riviera the very worst thing you can do— You will thank Jenny someday . . . didn't have a foundation in mind, of course—her idea much more modest— Jenny said that after her husband died you carried on his work for a time at the clinic, some special clinical research in the problem he was involved in—Queens General Hospital—experimenting with his drug on some of the clinic patients there—"

"Jenny. Jenny. Jenny!"

"—says she has always known, since you first suspected you had the same constitutional disease her husband had, that the only salvation lay in continuing his work. A blessing if you could continue—not merely earning a living—not enough to merely earn a living—punch a time clock— Jenny blames herself for thinking of the years when there would be no one to help her and the children so that every dollar you could earn was welcome— She blames herself. She feels guilty and that was why she gave me this advice the moment you released her from her promise not to tell me about your—illness—until you told me about it— Where are you going, Milton?

"Milton, ah, don't go off and sulk!

"Milton, if you mean to sleep in the next room, you will not only have to make up the bed—and I most certainly will not help you—but Mrs. Austen showed me some moth eggs in the carpet and I sprayed it with that smelly stuff.

"Ah, that's better, Milton. Milton.

"I am sorry. I simply cannot stay on my side of the bed. Ah, Milton, there is one immortal line from Hemingway where the heroine says the hero has such a lovely temperature. (Or was it the hero said it to the heroine?) Well, I feel such a heroine tonight, Saint Sloane! I say it to my hero: You have such a lovely temperature! You're such a hero! Don't think I don't know it. Such a hero, but not unsung, you won't be unsung, Milton darling, doesn't that matter to you at all? Don't deny me your lovely temperature!

"Still sulking? Darling, only shopgirls and clerks dream of the Riviera. Antibes is really only one step removed from Coney Island, Milton! The Coney Island of the well-heeled, believe me. Common!"

He clamped both hands onto the edge of the mattress and pulled himself away from her clinging body.

"Milton, I warn you! 'Then worms will try that long preserved virginity.' " She flung herself at him, weeping. "Oh, forgive me, forgive! That was unforgivable, Milton! You make me so beside myself when you deny me! Don't lie there, beat me! I deserve it! Kill me, *kill me*, Milton!"

The desk on which Sloane's suicide note had lain that first morning was covered, this morning, with papers. Sloane, wearing the glasses she used for reading, was sitting at the desk. A tray with the coffee pot and a cup and saucer were at her right hand, the cup stained with the brew. When she saw Milton in the hall, she called to him. "Good morning, darling! I've been up since dawn. No sleep at all. It was more restful to get out of bed and just jot down my ideas than lie there and let them dance in my head—like sugarplums!" She waved the batch of papers at him. "These are my sugarplums, Milton!" She took off the reading glasses to see his expression. "All forgiven? Please, please, I need you to help me get the plans all down so that on Monday I can take them to my lawyer and get him started drawing them up. You must help, Milton—there's just today and Sunday to get it all down. And then, after the lawyers on Monday, I have a luncheon appointment with Jenny— What is it, Milton? No, my dear, it will take too much time, obviously, to get the Foundation rolling, and—and obviously, we need something for you to occupy yourself with. At lunch, Jenny is going to explain to your ignorant wife, in words of one syllable, exactly what you did at the clinic. What is it, Milton?"

Not in words of one syllable, he thought, in three syllables. Pla-ce-bo. "Nothing. It's nothing."

"Jenny and I are going over the technique by which you tested this wonderful drug of her husband's so that I can work side by side with you in your clinic!"

Jenny, he thought. Jenny, Jenny, Jenny! "Monday. Yes."

Chapter IX

WHILE Jenny waited impatiently for her son to open the front door of the apartment, Maureen showed her the step she had just learned in tap class. "Looka this, Mom!"

"If that boy went out! He knows perfectly well we have to catch that train. We would have been there already and had the whole weekend if you hadn't had your tap class this morning!"

"What will I do if there's no tap class out with Uncle Frank?"

Jenny pressed her finger on the bell and kept it there. "You'll become an opera singer." The door opened. "For the love of Mike, Bud!"

"For the love of Mike, Mom, I just happened to be occupied!"

"Maureen, go on now, you better pack your little bag and don't forget the toothbrush. Are you all packed, Bud?"

He nodded. "Mom, while you were out, Uncle Miltie called. He wants you to call right back. A matter of life and death!"

"What? Oh, you're just kidding! You trying to scare the life out of me, Bud? Maureen, I give you three minutes to pack.

215

Don't forget the toothbrush, you know what the teacher told you about cavities!"

"Aren't you going to call Uncle Miltie back, Mom?" Bud, watching his mother hurry to the bedroom, was genuinely startled. "Right away, he said."

"Right away we have to catch a train. We have to walk to the subway and go all the way to Penn Station, and get to Uncle Frank's. He's meeting the train." She had no intention of missing the train just to let Milt burn up the wire telling her what he thought of her nerve for doing him the best turn anyone could. Someday Milt would thank her, but not yet. "Look at those fingernails, Bud! You can plaster your hair down all you like, but it doesn't help much with black fingernails! Two minutes, Maureen!" Bud was like Milt. You had to do what had to be done and not expect to be thanked. "Don't answer that phone," she told Bud. "Let it ring!" He and Maureen, dressed in their best, looked at her with big eyes. "This isn't a doctor's office any more so we aren't obligated to answer the telephone and miss that train." If it was Milt again, it wouldn't hurt him a bit to stew in his own juice a while and simmer down.

"It will be nice getting into the country at that," Jenny said, sitting between her two children on the hard subway seat. "I don't know what they use for air in these subways but it isn't air. Nice to breathe air for a change."

Maureen became excited and began to ask a slew of questions about the country. It was hard to realize, Jenny thought, setting Maureen's brown felt sailor straight on her head, that her kids were city kids through and through. You didn't get to know about cows and chickens through your mother's milk. Bud was trying to act sophisticated about going away for the weekend, but he was excited too. Jenny had to turn her face away so Bud wouldn't see her grinning at some of the information about farm life he was handing out to Maureen. "Mr. Know-it-all," she thought fondly, "Mr. Man!" She thought about Milton who looked, if you asked her, quite a bit like the man in the Calvert ad there. The girl in the Life Bra ad could have been Cissie, too. It was then, just as the subway was approaching Fifty-ninth Street, that Jenny realized she could have been mistaken about Milt calling just to burn her ears off. It could have been that Mrs. Parker had told Cissie about the Chanel Five; from that it followed that Cissie, who need not be dumb just because she looked like the girl in the ad, could have figured out for her little self why Jenny had come upstairs with the present. Cissie didn't even need to have figured it out; all she had to know was that Jenny had been up there asking questions. Then—it was natural—Cissie could have contacted Milt some way and reported. It didn't take a genius to suspect Jenny might have guessed he and Cissie had been out together. The call could have been about that.

"Mom, when you were a little girl did they have tractors?"

"I'm not Methuselah, Maureen!" If Milt didn't know her well enough to know she wouldn't tell his wife a thing like that! No matter how often it should have been proved to him that when she did stick her two cents in it was only for his good, he still wasn't convinced. (She remembered, blushing, the nasty cracks he had taken at her!) Suppose Milt didn't take it for granted that if she had a date with his wife on Monday, it would be for his good only?

"Bud, when we live there, we'll get to go to the movies! Mom, Bud is just trying to tease me, isn't he, Mom? Mom, when we go live with Uncle Frank, we will too get to go to the movies, won't wc?"

"Don't worry, you will, although if you ask me it would be all to the good if you didn't. What do you get out of those movies but a lot of killings!" Jenny turned sharply to stare at the Calvert ad man again, searching his face as if he could reassure her that if she let Milt stew in his own juice over the weekend nothing much would happen. If Milt couldn't reach her and thought she was purposely not calling him back because on Monday she intended snitching to his wife about his little girl friend Cissie?

"Next stop, Mom!"

"I know, I know!" When there's a pile of money concerned, do I know? For sure? If Milt really thinks that by Monday the truth will be known? Money is the root of all evil, she thought, I don't know for sure. I didn't know he'd ever get involved with a girl like Sloane in the first place. I didn't dream he'd marry her! "Get up," she said, standing, swaying," don't forget the bag, Maureen!"

"Mom, the *next* station!"

"There's a telephone somewhere on this platform," Jenny said. "If you would stop asking questions and use your eyes and find the telephone we'd waste that much less time, Bud!" She slapped Maureen's clutching, nagging hand off her coat. "Stop hanging on me!"

Milt must have been hanging on the telephone. "I can't hardly hear myself think here, Milt. I'm calling from a phone on the middle of the station platform on Fiftieth Street. Milt, I don't want to yell and I don't want to spell it out, so will you just listen to me, Milt!

"All I want to tell you is that on Monday, when I see Sloane, it's to talk business, do you get me? Business," she repeated, "just *business*, Milt! Plain business, not monkey business, do you get me? So don't worry your hcad about Monday, Milt!

"I can't hear what you're saying, Milt, and it doesn't matter. I just wanted to get that point across. All I'm going to do Monday is bring Sloane Phil's publications and explain to her how you were carrying out the clinical experiment in Queens General. You got to lose yourself in work, Milt, you can't bury your head in the sand on some foreign beach like an ostrich, Milt. I know whereof I speak. Whatever you do on the side, Milt, that's between you and your conscience! I can't be any plainer," she said.

Milton ground his teeth. "Listen! Suppose you let me be plainer! It's all right. My wife is in a room a mile off. Nobody's here. I can talk."

"O.K. I have no intention of telling her about Cissie Parker, Milt. As I said, what you and Cissie do is your own business."

"What she does is her own business! You've got her on the brain, I tell you! Listen, I have to see you today or tomorrow. Before Monday."

"Now, Milt!"

"Shut up for a second, will you? Why are you calling from the subway?"

"For the love of Mike, Milt, don't you remember? We're on our way to my Uncle Frank's. I wouldn't give my final say-so whether I'd take up his proposition to live there without trying it, so we're trying it this weekend."

"Go home. I got to talk to you."

"Did I hear you? Milt?"

"Go home. I've got to talk to you before you talk to Sloane."

"Don't worry, don't worry! Why don't you trust me? I told you there's nothing to worry about. She's so sorry for you, Milt. She wants to help you keep busy so you won't brood over it. She wants to be intelligent about your work, so I'm just talking to her about the clinic, how you conducted the experiment, the placebo, stuff like that."

"Jenny, can't you understand English? To hell with that. I'll tell you what I'm worried about when I see you. Remember when we had it all fixed you should call and say Bud was sick and I should come over right away? I want you to use the same gimmick so Sloane won't know I'm talking about her to you, see? It's the same thing as that time all over again, only worse. You've got to turn right around and go home!"

"Milt, I can't! Listen, Milt, I'll see Sloane Tuesday, then, not Monday."

"No."

"You honestly want me to—"

"I want you to. Jenny, you're always yapping about how much you'll do for me. Well?"

"All right, Milt."

"I'll call you tomorrow morning when I go out for the Sunday paper, around ten, and make all the arrangements."

Jenny remembered, while she tried to get Maureen to stop her bawling, that Milt hadn't even said thanks. (The fact that Maureen was drawing a crowd made her even harder to stop than usual.) Bud didn't bawl, of course, but his disappointment over canceling even such a tame weekend made Jenny realize how little Bud had, how rarely he went anywhere. And his sports jacket was too tight in the rear now he had his shabby old coat hung over his arm, she saw that. Bud's rear in the tight sports jacket, as he walked away from his wailing sister and tried to be nonchalant, did it. Jenny could see no reason why Milt (who hadn't even bothered to say thank you) should expect her to disappoint both her orphaned children, maybe make Uncle Frank change his mind about letting them live with him. Milt hadn't offered her or the kids any of this money he was going to have. She simply did not see why she shouldn't at least go to Uncle Frank's as planned.

They could come home early tomorrow instead of waiting until Monday morning when Uncle Frank expected to be driving into New York with a load.

Jenny had forgotten how cold a bedroom could get in the country. Lying on a big double bed with a room to herself for a change, without Maureen in the bed in the opposite corner, singing or playing games or practicing dance steps lying down, Jenny decided the whole darn thing might be a fake. She simply did not believe now any more than she ever did that Milt was so concerned about his wife that she had to get out of the warm bed on a Sunday morning, into the cold room, and hurt Uncle Frank's feelings leaving the minute they arrived. Lying there, hearing the farm sounds outside, feeling twenty years younger, Jenny decided it could just as well be that Milt wanted her to call him and say he had to hurry over, Bud was sick, for reasons of his own! *Cissie*, she thought. Ten to one, she thought, this has something to do with Cissie and not with Sloane at all! Couldn't it be that Milt wanted to see Cissie again today? Couldn't it be he thought because his fool sister-in-law was so darn loyal to him, he could make a bigger fool of her than she was with his mysterious telephone calls and his arrangements?

Jenny felt hot all over, all of a sudden; sudden sweat tickled and stung her armpits, like hot flushes, only it wasn't a hot flush. (She wasn't Methuselah!) It was what happened to her when she felt that Milt was trying to put one over. It always affected her like that to think that Milt, Milt, felt he was so darn smart and she was dumb enough so he could put one over on her!

She had not yet told the poor kids that their visit was to be cut short and instead of driving in with Uncle Frank they would have to make the dreary trip by train and subway, so she didn't have to tell them she had changed her mind.

And she didn't have to tell Milt, either. Thinking he could use her and the kids, too, for his monkey business with Cissie! If he had only been a man and come out with it, Jenny thought. If he had confided her the honest truth instead of making up a lot of hogwash, she would do anything for him, kids or no. This way—it was Milt's hard luck. It would teach Milt a lesson, she thought.

When Milt went out to get his paper—ten o'clock—and

nobody answered, he would know she hadn't turned straight around and come back to the apartment. He would know that she had put her kids and what they wanted before what he wanted, and if he had the sense he was born with, he'd know that was only right and decent, and he'd know (Jenny stretched under the warm covers) that he couldn't fool her with his stories about how important it was and Monday wouldn't do.

Milt could like it or Milt could lump it. Monday would have to do!

Lady Constant looked with loathing at the untidy hotel room, impatiently kicked aside her fur stole which had dropped onto the floor, went to the bed where Day was lying nursing a spent highball and stood over him, hands on hips. "Day, are we going to the Thomases' or are we not?" She looked at the traveling clock on the bed table. "Pretty soon that will be a purely academic question, Day! On your insistence, I spent practically all yesterday in this damned room waiting for the good doctor to return my telephone call. I mort-u-ally wounded Aggie's feelings by backing out of the weekend to do so."

"Since he *is* the good doctor. Amory, since he didn't murder your mother as you now realize, call him again."

"It turns my stomach."

"Humble pie does that, sweetie."

"It's not that. I don't know, Day— Yes, I do! 'I do not love thee, Doctor Fell, the reason why I cannot tell.' Even if I was wrong about Mother, I still do not love thee, Dr. Fell!" Day shrugged and looked into his empty glass, not at her. "You are shameless, Day. It is shameless to crawl to him to get the money and you know it."

"I know it. You know it. Very well."

"It is not very well. Here Sunday is almost gone and I have

222

spent it calling him at intervals and being told he is not at home when I know damn well he is!"

"Once more."

"I will not," she said, sitting on the bed and reaching for the telephone. "Once more and then we go to the Thomases'?" She dialed the number. "I don't know why I put up with you, Day. This once more and then we will go to the Thomases' do, and I will figure some nice clean way of getting some funds— like going on the streets! They're not answering, Day!"

Milton heard the telephone and waited for Mrs. Austen to get it, but it kept on ringing. Then he remembered that she was up on the third floor, dolling up to go out, he thought.

On the third floor, Austen heard the telephone. It would be madam's sister again and she would only have to say nobody was at home.

Sloane, who was sitting at the desk, remembered that Austen had gone upstairs. She didn't want poor old Austen walking down; on the other hand, she couldn't concentrate with the telephone ringing. She pushed the chair back and found Milton. Whispering, as though Amory could hear her, she asked Milton to speak to Amory, to make her stop telephoning, put her off; then she ran back into the small sitting room again and slammed the door. (As if Amory could reach in otherwise.)

Milton answered the telephone as Sloane had asked him to because there was one chance in a hundred it might be Jenny.

"Hello? Dr. Krop?" Lady Constant nodded and, behind her, Day sat up on the bed. "I telephoned you on Friday, Dr. Krop, to eat humble pie. The results of the exhumation—the exhumation was finished on Friday—mother died of heart disease. If one can apologize for such a thing, I apologize." She waited but there was no response. "Obviously you weren't concerned about what they found or you would have called me back, wouldn't you? Well, that's what a clear conscience does for you!" Day squirmed around and showed her his grinning face. He touched the corners of her mouth, directing her to put a smile in her voice. She slapped his hand away. "Well, interested or not, you and Sloane are in the clear, Dr. Krop—and I am in the doghouse for having cost the borough whatever it does cost to do all the extensive and completely conclusive tests I have been assured they did on poor Mother."

"I see."

Lady Constant shrugged at Day and made a "now-what" face.

"Go on," he whispered. "Continue."

She continued. "I could go on apologizing but I am certain you'd be disinterested."

"A hundred per cent," Milton said.

Lady Constant could tell that he was about to hang up. "But, why, Dr. Krop? Why disinterested? Have you forgotten? When I last saw you—when I first and last saw you, Dr. Krop—you made me promise that I would telephone you the moment I made sure you weren't a murderer. Which is why I telephoned on Friday. You assured me that once I knew this, you had something you wanted to discuss with me. Well, now we may discuss it, may we not? I am right here in my little room waiting to talk to you about it."

"I don't want to talk to you," Milton said. "Not interested."

"He hung up." Lady Constant held the phone toward Day so he could hear, then put it into the cradle, got off the bed and took the highball glass out of Day's hand. "That's that. He doesn't want to talk to me. Not interested." She set the glass down near the clock. "Too late—but not too late for the Thomases'. Come on, Day, I've done my best, and that's that." She went to the littered dressing table. "I'm going to put on my face and when I'm through if you're not off that bed and ready to come with me, I'm going alone, and in that case, I assure you when I do go on the streets, you won't see a penny of it!"

Day said, "I don't understand. What happened? He was eager enough before."

"I have done trying." She renewed the faint blue line on the edge of her upper lids, drew back from the mirror, nodded and then began to gather up her handbag from the chair, her gloves from inside a red hat and her furs from the floor. Day reluctantly left the bed. He was the kind of man who could lie around in a suit all day, shake himself and be perfectly groomed; it was one of his talents.

"Just time to get to the Thomases' before our arrival looks like sour grapes. Fanny is allergic to being second-best hostess, the hostess with the leastest."

Milton did not even see Sloane standing a little way off from the telephone. She was wringing her hands and it was that which caught his attention; he looked at her sullenly.

"You hung up on Amory! You've made her angry with us!" She hurried to him, her face white. "Call her back, Milton! Apologize!"

He walked away from the telephone. "You call her up."

"I can't. I cannot. I would if it were possible, but I can't. Milton, please, you must see that it is dangerous to make her angry with us until the papers are drawn up! All this time you insisted Amory must be propitiated, you were all ready to run to her with my money to sweeten her— Now, when tomorrow I am going to the lawyer's, when in just a few days we will have all the money tied up so she can't get her claws into it, you do this!" She ran after him, caught at his jacket.

"Let go of me."

"Milton, you're angry with me now, but you will come to see I'm right. I promise you will, so please telephone her and smooth this over." She looked into his indifferent face and stamped her foot. "Don't be so stupid! Call her at once! Don't be such an abysmal fool!"

He didn't even trouble to repeat that he had disassociated himself from what she wanted.

"Milton, at dinner—when Austen goes out, we will go over all of it again. When we are alone here, I know I can convince you, but the whole thing will be jeopardized if you make Amory so angry she does something—" she made a gesture "—desperate. *Official.* I have been sitting all day yesterday and today trying to figure the Foundation out with no help from you. You've wandered in and out of this house all day long as if it weren't your concern more than mine! I can't stand it," she said, beginning to cry. "I can't stand it!" She threw her hands over her face. "It is for your sake, Milton—what is best for you, too, and you simply won't see it!" Then Sloane saw Austen's shadow trying to back away upstairs again, and that was too much. Sloane ran sobbing past Austen, upstairs.

Milton saw Austen, too, but what did he care? He walked away from her, away from her pursed lips, her shaking head, her frown as she watched Sloane run bawling up the stairs. What a setup it would have been, Milton thought. Perfect. *"I can't stand it! It is for your sake, Milton. What is best for you!"* Sloane screaming at him that she couldn't stand it. The old woman was certainly thinking Sloane was suicidal again. She would certainly have decided it was all the phone calls from the sister that set Sloane off. Perfect, and everything washed up once and for all because that bitch Jenny, that damned stubborn mule, decided for the last time to run things her own sweet way!

There was no reason for Milton to head for the front door and grab his coat and walk out of the house except that he had been facing that way, away from old Austen, from Sloane upstairs. It was not until he approached the iron gates that he had the flash, the inspiration. After that, he did not dare run until he was out of sight of any of the windows in the Haunted House. After one block, he had to slow down again because what was the sense of dropping dead on the street, what was the sense of that, now, so that it took him ten minutes to reach the drugstore, sweating and breathless.

"I am sorry," the desk clerk said. "Lady Constant's room does not answer, sir."

"She's got to answer. This is Dr. Krop. This is important, do you hear me? She's got to answer!"

"I'm very sorry, sir. I will ask the man at the door. Lady Constant just went out, sir. The doorman saw her go."

"Where did she go? Where can I reach her?"

"I am sorry, sir. Lady Constant didn't say."

"Ask around, ask around, maybe somebody there knows!"

"Excuse me, sir. I have another call."

Milton was suspended in space. He was hanging by his toes.

"Hello? Doctor? Are you there? I am sorry but nobody here knows. Can I ask Lady Constant to telephone you when she returns?"

"When will that be? When?"

"I have no idea, sir. What would you like me to do, Doctor?"

Go jump in the lake. Take a flying leap— But Milton was just too gone to say so; he leaned against the wall of the telephone booth with his eyes shut, the receiver still clamped to his ear. "Doctor?" he heard. "Sir? But, he's still on the line," he heard. "No kidding, you'd think it was my fault she goes out!" He heard the hotel noises, the switchboard operator, then he heard a man's voice, a different man's voice, and it was only the deadly fatigue that kept him standing there like that with the telephone clamped to his ear because he didn't realize at first that the man's voice saying "Hello? Hello?" was Lady Constant's pet bloodhound, sent, he was explaining, to pick up the trail of one of her damned gloves which she had apparently dropped somewhere between the taxi and her room. Just in time, just as the fellow was telling the switchboard that there was no one on the line any more, and who had it been, anyhow, that Milton pulled himself together and said "Hello" to her guy, the sister's guy, "Hello, this is Dr. Krop."

Chapter X

*A*MORY wondered why New York seemed a European city, why she had this persistent sensation of riding through a foreign city. Because death was a foreign city? "No," she said, "that isn't it. I must stop thinking about it," she thought, and, as if she were a schoolmaster, called herself to order and questioned herself. "Why does New York seem foreign?" Sitting on the low bucket-seat next to Day driving in his fire-engine-red MG, she kept her red-eyed swollen face turned away from him and tried to find the answer to her question at First Avenue, Second, Third, Lexington, as they drove up Fifty-ninth Street from the bridge. It was not that the early morning smells were reminiscent of London or Paris, the almost empty, somehow clean winter streets, the air as yet uncharged with the New York ozone generated by New York energy, but only that in Paris and in London and Venice and Rome she had often driven through the streets so early; in New York, she did not. When sightseeing, you often got off to an early start; in your home town, you didn't. Lady Constant turned to Day, to tell him this, to say something, to break the silence that was like the foreign city death, but it didn't come out and instead she heard herself repeating the only sentences she had been able to utter since Day drove out to Queens to pick her up and take her back to the hotel. She said, "He murdered Sloane. I know he murdered her."

Day once more repeated his part of the dialogue. "You have no proof. For God's sake, Amory, drop it, you have no proof."

Amory put her head down to hide the tears which started again.

"It's Monday morning, Amory. Last Friday evening, three days ago, you were given positive assurance—from the horse's mouth—that he did not murder your mother. You better drop it, Amory. If you start this with the police again, in the teeth of the sworn statement you just made to them which, according to you, you yourself, proved his innocence, and tell them that he murdered your sister you know what they'll do, don't you? Amory, for Christ's sake, don't you realize they'll send you to Bellevue psychopathic ward if you pull this sort of thing with the police?"

"Do you think I'm crazy, Day?"

"It was you who— You were his alibi, Amory! You were there!"

"He used me. He dared to make use of me as his alibi!"

"Amory!"

"I could kill him," she said.

"Now, that's nice."

"He killed my sister. I know it," she said. "He murdered her, I know it! You think I'm insane. So now he has you believing I'm insane, too!"

"He hasn't got me thinking anything. If I think anything, you're the one who is making me think it."

"He has you fooled. He has the police fooled."

"Everyone but our Amory! The whole world is out of step but Amory!"

"Day, let's stop and have a cup of black coffee," she said.

230

"Day, pull up at that drugstore there and let's have a cup of hot black coffee."

"It's closed. It's too early. It's six o'clock."

"You want to get rid of me. Now you want to get rid of me."

"Amory, stop it!" He pulled the car up to the curb. "We can talk here if you like. You don't need any coffee, anyhow. How many cups did you drink all night long? I think you're going on this way because you're jittery with coffee and the night up—what happened, and the police—Amory, darling." He turned toward her, the reddened eyes, the swollen flesh of her face, then, in charity, looked instead at his hand in its yellow glove which was jiggling the gearshift. "I'm sorry, love, but it all seems perfectly straightforward to me and that lieutenant told me it seemed perfectly straightforward to the police. Your sister killed herself. No one killed her. Certainly the part I was in on was straightforward! When you called and told me, I wasn't surprised. Shocked, yes. Oh, Amory, darling, I am shocked at your sister's death, but not particularly surprised. It was in the cards." His hand left the gearshift and touched Amory's thigh, but she jerked it away and kept her legs as far away from him as the limited space of the car would permit. (An MG was wrong for death!) "Amory, I'm sorry, but this sort of thing seemed in the cards after what he told us about her last night. It was bound to happen. She was for it, darling!"

Day remembered how gone the doctor had sounded on the telephone when by the merest accident he spoke to him. Washed up. At the end of his rope. Amory saw a killer, a murderer, but he had spoken to a worn-out, pathetic guy with an insane wife. Of course insane. A wife who wouldn't talk to her own sister. (Which Amory knew.) A woman who wouldn't let her husband see her sister, so Dr. Krop had to ask him to ask Amory to telephone at seven-fifteen exactly so that Dr. Krop might tell his insane wife that it wasn't Amory calling but his other sister-in-law whom Sloane did not mind him seeing. How could Amory believe that the man had planned an elaborate fool-proof murder with herself for the perfect alibi when it was just by the merest chance, just because Amory had lost her gloves en route, that she happened to be in on it at all? How could Amory believe that the man had planned to use her as his alibi for a planned murder when ten minutes before he spoke to Day, he had refused to have anything to do with Amory? ("One hundred per cent not interested," Dr. Krop had told Amory, ten minutes before.) Day asked Amory how she could believe that she had been set up to be the doctor's alibi when his being there at all had been as chancy, as haphazard as it had been?

"I don't know," she said.

"Unless you think he knows you well enough, darling, to be pretty damn sure you'd lose something or other en route to the Thomases' and send me back for it so that I'd happen to pass the desk while he was hanging on the other end of a wire?" Amory did not smile. Well, it was a feeble effort even at a happier time. "If you hadn't dropped your glove, angel, you would have been out of his reach and wouldn't have known about your sister's suicide until this morning." Except for her lips which trembled, Amory's face was set and stubborn. No impression. "Darling, come on, try to be impersonal about this. What would you think if I came and told you this story about two strangers —about a murder in the newspapers—if you didn't have a down on the doctor—Dr. Fell?"

When Dr. Krop had begged him to ask Amory to telephone at seven-fifteen, he had said he would ask. Beg was more like it. Amory had been, Day thought, fanatically determined to cut off her nose to spite her face and had needed a heap of persuasion to put the call through, to give up the party at the Thomases', go back to her room and, at seven-fifteen, make the second call, the one to her old home, when Dr. Krop had addressed her as "Janey" and said he would be right over to attend to the child who had been taken ill. "Amory, last night when Dr. Krop finished telling us about it you certainly believed him."

"No."

"That's a downright lie, Amory! You did believe him last night! Come on, it was a perfectly straightforward story that no one could help believe. Didn't he come over to see you that first time to tell you the same story, didn't he say at the time that he wanted to tell you about your sister but what with me hiding in the bathroom, snatching those perfectly harmless sea-sickness pills, telling him to his face that you were having your mother exhumed, you can hardly blame him for not telling you. Nobody could have told you anything then and you know it. You *told* your lawyer, didn't you, you made *him* tell the medical examiner? You were hell-bent on your sister and her husband having murdered your mother between them and wouldn't have believed the angel Gabriel if he came down and told you that your mother hadn't been done in!

"Oh, be fair, Amory—if you think back to that day you'll realize that he was hinting at the state of mind your sister was in. Didn't he ask me how long I knew you? Whether you were —tetched, too? He had to wait until it was proved that he had nothing to do with your mother's death." Her lips had not relaxed their stubborn set at all. "You do agree now that your mother wasn't murdered—your mother, anyhow? Amory, you have to believe that much. It's a fact! Amory, love, anyone who believes that a woman was murdered after the medical examiner boys tell her she wasn't is out of her mind. I'm referring to your sister, I hope, and not to you, love!

"Amory, last night when Dr. Krop sat in your room and told you that Sloane insisted she had killed your mother when your mother died a natural death, you agreed she wasn't—quite sane. Dr. Krop, who is a physician, after all, and possibly has had more experience along these lines than you have, believed it. I believed it and so did you, last night. He came here to ask your help."

"That I do believe!"

"Help for your sister, Amory, and you know it. He came hurrying here last night out of concern for your sister and for no other reason. Amory, remember what he looked like last night —the way he paced the room—how he sweated trying to get it across? He knew you wouldn't like hearing such a thing about Sloane— I've known a couple of instances myself where the family refused to believe in the insanity of a close relative. The family—you know, ducks, like husbands—they're the last to know. No, I'm serious, families often refuse to believe there's insanity until it's too late. He mentioned that, remember?"

"I remember everything," she said with emphasis. "I remember he was bright enough to know you'd read Freud in the Modern Library and kept consulting you. A real psychiatric consultation. I remember!"

"He is bright enough to feel unsure of himself, that's true. He was kind of humble, Amory. I thought it was touching. Perhaps he'd done the wrong thing? Perhaps he should have forced her to go to a psychiatrist—twenty-five dollar edition, not Modern Library! And if you think it's easy to insist a patient see a psychiatrist— Well, it isn't."

"Sloane was herself. Not insane."

"I've heard that before. 'Aunt Emily is eccentric, that's all!' Amory, how often have you spoken to your sister in the past couple of years? This man, this physician, lived with her, remember. Don't say you remember everything that way again! Don't be so damned stubborn, Amory. And don't be such a damned snob because that's what it comes down to."

"No."

"Yes. Yes. Yes. And don't think because you had a crush on that fisherboy in Antibes— You're a snob about the middle classes, Amory, don't kid me. I like him."

"Because he consulted you. You're no psychiatrist."

"And you're no detective." He turned on the ignition and started the little car.

Now Amory laid her hand on his knee. "Day, I'm sorry. I hardly know what I'm saying, Day. He was convincing last night. I almost believed him when he told about Sloane being—ill— Oh, Day, certainly I believed him enough to trot along with him when he explained his sudden change of mind about not having anything to do with me for Sloane's sake. I did believe his change of heart about not telling Sloane about the exhumation. That first he believed it would send her over the edge if she found out I was so convinced that she and he between them had murdered Mother that I'd gone to the police, and that later—that night—decided that the other way round would be better for Sloane. It made sense."

"Kindness! Certainly it was kinder to you not to tell your sister you had gone ahead and bullied the authorities into doing the examination. You can't tell me it would have made your sister fonder of you to know about it?"

"Fonder, Day, or—generous?" Amory's fingernails rasped on Day's trousers, drawn taut over his knee. "Never mind. It could not have made Sloane fonder of me to know I'd gone to the police. I agree. I agreed when he said so last night. I agreed that since—according to him—Sloane was in even a worse state than ever before, it was worth a try to go and tell her the truth. I agreed with him that Sloane being—fonder—of me or not didn't matter any longer and that perhaps finding out about the exhumation might act like—"

"Shock therapy, darling."

"Shock therapy. I agreed last night that if I told her what I had done and then produced proof that the whole thing was in my imagination and in hers, it might shock her back to herself."

"Anyone would have agreed," Day said. "That's my point,

Lady Constant, love, you were rational last night, you must be rational now, that's all. Your mother died a natural death. We know that, your sister believed she killed your mother. We know this. Now this is insanity, darling. We aren't taking his word for this, Lady Constant, are we? Your sister left a note in her own handwriting addressed to you saying that she was taking her life because she had killed your mother; therefore, I really can't see any reason to disbelieve, when we find your sister dead, that, as she herself wrote—she did commit suicide."

"No, he killed her," Amory said wearily. "I know he did."

"Seth" Thomas was really beginning to believe that the reason Amory Constant had reneged on Fanny's party last Sunday was because she wanted to avoid him. (Because she was attracted to him she wanted to avoid him. Because she was scared of Fanny. Everyone knew what a terror Fanny was.) Otherwise why had it been so easy to see her tonight? Otherwise why was he in Amory's bedroom at 7:30 P.M.? He nursed the martini room service had sent up because when the martini was finished he would have to make a move—or else why was he up in Amory Constant's room? Since it had been so absurdly easy to see her, it must mean the rest would be easy. He held the remainder of the martini up to the light. He said to Amory that they could never make them dry enough for him.

"I beg your pardon?"

"Dry enough. For me." Why else was she just standing there with her martini untouched, just staring at him? "Bottoms up," he said.

"I beg your pardon?"

Under her steady stare, "bottoms up" became an impossibility to repeat. It was just one of those things you said, but once you really started thinking about the words—

Lady Constant, holding her untouched martini, was thinking

236

that, in a nutshell—and nutshell was the *mot juste* because insanity was the whole thing in a nutshell. Nutshell. Pun, she was thinking. Sloane was not insane. I know he killed Sloane and I am not insane and Sloane was not insane either. Just eccentric, eccentric, eccentric. Trick, trick, trick, that was it, wasn't it? There was a trick. There had been some trick. Sloane certainly believed she killed Mother when Mother died a natural death but that doesn't mean Sloane was insane. She could have been tricked, somehow, into believing she killed Mother, couldn't she? And then she could have written a note saying so. How, Amory thought, how tricked? Aloud she said, "I don't know!"

"It's just an expression," Seth Thomas said. The more he thought about it, the worse it became: *Bottoms up!*

Amory set her martini down on a table and walked to the window. Seth Thomas' face called for attention by its extreme ruddiness and because his eyes were protruding, so Amory turned away and looked out of the window. She wondered how Sloane could have been tricked into believing she had killed Mother, but did not know, only that Sloane had been tricked, was not insane. On the street, below, a woman suddenly pulled away from her escort's guiding hand. The woman down there was angry. She would not—something or other. Go with the man. The man spoke to her, spoke to her, gentled her, then slipped his hand under her arm, bent her arm upward so he could take her elbow and tricked her, tricked her into going along with him again.

Seth Thomas said, "Where? What? You're sore at me!" She was moving swiftly from bed to chair to dressing table. It was really remarkable how she knew that under that pile she would find an alligator purse, under another mess of stuff, her gloves, how she knew her coat had slipped, or been flung, beyond the bed there, or her hat—it must be a hat, although she did not put it on—was folded between the pages of *Vogue*. It was even more remarkable how from such a mess, with no apparent effort, she could come out the knock-out she was. "If I've stepped out of line, I apologize," he said.

She walked right by him and would not listen to him in the elevator, or in the lobby, and on the street he began to be afraid he would make himself conspicuous, so he just stood by while she got into a cab as if he were seeing her off rather than being left flat.

The friend who shared the *pied-à-terre* with Day would not have been pleased to see where Day settled himself after letting Lady Constant in. Day had pulled the huge circular green marble coffee table directly in front of the television set and was sitting on it, rather like a frog on a lily pad, with his knees pulled up to his chin and his bare feet planted on the green marble. He had discovered, he told Amory, that with his feet resting on cool marble, he did not mind steam heating so much; it was his great discovery, he said, and then fixed his eyes on the television program.

"Day," she said, "Day, will you turn that damned thing off and listen to me? I came here to tell you something."

"To tell me something. You don't ever ask me, do you? You tell me. Over and over. Leave that set alone! Lady Constant, I live these days for Thursdays and Groucho; I'm a simple-minded fellow and I adore Groucho. I am not a master-mind like you, Lady Constant darling, smarter than the whole police department of the Great City of New York. Leave it alone!"

She turned the volume control down and came to the coffee table, kneeling on the floor, resting her elbows on the marble. "As you said, Thursday—and you haven't called me since Monday morning. Four days."

"I'm sure you've been very busy, Amory. You can't have had a free moment, playing Sherlock Holmes all over the place.

Haven't you been snooping all over the old place in Queens with a magnifying glass looking for clues?"

Amory shoved her sleeve up so that her arm was bared against the marble. "No. I haven't tried to go there. There wouldn't be any clues. Why would he leave any clues?"

"Clever Lady Constant! But haven't you interviewed the servants?"

"There's just the old cook. Why should I bother with her when obviously he has her in his pocket, Day; what would be the point trying to get around her? They let me see her statement and that proved whose side she is on! According to her, she was present when Sloane wrote a previous suicide note and besides that she once heard Sloane threaten to take her life and heard him trying to keep her from it. Stuff like that. Oh, she knows on which side her bread is buttered, that's obvious! And there was another cook too, testified; he's a grand man with cooks whereas if you knew Sloane— She was like Mother, modern servants don't take that kind of treatment kindly. Compared to Sloane, he'd be the servant's delight, cook's delight. Of course he would be, Day! No, I haven't seen him and I haven't heard from him."

"You do surprise me, dear! You've done *nothing?*"

"I've thought," she said. "I can't stop thinking."

"Using the little gray cells, Lady Poirot, eh?"

"Stop it. I have thought, Day." She told him about eccentric-trick and watched his response eagerly, but he only got off the lily pad and went to find a bottle and two glasses and then offered her a drink. "No, thank you, Day. Well, that's what I came to tell you." Eccentric-trick. She remembered Seth Thomas and wondered what had happened to him, was he still in the hotel? "I must go now." She looked helplessly around the room. "Will you do me up the back now, Day?"

That meant collect whatever she came in with. Today, Day thought, there wasn't as much to collect as usual. She had stayed in one place, kneeling there, kneeling but stubborn, a stubborn piece. He put down the bottle and the glasses and found her gloves, her pocketbook and, shoved under the marble table, the little hat, one of the little hats she always carried with her but never wore. It was the little hat undid him. "Don't go, Amory!"

She walked to the television set and turned up the volume again.

"Amory, you're wrong to think it is because he holds any purse strings there might possibly be going, honestly you are. My dear ducks, the man is in the clear with the police! They haven't even held him! You must let him go, Amory; let it go. Do, ducks!" He bent forward to kiss her but she turned away. "Amory, you haven't got anything. You've decided he tricked her into thinking she killed your mother. You decided. You have no idea how anyone could be so tricked. You're exactly nowhere, darling; let it go!"

She shook her head. "That's all I have. I've gone over it and over it and over it."

He took back the gloves, the purse, the little squashed hat. "Go over it again, then. Sit down, love, and we'll go all through it again, once and for all. Start from the beginning, when you reached the house, about ten-thirty, wasn't it? No, set the mood first, then it will come out more—emotionally correct. You left your place trusting him. More or less," he added quickly, because she flicked her head restively. "He asked if you'd go home with him and confess to your sister about the exhumation and what it had shown and you said you would. I was here, Amory love, I know that at the time you were—reasonably sure—he had your sister's best interests at heart."

"Do you think I've forgotten that?" she said, sitting down, jumping up. "Do you think I've forgotten for one instant that I trotted along with him—trotted obediently along like his puppy dog! Like a sheep being led to the slaughter, which is literally correct as it turned out. Trotting along so I could be the witness for the defense!" She stamped her foot.

Day pointed to the narrow foot she had just stamped. "Don't you see, Amory? Don't you see?"

"That I resent it? I do resent it! It is the last straw that he should choose me to be there and be his witness! It is ignominious—that besides killing my sister that man should do that to me!"

" 'That man!' " Day pointed to the foot again as if had spoken. "That 'that man' should plan to deceive the entire police force is one thing, but that he should also pull the wool over Lady Constant's eyes!" Day grabbed a handful of his hair and pulled. "You're going to see that he rues the day he thought he could pull the wool over Lady Constant's eyes—as well as murder her sister, aren't you, Lady Constant, darling?"

"All right," she said, "that's enough, Day."

"Enough? It's everything! It's all there is! It's your whole case against the poor fellow! No, that and your own guilt which you are projecting—"

"Projecting!" Amory ran to the bookshelves on the fireplace wall and grabbed the first thick book and flung it at Day, who stepped aside in time but did not dare turn to see what she had hit. He let her fling the next book and then caught her hands and took the third volume from her, glancing at it.

"William Blake, Amory, not Sigmund Freud, and never mind." The book throwing had taken the fight out of her and he could lead her to the round marble table and help her step on it, and wave her grandly to sit down. "Tell me from when you got to the house, Amory, go on." Now he knelt before the table, and gently pulling her left foot so that her leg stretched toward him, removed first the narrow shoe and then the filmy stocking.

Amory steepled her fingers and stared down at them, as if she were praying. "It is not my private mania, Day, and he did kill her and I was there and I must have seen something which would prove it—could prove it—only I don't know what." He was nodding for her to start and give him her other foot. "It was too dark when we got there for me to see, but I could see the grounds had been mucked about somewhat—that was therapy for Sloane, he said. He'd tried to keep her occupied gardening. Nothing was changed about the house, though. It was the same outside. It was the same inside. Gog and Magog—the two suits of armor—were still one on either side of the door— No therapy for Sloane inside, just death." She waited a moment to quiet down. "He called Sloane the moment we entered the house, but she didn't answer. Of course she didn't answer! He stood at the foot of the stairs and called her again, but she didn't answer. He thought that she must be upstairs. There was no question about his wanting me to come right up with him and find her, Day—he did! We had discussed whether he should prepare her for me or whether I should burst in on her. We had decided I'd better burst in on her and not give her the chance to lock herself in somewhere— She'd refused to see me until then, all right. I was the one who wouldn't go straight up with him. I balked at the last moment, Day— I'm being completely accurate, you see that? He asked me to come upstairs with him so that he didn't plan any time by himself to fix anything. I was afraid—I don't know why."

Day put his hand around her ankle. "You do know why, darling. You were afraid to face your sister."

"Very well. I was afraid to face my sister. I stood there and said he should go up first, after all, and tell Sloane. He started to protest, then he shrugged and went upstairs."

"What did you do when he was gone?"

"It wasn't more than a couple of minutes, Day. What did I do? I'd come home. I looked at home—into the ghastly taipan room, the dining room— The table was all set, same awful table, same awful dining room, same china, silver, everything the same;

242

so help me God, Day, the same cold Sunday evening meal we used to have. Cold roast. Salad. Time standing still that way, nothing different but little me. You know. Then I heard him coming downstairs. I could tell immediately—from his steps— the way he was walking—that something was wrong up there. One can, you know." She closed her eyes and shivered. "I came out into the hall and he walked right by me to the telephone. It's on a beastly black carved monstrosity two-thirds down the hall. No extension upstairs, of course. He went straight to the telephone and called the police. I crept after him down the hall —petrified. When he finishing dialing, while he was waiting for the phone to be picked up in the police station, he handed me Sloane's note."

"Amory: I am committing suicide because I poisoned Mother. Sloane."

"Sloane's notepaper. Sloane's handwriting—"

"In fact, Sloane's suicide note, darling."

She glared at him, then closed her eyes again to visualize it. "Then the police got on the wire. He said who he was, where he lived— 'Dr. Krop. My wife has just committed suicide. No, don't bother with that—'"

"Ambulance."

"He told them she was dead, all right, that he was a physician. She had been dead from one to three hours, he said. I read the note and heard him saying this at the same time, and I started to run upstairs. The door to Sloane's old room—next to my old one—was open so I knew she was there. She was lying on her bed. She looked smaller, shrunken, but that is because one has become unaccustomed now to such huge beds, I think, Day. She had on a black dress. Her hair was up—more or less. Sloane never had her hair cut and never had a permanent wave and never— Eccentric." Trick. Trick. "Sloane was completely dressed, only her shoes were kicked off. Her clothes and the bed-clothes were very much—disarranged—" Lady Constant pressed her fingers hard against her eyeballs, then steepled her fingers again and held her head propped up straight. "He followed me upstairs when he finished the call to the police. He stood next to me in the doorway looking at Sloane. He started moving away. I asked him where he was going and he said just going to wash his hands. You know—but I didn't understand what that meant at the time. I made myself look at Sloane again."

"Punishing yourself," Day said gently.

"I couldn't take the punishment. I couldn't be alone. I began to panic and ran down the hall to the bathroom and yanked at the door—it wasn't locked—and ran in. I startled the bejesus out of him; he threw me out. 'Out! Out!' When he had recovered somewhat from the shock, he came after me and we went downstairs to wait for the police.

"The police didn't come right away," Amory said, "or maybe it never seems right away with police and doctors and stuff— It seemed forever; anyhow it was long enough to start eating supper. Then the police came and after they went upstairs and decided Sloane had taken poison, they were pretty startled to find us eating the same food she'd had—not from her plate, of course—her plate was clean. I was the dirty-plater in the family always, not Sloane; she couldn't bear to see anything wasted, even when we were children. It started early with her."

"Don't get started on that, Amory, love—if you go off into your childhood, you'll get this all wrong. You were saying that the police had been surprised to find you eating the same food that your sister had eaten."

"When the police were surprised—annoyed—I realized— For a few minutes there I had some sharp stabbing pains in my belly, and expected to drop down dead any moment."

Day nodded. "Psychosomatic."

"Whatever you call it, but he—Dr. Krop—explained to them that I had been on the verge of collapse. We had to wait. He had decided that if I didn't have something to do, I'd blow up, so he had made me eat. Therapy! He had eaten, too, you see, the same food I ate. We know now that the cook had the same food as well. She always had her dinner before going off. Dr. Krop was more interested in explaining what Sloane had taken (he was pretty sure, anyhow) and why it had been in his medical bag left around when he knew of her suicidal tendency. This stuff—I forget the name—was the only poison he had around and he had it for Sloane's sake. It is both a poison and an antidote, it seems. Sloane had been doing very little sleeping and he had been giving her sleeping pills. She was just as much afraid, according to him, of dying of an overdose of sleeping pills as she was anxious to die. Both, I mean, but not at the same time. One or the other. He had to keep the stuff around so that she would take as many sleeping pills as she needed—so he could pull her out if she overdosed."

"They do that," Day said. "The ones who want to kill themselves have this pendulum thing. Because they want to die they are more afraid that they will. They swing to either extreme. That figures."

"Ironic," Amory said. "Ironic is the word, I suppose, that she should take this particular stuff— He had warned her that it was a double-edged sword, of course. I know, it was his duty to warn her. Anyhow, he was pretty sure that was what she took and it was. What she took."

"Did you see the stuff, Amory?"

"He showed it to the police. I saw it, yes, a white powder—like salt."

"Now you've told me the whole thing?"

Amory nodded, leaning toward the table edge and Day's face to see whether she had told him something she had missed, then straightened up again.

"You haven't omitted anything and you haven't added anything? Well, what did you see? What did you see that would prove he killed her?" She didn't know. "Amory, was there any time during the evening that he acted peculiarly? Did anything he did stand out of context, I mean?"

"No. I have gone over it and over it, but it seems to me he acted perfectly—correctly. He was exactly what he should have been."

"The only thing that strikes me, darling, is the eating. I am now leaning over backward to make a case out for you, Amory. Doesn't it look as if he wanted to make certain the police knew she wasn't poisoned at dinner? I mean—his class is strong for decorum—at a time like that, his wife just dead, urging you to eat?"

"I know, but he is a doctor, Day. Surely your psychiatry books tell you that it is natural to feel hunger at times of extreme emotion—maybe one uses up something or other, or it shoots something or other into the bloodstream which makes one hungry. Anyhow, I know I was, hungry and shaking and faint— No dinner, if you remember. Certainly the food had no taste—'The salt hath lost its savor'—is that from the Bible or Shakespeare? The salt had lost its savor, all right, I remember everything tasting 'stale, flat and unprofitable,' Day, but I ate. I wolfed, in fact. But, oh, Day—what you said—'middle-class decorum'—in spades, Day! You see until I realized that I had trespassed on his sacred middle-class prejudices about what is simply not done, what I couldn't quite understand was the way he acted when I barged in on him in the john. I told you that, but, Day, I don't think I've ever seen anything quite as scared and horrified as his face. It struck me. It was absolutely convulsed—much more shocked than he had been the time in my room when I told him I thought he'd murdered Mother. Much more! But probably it was much more shocking to have a lady walk in on you than to accuse you of murder."

"Lady Kinsey."

"Literally, of course, I didn't walk in on anything— He was just standing there about to flush the toilet—Mother's house still has one of those chain things. One arm in the air— It seemed so preposterous, that expression on his face at such a time for such a thing, that I became hysterical and screamed at him, 'Oh, flush it, flush it and let's get out of here.' You know, Day, 'Flush your prudery down the drain,' 'I don't want to be alone,' something like that, I meant. He was struck absolutely speechless, one hand in the air like that, and then he started screaming for me to get out, get out. 'Out, out, damned spot'— Dr. Macbeth, caught in the act of trying to flush down the evidences of foul murder!

"He threw me out and standing outside the door—I could *not* be alone—remembering the expression on his face, how he *hated* me for walking in, I was scared, Day. Day—you— How many times you've said one's expression—wait—one's expression speaks truer than words, only not as loud as. And he looked— he looked *daggers* at me, I tell you. He hated me! There can only be one reason! I tried to apologize later. I couldn't figure out why, if it did that to him to have anyone barge in, he didn't lock doors."

"No need. Barging in isn't done. It would never have occurred to him that you would."

"I wondered why he hadn't made it plain—but he thought he had, Day. He had told me he was going to wash his hands, that is a polite euphemism, I suppose. I certainly thought he meant wash his hands." She was smiling faintly, then she frowned. "Washing his hands of Sloane's blood, that's what he looked like, as if I had caught him in that act."

"Now, Amory, you shocked the fellow down to his grass roots!"

"Not only him, Day." She smiled again. "That night when I was telling the policeman what happened, and he asked me—the same thing you asked: 'Do you remember anything out of the way?' I told him about the john episode, about how—flabbergasted Dr. Fell had been, and you know what, Day? The two

247

young cops turned bright red and the older one began to cough. They were just as flabbergasted—they were just as shocked! Apparently they would have thrown me out and given me the same look Dr. Fell did."

"And that's all? Then you have nothing, Amory. There is nothing." He stretched out his arms and stood up. When Amory was off the marble table, he took her in his arms. "Bury the hatchet, darling. Let the poor man know you forgive him what he did do—which was not to get her psychiatric help—"

"You want me to suck up to him for the money!" Pulling away from Day's embrace, Amory stubbed her toe. She stood there, frowning, holding her foot in her hand, staring at Day, then she smiled. "Oh, all right! I'll do as you say, Day. I'll bury the hatchet. We will be bosom companions, he and I!" Gingerly she put her foot on the floor again.

"Amory! For Christ's sake, Amory, you're still at it! You don't want to be decent—" She was moving away from him and he could not see her face. "What do you want now? What do you think—?"

She was at the television set. She turned up the volume control and listened, it appeared, to Groucho, then nodded and whirled around.

"He just said what I want, Day! Your Groucho! Did you hear him?" She tried to imitate the famous voice, "—the magic wordie, that's what I want! 'It's a common word—something you might find around your house— Say the magic wordie and get—' I'm through thinking. Yes, I'll call Dr. Fell now, and I'll see him and listen to him and perhaps, sooner or later, he'll say the magic wordie and then I'll know!" She turned and pressed a kiss on the television screen, then turned it off. "Where's your phone, Day?"

Chapter XI

MILTON thought of the Haunted House as being finished but it didn't look finished. Even though the house was going to be torn down and the stuff in it, except for what Sloane had offered to the museum near Boston, was going to the Salvation Army, it looked as it always had and what was worse as if it would always stay that way. (As if he couldn't order it torn down.) He had, however, pulled the most comfortable chair in the small sitting room out into the hall near the telephone. At least he could be comfortable while he kept an ear to the phone and an eye on the front door and the other eye and ear on Mrs. Austen as she went about her business. So far nothing had happened. Nothing would happen. Only one week more not counting tonight. (He would go to bed early and then it would really be only one week more. He looked at his watch. Eighty-twenty; he would go up to bed around ten.) When the telephone rang, Mrs. Austen was in the kitchen cleaning up after dinner and he was making the final "arrangements" with Joe Dinton. (*Final* arrangements meant finished. *Finished.*) When the phone rang, Joe Dinton stopped talking and his pencil point stabbed into the dollar sign on the "estimate."

249

Milton called toward the kitchen, "I'll get it, Mrs. Austen, don't bother." He had already explained to Joe why he was camped in the hall like that. He didn't want to go to the bother of hiring strange people to clean up the odds and ends before the place went but that meant a lot of work for the old lady, so, to save her strength, he was picking up the telephone and seeing whoever came to the door. "I'm getting it, Mrs. Austen!" Milton wet his lips before he lifted the receiver. Every time he had to talk to anyone these days he did that. "Hello? Hello? Oh, Lady Constant!" As he listened to her he kept moistening his lips.

After he hung up, in the few moments of respectful silence Joe Dinton obviously believed was due a conversation between the bereaved and the closest blood relative of the deceased, Milton went over in his mind what he had said to Lady Constant: "Now, that's very nice of you, Lady Constant." (To want to see me.) "I appreciate that. It takes a load off my mind. Frankly, I didn't have the guts to call you. What do I mean by that? My God, I've been scared you might be blaming me for not preventing what happened, so I certainly appreciate your calling, but if you don't mind, I'll take a rain check on that." (She wanted to come here and see him. Like hell. She and the old lady crying on each other's shoulders. Like hell.) "Well, I'm up to my ears here. I'm working every minute on the Foundation—the plans for the Foundation Sloane wanted. You know about that? I'll ask Sloane's law firm to give it all to you, they're the ones handling it, but where my medical knowledge can help— The Foundation was your sister's dearest wish and believe me it's got me all tied up in knots here. I want to get my part off my mind before I go." ("Where are you going?" Lady Constant had asked.)

"You didn't know? No, I guess you didn't. I'm sailing on the *Elizabeth*, the next sailing, Friday a week. That was the sailing Sloane got us and from sentimental reasons—because she arranged it all— We were going together. We didn't have any— wedding trip— Well, I'm going alone, because I want to get away, you can understand that, Lady Constant, my wanting to get the—excuse me, out of here. All I want to do is get away and forget, that's all I can do now." Then he had paused and then quick, as if, if he thought it over he might not say it, "And, excuse me, Lady Constant, but—it's not only I'm tied up in knots here with the Foundation but—you remind me. You remind me. It's natural." (He had given a kind of laugh.) "All I want from you, if you'll excuse me, is what you just did. I appreciate that. I appreciate your telling me you don't blame me— but besides that—I'll take a rain check." (He had looked at Joe here and Joe looked and nodded as if it was natural he should feel that way. Anyone would think it was natural.)

"Now that's real nice of you. . . ." (She said how about a bon voyage party then.) "But I'm not in the mood." (Joe had looked as if this was only right—for him not to be in the mood.) "All I want is for that boat to leave the pier, that will be all the bon voyage I need, no champagne and caviar, thanks all the same!" (She had said that if he didn't see her once, didn't let her bury the hatchet, she would go on thinking that he blamed her, but he had the answer to that.) "Lady Constant, you don't need to worry about my blaming you. You'll be hearing from Sloane's law firm one of these days and you'll see I didn't blame you. I'm doing the fair thing, Lady Constant, you're getting what you said was yours and more; you'll see. The bulk goes to the Foundation, of course, because that's the way Sloane wanted it, but I'm doing the right thing by you. They'll give you the details if you want them, I guess; ask her lawyers." (The lawyers had told him his demands were modest. Modest.) That had been about it. Milton wet his lips again, satisfied, and turned back to Joe Dinton and the "arrangements." "That was my dead wife's sister, Lady Constant."

Joe ran his pencil down the estimate sheet. "She'll be in the first car with you and your sister-in-law, Mrs. Krop."

"Let's skip it, Joe. I haven't mentioned the funeral to her; you heard me."

"You haven't mentioned—"

"I don't even know if she knows the police released the body yet. You heard me, this is the first I contacted her. You heard why, Joe, I've been thinking maybe she held it against me that her sister took her own life." (Joe was shaking his head. For the first time, Joe disapproved.) "She should attend, you mean? It would look funny? O.K., then, Joe, but wait a minute—" (Wait a minute. Think. Look before you leap, Milt!) "It's bad enough she'll have to mingle with me, Joe, but I just can't see her with Jenny—Mrs. Krop! You know my sister-in-law, Joe? Well, take my word for it those two are like oil and water. O.K., Lady Constant goes with me and Jenny goes in the second car." (That set all right with Joe. The more cars the better as far as Joe was concerned. Milt had had to convince him that because it was a suicide—a disgrace, no matter how you looked at it— he wanted it as private as possible.)

"O.K. by me, Doc. You and Lady Constant in the first car and Mrs. Krop in the second Caddy."

Milt wet his lips. "Wait a minute, Joe—" Joe held his pencil in the air. "There's someone I don't want to go to the funeral, Joe, and here I'll want your help. It's a—it's one of those things, Joe!" He pointed toward the kitchen. "The old lady, the maid —I don't want her attending. Now, this is it—I don't want her thinking it's because she's the help. You know me, whatever I am, Joe, I'm no snob. I'm a physician and I don't want the poor old biddy exposing herself in this weather. I want you to put it to her, Joe—from an outsider it will sound better. How many people do you know were the next ones buried because they insisted on attending funerals when they should have stood in bed? She can pay her respects right here. Before you leave, put it to her strong, Joe." Milton tried to laugh. "You're not the Doc, maybe she'll listen to you!"

"Glad to, glad to—and talking about taking care of yourself, I'm glad to hear you're going away for a trip, Doc, you don't look well. In my business you see plenty of suicides; you can't stop them, believe me. If they gotta go, they gotta go, as the saying is. You shouldn't blame yourself."

"I'll be all right once I get on that boat, Joe." Why the sudden urge to see him? Bury the hatchet, she said. In my head, Milton thought, sour coming up in his mouth. I have no head, he thought. I can't think again. I still got to be prepared—one more week to go, but I can't think. "Once that boat leaves the dock, I'll be O.K., Joe!" I've got to leave that dock. I've got to go. I'm not going to let her stop me now. If you gotta go, you gotta go.

"What a boat, boy," Joe said.

"You took a trip on the *Elizabeth*, Joe?" Everybody but him. Milton. Milton was going to go and she wasn't going to stop him now. But why the telephone call? Bury the hatchet. In my heart. Any news from Lady Constant is bad news. "Did you happen to get to the Riviera, Joe?" I'm going to get to the Riviera. Steps of living stone. Bikini bathing suits. Air like a fin. "Where did you go, Joe?"

"Me, Doc? To the pier on West Forty-sixth Street, that's where I went! When I came home I said to the wife, well, we took a trip, Amy, a tour. We took a tour of the *Queen Eliza-bath*, I said, we're different. Other people take tours on her; we took a tour of her! We got to be different, I said."

"A tour of the *Queen Elizabeth*?"

"Don't you get it, Doc? They let you go on when she's in port. It's good advertising, I guess. They got little maps of her for the sightseers in the Cunard Line place. What would Columbus think of a boat so big you need a map to find your way around, Doc, huh? Anyhow, we took a tour of her, as I said.

Nobody stopped us. The works, the whole shebang, top to toe, port to—I know it isn't rear! We saw all the fancy fitting and that stairway they have, and the dining room and all." He cupped his mouth with his hand and lowered his voice. "As a matter of fact, we have a little souvenir ashtray in our place right now that says Queen Elizabeth on it!"

Milton's hand thrust itself into his pocket and felt the vial of picrotoxin he kept there all the time, for no reason. Just because. (There would be no reason. Nobody was going to stop him this time.) He said to Joe, "Port to bow!" His thumb ran over the top of the vial, as if he were testing its edge. "Dining room and all? Port to bow?"

"That's it! Sure the dining room, the dining room is one of the sights, and we covered the whole shebang. We covered the waterfront."

"That's something, Joe, that's sure something!" He took his hand out of his pocket. "Joe, while I'm telling Lady Constant about the funeral—" His hand stretched toward the phone but he did not dial. "I want your opinion on this—" He told Joe about the *bon voyage* party she had wanted to throw and which he had turned down. Well, on second thought, should he turn it down? She—Lady Constant—said she wanted it to prove he had no hard feelings. He'd been thinking she blamed him and she'd been thinking he blamed her. Well, he asked Joe, who would it hurt? Why not, Joe, right? Now he had a witness, Milton thought, who could, if it ever came to that, swear that he, Milt, had only agreed to a little party—just the two of them, of course, a big party certainly wouldn't be the thing—because he didn't want to hurt his dead wife's sister's feelings. "You heard me before, Joe, I figured she might be holding the suicide against me, but it turns out (the way she talked), it looks as if she had a guilty conscience because of the way she was in Europe on the Riviera all these years leaving my wife here with the old lady holding the bag! Could be, right? And so, if I let her see me off, give me this little party, it will be a way of saying I don't blame her, she shouldn't go blaming herself. Tell me what you think, Joe?"

While Joe—who was the gabber of the world—told him what he thought, Milt went over it. (Wetting his lips. Making his hands stay out of his pocket, away from the vial.) If the worst came to the worst—in half an hour she'd have a bellyache. (By that time she would be off the boat. He would see to that.) Within three hours she would be gone. (If worst came to worst. If he had to.) Of course they'd autopsy. Of course they'd think of him. (If worst came to worst.) To think and to prove were two different things entirely. Of course they could radio the *Elizabeth* and get him; he knew that. Even if it took longer than four and a half days to get around to thinking of him they could get him. Europe wasn't the wilds of darkest Africa; he knew that! But to pin anything on him would be a different story. "My God, I didn't want to see her. I didn't call her up and ask her; she asked me." (Ask Joe Dinton, he was present.) Her party, not mine. She supplied the food. (Ask Joe.) How would I give her poison? Prove it. Her hamburger, her beer. The salt from the dining room of the *Queen Elizabeth*. How did I poison her, prove it. No, Milton thought wearily, it wasn't if he did it once, he could repeat it. (He nodded at Joe who was gabbing away at a great rate.) It wasn't that he figured it would be so easy, it was just the best he could do. (If he had to.) "That's just what I thought, Joe. It's the decent thing to do." (It's the only thing to do. She's in port, now, the *Queen Elizabeth*. Get a map like Joe had. Go to the dining room. Get the shaker. Yes. For insurance, just insurance, that's all.) He dialed the hotel number. "That's just what I was thinking, Joe."

Day was sitting cross-legged on the floor watching Amory perched on the coffee table, putting on her stockings. He had just about given up trying to fit together the pieces of ceramic tile which Amory had broken when she flung the book at him. It was one of the Picasso tiles and he couldn't tell what went where.

Amory stuck her leg out in front of her and stared at it. "I guess having the Folsom Mausoleum is a lucky break, Day, otherwise—Sloane being a suicide—" She set her foot on the floor. "Day, where *is* unhallowed ground?"

"I'll come with you, Amory."

"Oh, you hate funerals," she said.

"Everyone hates funerals. Don't be ridiculous. Amory, I don't want you to go alone."

"My dear! Now are you becoming suspicious of your driven lamb?"

"I liked it better when he wouldn't see you. I preferred it when he gave you the back of his hand, darling."

"And the money."

"And the money. He shouldn't *want* to see you, Amory."

"He didn't want to, did he? I forced my attentions on him, didn't I? Dear Day, this is going to be Sloane's funeral, what could happen?"

"Nothing, I suppose. The *bon voyage* thing worries me."

"It was the best I could do and it's going to be my party, you know. I'm supplying the food, didn't you hear? I was ready to run to caviar and champagne but he prefers beer and hamburgers—and that was the only objection, Day. He didn't in the least object to its being my party, I mean. I'm ordering the hamburgers from Hamburger Heaven and they'll be sent down to the boat just in time, *intact*, so there can't be any hanky-panky there, can there?" She scratched her calf. "If I'm found dead, Day, you won't need to analyze the food." She remembered about the Dramamine. "Golly, I'd have to be damn suspicious to have anything analyzed any more!"

Day kissed the top of her head. "I shouldn't like finding you dead, darling."

She frowned. "I didn't like finding Sloane dead." She was silent while she put on her other stocking and fastened her garters and stood up and gave herself the necessary smoothing down.

Day said, "Amory—let it be!"

She shook her head. "Uhuh!"

"Drop it, Amory, please!"

"Uhuh. I'm going to see him, ducks, before he leaves and this party is the best I can do. Remember the magic wordie, Day!" She flung one arm out toward the television set. "Going, going, Day! The funeral and the party—last two chances for the magic wordie, Day!"

The ceremony, such as it was, was over. Amory was sitting in the black Cadillac into which Dr. Krop had just handed her, his fingers firm on her elbow. It seemed to her that she could still feel his fingers on her elbow and she rubbed at her black sleeve. It nauseated her to feel his fingers on her elbows and to take her mind off it she read the sign over the glass canopy: J. P. Dinton Funeral Home. Toward the rear of the sidewalk, in the shelter of the canopy, she could see a thin scatter of black coats and hats who were vaguely recognizable as distant relatives, Folsoms, Drubakers, Vanderpeels—all of them obit readers, evidently, because how else would they have known this was Sloane's funeral? (She remembered Sloane's twelfth birthday party then. Mother had not let Sloane take off her brace and she had scarcely been able to eat anything. Poor Sloane.) At the front of the sidewalk, Dr. Krop was arguing with some woman who had stepped up and tried to climb into the car. Amory watched.

Jenny knew that Milt thought she was trying to push in where she wasn't wanted, but it wasn't that. Since the suicide, she had certainly not pushed in, had she? The reason she was standing here now, insisting that she go to the cemetery in the car with them, was because of the way he had kept his eyes on the Duchess all during the ceremony. The Duchess looked like her dead sister but—different. *And how different!* What a whale of a difference a lipstick, rouge and an eyebrow pencil could make. And that woman was poison for Milt! Look at the way he had held her by the elbow and rushed her into the first car with him as if she was his best friend. That woman was bad news; from the first minute she'd heard that voice coming over the telephone, asking questions, nosing around, she, Jenny, had known her for the bad news she was— Look at her sitting there in the car waiting for Milt to come into her parlor, snug as a bug in a rug!

He is furious with her, Amory thought, pressing closer to the window of the car. Why is he so furious with her? She could not hear what Jenny was saying, but her gestures were easy to interpret: She wants to come along with the two of us. He does not want her to come with us and therefore is furious at her persistence. Obviously he could wring her neck, but why? Day would probably say, "Oh, for Christ's sake, Amory, because the good doctor wants to climb out of his class and a woman like that, so unmistakably what she is, places him. A woman like that is *de trop* in his new life and that is that."

But *would* Day say this any longer? Day hadn't wanted her to be alone with the good doctor. Day said he preferred it when the good doctor gave her the back of his hand. Perhaps, Amory thought, watching Milton, perhaps Day wouldn't attribute his desire not to have a third person in the car to anything as innocent as social climbing. Once the car started, she would be locked into the tonneau of the Cadillac by the motion; the tonneau in motion was a black steel room. She would be locked in here alone in this black padded steel room with Dr. Fell during the long ride to the cemetery. The chauffeur would be behind thick glass, his eyes would be front, on the road. She recalled, trembling, the etiquette of funeral processions. No cars would pass them because one did not break up funeral processions. It was not done.

Amory, fumbling, her fingers stiff and clumsy with panic, thought that the door was locked already, that it was already too late; but it was only fear which locked the door. She could get out. She was out, on the sidewalk with both Dr. Krop and the woman staring at her.

The woman, she found, was Dr. Krop's sister-in-law, Mrs. Krop. "But Mrs. Krop should be riding with you, she is your side of the family," she heard herself saying, as if this were a wedding. "Mrs. Krop takes precedence over me, I believe." But he would not allow his sister-in-law in the car with them and Amory would not go alone with him. Impasse. The three of them were locked on the sidewalk; then Amory saw Dr. Krop's face disintegrate. He gasped and swallowed. He wet his lips.

"O.K., O.K.," he said, shouting, "you two go together, O.K.!"

Amory noticed how for one moment he turned to his sister-in-law and searched her face longingly. Longing for what? For reassurance. Reassurance about what? Reassurance that it would be safe to have the two of them locked together in the black steel padded room of the car. Amory turned to the sister-in-law but she seemed to be merely bewildered by the sudden switch. As Dr. Krop began to move off, leaving them together, Mrs. Krop stretched out her hand to stop him.

"Milt! Where you going, Milt?"

Dr. Krop didn't answer his sister-in-law and the two of them watched him hurry to where an old shabby woman was standing alone. Both of them saw the doctor take the old woman's elbow and hurry her toward the big car. Amory could feel the pressure of his fingers on her own elbow and knew how insistently he was bundling the old woman along. His face was so set, his determination was so obvious that both she and the sister-in-law stepped out of the way. The old woman was, as far as possible, hanging back and both Amory and her companion had a good look at the old face as Dr. Krop unceremoniously shoved her into the first Cadillac, got in after her and, ignoring the chauffeur, pulled the door to. Amory turned to Jenny. "Well! Mrs. Krop, is that Dr. Krop's mother?" Jenny shook her head in a dazed way. "His aunt? Who?"

"I'm Milt's only blood relative here; that old lady is the maid."

"The maid? Sloane's maid? I didn't know she had a maid, I thought there was only the cook."

Jenny was blinking after the first car. "That's what I said, the maid."

"But I thought the cook was in his pocket—"

"You thought what?" A second Cadillac drew up, a chauffeur stepped out and held the door for them. Jenny climbed in first and when Amory followed, she repeated, "You thought *what?*"

Amory was trying to collect her wits. She had imagined such a different kind of servant, the kind Mother used to call "ungrateful, impertinent, overdressed chits," but this one with the decent black, the thick silk stockings, the Queen Mary hat, was old school tie—yet the look she had given the doctor wasn't old school tie one bit! For a servant of that type to glare with such unmistakable hate at the master meant something. Yes. Yes!

"What do you mean, 'in his pocket'?"

"Oh, nothing."

"In his pocket" means on his side, Jenny decided. On Milt's side. If she didn't mean something she'd have told me what she meant.

"I didn't think anyone but a relative could glare that way at anyone, that's all."

"A glare," Jenny said, but she was shaken, too.

"Now why do you suppose Dr. Krop chose to ride with the cook, Mrs. Krop?" The car moved off smoothly.

"Why not? Milt's democratic. This happens to be a democracy, in case you didn't know." Her uncertainty made her belligerent.

"Oh? Well, cook certainly didn't want to ride with him, did she? Perhaps cook isn't democratic."

"What kind of crack is that, Lady— Look, if you don't mind, I'm democratic and that Lady business just goes against the grain."

"Won't you call me Amory, Janey?"

"Jenny is the name, plain Jenny, and over here when we want to find something out we ask the person who knows. Ask the maid these questions, not me."

"Now that's an idea," Amory said. She was positive from Jenny's tone that she was wondering about the hate on the old woman's face and that she had noticed how frightened of her Dr. Krop had been. Amory badly wanted a cigarette but she didn't want to offend any prejudices Jenny might have. She wanted Jenny to talk, to say the magic wordie. "Why do you think? Why do you think she hates Dr. Krop, Jenny?"

"Ask her."

"I don't think Dr. Krop is going to give me the chance." She sighed. "Alas."

"Alas! My God! You're very curious, aren't you?" Curious— on the edge of the seat with curiosity, Jenny thought. (Me, too, she thought, only Milt's a damn fool not to tell me!) Then it occurred to her that the Duchess might be curious also about why Milt wouldn't let her, Jenny, ride along with them. "You'll have to ask the maid about her, but in case you're interested, I can tell you why he didn't want me riding with him."

"Do," Amory said. "Please do."

"There's no need for you to make a mystery about that. Milt's sore at me, is all. Because of Sunday. When she died. Milt gave me hell, let me tell you. I'm in the doghouse, but good! You'd think I was responsible personally, you'd think I personally killed your sister. Didn't he tell you about it?"

"No."

"I thought he might have told you— It would be like Milt to blame it on me; everything is Jenny's fault! Anyhow, he told me. Plenty. You see, we had it fixed for me to call him Sunday morning. I was supposed to say my Bud was sick and I needed Milt. The thing was he wanted to come and talk to me and Bud was the excuse. He wanted to talk to me about your sister —he was worried, with reason, it turns out! I'm an R.N. in case you didn't know and in the past I've had plenty of experience on the psycho wards, more than Milt, really, and he wanted to ask my opinion before he went over her head and called in a psychiatrist. As we know now your sister had the delusion she had killed your poor mother and Milt couldn't knock it out of her head, no matter what. I didn't know this was the way it was with her until after she killed herself, of course. Well, it so happens that weekend it was all fixed for us to go to Connecticut, the kids and me. It was all set—you know how kids set their heart on things? Well, I couldn't bear to spoil their good time —they don't have many, let me tell you—so I didn't get back in time Sunday and that's why Milt's so sore he wouldn't ride in the same car with me. So now you know." She looked out of the window. The car stopped for a traffic light and a middle-aged woman standing at the curb whipped her hands behind her back as she sighted the hearse. Jenny thought of her mother who had had the same superstition. She sighed.

"So that is why he didn't want you riding with him!"

"The one time I fail Milt— The once I put my kids first before Milt a thing like this happens! Isn't that life for you? Naturally, if I'd known if I had an inkling— Was I supposed to know that on that particular day your sister would—" She turned to the Duchess for acquiescence, for comfort, and the Duchess was staring, her mouth had dropped wide open. What did I say? Jenny thought; she pressed her palms together. I didn't say anything much. Of course not.

Day had insisted that it could not possibly have been murder because a murder would have to have been planned for that evening. Day had insisted that since we knew my being with him then had been such a matter of pure chance that Sloane's death couldn't have been anything but suicide! So was this the magic wordie? Was *substitute* the magic wordie? (How right I was to come! Amory thought.) Substitute, understudy? If she had merely been this Jenny's understudy, if she had merely been a stand-in for the sister-in-law, called in at the last moment only because at the last moment the star—the star witness—had failed to show up for the performance? Amory's eyes were caught by the movement of Jenny's hands, the way she was grinding her palms together, and she knew that if she wanted to hear any more she better reassure the poor creature. "You mustn't blame yourself, Jenny. You and I both know that nothing and nobody can prevent an insane person from doing away with herself, if that is what she wants to do." Amory knew, from the way Jenny threw her head up, from the worried flicker of her lashes, that she had not put this strongly enough, that she had woven doubt into her words, but because she was so sure now that she was getting somewhere at last, that was how the sentence came out.

The sentence did have Jenny worried. "If" is a big word, Jenny thought. "*If* that is what she wants to do," the Duchess had put it. "Nobody can prevent an insane person from doing away with herself *if*—" That wasn't saying her sister had been psycho and that even if Jenny had been there she couldn't have saved her! *If!* Jenny saw that the Duchess was spying on her grinding palms and pulled out her handkerchief and blew her nose so as to give her hands something to do. She didn't like the way the Duchess was waiting, almost smiling. Waiting. Say something: Milt. What a good guy, always, from way back. Respected. How good to her and the kids, always. The Duchess looked as if she was chewing on something she, Jenny, had given her, and as if it was good to the taste. Jenny went over what

263

she had said: There was no mystery why Milt hadn't wanted her in his car; he'd been sore because she hadn't helped out his wife. That was nothing against Milt, that went to Milt's credit or she wouldn't have said it. She couldn't explain to the Duchess why the maid hated Milt so she had told her why Milt had her, Jenny, in the doghouse. Surely that could only prove to the Duchess how much Milt had wanted to help his wife? For a moment Jenny wavered, wondering miserably whether she shouldn't have stood in bed, kept her two cents out of it, but then, sneaking another look at the younger woman from behind her busy handkerchief, she decided better her here than Milt here; any man sitting in a car next to that one in that kind of black dress, that kind of hat and shoes, seeing those legs, wouldn't keep his mind on his business. Better her than Milt, Jenny decided, putting the handkerchief away, snapping her purse closed. She began to talk more easily. "If anyone could have stopped your sister doing what she did, Milt was the one. Milt took care of her like a baby, hanging over her all the time. He didn't stir from her side. I didn't know why, of course, and I admit I was kind of sore about it, you know how it is. We'd always lived so close and then when he married your sister— pffft—I didn't see him from one week to the next! It hurt me that he dropped me and the kids like hot potatoes. I admit I thought maybe now we're not good enough for Milt, marrying into the Four Hundred, but I should have known my Milt! He couldn't come round the old place because your sister was psycho. I tell you Milt's the world's best! Everyone loves Milt!"

"Everyone but the old cook," Amory said softly She leaned toward Jenny. "Ah, Jenny, you saw it! You were shocked, too. You wondered!"

"Wondered! The maid was the one testified about how your sister tried once before, did you know that? Did you see that? She was the only one living in the house with the two of them and if she hated Milt she could have made him plenty of trouble, but did she? She did not! She was the one wrote a sworn statement how your sister wanted to end it all, how Milt stopped her, et cetera, et cetera. Do you think if she had anything against Milt she would testify like that?"

"She would testify to what she had seen," Amory said. "She would tell the truth as she had seen it."

And that was another funny way of putting it! Oh, God, Jenny thought, she believes Milt killed her sister, murdered her sister in cold blood, that's what she means! And what do I believe? Jenny wondered. No. She told herself, no, he hadn't. Never. Not Milt! She left a suicide note, didn't she? She killed her own self because of thinking she murdered her mother!

And because of Cissie, Jenny thought. She killed herself because of Cissie! Jenny deliberately turned toward the car window and stared out to keep from talking before she thought it out. Should she tell the Duchess about Cissie? That Sloane had found out about Cissie and jealousy had been the last straw that broke the camel's back? Plenty wives, *plenty* wives killed themselves because they found out one fine night there was another woman. Should she tell the Duchess about Cissie so that she would know posi*tive*ly her sister took her own life? Or should she make her take pity on Milt by telling her how long he had to live? But if she told about Cissie and the blood pressure, wouldn't she think that was the motive? That Milt had wanted out? That he wanted her sister's money but without her sister because he was in love with Cissie and had only so long to live?

Amory said softly, "A penny for your thoughts."

Jenny shot around and faced the Duchess formidably. "My thoughts are you must have bats in your belfry. My thoughts are it must run in the family!"

Amory laid her narrow hand in its fine black glove on Jenny's black glove. "But I will never kill myself," she whispered. "Remember that whatever happens. I will never commit suicide!"

Jenny finally found Milt standing at the gate of the cemetery, still holding onto the old woman, and hurried to him. Milt saw Jenny but his eyes passed over her as if she was nothing to him, stared right through her and made her so furious that she came right out with it even though she meant to keep her mouth shut while the old woman was around. "If you're looking for the Duchess, Milt, she's gone back in a Rolls-Royce—1935 model—with some tatty old ladies. More royalty, no doubt! Crowned heads, no doubt!" She smiled at Mrs. Austen in a democratic way. "Anyhow, I figured they were crowned heads because their hats fit so peculiar—I figured they must have their royal crowns on underneath."

"Very funny," Milton said. He waved and the big black Cadillac pulled up and he opened the door and handed Mrs. Austen in.

Jenny tugged at Milton's sleeve. "They made her ride with them, Milt; she wanted to ride with you, I think—but not because she's so crazy for your company, Milt! You're the one crazy if you think that."

"I'm not crazy." Milton tried to pull his sleeve free and get into the car.

"I'm coming with," Jenny said. "Don't try to stop me this time, I'm coming with. I got my reasons, Milt!"

He decided it wasn't worth another scene, shrugged and let her step into the car.

Milt made no move, so Jenny introduced herself to the old woman. The doctor's sister-in-law. What an awful thing. Awful. A young woman like that, her whole life in front of her.

Mrs. Austen said, "Yes, madam. Yes, madam."

"I always think though it's worse for those left behind. Milt —Dr. Krop looks terrible!" Take pity on him. Don't hurt Milt.

"Yes, madam."

If there was any guarantee she'd never say anything but "Yes, madam, no, madam," to the Duchess, but then she'd probably talk plenty to royalty. "I'll bet the doctor hasn't had a square meal since it happened."

"He has not, madam. No."

"It's only to be expected," Jenny said hastily, catching Milt's glare. "He should get out of that house more. You know what? Milt, Mrs. Austen certainly hasn't had time to fix a meal today and a funeral takes it out of you—it would be a charity to Mrs. Austen if you came to my place for a meal, Milt." She leaned across and smiled at the unsmiling Mrs. Austen. "I know how a woman is—if she can have a cup of hot tea and a slice of bread and butter and go to bed that's O.K., but not with a man, isn't that right? Well, I have a nice pot roast all fixed with browned potatoes just the way the doctor likes it. Maureen will have the table set—Mrs. Austen, at a time like this, isn't it so? There's nothing like having kids around to cheer you up. They bring it home that life marches on. The doctor has been a father to my kids, Mrs. Austen. They'll be beside themselves to see their Uncle Miltie again. So, is it settled, Milt? You ask the chauffeur to drop Mrs. Austen at your place and then come home with me?"

"No."

"No! I talk and talk and 'no'! Maybe that's why! Milt, if I shut up? That's a bargain, Milt, I'll shut up if you come. The doctor made a good bargain, right, Mrs. Austen?" Not knowing what to answer to that, "No, madam" or "Yes, madam," the old lady turned to Milt and again Jenny saw—it stabbed her to the heart—that she hated Milt like poison. The minute she looked at Milt the hate showed up. It wasn't difficult to keep quiet after that look, and anyhow, the ride back to her place was much shorter than out from the funeral parlor. No longer decorously trailing the hearse, the Cadillac could show what it could do. When the car stopped, Milt—in such a hurry to get rid of her, Jenny thought—opened the door, not even moving! "You got to see me to my door," Jenny said. "What kind of manners will

Mrs. Austen think you have, Milt!" She said it like a joke, but Milt knew her well enough to know she wouldn't budge unless he escorted her.

As they approached the apartment house, Jenny turned and looked at the old woman sitting stiffly in the car, her back like a rod, her black hat straight across her head. Jenny said softly, "Why does she hate and despise you, Milt? What does she have on you?"

"What?" Milt said. "*Her?*"

"*Her.* Why does she hate and despise you? It's peculiar. She swears all kind of stuff to the cops that shows them you're kosher, Milt, strictly on the level, but she hates and despises you." There was that smell to Milt, she got it so strong now because he hadn't been around for so long; she drew in her breath. "If I was the only one that thought it was peculiar, Milt, it wouldn't matter." She nodded vigorously. "You got to listen to me, Milt." All she got out of him was a shrug of his shoulders that she could go ahead and talk. "Milt, I didn't push myself in with you because I have no pride. I have pride, I have pride, but not where you're concerned, Milt. I didn't ask you home for a pot roast. Because of *her.*" She pointed toward the car. "The Duchess noticed also."

"You don't say? Noticed what? For your benefit, Jenny, once and for all, and for Lady Constant, also—it just so happens that Austen always was and always will be a sourpuss. She just happens to have been born with a sour pickle in her mouth. Listen, I've seen her around for four years at the clinic in Queens General off and on and I never yet saw her crack a smile and neither did anyone else."

"She hates you, Milt. Why?"

"Why? She hates the whole world."

"The world will get by, the question is you."

"I'll get by. By the nineteenth I'll be out of the house and so will Mrs. Austen."

"Does she know that?"

"Of course. She's just staying on until the nineteenth."

"Then she'll be out on her ear?"

"Out on her ear? I'm giving her two months' salary. Out on her own two feet. She's no relative of mine."

"So she's no relative, so what? She's an old woman, isn't she?"

"She'll get back on Social Security or Old Age or whatever she had before."

"And she's not a well woman, either."

"The clinic will handle that."

"Milt, Milt, what's the matter with you? Maybe that's why she gives you those looks—if looks could kill! Because maybe, as the Duchess said, she told the truth as she had seen it, but—but, Milt! She helped you plenty, don't you forget that, and now you've got to help her, not throw her out on her ear! You've got to make that old woman love you like a son!" The reason the Duchess was taking the look Mrs. Austen gave Milt so big must be that it was all she had to go on and he wants to leave the old lady flat so the Duchess can ask questions to her heart's content! *The Duchess thought Milt murdered her sister!* "Believe me, Milt, the last thing you should do is leave the old lady flat in New York City. Where's her home town?"

"I don't know. Canada, somewhere. What do I care?"

"You care, you care, Milt! Milt, you're a rich man now. You know what rich people do with their faithful help? They don't just leave them flat! An old woman like that—from the clinic—a cardiac! They just don't throw them out, Milt, they give them a pension. The old lady knows that, if you're too ignorant, Milt. You got to go to your lawyer tomorrow and fix it legally so she has a little income that will make her independent for life and make her go back to Canada, that's the thing you have to do. 'In gratitude for her faithful services'—I've read that lots of times in the paper! That's exactly what you better do—a man in your position!" She flicked a bit of lint from his coat collar. "If you know what I mean, Milt!"

He set his chin stubbornly and reached for the door. "No, I don't know what you mean."

"Milt, you do! A man in your position! That's all I can say. Leave it at that."

He managed a laugh and shoved the door open. "Now I've heard everything! Something you don't say!" But damned if she wasn't right for once. Of course he didn't want the old lady hanging around when he couldn't be here to watch her. The reason he hadn't thought of it himself was he grudged giving her anything because of the way she had never shown him any respect, the way she had never hidden that she thought he was dirt.

"Milt. My last word. Give her a pension."

"The way you're talking—or rather, the way you're not talking —why bother with a pension? 'A man in my position'—why don't I take her for a ride; after all, dead men tell no tales? Why don't I take Lady Constant for a ride? Hell, all of you, all three of you?"

"Milt! Milt!" She walked into the vestibule.

He forced himself to be angry rather than frightened. "You, too, remember! 'A man in my position,' whatever that may mean! You're driving me nuts! The police give me a clean slate. I can leave the country. I can do anything I want; it's O.K. with the police, but with you—'Milt! Milt!' Why do you look at me that way? 'Milt! Milt!'" He grabbed both her arms. "What's going on in that head of yours?"

She pulled her arms back and his hands pressed against her side, her breasts. She closed her eyes, feeling faint. Her voice came out unlike itself, soft. "Milt."

"What's going on in your head, I say! You have the facts! Sloane had this delusion she killed her mother because she wasn't right in the head. Because she was insane, she killed herself on Sunday. Those are the facts!" He pulled his hands away from between her arms and her firm body whose warmth came through the cloth of her coat.

Jenny said softly, "I think you made Sloane think she killed her mother, Milt. Somehow, that day the old lady died a natural death, you made your—Sloane—think she killed her poor mother, that's what I think the facts are, Milt."

"Just like that I made! Jenny, how?"

"Oh, Milt, if I only knew!"

"Then what?"

"Then you would listen to me! That's what! That's all! Then what do you think? Then I'd run to the cops and tell them?" She came very close to him. "Then you would realize I'm your only friend and you'd listen to me!" Milt turned away so that she could only see his ear and the side of his cheek. "My God, what a kid you are! Worse than Bud! You act like this was some kind of guessing game, Milt. 'How?' The way you said that. If I guess, I win. I win the booby prize! Well, I can't guess how, I don't know how but maybe I do know something! Maybe I know what the last straw was, what drove her to it Sunday. Maybe not insane, maybe insanely jealous!"

"My God!"

"Look how innocent he looks! Yes, insane with jealousy. You heard what jealousy does to a woman! A woman can stand anything but not jealousy!"

"Jealous! Of you? Jealous of you, Jenny?" He turned back and saw how white in the face that got her. "Of you?"

Jenny tried to stop trembling. She could not stop trembling. "No, Milt, not me. Your Sloane called me up on Friday before she killed herself. I only realized later she was suspicious. You told her you would be with me. You thought she wouldn't suspect or check up and you didn't have the good sense to tell me first so if she called I'd go to bat for you. You don't trust me, Milt! You'd rather trust to luck she wouldn't check up, so I didn't back you up and you were out at the Stork Club with Cissie Parker. I did a little checking up myself, Milt! So what I think is maybe Sloane found out, too, and Cissie is who she was jealous of and it was little Cissie who was the last straw that broke the camel's back."

"Cissie Parker! I'm in love with Cissie Parker!"

"Don't say that out here in the vestibule, Milt—anyone could come in. Milt, go on and send the old lady home in the car, come into the apartment where we can be private."

"No."

She saw that he would not let the old lady go to the Haunted House alone where the Duchess could stroll in and get to work on her. Good. "Then lower your voice, Milt." She spoke very softly. "You're in love with Cissie Parker, Milt."

"I'll show you how much I'm in love with Cissie Parker!" He reached into his pocket and pulled out an envelope. As he did so another paper fluttered to the floor and Jenny bent and picked it up. "Give it to me. It's nothing. Give it to me."

Before she gave the paper back to Milt Jenny saw that it was a kind of map of the Queen Elizabeth. "What's so private about that?"

"Who said private?" But he saw on Jenny's face that he had snatched it, that he had showed anxiety. "Okay, I'm embarrassed, can you understand that? I didn't want to act like a greenhorn when I get on that boat because I never set foot on a boat in my whole life!" He put the map in his pocket and opened up the reservation notification from the Cunard Line and waved it in Jenny's face. "If I'm in love with Cissie Parker then why am I going to France?"

Jenny fell back against the wall. Her hand went to her throat. She shook her head at Milton. "To France?"

"You're so sure I'm in love that's all you can think of. Yes, to France, that's what I'm trying to tell you."

"No, Milt. Your wife told you no, Milt. You mustn't go. It will be the worst thing for you, Milt!"

"Should I stay with you?" He waved toward the door of the apartment. "I should stay put here and drop dead in harness? Nix. No." He folded the letter and put it back into his pocket, then strode to the door and held out his hand for Jenny's key, but she wouldn't give it to him. "Milt! Milt!" He laughed at her. "Milt! Milt! Listen, Jenny, Milt knows what he wants and Milt can take care of himself. I can take care of myself, do you hear me?" She had moved up to him. "All I ask you, Jenny, is to butt out. Leave me alone. Keep your nose out of my business." They stood close to each other in front of the apartment door silently. Jenny's eyes were big and full of tears. Milt swallowed, his hands went to her arms again but this time he pressed them against her side. "Ah, you mean well, Jenny, but every time you open your mouth, you put my neck in it." He mocked her, but tenderly, pressing her arms tenderly. "'Milt! Milt!' I'll be the death of you; I'll be the death of you! Jenny, Jenny, listen to me for once! Butt out, butt out or you'll be the death of me!"

THURSDAY, THE EIGHTEENTH

The dining-room steward was very much annoyed at having to go down to supplies at the last moment like this. The waiter said that he most certainly had checked his tables earlier, but for missing ashtrays, lifted silver. "Now, I ask you, wot will they steal next? Wot," he said, "would any sane person want with a *salt* from the First Class Dining Room, sir?"

And the steward couldn't rightly blame him. "Wot, indeed! a *salt!*"

Chapter XII

$\mathcal{M}$ILTON tore off the flap of the calendar and looked at the circle he had marked around the date, tore the calendar across and dropped it into the fireplace, then took another look at his watch. Twelve-twenty. The minute hand hadn't moved since the last time. It seemed to him that the twenty-four hour interval between tearing yesterday's leaf off the calendar and today's leaf was shorter than the interval between minutes today. Because today was the day. *Der Tag.* He had lived twenty-four hours since he woke this morning. You didn't have to be any Albert Einstein to know what relativity was, just live through one day like today.

But now he was set. He couldn't make any mistakes now and she wasn't going to make any move now. *Bon voyage* was all it was going to be. She was just coming to see him off, to let him go, to let loose.

She'd better, he thought, and his hand went to his pocket; she'd better. He heard the pugnacity in his inner voice and knew how false it was. He had nothing against her if she didn't start anything. Live and let live—start something and— He took his hand out of his pocket.

She was just coming to see him off. She wasn't going to make a move now. Any move, she'd have made it before now.

He hit the side of his head with his open palm as if he could jar the revolving thoughts loose, stop the wheel turning in there.

He looked at his watch again. He had planned not to leave the house until one-thirty, plenty of time to get to the boat and say *bon voyage* to Lady Constant. (And that's all it would be.) Milton looked around the big bedroom and ran out into the hall and down the stairs. He would burst a blood vessel waiting around here another minute.

Milton walked out into the hall where his new pigskin luggage stood near the door with his new gray overcoat from Tripler's folded neatly across it and the cap the salesman had said was the latest thing for boats on top of the coat, then walked back to the foot of the stairs and, as he called Mrs. Austen, felt in his pockets. First the breast pocket for his wallet with the passport and the letter of credit, then for the envelope with the confirmation of reservations. He did not need to touch what was in his trousers pocket again, that he had felt for twenty-four hundred times since the morning. It was insurance, that's all. He wet his lips and called Mrs. Austen again, hearing, as he did so, her steps on the third floor. "Mrs. Austen, you all packed?"

"Yes, sir."

"Swell. Look, Mrs. Austen, I've got a couple of things I have to do before the boat sails. "He started up the stairs. So I'll come on up and get your valise and we'll get out of here now."

"But, sir—the gentleman from the Museum hasn't come yet."

"I forgot to tell you. I got a letter this morning; they put it off again until tomorrow. Boy, I knew they were looking this gift horse in the mouth, but now you'd think even looking was too much trouble."

"But, sir—"

But, sir. Take it easy, he told himself, moving steadily upward.

"Sir, someone must show them."

"That's okay. My sister-in-law, Mrs. Krop, is going to do that little thing. It's going to be just the way my wife wanted, don't worry." What he wanted to do was to run upstairs, grab the damned valise in one hand and the old mule in the other. "I'm on my way over to give my sister-in-law the keys to the house now and tell her just what's what. And say good-by," he added, his heart lurching at that thought. "So it's O.K., Mrs. Austen."

"Mrs. Krop. Yes, sir, I see." She stepped to the side of the landing and waited for him to come up; when he reached the third floor she walked to the door of her room and threw it open for him.

Milton pointed. "I thought you were all packed?" The battered suitcase lay open on the bed.

"Yes, sir, I am." She followed Milton into the room. "I am all packed, sir. I would just like you to go over my things before I close the case, sir."

"What the hell for?" Why did her "sirs" always sound like dirty cracks?

"Sir, I would just like you to go over my things, so that—so that you will know I haven't taken anything that isn't mine." She spoke very quietly, so softly and hesitantly that he could barely hear her.

"Nuts." The way she turned on him then, the look she gave him! Sir! He could hear Jenny advising him to go look at the damned bag so the damned old mule would love him like a son. Nuts to Jenny's advice. Milton bent over and pulled the lid of the suitcase down and it groaned as if he had hurt it.

Mrs. Austen tried to stop him. "Please, sir, it's customary."

"Not with me it isn't. It isn't my custom, Mrs. Austen. No, look, I don't think much of the custom, no kidding—if I had more time I'd explain you why—" The old biddy looked at him as if a whole lifetime couldn't explain her to him or him to her. "Sorry," he said, trying to smile agreeably, "no can do today, Mrs. Austen." He lifted her hand off the old valise and, leaning on the lid, snapped the lock shut and then fastened the sides. Service. "I've got a boat to catch and about a million things to do. Put on your hat and coat and let's go." But, sir. "Let's go, let's go!" He picked up the valise and heard her reluctantly following him.

As he walked down the stairs, he talked to her. "Now, Mrs. Austen, if I didn't think you were one hundred per cent honest —and faithful—would I give you the pension? For the love of Mike, what would you want to take from here, anyhow? You just forget what's customary and I'll drive you to Roosevelt and you go down to Pennsylvania Station the way we planned and get on that train for back home and take it easy. On Easy Street." But that was enough to start her again and she began playing the same record, her good name, customary, just look through— Enough of that. Enough of her, Milton thought. He had said he'd put her on the subway himself but suddenly felt he couldn't. He hadn't let her out of his sight since they came home from the police station together. Old Lady Picklepuss. He hadn't let her out of his sight day or night and now he couldn't take one more minute of it.

He carried her bag and then his own out on the front steps and standing there, rubbing his arms, heard a car on the street and thought why not a cab? Why not turn her over to a cabby and pay him in advance, plus a fat tip to take old sourpuss straight to Pennsylvania. He could do it. It would look better than dropping her at the station himself. He could afford it. Today, now, soon—he could afford to do anything he wanted to and nothing he didn't want. Soon.

Milton carried his bags and Mrs. Austen's down to the gate, set hers on the sidewalk and put his into the car, then, nodding soberly to the baby carriage brigade who seemed to be picketing the gate the way they walked up and down in front of it, he went back to the house for Mrs. Austen.

She was standing in the hall waiting for him. He left the door open behind him and waved for her to go out, then went into the drawing room and tested the windows, then the taipan room, then the sitting-room windows. The dining room, however, was too much for his stomach. The dining room would have thrown him. He didn't see Sloane sitting there as he had last seen her, nothing like that, it just threw him. He went out quickly and locked the front door behind him.

"Did you do the back door, sir?"

Milton shook his head and moved off to the side, then stopped. "Hell with the back door," he said. "Hell with it." The dining room threw him. As he put the key into his pocket to give to Jenny, he could feel the saltcellar from the *Queen Elizabeth*, the souvenir. (That was all it would be, a souvenir. She wasn't going to make a move. He was just carrying insurance, that was all.) "Let's get going," he said, and Mrs. Austen started down the front path for the last time, and he followed her slow footsteps for the last time.

Milton whistled at a cab and pointed left to the cabby, who nodded and started a U turn. He had to wait for that and for the cabby to figure how much the ride to Pennsylvania Station would come to and that gave the baby brigade time to ask questions. He was sailing for Europe on the *Queen Elizabeth* that afternoon, he told them. The old lady (she stood there like a statue; wisps of her hair blowing in the wind were all that moved) was going back home. The house was going to be wrecked starting next week and until then the house would be empty, he said. He gave the cabbie a ten-dollar bill and told him to keep the change and then, because he wasn't sure whether he should or shouldn't shake hands with old sourpuss, he sort of waved at her and at the baby brigade, said a kind of general good-by, got into the Studie and drove off.

Mrs. Levinson took her hands off the rail of the baby carriage and rubbed them together. "Empty!" she said, tossing her head at the Haunted House. "Little does he know! I'll bet you anything the minute word gets around that the doctor is out of the way that house will be full of teenagers wrecking the place for the heck of it!"

"Like they did to that old house where your apartment now stands. Oh, you wouldn't know. You weren't here, Mrs. Olson. That was something!"

"Teenage gangs," Mrs. Olson said, "I can imagine!"

The cabbie reached back and opened his rear door. "Which one is going?"

Mrs. Austen picked up her valise and started toward the taxi. Mrs. Levinson went to help her and shoved the valise in. Mrs. Austen thanked Mrs. Levinson, turned back to look at the Haunted House and then got into the taxi and it moved off.

"Did you see her face?" Mrs. Levinson asked. "She didn't want to go! If it was me," Mrs. Levinson said, "I'd run so fast—!"

"Yes, Milt," Jenny said. "I got it. I got it. The guy from this museum in Boston will come around noon tomorrow. I have the key to the front door." She held up the key but did not take her eyes from Milton. "I should be there and show him what you told me and he will make arrangements to get it to the museum if he wants it. A big if! And what he doesn't take, I can take. Any old thing my heart desires. Thanks."

"Now, listen, Jenny, I'm not offering you my secondhand clothes, you understand. This is old furniture and it could be valuable and the car isn't three years old, yet. You got the car keys there?" She held them up. "You don't have to be so sarcastic."

"I'm not being sarcastic, Milt, it's not that. Can't you sit at least? You've been walking up and down this room since you got here. You'll wear out the rug." She patted the Hide-a-Bed next to her.

"You can take all the rugs you want from the house if I wear this out."

"Oh, Milt, what do you think I care about rugs?" She jumped up. "What's the matter with you, Milt?"

"What's the matter? In a couple of hours I'll be waving good-by to the skyline of New York. I'll be—off to the races! What's the matter with me!"

Jenny put both hands over her face. "Do you think I forgot that, Milt? For a minute? For a minute since you told me?"

Milton saw her body shaking. "That makes two of us."

"I worry so about you, Milt. I yell at the kids. I lose my temper over every little thing. In bed at night I stuff the pillow in my mouth so they won't hear me." She took her hands away from her face. "I worry so! Don't stay away too long, will you, Milt? In Europe. What's Europe?" She bit her lip. "You're an American, Milt, come back home to America."

"Come home to die like an animal crawls into a hole? I'm going to have something, and then I'll die big, Jenny. I didn't live big but I'll die big."

"Have something! Nothing! Who's going to look after you, Milt? Who's going to watch over you? Milt, if you want, I'll park the kids with Uncle Frank. I'll get like a housekeeper, or both the kids could go to boarding schools. You're a bigger kid than my two, Milt!"

"Why sure, if you only had a passport, you could come with me," he said, pulling out the envelope, tapping it. "If you look, you'll see. A suite. Two bedrooms. A regular apartment."

"Two? For who, Milt?"

"One for you and one for me, of course."

"For who, Milt? For Cissie? Is it for Cissie?"

"Ask her. Go upstairs and ask her, Jenny. I took her out one night to make up for being a stinker to her—on account of you, Jenny—so go on up and ask her if we're eloping on the *Queen Elizabeth!*"

She searched his face, shook her head. "I believe you, Milt."

He laid his hand on her shoulder gently. "One room was for my wife, Jenny. We were going in style. She ordered the suite and I'm stuck with it. One bedroom is going to be empty, but ishkabibble, I always liked space." He looked at the small room scornfully. "Don't fence me in!"

"I believe you," Jenny said. She was still thinking about Cissie.

Milton wondered, looking at Jenny, whether if it hadn't been for Jenny he would have given Cissie a second thought. (A look, yes. A pretty little kid like that, a pretty little bird, but if not for Jenny, Cissie might not have been more than a ship that passed in the night. Yessie-Cissie with her "yeses" and Jenny with her "no's." "Boy, Jenny, it's too bad you haven't got a passport— You'd look swell in a bikini!" It was a nasty crack and Jenny's hands went to her generous hips and her head came up. "Boy," Milton said, and then he couldn't look at her any longer. "Well, I better get going."

She let him move away, across the room, out into the hall, and then ran after him. "I'm coming with you. To the boat, Milt. I'm going to see you off." He shook his head. "Oh, my God, Milt, what's wrong with that? You see people off. Maybe I never been to Europe, but I know that much. People see people off." She put her hand on his sleeve and began to stroke it. "Milt—I got to—maybe I'll never see you again. I got to at least see you off, Milt."

He stared down at her stroking hand, then removed it and held it. "Jenny, no. Stay away, Jenny, don't see me off. I'm asking you, Jenny, keep hands off!" Her mouth began to work. "Jenny, I told you a hundred times, butt out. Butt out, Jenny! And, by the way, don't be surprised if you hear from a certain lawyer one of these days informing you you and the kids are provided for." He looked down at the hand he was holding, then dropped it and walked out of the apartment, not turning back once.

For at least five minutes, Jenny stood where he had left her. For five minutes at least, then she began to walk up and down where Milton had walked five minutes before, the way Milt had walked, like a caged lion, unable to sit as he had been unable to sit or rest. Then she ran out of the room, picked up a silk scarf which Maureen wore on her hair and made a babushka out of it. She was going to do what Milt asked. She was not going to the boat to see him off, but since she couldn't sit still, why shouldn't she go to the Haunted House today? Why wait?

For Milt's sake wouldn't she be a fool if she carried out his orders like a moron and waited until the man from the museum came tomorrow and walked in cold and maybe saw something he shouldn't see? For Milt's sake Jenny slammed the door behind her and, thrusting her arms into her coat sleeves, hurried out of the apartment house.

Jenny pulled up to an empty sidewalk. It was lunch time. Jenny, hearing only her own hurrying footsteps on the path and the wind in the dead leaves and dry grass, was made a bit nervous. She had become so accustomed to voices and cars and other people's footsteps. She was disconcerted when the big front door opened so noiselessly, and did not like the solid sound of it closing behind her. She stood in the wide hall swallowing hard, feeling as if she had been locked in a vault. "With two skeletons," she thought, catching sight of Gog and Magog.

She put the key carefully into her coat pocket and started down the hall to look. For what? "I'll know what it is when I see it," she told herself, and then heard sounds from upstairs. It was only the thought of Milt saying "I told you to butt out" that prevented her from running away. "Who's there?" she called.

Like an echo, from upstairs someone said, "Who's there?"

282

"Who's that up there? Oh, it's you. The maid. What are you doing here?" she asked Mrs. Austen.

"Mrs. Krop! Madam! I thought you were coming tomorrow, Madam!"

"Come on down here. What are you doing here, anyway? The doctor said the place was empty and you were on your way to Canada. What are you doing here?"

The old lady, holding on to the banisters, walking carefully, started down, talking a mile a minute. Yes, Dr. Krop did think the house was empty and that was so. He had started her toward Canada, yes. She had been waiting by the gate for the taxi when she heard some ladies there talking about—gangs. They said the house would soon be swarming with these gangs by nightfall. They would break windows and get into the house and destroy the property. She had been brought up to respect property. She had driven off in the taxi Dr. Krop had so kindly provided, but she had turned back. She couldn't leave this house and madam's things ("madam's things!") to be destroyed like that. She had been told by Dr. Krop that madam ("Me," Jenny thought) was coming tomorrow and that the gentleman from the museum would be here then and she had decided that it was her duty to stay behind a day and look after madam's things until tomorrow. (There was something fishy about the story, Jenny decided. The old woman was sweet-talking too much.) "Well, I'm here now," Jenny said. "I'll take over."

"Yes, madam."

"In other words, you can go now."

"Yes, madam."

For whatever reason she had sneaked back, she was meekly going to go now. Why? With what? What had she really come back for?

"Madam—might I ask you I would feel much better, since you are here—I wonder could you go over my things, madam? I have my suitcase right here in the hall." She hurried past Jenny

283

to where the shabby case lay on a bench and began to work the fasteners open.

Jenny had a feeling that she was being manipulated. "Wait a sec—how did you get in? Did you break a window?"

Mrs. Austen had the fasteners open. "The back door was unlocked, madam."

Just like Milt, Jenny thought. Leaves a door open. Lets her sneak back this way.

Mrs. Austen carefully lifted the lid of the suitcase and stepped aside. "If you will be kind enough to go over my things. Before I go, madam. It is customary."

Whatever she had sneaked back for, it certainly wouldn't be laying right there in that suitcase since she was so anxious for Jenny to look it over. "Now, Mrs. Austen—" The old lady stood like a block of stone. "Come on, Mrs. Austen, why bother? I know you're honest!"

Mrs. Austen's thin lips began to tremble. "If you please, madam! Madam, you must! I begged Dr. Krop to do this and he would not. It wasn't only the gangs, madam, I came back so that you could look my things over. Dr. Krop said you would be here tomorrow. I will not leave until you do, madam."

She meant it. Jenny took off her coat. She wouldn't leave until her junk got the once-over. Jenny, shoving her sleeves up, paused. "I'll do it but first you tell me why it's so important to you. Why is it so important?"

The old lady clamped down her trembling lips, then opened them, but good. In two minutes Jenny heard all about the missing brooch, what it meant to her who had worked all her life in good houses to be suspected of stealing, her helpless fury when, having accused her, the only proper thing was not done, they would not, would not call the police in and settle the matter once and for all time. Her good name. Her good name. The old lady was shaking so that Jenny thought she would fall apart. She got up so much steam that Jenny was afraid she would blow

284

her top. She was like a witch, blazing away; her eyes shot darts. Jenny, staring at the old woman, suddenly remembered the Duchess at the funeral. The Duchess at the funeral, Jenny thought, imagining God-knows-what about Milt because of the dirty look this old lady had given Milt. Jenny squatted down in front of the battered suitcase and smiled up at the old lady. (She could have kissed the old lady.) "Shhhh," she said, "shh, calm down, calm down. You'll blow your top if you don't calm down, Mrs. Austen. Sure I'll look over your—stuff for you—" (She almost said *junk!*) "But tell me something first. This is important to me, Mrs. Austen, like your good name is to you. I can see that your good name means more to you than all the pensions, right? Well, this means a lot to me. Now tell the honest truth, so help you God! Mrs. Austen, you hold a grudge against the doctor. Don't bother to contradict because I know better." She pointed at the old lady. "Your face says better. You have an honest face, Mrs. Austen. It tells the truth."

"I am honest, madam. I was brought up to be honest."

"That's right. Now, are you sore at Milt for not calling the cops in about the brooch, is that it? Poor Milt, he'd think he was doing you a favor but that's beside the point. Now, that's what you have against him, isn't it, Mrs. Austen?"

"But that was *madam*," Mrs. Austen said, shaking her head. She held her hand against her knocking heart in a real-life gesture but spoke with her servant's voice. "It was *madam* who wouldn't have the police in! Dr. Krop wouldn't understand, madam, and I wouldn't expect him to, but *madam*—and that put me into black despair!" Now that she had broken her rule of "keeping herself to herself," now that the dam was broken, she could not stop. She had felt there was no one left in the whole new world who understood her sense of values, so what was the need to go on? She had felt that she could not stay on with madam after that, but what would she do then? Where could she go? Back on the dole? Madam was the only person who had been willing to take her on. Madam had been so kind, working out the plan so that she could cook for madam. No one else would go to that trouble, only madam—and then madam had let her down! The old lady held up her trembling hand as if Jenny had been about to interrupt her, although Jenny had no such intention. That, Mrs. Austen said, was how she felt at the time, although now, of course, she understood. Now that poor madam was gone and the story was out in the open. "Poor wandering creature, believing she had killed her mother like that, naturally madam would refuse to have the police in. She couldn't help herself. No, Mrs. Krop, that was madam, so I can't blame Dr. Krop for *that!*"

"For *that?* Then what do you blame him for?"

"You are mistaken, madam."

Like fun mistaken, only the old lady had herself under control again. Jenny shrugged and, bending over the suitcase, began to go through the things in it.

". . . bolt of good Irish linen my old madam brought me— keeping it to be buried in, madam. Lace—*real* lace, madam, not machine made—"

Jenny lifted each of the sad objects in the suitcase and heard faintly Mrs. Austen's descriptions, the proud old voice coming from far off. If it had only been the brooch that made Mrs. Austen hate Milt, she could have called the Duchess and told her off. What a pleasure it would have been to tell the Duchess off—"So you thought the old lady had something on Milt, well, she did. You know what she had on him? He insulted her good name. He wouldn't call the cops in to give her the once-over— he trusted her but that isn't the way she wanted it—so now you know what you can do with your suspicions of Milt!" Jenny lifted out the bottle which was tucked into the corner of the suitcase, laid it on the floor, then picked it up again, and recognized, from the way her heart gave a sudden squeeze, that it was Milt's handwriting on the label. CAUTION, POISON, DO NOT

OVERDOSE. NO MORE THAN THREE PILLS DAILY. Jenny held the bottle toward Mrs. Austen because it was such a nutty thing to steal.

Mrs. Austen took in the expression on Jenny's face and a white ring formed around her mouth. "If you mean that I—took that, madam, you are quite mistaken."

"Aw— Who cares? My, you're touchy!"

"That bottle is mine, madam. Dr. Krop gave that bottle to me more than three years ago in the clinic, madam."

"Of course he did! It slipped my mind— Sure he did! I remember now Milt said you'd been a clinic patient from way back." She smiled sadly at the bottle. "This happens to be a drug my husband worked on. You didn't know that, did you? My hubby was a doctor, too, Mrs. Austen. Milt—Dr. Milton Krop was carrying on the clinical side of my husband's research on this drug in Queens General cardiac clinic." She made her face quiet and serious. "I hope it helped you."

"No, madam, it did not." The white ring deepened with distaste.

"Well, it didn't hurt you anyhow."

"Neither helped nor hurt, madam."

Now what was eating her? Jenny looked up from the label at Mrs. Austen's face. (Like she was smelling something bad.) "What do you mean by that? Why do you say that? Mrs. Austen—"

Mrs. Austen told Jenny what she meant.

"Mrs. Austen," Jenny said, "you've got to tell the Duchess what you just told me."

"The Duchess, madam?"

"Lady what's-her-name—"

"Madam!"

"Mrs. Austen—I won't take no for an answer. Now, wait, I know you're not one to broadcast your troubles, but you've got

287

to tell her. If I tell her she won't believe me—she's got to hear this from your lips."

"I don't understand, madam."

"All right. I'll tell you. Lady what's-her-name saw you at the funeral. She saw you giving the doctor a dirty look. She got the idea in her royal head that the dirty look meant you had something on Milt, something you weren't telling the cops. About her sister, Mrs. Austen—about her sister dying. You know."

Mrs. Austen looked thoroughly shocked. "I told the police all I knew, madam."

"Sure. I know. That's what I told the Duchess, but— Mrs. Austen, don't you get it? She wants to make trouble for Milt, so we have to set her right on this. Mrs. Austen, you know as well as I do what kids men are. They set their hearts on one thing and beyond that they will not see. All Milt will see is getting off on that boat today. He should worry about what's going on in the Duchess' head. He should worry what comes next, but I worry. I give a thought to tomorrow even if Milt doesn't so I tell you we have to tell her." Jenny jumped up and brushed her skirt off. "Now, Mrs. Austen, have a heart! Now I've explained the whole thing to you you don't hold any grudge against my brother-in-law any more, do you?"

"No, madam. I understand now."

"Good. Then, if you don't hold any grudge any more it's up to you to tell the Duchess." (Get her off Milt's neck, stop her smelling around, poking around.) "O.K.?"

But Mrs. Austen would not be rushed. "Her ladyship thinks I kept evidence from the police?"

Jenny nodded. "That's it."

"But I wouldn't do that, madam! Why, madam—her ladyship's sister was ever so kind to me, madam. I told you. She was the only one— I told you, madam! If I knew that Dr. Krop had done anything to harm madam nothing would have kept me from speaking out! How could her ladyship think such a thing!"

"In plain English, Mrs. Austen, her ladyship thinks you were bought off."

"Madam?"

"The pension, Mrs. Austen, you're forgetting that."

"The pension! The pension!"

"Her ladyship thinks Milt gave you the pension so you would keep your trap shut."

"Oh, madam!"

"Why else? So O.K., then? You know that Milt gave you that pension out of the goodness of his heart, don't you think you owe it to him to explain the reason you gave Milt that dirty look?" She was nodding. "Is the telephone line shut off yet? No? Not?" Jenny pointed to the old suitcase. "Lock her up." She hurried along the hall to the telephone.

Jenny could tell that the old woman must be wondering what had hit her, why she was standing there now, holding onto the black carved table where the telephone sat as if she had all the wind knocked out of her. She had to hold onto the black table because her legs felt so weak they'd give way otherwise. When the desk clerk at the hotel had informed her that Lady Constant was on the Queen Elizabeth this minute, it had knocked her for a loop! She was seeing Milt off when Jenny couldn't! Jenny couldn't go to the boat with him, oh, no, but she could! "Lady Constant isn't at the hotel. She's on the boat."

"On the boat, madam? Then Lady Constant is returning to France, madam?"

"To France?" Jenny glared.

"Well that is where her ladyship lived, madam."

Jenny groaned and straightened up, thinking, that fool, Milt! Oh, God, that dope, Milt! The royal suite was for royalty, who else? Milt had the royal suite, didn't he? Two bedrooms. She,

Jenny, was the dope. Hadn't Milt himself told her that the Duchess was the one who had given him the idea of the Riviera in the first place? He had such a yen to go to the Riviera it was all he could think of. My God, could he be taking her along, letting her use the extra bedroom so she could introduce him to the Four Hundred there? A brilliant idea—brilliant! No matter what he said Milt didn't speak a word of French. Brilliant idea. That the Duchess was poison, that from the minute she had arrived on the scene she'd been after his head, that she still was, that didn't matter to that dope, Milt! Of course, Jenny thought, that was why he wouldn't let her go to see him off, of course! There was no other reason in the world he wouldn't have let her come to see him off! She had a vivid mental picture of the delicately made-up face. Was Milt the first man to forget everything because of a pretty face? Because she had a size twelve figure? Because she would look good in a bikini? Because the hardest work she had ever done with her hands was rub cold cream into her face—not scrubbed Milt's floor or cooked Milt's meals or washed his dirty socks! "What?" Jenny asked the old lady, who had been saying something, what Jenny hadn't been able to make out because of the way her heart had been going like a trip hammer. "What did you say?"

"Do you think we might catch her at the pier, madam?"

Jenny shoved herself away from the black carved table, "Sure we could!" The strength came back to her legs. "We could try!" She started down the hall, then returned for Mrs. Austen's suitcase. "Come on, I've got Milt's car outside."

"Yes, I do want to speak to her ladyship, madam."

About halfway down the path to the gate, Jenny stopped abruptly. The old suitcase had been banging her side the whole way, "Butt out, butt out, butt out." She set the valise down, rubbed her side and considered the warning. She heard the old lady breathing heavily. Her? The old lady? Jenny rubbed her sweated palms down the side of her coat. "Mrs. Austen?" She heard how silky her voice sounded, how coaxing. "Mrs. Austen, why do you want to talk to 'her ladyship'? I mean, the most I expected was you'd back me up and I'd do the talking. What do you want to say so special to her?"

Mrs. Austen's lips were tinged with blue from hurrying down the path after Jenny. "It's difficult to tell you, madam."

"You better."

"Madam— Her ladyship—"

"I told you what her ladyship was trying to do. I have to know what it is you want to tell her to make sure it's nothing she could twist—"

"Oh, madam, it is nothing like that. This is about me, Mrs. Krop. I wish explain something about myself." She was talking more easily now, having stopped moving. "I'll tell you, madam, and you'll see it is nothing to do with Dr. Krop. I want to explain to her ladyship that I took the pension even when I —I was very angry, you know, madam! It was only because I felt Mrs. Krop would have wished it. I want to explain to her ladyship that I could not face the dole again. If I could have got employment, I wouldn't have taken it, madam. Not feeling the way I did, madam. But it was no bribe, madam! I want to tell her ladyship why I can't hope for employment now that madam is dead."

"Oh, that," Jenny said. She narrowed her eyes and looked straight at the old woman. "You mean your cardiac condition?" She was sour but she was honest. You could see she was honest. "Come on," Jenny said. "There's no reason you shouldn't tell about your operation." She saw the old lady was puzzled. "That's supposed to be funny. 'Let me tell you about my operation,' they say." She could not help smiling.

All the way down to Forty-seventh Street, the old lady kept going: She was used to a good class. There were no more good classes. They didn't want servants nowadays. If Milt had shown the good sense he was born with, Jenny thought, she wouldn't butt in, but when he started cuddling up with a cobra, how could she not butt in? If Milt were taking Cissie, Jenny thought, she wouldn't have butted in again—she had butted in once with Cissie, and that was enough, but not Cissie—that one!

"Madam was willing to put up with the salting all food at table because she knew what a good servant was and it was worth it to her, but these others— No one else would put up with it. I want to explain to her ladyship."

"That's right," Jenny said, "explain to her ladyship."

A steward led the gaping Jenny and a blue-lipped but determined Mrs. Austen through the first class lounge, which was full of people seeing other people off, and upstairs to A deck, and along the carpeted, faintly oil-smelling, heat-smelling, antiseptic-smelling corridor to the door of the suite; then he knocked smartly. When Milton gave him permission to enter, he threw open the door. "Mrs. Krop and Mrs. Austen to see you, sir."

Amory had been sitting in a blue upholstered chair which Day would have called "Marine-*moderne*." (Day was going to have the laugh on her, wasn't he?) She was becoming very tired of hearing Dr. Krop say all the usual things about a big boat. "A boat is a boat is a boat," and Dr. Krop paused, shrugged and then continued. To Dr. Fell a boat was not a boat—it was a ticket to Paradise, he explained. He was not like her, remember. She had probably been back and forth so much it was like a trip on the subway to her, but not to him.

"Believe me," he said, "Sloane knew what it meant. She got the reservations, you know." He swallowed. "And you know Sloane." His hand ran over a green upholstered chair in appreciation of the fabric.

Amory hated her sister's name in his mouth; it made her flame inside. "Yes," she said. "I know Sloane." *Sloane was not insane.*

"All this—" He took his hand off the green chair and waved at the sitting room, toward the bedrooms. "She did it for me."

And what did you do to her? "Yes." He was getting an enormous thrill out of it but what was she getting? Exactly nothing. Just before the steward knocked on the door she had been getting so much nothing that she had announced she must go and he had said, oh, must she? He had been so ecstatic (so confident, so cocksure!) that he had insisted they must have their little party first, there was still an hour before the visitors had to leave. His hand had trembled with excitement and he opened the box Hamburger Heaven had sent down. He had offered her a hamburger but she would have choked on it, and when she refused—just before the steward knocked—he had unwrapped a hamburger for himself and had taken a big bite out of it.

When the steward knocked he had his mouth full of hamburger.

Amory had been quite uninterested in the knock until she saw Dr. Krop's face. His eyes seemed to sink right back in his head and become hollow. He stopped chewing. Amory jumped up off the blue upholstered chair. Sloane. Sloane. Now! Amory thought. Now! She hurried to the two women who stood uncertainly just inside the door. "Well, Jenny! And it is Mrs. Austen, isn't it? I saw you at Sloane's funeral, Mrs. Austen. I'm Amory Constant." She held out her hand which Mrs. Austen took after wiping her own down her coat. "Just in time for the party!" It was obvious to Amory that Dr. Krop wanted to throw the pair of them out on their ears—to the steward, also. The steward looked as if he were waiting, not for a tip, but for Dr. Krop to order him to show the ladies out. Amory hurried to the Hamburger Heaven box and began to lift the hamburgers out onto the table. "Do sit down, Jenny. Mrs. Austen."

"Sit down, sit down. Now you're here take a load off your feet!"

His voice was so peculiar, now he found it again, that everybody stared at the host standing there with his hamburger in his hand. He was still pale, Amory noted, but now he seemed different somehow. Fatalistic? No, determined, Amory thought; he looked ready, get on your mark, go. Go? All he did was lift his hamburger to his mouth, take another bite and start chewing. *Faute de mieux?*

He made a face. "Not enough salt! They never put enough salt!" He laid his hamburger down on the table next to the others still in their wax paper and took the onions, relish, pickles, out of the box. "Nope." He walked to the hovering steward, his hand working his wallet out of his breast pocket. "Could you get me a salt shaker before these get cold?" Using his wallet as a shaker, he pantomimed shaking salt.

"A salt, sir?"

"That's correct."

Now something was going to happen, Amory thought. Ready. Get set. Go. Either Jenny or the old cook was going to say the magic wordie now. Because she believed that Milton was simply going to try to stop up the two mouth with this complaint about her hamburgers, she spoke sharply to the steward. "They must have salts in the dining room, steward! Fetch one, please!"

"Rush it, will you?"

The steward bowed and disappeared.

Immediately, Jenny, explaining that she had never been on an ocean liner before, began making a tour of the suite.

"I was just telling Lady Constant, me neither, Jenny," Milton said. "I never set foot on one in my life either. You probably did, Mrs. Austen, but not me or Jenny." That was established now. Insurance.

"Well, I better take it all in while the going's good. You're going with, Milt, but not me."

"I'm going with. I'm sailing. This is *der Tag* for me, Jenny. D-day! Finally, at last, I'm sailing!" He moved closer to Jenny. "Jenny knows how much this means to me, Lady Constant. I was just telling Lady Constant, Jenny, how much this trip means to me!"

He was trying to give Jenny some message but she had her mind on other things. Jenny was searching for something in the cabin; not finding it, she walked to the door of the first bedroom.

"That's a knockout new suitcase! Pigskin! Yours, Milt?"

"All I had was Hut's old wreck." With the slit in the lining.

"The last word!" She went to the door of the other bedroom. "No baggage or anything in here. Empty, Milt?"

"I told you."

"That's right." She turned away from the bedroom door. "Don't fence me in, Milt! Milt likes the great open spaces!"

"Don't we all?" Amory asked. Innocent chitchat? But he did look fenced in. "I wish Dr. Krop had told me you two were coming to our little *bon voyage* party, I'd have ordered more hamburgers."

Four will be enough, Milton thought. She'd ordered four. Turns out the right number. But only if she makes me. "This is Lady Constant's idea, Jenny. Went to all the trouble of ordering the eats sent up from Hamburger Heaven. Nice to get a *bon voyage* party, huh, Mrs. Austen?"

"Very nice, sir."

"A *bon voyage* party? Correct me if I'm wrong," Jenny said. "Were they surprised when she sat down at the piano and talked French! *Bon voyage* means so long, farewell, good-by, right?"

"Quite right—only Dr. Krop should have told me!"

"Milt didn't know. I'm the uninvited guest. I crashed, didn't I, Milt?" She pointed at Milton. "Look at him! I'm the regular bad penny always turning up. Look at Milt's face!"

He had told her not to come here. He didn't want her or the old cook, either.

Jenny took a step toward Milton, who moved away. "Don't worry, I had good reason to come, Milt. Don't worry."

The way he was backing off made it obvious to Jenny that Milt wasn't going to take her word for her reason. She turned to Lady Constant. "The reason I had for butting in like this and bringing Mrs. Austen is I found out what you wanted to know so bad at the funeral. Do you remember what you said? 'Oh, Jenny, she does hate him!' Big mystery! Well, I just found out why. Big mystery!"

"Oh, madam!" The old woman's chin began to quiver.

"Now, Mrs. Austen. I told you why we had to call a spade a spade, didn't I?" She swung toward Milton enthusiastically. "You'll die when you hear this, Milt! Honestly, you'll die! Milt, when you hear this, you'll thank me. After—by dumb luck—I found this out, I had to come." His face didn't soften. "This is the way it was, Milt. To make a long story—One: When you said good-by to me before, I felt kind of restless. You know."

"At loose ends," Amory said, to encourage Jenny. "Go on. Hurry."

She ignored Amory. "Two, I figured why shouldn't I run over to the Haunted House today instead of waiting for tomorrow. Why not? I had nothing better to do. I can't claim it was a hunch, Milt, I just went. Then when I ran into Mrs. Austen there and found this thing out, I had to come here with her while she was around to back me up; otherwise who would believe such a thing? Do you see, Milt?"

Amory saw one thing. Jenny was the type who bulldozed her way over other people's objections but at the same time wanted their approval. Dr. Fell's approval, anyhow. He had told her not to come, she had ignored his order but she was determined he should thank her for coming. Very interesting, Amory thought. So she is *cette type*, but where did that get one? Nowhere. "What is it I wouldn't believe, Jenny?"

"We'll get to it, don't worry. We're going to take our hair down, don't worry!"

"Shut up, Jenny!"

"No, Milt, let me talk. She's been dying to pin something on you. She knows it and I know it and now Mrs. Austen knows it and if you don't, Milt, it's just too bad about you!"

"Do go on and take your hair down, Jenny."

"From the first minute you heard about Milt, you were looking for trouble. You didn't like Milt marrying your sister and I'll bet you didn't like him coming into her money, either. In spades: So you made up your mind there was something fishy about your poor sister and the best you could rake up was that Mrs. Austen hated Milt's guts."

Mrs. Austen groaned and wrung her hands.

"I'm sorry if I'm too plain-spoken, Mrs. Austen, but better plain-spoken than a snake in the grass as far as I'm concerned. I was brought up to call a spade a spade and I'm going to do so." Milt was waving his hand with the hamburger in it. "Just wait, Milt!"

"You wait, Jenny! Hold on a second. This is a party, or it was until you came in. You want to take your hair down, do it later. After the party you girls can get together all you want, but not now."

"Now. Oh, for the love of Mike, Milt, you're just like the time with the impacted molar and you wanted to wait until after that benefit we had those tickets for. Didn't you tell me I was right and you wouldn't have enjoyed the show with it hanging over your head? This is the same thing. You want to go away with a clear mind, don't you? So let me spit it out and I'll butt out of your party!"

"Do let her spit it out, Dr. Krop!" Try and stop her.

"You know as well as I do she's trying to pin something on you— My God, he's so polite since he married into the Four Hundred! What I say is show her how nuts she is about Mrs.

Austen, then she'll use her imagination on something besides you, Milt."

Outside on the deck someone called, "Richard! Rich-ard!"

"I had no intention of coming here, Milt. I called her hotel—Amory's. When they said she was here, I had to come here."

That's why she was peeping into the cabins, Amory thought. She was looking for my luggage. She thought I was going with him. What an extraordinary idea! Her face tightened with distaste, then she shook her head; not extraordinary when you were in love with a man. Jenny was in love with him, poor Jenny. Jenny was jealous, poor Jenny!

"Amory, Mrs. Austen is letting me tell you this because she's a good woman, God bless her." Jenny smiled at Mrs. Austen. "She wouldn't be able to take it easy on the money Milt's giving her if she didn't give him a break when she could. She knows, even if you don't, that the only reason Milt is giving her the money is because he's a good Joe!"

"Your ladyship—"

"Rich-ard!" someone called again.

"Listen, Milt, this is good. You couldn't make this one up in a million years. Listen. Mrs. Austen tried to commit suicide in the Haunted House, when Sloane was living, I mean. You didn't know about that, did you, Milt?" He shook his head automatically, wanting only to stop her. "There's more you don't know, Milt!"

"O.K., but she's still with us, isn't she?" He was almost shouting. "I don't want to hear about a suicide! Haven't I had enough suicide to suit me? My God!" He waved the hamburger. "And Lady Constant had enough suicide to suit her, too!"

"Ask her if she's had enough?" Jenny pointed scornfully at Amory's face. "She's interested about suicide, don't worry!"

"I'm interested," Amory said. She met Milton's eyes. "I'm afraid I am."

The knock on the door came then.

298

Milton kept his eyes on Amory's face an instant longer, then shrugged. "Come in." He went to meet the steward, who had a saltcellar on a tray. Milton threw a crumpled bill onto the tray. "Thanks." He took the salt, lifted the top half of his roll off the hamburger and ostentatiously salted it. "Now it will taste like something." Turning his back, he walked to the table where the Hamburger Heaven box was. "You girls can gab. I'll eat."

To show her how to be discreet, Amory thought. (*Pas devant les domestiques.*) Jenny waited until the steward closed the door after himself.

"The whole point, Milt, *is* that Mrs. Austen is still here! Anyhow, she tried to take her life. Why is her own business. Let me say this much, Mrs. A.—The way she blames Milt for everything—Mrs. Austen tried to take her own life because your own sister let her down."

"I understand now, your ladyship, but at the time— Oh, your ladyship, it turned me against the whole world at the time!"

"What did Sloane do?"

"It was what she didn't do. Mrs. A. can tell you later if she wants." Milt wasn't eating, he was listening, all rightie. "As far as Milt is concerned, it was what Mrs. A. took to kill herself with that counts." Jenny hoped for encouragement from Milt, but he wouldn't give her any, just set the salt shaker down on the table next to the Hamburger Heaven box. "Just by luck, just by dumb luck, Milt, I found the bottle when I was going through her stuff for her. If you hadn't been in such a rush to get to the party here, Milt, you'd have found it and you wouldn't have needed me putting my two cents in, but, no, you wouldn't be bothered. Would he, Mrs. A.? By dumb luck I came back to the house and when Mrs. A. asked me, I bothered. I didn't have any party I was in a hurry to get to. What Mrs. Austen took happens to be Milt's business because she got the particular medication from Milt. I recognized the label." No sign from Milt. Jenny sighed. "Well, it says right on the label, POISON.

CAUTION. DO NOT OVERDOSE. So, because Mrs. A. wanted to over-dose she took—how many, Mrs. A.?"

"Eleven," she whispered. Ten, eleven, go to heaven. She was back on the third floor again. Ten. Eleven. Heaven. Now I lay me down to sleep. Like a child. Treating her like a child. Her voice trembling with retrospective anger, Mrs. Austen took up the explanation. "I had this bottle which Dr. Krop had given me. I kept it because it was a—comfort to me." She glared at them. "Many the time when the investigator person called I would think little do you know, young woman! I don't have to sit here and answer all those questions if I don't choose to! It was a comfort," she repeated furiously. "So when I took them—when I woke up, still in that lumpy bed—"

"Do you get it now, Milt? Are you beginning to see the light? The label said more than three was an overdose and she took eleven and she's still with us as you said, Milt!" Jenny turned to Lady Constant. "Let me tell you, if you are under the impression that because Milt's medication didn't kill her she should be grateful to him, that shows you've never been a nurse! You should hear them in emergency when someone stops them—Grateful!"

"I thought he made sport of me," Mrs. Austen said. "No one had the right to make sport of me!"

"Now, Mrs. Austen," Jenny said. "Are you convinced, Duchess? Even thinking about it after I explained it all to her, she still sees red!"

"Sir," Mrs. Austen said, "excuse me, please. I thought it was because I was a charity patient."

"She's sensitive, Milt. But now I explained it all, it's okay."

Amory could not see how Mrs. Austen and her abortive suicide was going to help her but when she glanced at Milton's stricken face, she said hastily, "You haven't explained it to me, I assure you!"

"Placebo," Jenny said.

"And what is that?"

Jenny smiled. "I guess they don't teach you everything in college, do they? Your sister didn't know, either."

Sloane didn't know? Sloane? *Now*, Amory thought. She didn't dare speak.

Jenny's eyes filled. "I thought I'd be explaining placebo to your sister. I was going to tell her Monday—and on Monday—"

"On Monday Sloane was dead." *Now.* "Tell me about placebo, Jenny."

"Nothing." She took out her handkerchief and wiped her eyes. "Sugar pills."

"But why would they give Mrs. Austen sugar pills?" Why was Dr. Fell's Adam's apple sticking out that way?

"I thought it was because I was charity, your ladyship—but Mrs. Krop explained it all to me. I thought they never would give such things to regular clients."

Jenny saw Milt's Adam's apple sticking out, too. "Patients, not clients," she said mechanically, "the word is *patient*."

"They do give them to other patients, your ladyship; madam explained. If only I had known before! Madam explained that they give sugar pills to— Madam?" she turned to Jenny.

"To chronics, I said. To a certain type of chronic. Some people know they can't have relief all the time, but when they're the type insists— You have to give placebo or else you'd have cases of drug poisoning on your hands right and left."

What's with Milt? Jenny wondered.

"If only it had been explained to me before, your ladyship! I understand now that in the clinics such pills are given to help others, madam, for medical research. I would be the last one not to want to help others! Madam said that these particular pills were the same size and color and taste as the medicine her own husband was discovering and sometimes in the clinic we were given these, and sometimes the sugar pills, so that the doctors would know definitely whether the new medicine really worked."

"When you're testing out a new medication you have to rule out how people fool themselves." Uneasily, Jenny attempted a laugh. "Some people fool themselves about medication and some people fool themselves about other things!" She glared at Amory, but feebly. She was beginning to be frightened.

Mrs. Austen was very animated about it. Her cheeks had become pink with animation. "Madam explained that they could not tell us—why, even madam didn't know when she was giving sugar pills or the heart medicine. Madam explained that if she knew she might convey something in the way she gave it. Imagine!"

"You can give away a lot in a look," Jenny said. If Milt would look at her. If he'd *give!* She could only see that he was like a cat on a hot roof, but why? In order to give herself a minute to think, she walked to the porthole, pulled aside the pretty curtain, and began working the catch open.

Amory walked toward Milton; reaching the table, she turned to it and picked up one of the hamburgers and began to undo the wax paper wrapping. She spoke very fast, in a low voice. "Mother was a chronic—patient—wasn't she? And definitely the type who would not suffer patiently. So you could have given Mother placebo, couldn't you?" She crumpled the wax paper. "And—if you wouldn't tell Jenny when she was giving it, you wouldn't tell Sloane, either!" Jenny's head was out the porthole.

"Warm in here," Jenny said, pulling her head back inside the room, smoothing her hair. She saw Amory standing next to Milton. "What are you talking about?"

Amory wadded the wax paper and threw it at the wastepaper basket. "Placebo. It's very interesting. I never knew doctors were so—devious. Jenny, why were you going to tell Sloane about placebo the morning after she died?" She saw Jenny's glance at Milton and moved in between the two of them. "That's what you said, Jenny—" She lifted up the top half of the hamburger roll and studied it. "Why?"

"Why? Why?" Milt wouldn't even look at her. Milt was busy now putting salt on the Duchess' hamburger for her so of course he couldn't pay any attention to her! Couldn't she put salt on herself? *Helpless?* "Why?" When she began to talk about why Sloane was interested in placebo, the work Phil and Milt had been doing, the bottles of placebo in Milt's closet, waiting, she was really referring to herself. What she had done for Milt. How she knew better than he did what was good for him, how she intended to see he did what was good for him. Sloane, she said, meaning herself, had to know about placebo so she could talk Milt into getting back to work again. Sloane cared for Milt's best interests— Then, her anger having satisfied itself, Jenny took another look at Milt, at his back, rather, because now he had his back turned, seeing him as he was rather than as she wanted him to appear, and forgot about herself. "Your sister cared about Milt, whatever you think! We were going to talk on Monday for Milt's own good!" Be good to him, she meant. "Little did I know." She could not look at his back any longer. She had to see his face. "Hey, Milt, turn around, hey? Turn around and let us see your face. Maureen plays a game that goes like that. *Turn round, turn round, and let us see your face—* Milt!"

Maureen. *Funeral marches to the grave. Still, like muffled drums, are beating.* Still beating! He had to turn around and face them as if nothing was wrong. He had to. *Still.* He turned around. "O.K., Jenny? Now has everybody got everything off their chest? Now, is this a party or is this a party? Live it up a little. Jenny, have a hamburger." He motioned toward them. "Live it up!" He stuck his own hamburger in his mouth and began to work on the beer bottles with an opener.

Amory put her hamburger to her lips: Sloane didn't know what she had been giving Mother, of course, but on Monday she would have been told about placebo. On Monday, poor Jenny would have told her about mislabeled sugar pills given to chronic sufferers like Mother by a doctor who had a closet full of them. By Monday I would have told Sloane that the autopsy showed that Mother had died a natural death and then Sloane would have known the trick as I know it now. So Sloane had to die before Monday. But that's not enough to know, Amory thought, looking at the hamburger with great distaste and surprise, wondering how it had gotten to her lips. I know placebo now. I know the trick but placebo is not the magic word. She heard the first gong swooping through the corridor which meant there wasn't much more time left to find out.

Mrs. Austen pulled herself out of the chair. "The gong just went, madam."

Amory did not want Mrs. Austen to leave. She moved to her. "Oh, no, Mrs. Austen, you haven't had the party yet!" She held out the hamburger toward the old woman. "Do have some party!"

Mrs. Austen shook her head. "No, thank you, my lady."

By Monday Sloane had to be dead and was. But how? "When in Rome you mustn't scorn hamburger, Mrs. Austen! You must be democratic, my dear!" How?

"She said she doesn't want any, isn't that enough?" Milton set the beer bottle on the table with a bang, and got the old woman by her old quivering arm.

Amory saw Mrs. Austen gasp. "But it *is* un-American to scorn hamburger!"

"My lady, it's not that! I cannot eat—"

"Un-American yet! She said no and that's enough!" Milton began hauling Mrs. Austen to the door of the suite. "Now, I'm not being undemocratic, believe me, Mrs. Austen. You know me, don't you? You came here and you said your piece and I'm grateful, believe me. I'm happy to know there's no hard feelings any more, but you heard that gong—"

"Of course, sir—I just—"

It was like the funeral again, Amory thought. He's got hold

of her again and he's determined not to let me get at her. She moved swiftly.

As Milton shoved Mrs. Austen toward the door Jenny saw the starting sweat on his face, the beads of it on his temples, the way the sweat stood out against the color of his skin. The death sweat, she thought, oh, my God, the death sweat! Only to help Milt, for no other reason, Jenny dodged in front of the Duchess and got to the old lady's other arm and helped Milt haul her off. "O.K., Mrs. Austen, you go on up. Wait in the Studie, Mrs. Austen. Remember where we left it? You can't miss it, pastel green with an M.D. license." Milt dropped back and Jenny got the old lady out into the corridor and gave her a shove.

"Jenny! The *Elizabeth* is a perfect maze. I'll see Mrs. Austen off and you stay and say your good-by to Dr. Krop."

Good-by to Milt. She wanted to, she wanted to, but looking at him, she saw that wasn't what Milt wanted. "No, I'd better go with her; after all, this is your party. I'll run along now, Milt."

Mrs. Austen, puffing, detached Jenny's hand from her coat sleeve. "If her ladyship will be so kind—I would like a word with her ladyship."

There was Milt in the doorway with that face of death. "Look —Amory, you haven't had a bite of your hamburger even. Lady Constant should stay, Mrs. Austen. It's her party, you know. Come on, Mrs. Austen!"

Amory, smiling, gave the hamburger to Jenny. "Keep it for me. Mrs. Austen would like a word with her ladyship!"

So they were alone at last. Alone at last. Like love stories alone at last. Jenny came back into the cabin holding onto Lady Constant's hamburger. She didn't know what to say. She wished Milt would say something. Not look like that. Jenny put Lady Constant's hamburger down on the lid of the Hamburger

Heaven box and unwrapped a fresh one. If Mrs. Austen was entitled to one, she, Jenny, was entitled to one. She took a bite.

If she gave a party for Milt, it would be a better party than this. Some party, she thought, staring at Milt's face, what a party! She took another bite. My hamburgers are as good, if I say so myself. Oh, she thought, *salt*. She held the hamburger toward Milt, seeing the shaker still in his hand. "Salt, Milt!" For her ladyship he was all service, for Jenny he wouldn't even give her the salt. He shook his head.

"Jenny—what did she want to talk to her about?"

"Mrs. Austen? Nothing." He looked so terrible, so lousy with that face with the death sweat on it, that she could not look at his face another minute and lowered her eyes to his big chest. Swallowing the bite of hamburger which was like dust and ashes in her mouth, she saw, instead of Milt's big chest, a fluoroscope of a heart. She saw the black ribs like a cage and the terrible heart sucking and swelling and hitting against the black bars. "Milt—"

Jenny put the remains of her hamburger on the table and, opening her purse, pulled out her handkerchief. Holding it out to show Milt what it was, she moved toward him to wipe that sweat off his face. "Oh, Milt," she whispered, "Milt, what is it?"

He couldn't take his eyes away from the doorway through which the Duchess had gone with the old woman.

"What did she have to talk to her about? What hasn't she told her yet? Jenny? Jenny?"

He let her wipe off the beads of sweat. He *let* her! "*Jenny? Jenny?*" It was her heart under the fluoroscope. At his voice saying her name like that it began to bang so hard against the black ribs it would break. "What do you care? Oh, Milt, you don't use your head! If that old lady knew anything against you— That much, Milt!" Jenny flicked the tip end of her little finger with the thumb nail to show him. "If she knew that much, feeling the way she did, wild horses couldn't have kept her from

306

spilling it to the cops! Let her talk to the Duchess, Milt! Every word out of her mouth is one more proof there was nothing. Relax, Milt!"

"What is she talking to her about, Jenny?"

"You won't take my word for it, nothing? She wants to tell the Duchess that she insulted her good name thinking for a minute she could be bought off with any hush money. She wants to say feeling the way about you she did—even knowing nothing against you she wouldn't have taken a red cent except she can't get another job." Milt and the kids used to split their sides at some of her imitations in the old days. The H.N. from St. Agatha, old Mrs. Levinson, Bud's school principal—now Jenny began to take-off Mrs. Austen: Good class. Bad class. Madam. Poor madam. How madam appreciated a real servant. How madam picked her up out of the ash can. How madam worked out this wonderful system with the salt. "Milt!" She screamed, running after him into the bedroom. "Where you going, Milt?" He slammed the bathroom door in her face and she heard the lock turn. "I'll be in the other room, Milt. I'll go in the other room," she repeated to herself, for company against the silence.

The Duchess came back right after that and asked where Milt was. Jenny, jerking her head toward the john, said he was washing his hands. "He'll be out in a minute. You want your hamburger meanwhile? I laid it on the table there, for you. What are you looking at *now*?"

Amory was goggling at the table that had the box and the hamburgers and stuff on it. Jenny came up beside her and stared also.

"Something is missing," the Duchess said.

"I don't see nothing missing. What's eating you?" The Duchess tapped her red lips with her finger. "Listen, the old lady wanted to tell you her hard-luck story, didn't she?"

307

"I beg your pardon?"

She wasn't paying attention. She made Jenny beside herself goggling at that table as if she was expecting God-knows-what. Out of nervousness, Jenny began talking, off the top of her head, while she, too, studied what was on the table to see what this was all about. Never say die, that was the Duchess, wasn't it? Went with the old lady still expecting to hear God-knows-what. Got an earful of good names and bad names and good classes and low classes and heart disease and salt-free diets, right?

Amory swung round, her eyes widening. Her finger moved from her lips to her cheek, the fingers spread over her cheek. "Salt! That's it, salt!" Her hand pointed at the table. "The salt! The salt is missing, that's what's missing!

"Where is he?" she asked. "Where did you say he went?"

Jenny wouldn't say. Jenny wouldn't say another word. Jenny wouldn't open her mouth.

" 'Washing his hands,' you said! You said 'washing his hands' and that's just what he said the first time!" She ran to the blue upholstered chair and unerringly drew her pocketbook out from between the cushion and the seat and opened it.

Amory took out her handkerchief and, my God, she picked up her cold hamburger and wrapped her handkerchief carefully round it.

"What are you doing there? Are you nuts?" Jenny asked.

No, she was quite sane, she said.

She wasn't going to eat the hamburger, she said, only going to preserve it. She opened her purse wide, put the hamburger wrapped in the handkerchief into the purse and closed the purse.

She said it was her evidence. She moved to the cabin door.

She said she was going to get off the boat this minute and she was going straight to the police.

She said she was going to ask them to have the hamburger

analyzed and if they refused to do it, she said, and they might, she would have it analyzed somewhere else.

The police would almost certainly think she was insane, she said. And she was insane, she said. She was just exactly as insane as her sister had been.

Crazy like a fox, she meant.

Eventually—unless she was very much mistaken, she was going to have Milt arrested.

And she was not mistaken, she said. She had not been mistaken at all, she said, standing by the door, ready to run.

Wait until Day heard this, she said. Her light blue eyes had turned a dark and thundery blue.

She said that Jenny had said the magic word. (Poor Jenny, she said.)

Didn't Jenny know about the magic wordie? Didn't Jenny have television? Didn't the children listen to Groucho? To Day's precious Groucho? "Say the magic wordie and get a hundred dollars?"

Placebo was a magic wordie, she said, salt was a magic wordie. Salt. Salt. Salt.

She said certainly "washing his hands" was a euphemism, but not the conventional middle-class one. She said Milt was in there flushing down the poison out of the saltcellar and refilling the saltcellar with genuine salt. No, she said, not this time! The first time, last time, that was what he had done, but now he was in there tossing the saltcellar with the poison out of the porthole. But that wouldn't save him, she said, patting her purse, smiling at her purse.

The other time, she said, Sunday, she said, oh, yes, Jenny, the Sunday he murdered Sloane, he had flushed the poison down the drain, all right. She opened the door.

She said that this was what she had seen when she had been upper class about the euphemism, only she hadn't known it then.

But now she knew, she said, and now she wouldn't for the world barge in on him while he was "washing his hands." She would run along now, she said. She patted her pocketbook gently. She and the hamburger would run along. The party was over, she said.

"Oh, my God," she said. "Did you eat one, Jenny? No," she said, "he couldn't have poisoned yours!"

He was in love with you, she said, didn't you know that?

"Well," she said, "he probably didn't know it, either," she said, and left the cabin.

Milton. Milt.